A HEART EXPOSED

"In the café," he began, "why did the man call you ugly?"

She reached for the pen and curled her fingers around it. "Is that your idea of humor, Kieran?" she asked hoarsely.

"I don't understand."

She stared at him, and he felt her disbelief. With a sharp movement she gathered up her thick red hair and pulled it away from her face. "You asked me once what I saw when I looked at you. What do *you* see?"

He looked as she bade him, at the clear blue of her eyes and the dark red lashes, gentle nose and full lips, delicate bones and stubborn jaw. "I see a memory," he said slowly. "A child I played with when I was young. My friend."

Her lips parted. "Is that . . . all?"

"No." He leaned forward, holding her gaze. "I see a woman who is also my friend." He hesitated, searching for the right words. "Hair like the leaves when they fall before the first snow. Eyes—like the lake where it's too deep to see bottom. A beautiful woman. I remember what beauty is."

The pen slipped from her fingers and rolled across the table. She let her hair fall back around her face, the curls swinging forward like a shield. "Your memory isn't reliable, Kieran," she whispered.

Bantam Books by Susan Krinard:

STAR-CROSSED

PRINCE OF DREAMS

PRINCE OF WOLVES

Prince of *Shadows*

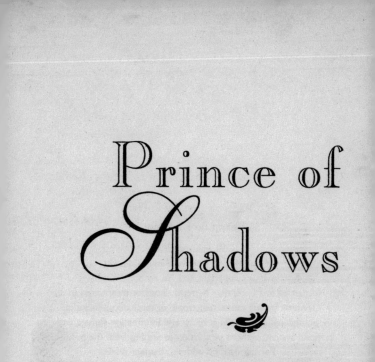

Susan Krinard

Bantam Books
New York   Toronto   London   Sydney   Auckland

PRINCE OF SHADOWS

A Bantam Book / August 1996

ISBN 0-553-56777-2

Published simultaneously in the United States and Canada

Bantam Books are published by Bantam Books, a division of Bantam
Doubleday Dell Publishing Group, Inc. Its trademark, consisting of the
words "Bantam Books" and the portrayal of a rooster, is Registered in
U.S. Patent and Trademark Office and in other countries. Marca
Registrada. Bantam Books, 1540 Broadway, New York, New York 10036.

PRINTED IN THE UNITED STATES OF AMERICA

OPM   10 9 8 7 6 5 4 3 2 1

Special thanks to:

Casey Mickle—fellow writer, critique partner, cheerleader and friend, who helps keep me
sane;

Jean Brashear, Ellen Breen, Laurel Chevlen,
Jennifer Doll, Betty Ivy, Kaelyn Johnson, Sandy
Miller, Pat Rouse, Cheryl Rovang, Kathleen
Stone and all those wonderful readers who wrote
to tell me how much they enjoyed *Prince of
Wolves*—your support is a lifesaver;

Bree Carter, Minnesotan and Ojibwe, for
her invaluable assistance;

And to wolf researchers and protectors
everywhere, who know the true worth of the
princes of the wilderness.

Prince of
Shadows

Prologue

Maheengun County, Minnesota, 1979

The beast stalked her silently, its paws drifting among the pine needles as if it were no more than the merest wraith.

Alex knew the wolf was there, right behind her, as it had been for the past hour. She had caught a glimpse of it once: black as midnight, yellow-eyed, frightening in its single-minded intensity.

Granddad had told her almost no one ever saw a wolf in the wild, even fourteen years after the wolf bounty had ended in Minnesota. But the old wolf hunters still told tales of massive brutes with glaring eyes, cunning and unpredictable and unfailingly dangerous.

Those stories were exaggerations. Alex knew that, even though the first time she heard them she'd felt chills up and down her spine. Granddad and Grandmother had lived in the north woods long enough to know the real truth.

Alex hummed a soft, steady tune under her breath and kept reminding herself that she wasn't afraid.

She had no reason to be. This was her special place. She had been coming here every summer since she was old enough to walk; now, at ten, she knew how to roam these woods like any forest creature. Granddad had taught her to watch and listen and understand, just as he'd once taught Mother. She knew all about the animals that made these woods their home: gray and red squirrels chattering in the pines; snowshoe hares and cottontails; raccoon, bobcat, black bear, and red fox.

But none was as mysterious as the creature that trailed her now.

Alex stopped, her damp tennis shoes sinking in rich, spongy earth, and listened. She'd thought the wolf would go away. They were supposed to be shy, never coming close to people. This wolf clung to her like a lost shadow, always a few yards behind.

I won't look back. I won't. I'm not afraid.

She shivered, though the early summer day was warm even under the trees. She pushed out her lower jaw and stared up through the canopy of birch, aspen, and popple, the deeper green of pine and spruce. A squirrel scolded and fell silent as she passed beneath a spreading sugar maple. A single narrow twig spun down to bounce from her shoulder.

"I hear you, Squirrel," she said defiantly. She listened again, but the wolf would not reveal himself.

She clenched her fists. *This is* my *place, Wolf. Mine as much as yours.*

Alex knelt down, a carpet of last year's autumn leaves and old pine needles giving under her knees. Even the birds were quiet. If the wolf wanted to pounce now, it had its chance. She cupped her hands around the petals of a trillium as if the brilliant white flower were so much treasure, wealth beyond counting and far more precious than all the things her parents' money could buy back home.

"Wolf," she said. "Can you hear me?"

She waited uneasily for an end to the silence. It came with a whisper of sound, a hesitation, a soft whuff of air.

"Do you hear me, Wolf? You can't scare me."

The fine hairs rose on the back of her neck. It was closer now; she felt it on the chilled skin of her cheek and in the very earth beneath her. She turned her head carefully, resting her hands flat on the ground. "You can't make me run."

This time the wolf abandoned any attempt at secrecy. A body crashed through the bushes. Alex scrambled around and rocked back on her heels, raising her hands to fend off the attack she knew would come.

It never did. A pair of amber eyes regarded her with bright curiosity. The wolf sat three feet away, huge paws planted squarely under its body, ears pricked and jaws agape, and tongue lolling. Alex felt her own mouth drop open in awe.

A wolf. A real wolf, close enough to touch.

It was not a monster. It wasn't scary at all. She knew in that instant, between one heartbeat and the next, that she had never seen anything so beautiful in all the world. Its coat was still lush and thick, even with the coming of summer, black fur rippling with silvered light. A single splash of white marked its chest.

But the eyes were the best. They were almost human. The wolf looked at her as if it knew every thought that passed through her mind. As she met its gaze its expression changed: ears dropped to the sides, eyes narrowed, and head ducked. It whined deep in its throat.

Alex felt her face unfreeze, her body grow boneless in relief. Without any thought at all she made herself like the wolf, crouching lower, ducking her head, echoing his soft whine.

And then a miracle happened. The wolf's tail, a thick plume of ebony fur, swept to the side and back again. Just like a friendly dog. Alex stared at the tail and watched it wag, a lazy drift back and forth among the pine needles.

She laughed. The sound escaped her before she could stop it, and she clapped her hand over her mouth. But the wolf seemed to understand. He crouched, paws extended, rump in the air, and laughed back at her, flashing teeth and tongue.

"You want to play . . . is that it?" she asked. "Is that why you've been following me?"

The wolf barked, a swift yip of agreement. He hopped toward her, muzzle thrust forward, and then retreated when Alex flinched. He sat up again, an expression on his mobile face that looked like a puzzled frown.

Alex sat back and tugged her knees up to her stomach. "Well, Wolf, you want to play, but I don't know how wolves play. You have sharp teeth, and I don't." She studied the animal—his gawky lines and overlarge paws, as if he hadn't quite grown into his skin and bones. He looked the way she felt sometimes.

"You're young, aren't you? I'll bet you aren't supposed to be alone."

The wolf cocked his head. Abruptly he stood, lifted his muzzle to take in some elusive scent, and flashed a glance at Alex that seemed to hold a wealth of meaning.

"Granddad told me you have good families," she said. "You all stick together. You take care of each other, just the way people do."

She could have sworn the wolf nodded. It was eerie and wonderful, looking into those eyes. Suddenly, and with all her heart, she wanted to know this wolf—every movement, signal, expression. If she could grow fur and become what he was, even for an instant . . .

A howl, low and quavering and thinned by distance, sliced cleanly through her imaginings. More wolves—at least two of them. *Her* wolf stood like a creature in a painting, perfectly poised, black silhouetted against rich forest color. And then he pointed his muzzle toward the sky and returned the call.

Sensations she didn't recognize washed through Alex from her toes to the roots of her hair. She'd heard that sound before, but never so close or so real. Never with her heart. She closed her eyes and tilted back her head. Just a little push, a little release, and it would come: a cry as full and rich as the wolves'.

Cool wetness touched her cheek; she jerked back just as the wolf retreated, his gaze locked on her face. With a sad little whimper, he backed away and began to melt into the undergrowth.

"Wait!"

Loss overwhelmed Alex, a sense of panic that sent her scrambling after the wolf. Her foot snagged a fallen branch; her fall was cushioned by the padding of leaves, but she lay where she was and sucked air back into her lungs.

A triangular black shadow filled her vision. Amber eyes regarded her from only inches away. A rough wet tongue slapped across her face, filling Alex with a singing joy.

She sat up, reaching for the wolf. It stepped back and then went very still as her fingers found the lush fur and slipped between the thick guard hairs to the silkiness beneath.

The wolf was afraid of her, as afraid as she'd been of him. She stroked the wolf once and let her hand fall.

"We're kind of the same, aren't we?" she asked. "Maybe you knew that all along."

The wolf whined and looked over his shoulder. Alex wrapped her arms around herself to keep from touching him again. He was a wild creature, just as he should be. She forced the lump from her throat.

"Listen, Wolf. I don't know where you live or how long you'll stay here. Granddad said your packs move around a lot. But I'm going to be here all summer."

She knew she was being silly. Wolves didn't understand people. They weren't meant to be pets. But the thought of being separated from the wolf—*her* wolf—so soon was an unbearable prospect. Not when she had the whole summer ahead of her.

And maybe, just maybe, *her* wolf was different.

She held out her hand, not quite touching him. "I'm going to come back here tomorrow, wolf. And tomorrow and the next day. Right here to this same place."

She looked around. This *was* a good place. She'd never run across it before, but it was made to be a hideaway, the kind she'd always wanted to make her own. A fallen pine had formed a framework across a hollow between two jutting rocks; dogwoods and ferns had grown to fill in the open spaces between the dead branches. Two yards away a stream bubbled, nearly hidden by the undergrowth.

Alex looked back at the wolf. "I know you can't tell me your name. But I want to give you one anyway, in case . . . in case you come back."

It was ridiculous to expect any such thing. She waited for the wolf to vanish like the wraith he was. Slowly he sat down, ears flickering forward and back in clear uncertainty. And then he nodded again; she didn't know what else to call the gesture. He dipped his head and looked up, watching her.

She needed to find a name. A name for such a wonderful creature, one she could hold in her heart forever.

"Shadow," she breathed. "You were my shadow today, weren't you? And you're dark like one."

Her smile widened. "You're like a shadow, Wolf, because you're something people are afraid of until they see it up close."

Shadow opened his mouth in a grin. Alex stepped toward him and held out her hand. With grave deliberation, Shadow lifted his front paw and set it gently on her palm, dwarfing her hand. The leathery pads of his toes were rough and warm.

Tears pricked her eyes. She closed her fingers as far around his paw as she could reach and then let it slip back to the ground.

"I know you have to go now, Shadow. Your family is looking for you. But I'll be here every day, waiting. In case you can come back. You . . . you won't forget me? My name is Alex. Alexandra."

Shadow whined again, and Alex could see the answer in his face and body. She watched as he turned away and trotted into the tangle of brush beneath a stand of quaking aspens. Once he looked back, a flash of yellow eyes glimpsed and then gone.

Silence settled around her. The squirrel, forgotten, resumed its raucous scolding. Until the howl came again, far away, circling back on the warm wind and bearing a promise in its wake.

The tightness in Alex's throat eased. She lifted her head, drew in a deep breath, and let it out on a soft and hesitant howl.

*S*hadow came again the next day.

Alex lay on the bed she'd made for herself, one of Grandmother's old blankets spread over the pine needles in the hollow under the fallen pine. A single shaft of sunlight cut down through the trees overhead, teasing her face and making her sneeze.

She was thinking of the wolf when the sunlight stopped and cool wetness touched her cheek in its place.

"Shadow!" She sat up and flung her arms around the shaggy neck without thinking, forgetting he was a wild creature. When she remembered, she went very still and waited.

Shadow wriggled in her arms and licked her face, his tail waving from side to side.

"I knew you'd come," she said. "I just knew it."

She let him go and sat back on the blanket. "I brought something for you. Leftover fish from last night's supper. I knew Granddad wouldn't mind."

Unwrapping the foil bundle she'd brought, she laid the fish out for Shadow's inspection. He sniffed it and then, with gluttonish enthusiasm, wolfed down the entire portion. Alex struggled to keep the foil from disappearing the same way.

"This won't spoil you, will it, Shadow? I've been reading more about wolves. You're only a pup and still learning to hunt with your family." She grinned conspiratorially. "But if you're like me, you're always hungry!"

Shadow squeaked and plopped down beside her, throwing all four paws up in the air.

That was the beginning of the magic summer. Magic because of Shadow, because all of nature conspired to make their friendship perfect. When it rained, it rained briefly; the humidity never grew unbearable, and the mosquitoes fled Shadow's vicinity as if he were a spirit creature and not a wolf at all.

Shadow took her to places she never would have found on her own. That first day when he rose, shook himself, and started off into the forest, Alex followed. He led her to dells full of wood sorrel and blue violets and showy orchis, almost too perfect to be real; showed her the half-buried hollow log where the lynx denned her litter and the meadow where the black bear sow foraged with her half-grown cub. She almost expected him to lead her to the place where the Fairy Queen held court. Granddad was Irish, and he'd told her the old tales every summer since she was small. Mother had done the same.

Old tales she was almost too grown up to believe in. Until now. Now anything was possible, and all the world was made of spun dreams.

They ran together through stands of pine and splashed in lakes still cool with the memory of winter. Alex would tumble to the ground, laughing, and Shadow would stand over her, licking her face until she had to get up again.

At the end of each day, when Alex and Shadow were tired, they would return to the secret place and wait until Shadow's pack summoned him home.

Never once did she see another wolf. It came to her in time that that was part of the unspoken bargain she'd struck with Shadow: only here was time suspended, the outside world forgotten. They must return in the end to their own separate worlds. No matter how much she might pretend, the forest could never truly be her home.

Alex often thought of telling her grandparents about Shadow. Granddad would understand; at least he wouldn't laugh. But her friendship with Shadow was a secret; like anything magical, it would surely vanish if she ever revealed it to another living soul.

So she took what she'd been given. On lazy afternoons, she lay beside Shadow and told him about home: how different it was in San Francisco, the big restored mansion on Steiner Street and her room with its antique dolls and beautiful furniture. She told him about the private school she attended and her friends there, going shopping with Mother and the way people said they looked so much alike.

"They say I'm going to be beautiful, like my mother," she said matter-of-factly, running her fingers through the fur of Shadow's chest.

He yawned, patently unimpressed. Rows of white teeth flashed.

Alex laughed. "That doesn't matter to you, does it? What I look like or that my parents have lots of money. You don't even know how beautiful you are." She sighed, stretching her hands high above her head and staring up through the trees to the slivers of blue between branches. "I can have anything I want in the whole world, almost. Except you."

She rolled over to face Shadow. Somehow his eyes seemed sad, as if he knew the summer would only last a few more weeks.

She thought about her friends back home, all girls and boys from families like hers. They had fun, but it was never like this. Never like it was with Shadow. At the end of every summer in Minnesota, she'd been ready to go back. She missed Mother; that was the only thing she didn't like about summer. That had always been enough to call her back to San Francisco.

Now she couldn't imagine what it would be like without Shadow. He was . . . some wild half of herself.

"Do you think when I'm grown up I'll understand, Shadow?" she asked softly.

He stretched his chin out on his oversized paws. With no effort at all she could imagine him a big black dog, sleeping beside her canopied bed in her room back home.

The image froze in her mind. Shadow, always with her. Not only here, but home as well. No parting when summer ended. No good-byes she could hardly bear to imagine.

Would it be so impossible? He was already tame, with her. She was sure he'd never hurt anyone. And he loved her; she knew it more than anything in the world. He loved her as she loved him. They could go on long walks in

Golden Gate Park; she laughed, thinking of Eric Mickleson's face when he saw Shadow next to the Rottweiler he was so proud of.

They could run along the beach, and she could show Shadow his first glimpse of the ocean. And the redwoods.

Alex imagined it all. It wouldn't be so hard. Shadow would follow her back to the cabin if she wanted him to. He'd let her put a collar on him; Mother could arrange a way to get him back to San Francisco. Alex would just have to convince her, and Alex knew she could do it. Anything Alex had ever truly wanted she'd been able to get.

She got to her knees and threw her arms around the wolf, fighting off the strange niggling shame that didn't want to go away. Shadow would be happy with her. She knew it. He wouldn't miss his family; he would rather be with her. And they could come back every year.

"You'd like that, wouldn't you, Shadow?"

A low growl answered her.

Alex looked up, clutching Shadow's fur. Shadow whined in his throat, straining toward the two great wolves that stood only a few yards away.

One of them was massive and black—pure black, without even the streak of white that marked Shadow's chest. The other was gray, smaller, beautiful and slender. They stared at Alex with ears pricked and tails raised; she stayed absolutely still.

She knew. These were Shadow's parents. As if they sensed her thoughts, they'd come to reclaim him.

For a crazy moment Alex almost defied them, almost rose to her feet to drive them off. Wolves were shy creatures. They would run away, and she'd still have Shadow.

Then Shadow broke free of her arms. He bounded toward the wolves, with the playful, sideways lope that begged for play. He thrust his muzzle against the black male's, squeaking and whining with obvious joy. The gray female licked Shadow's ear with a gesture of unmistakable tenderness.

Alex sank down to the ground. It wasn't wolves she was seeing now, but a boy and his loving parents, glad to be with them again, belonging with them. Just as *she* belonged with her mother and father and friends back in San Francisco.

Ignoring the tears on her cheeks, Alex hugged herself tightly. "You're right, Shadow. I couldn't take you back with me. I couldn't stay here with you and never see my mother again, either." She looked at the gray female, whose sharp gaze turned suddenly to meet her own. "But the summer's not over yet, Mother Wolf. Won't you let him stay a little longer?"

Three pairs of lupine eyes fixed on her.

"I won't take him away from you. I promise."

The gray female nuzzled her mate's ear, almost as if she whispered to him. She shoved Shadow's rump with a turn of her shoulder, and Shadow loped back to Alex, grinning from ear to ear.

Alex buried her face in Shadow's fur, wiping away the tears. "For a few more weeks, Shadow." She looked up. "Thank you," she said solemnly. "I'll take good care of him until—"

But the wolves were gone. Shadow licked her face, and she sprang to her feet.

"Let's run, Shadow. Run until we can't run any more."

And they did, leaving the world behind them.

$\mathcal{S}$hadow wasn't coming.

One of autumn's first bright leaves spiraled gently down from a maple sapling, coming to rest inches from Alex's scuffed sneaker. She snuggled deeper in the hollow under the fallen tree and stared around the special place.

This day of all days Shadow wasn't coming. The last day she would have with him.

Summer had gone too fast; Mother and Father had come to collect her and take her home to California. They'd arrived early this morning, before she had time to say good-bye to Shadow. So she'd run away. She'd never run away before, and now it was all for nothing.

Granddad had sensed her sadness last night. He'd

hugged her and reminded her she'd come back next year. This place would always be here for her. The trees would pass through another cycle of seasons, along with the birds and animals and cold, pure water. They would not change.

But Alex had been desperately afraid *he* wouldn't be waiting for her when she returned.

Shadow.

Alex hugged her knees and closed her eyes. All day she'd walked and called, desperate to find him, searching out all the places they had explored together. Places that looked strange without him beside her, strange and scary and dark.

Dark. Soon it would be night, and she would have to go back whether she found Shadow or not. But she stayed where she was, where she'd begun, at the secret place. Hoping. Trying not to be afraid that something was terribly wrong.

Shadow wouldn't be afraid, she thought, picking up the red leaf at her feet. She imagined herself a wolf, as she'd so often done during the summer.

But pretending hadn't made the summer last longer, and it wouldn't bring Shadow to her now. Granddad would be looking for her. Father would be angry, but Mother would be worried. Alex could never tell them the real reason she'd run away.

Alex dropped the leaf, pushed herself to her feet, and brushed off her pants. The thought of Mother's distress made her chest ache. Working her fingers against the late afternoon chill, Alex studied the fading light that filtered down through the canopy of trees above.

She had no choice. She'd have to leave without saying good-bye, though it felt like tearing herself in two.

I'll look for you next year and every year after that, she promised Shadow silently. But the scared feeling in her stomach wouldn't go away, no matter how much she tried to ignore it.

"Alexandra."

She jerked her head toward the voice. It came from somewhere hidden, and she didn't recognize it. Not deep enough to be Granddad's or even Father's. She hadn't seen anyone else out in the woods today, not even the Indian children she and Shadow sometimes spotted at a distance.

"Alexandra," the voice repeated. And a boy came out of the woods, a skinny boy in a T-shirt and cutoffs, tall and dark haired and pale eyed. Older than she was by a few years. His feet were bare, and yet he didn't seem to be cold at all. Alex had never seen him before in her life.

"Who are you?" she blurted.

He blinked at her, and she stared at his eyes. Yellow. Like Shadow's. The similarity made her shiver. She thought he wouldn't answer her, and wondered what she should do.

"I . . . came to find you," he said.

His voice was husky and low and he wouldn't stop staring at her. Alexandra took an involuntary step back and caught herself. This was *her* place—hers and Shadow's.

"How do you know my name?" she demanded.

He smiled. A strange, crooked smile, as if he wasn't quite sure how to do it or hadn't had much practice. "I've seen you many times," he said.

Spying on her. Was that what he meant? Spying on her and Shadow. But he didn't look like he could be from the reservation, and no other kids ever came here.

"I've never seen you," she challenged. "You shouldn't be here. This is my place, and I'm waiting for a friend—"

"I know." The boy crouched down, dropping his hands between his knees. "You're waiting for a black wolf named Shadow."

Alex felt shock and then jealousy, one right after the other. This boy she'd never seen before knew Shadow. How could he? Was Shadow his friend too?

"You know Shadow?"

The boy stared at the ground between his feet, poking at the earth with a twig. "Yes. Very well."

No. No one could know Shadow as well as she did. No one. He was her special friend, just as this was their special place.

"I don't believe you," she said, balling her fists.

"You'll scare Shadow away if you stay here. I have to see him. I'm leaving—"

"So am I." He met her gaze again and held it, an open challenge. "Today. I came to say good-bye."

To say good-bye. Like her. To Shadow?

"My family was here for the summer," he said. "Just like yours. Only now there's a place we have to go, far from here. I don't know if I'll ever be coming back."

Why should she care? She flung a glance around the glade, hoping against hope that Shadow might appear.

"I left my parents to find you," he said. "I had to talk to you, to tell you . . ." He gnawed his lower lip and broke off. "My name is Kieran Holt."

The statement was so abrupt and absurd that Alex almost laughed, but somehow this wasn't funny at all. "You came to tell me that, and I don't even know you?"

The boy frowned, and for an instant there was a glimmer of anger in his mild, open face. "You have to listen to me," he said. "There isn't much time. They'll be coming after me."

He had all her attention now. He'd run away, just as she had. To find her, he said. "What do you want?"

A lock of dark, ragged hair fell over his brow. Alex wanted to push it back up. "It isn't easy to say," he muttered. "I've never . . . had a friend."

Strange. The boy was so strange. He wasn't anything like the older boys back home who acted so stuck-up and rowdy. But there was something about Kieran she almost liked, something she almost understood. As she'd come to understand Shadow. Maybe if she'd met Kieran earlier . . .

She walked a few steps toward him and stopped. "If you know Shadow, help me find him. We can both say good-bye." She looked into his eyes. "You know where Shadow is, don't you? Please . . . help me find him."

He let out a ragged sigh and rose to his feet. "You can find him," he said. "He's here. Very close." His smile flashed and faded again. "I—I am—"

From somewhere very close the unmistakable report of

a gun snapped off the end of Kieran's words. His head came up. An eerie, familiar wail broke into a long sob of despair.

Shadow. Alex whirled toward the fading cry and began to run, forgetting the boy, hardly watching the uneven ground ahead of her. The howl sounded again, closer still.

"I'm coming, Shadow," she called. "Wait for me!"

She ran blindly, branches of sumac and dogwood slapping her face and catching in her hair. The violent crack of a second rifle shot froze her muscles in midstride.

"No," she cried. "No!"

Alex surged into motion again and broke through the final barrier of brush. On the other side lay a nightmare.

Two wolves sprawled prone on blood-soaked earth, one pelted gray and the other black. The gray wolf was very still, but the black one moved feebly, working its paws fitfully in a search for purchase, for some final hold on the life slipping away.

Beside the wolves stood a man. His back was to Alex, but she saw the rifle in his hand, and the way he stood over the dying animals with his head thrown back in victory. Alex crouched, wrapping her arms around her stomach to keep from crying out.

"Two less," the man murmured. "Two less monsters in the world." He lowered his rifle and poked at the heaving ribs of the black wolf. It jerked, and the great head slowly lifted to regard its tormentor. Alex bit her lip and stared at the animal's pain-filled eyes.

The wolf was Shadow's father.

As she watched, stunned, the spark of life began to fade in the animal's gaze. It lowered its head, and as it did it saw Alex; she felt the weight of its stare as she'd done so many weeks ago.

And then the life of the great wolf shuddered out and was gone. The man prodded the wolf a final time.

"There is one more, isn't there? Your offspring. I can't let him go to become what you are—"

He broke off. Alex forced her gaze up from the dead

wolf to the place where the killer stared, just beyond the massed trunks of a basswood.

"Shadow," she choked.

The man swung around. Alex watched him aim the rifle at her and pull it up and away. Only his eyes were visible above the scarf wrapped about his face.

"*Tabarnac*," the man cursed. "What are you doing here?"

Alex scrambled to her feet. "You killed those wolves," she said, voice shaking. "You killed them."

The poacher's eyes narrowed. In that moment, he looked a thousand times more deadly than any wolf. He could have been about her father's age, perhaps a bit younger; his green eyes were utterly without warmth, the deeply lined skin around them harsh as weathered stone under his fur cap.

"Did you follow me?" he asked. So deceptively soft, his voice—so strangely gentle. But Alex knew it was false. He had killed Shadow's parents, and now he was after Shadow himself.

Run, she urged her wolf. *Run away. I'll give you time*—

"I . . . didn't know you were here," she told the man, pushing the words past the lump in her throat. "I got lost. My grandparents' cabin isn't far from here, but I took the wrong way."

Shouldering his rifle, the man knelt in front of her and cupped her chin in his hand. She wanted to wrench free, but she held very still.

"Didn't they ever teach you how dangerous these woods are?" he asked.

She met his gaze, shivering. The man shook his head. "Foolish child." He looked up, cocking his head to listen. "I'd take you home, but I have quarry to pursue—"

"You aren't supposed to hunt the wolves."

The words were out of Alex's mouth before she could stop them. Any trace of gentleness in the man's attitude vanished. He dropped his hand and rose, staring down at her.

"Wolves," he repeated. "What do you know about them?" Suddenly he bent toward her and caught her by the shoulder. "Do you know what they are? What they do?" His fingers squeezed, and Alex bit her lip to keep from showing any pain. "Did you see the other—a young black one?"

"No. No wolves." She glared up at him. "Let me go."

He released her with a little push and looked away. "I see the anger in your eyes, child," he said. "As if you knew the pain of the world. But I had to do it. I'm the only one who can. It's the duty given to me. No one else believes. No one else knows—" He broke off. "They must die. There is no other way."

Alex stared at him, sickened and fighting not to show it. Fear choked her as she made herself walk past the man to the dead wolves. She knelt beside them, reaching out but not daring to touch the thick dark fur, so much like Shadow's.

Run, Shadow. Run far away from here.

She waited for the poacher to order her to leave and wondered what she would do. She didn't know how she could delay him, stop him from hunting Shadow. She felt numb—too numb to find her way home, to move, even to speak.

Brush crackled behind her. When she looked around, the man was gone. She thought then that she was alone.

She was wrong. Someone was watching her from behind the basswood tree. Someone she knew in her heart.

"Shadow," she whispered thickly.

Leaves trembled and branches swayed. A figure moved, flowed forward into the interwoven pattern of earth, dying leaves, and fading sunlight.

Not Shadow, but the boy. The boy she'd left behind. He'd followed her and circled around to the other side of the clearing. She stared at him, desperate, praying he was Shadow's friend as he claimed. That he would help her.

But he didn't see her at all. His gaze was locked on the dead wolves, his face white as birch bark.

Alex wet her lips. "Kieran?"

His mouth worked, but only a moan came from deep inside him. All her own sorrow was in that sound, and a thousand times more. He began to shake uncontrollably, fists clenching and unclenching.

Alex threw off her own numbness. "You knew them too," she said.

Kieran seemed not to hear. He walked with short, fitful steps to stand between the wolves and spread his hands to either side, as if he could draw them up from death. And then he fell to his knees. He crawled to the black wolf, stretched his body alongside it, looped his long arms around the maned neck. His black hair mingled with the animal's coarse fur, indistinguishable.

Something was wrong with him, more than just the wolves dying. She edged closer and struggled out of her coat. "You must be cold," she said. "Here, take my coat."

It was many minutes before he responded, raising his head an inch from the wolf's shoulder. With clumsy hands Alex tried to drape her coat over the boy's lower back. He turned just enough for her to see his face.

Never had she seen such a look of open pain. The boy—Kieran—looked at her with his pale yellow eyes and broke her heart cleanly in two.

Unheeded tears tracked through smudges of dirt on Kieran's face, and Alex felt her own sobs break loose. They worked their way up from her chest and spilled free as dry little hiccups.

The boy raised himself to his knees, fingers still buried in the black wolf's fur. He made no sound to accompany the torment in his eyes. Alex scrubbed her knuckles across her face, and in that brief moment of blindness she felt cold fingers brush her cheek.

She held very still as Kieran withdrew his hand, one of her tears trembling at the tip of his finger. He closed his eyes and touched the finger to his parted lips. Her tear mingled with his. And then, as if some spell had been broken, his silence ended.

He turned his face away, lifted his head to the sky, and howled.

Alex forgot her own grief. She crawled closer, drawn to him, driven to console the inconsolable. Her hand found his chilled back. His cry wavered for an instant and then continued unbroken, accepting her presence. Kieran's grief wrapped around her, pulled her within the circle of something she couldn't define.

"Alexandra!"

She felt the boy's muscles knot under her hand. His gaze snapped toward the sound of the shout.

"Granddad," Alex said under her breath.

"Alexandra! Where are you?" That was her Mother's voice, laced with anxiety.

Kieran flinched sideways; Alex's coat slid to the ground. He crouched between the wolves, folded in on himself, and looked around with wild desperation. His muscles bunched to carry him away.

"No," she urged. "No, don't go! It's only my family—"

His gazed fixed on her again. For a moment she thought he would listen. He lifted his hand, cupped his fingers in a gesture of entreaty.

"Help me," he croaked.

Tears blinded Alex as she reached for him. Slowly, slowly she brushed his fingertips, slid her palm along his, began to close her smaller hand over his callused one.

"Don't be afraid," she said. "They were my friends, too. I'll help you. I promise, whatever's wrong, I'll help you—"

Branches cracked behind her. The boy was on his feet in a second, leaving Alex grasping air. Like a deer the boy sprang for the nearest cover, vanishing so cleanly that Alex couldn't tell where he had passed. She sat where she was, frozen, as her grandfather walked into the clearing.

"Alexandra! Eve, she's here, she's safe."

"My God!"

Her mother's gasp compelled Alex to turn. She looked past her grandfather to Mother's white face, Father's closed expression as they saw the wolves. Before Alex could speak Mother gathered her in an urgent hug, scraping Alex's hair back from her face with shaking hands.

"Alexandra! Are you all right, honey? Did they hurt you?"

Alex struggled to find words, her mind still with the boy and his terrible sorrow. She returned her mother's embrace. "I'm okay," she managed. "The wolves—they were already dead. A hunter killed them."

Granddad moved behind her, rising from an examination of the bodies. "Poachers," he said grimly.

"God, Dad," Mother said. "They could have shot Alex—"

"But they didn't." He looked across the forest, the way the boy had run. "Whoever they are, they're gone now."

Mother pulled Alex in for a second hug, and Alex glanced up at Father over her shoulder. His face was set and unreadable, but she knew he was angry.

"I don't have to tell you how much trouble you made for us, Alexandra," he said. "We've been searching all day."

Mother sighed. "William . . ."

Alex swallowed. "I'm sorry, Father."

Granddad helped his daughter and granddaughter to their feet. He glanced down at the wolves, shaking his head.

"Poor devils. Some of the old wolf haters will never give up until every last wolf is dead."

Alex resisted the urge to bury her face against Granddad's ribs. "That's what the man said."

"You saw him, Alex?"

"He left when I came. But—"

Father took a stiff step toward them. "We don't have time to stand here and chat. The plane is waiting."

"Damn waste," Granddad muttered. He glanced at his daughter. "Don't you worry, Evie. I'll let the authorities know about this."

"All right, Dad." Mother knelt and touched Alex's cheek. "I know this has been terrible for you, honey."

"The wolves were my friends," Alex said. "They didn't deserve to die."

"No. Of course they didn't." Mother stroked back Alex's hair over and over again. "Sometimes bad things happen, and we can't understand why. We can only try not to forget the good things."

"Eve!"

Mother stiffened a little at Father's tone. "We'll talk more about this on the plane. If you're okay, honey, we'd better go."

Alex planted her feet. "No. There's something else." She looked at Granddad. "I met a boy, a stranger. After the hunter left, he came to the wolves. Something was wrong with him. He was crying . . ."

She trailed off, pinned under Father's stare and Granddad's puzzled frown.

"A boy, Alex? You didn't know him?" Granddad glanced at Mother. "Could have been with the poacher—"

"No." Alex tried very hard not to cry. Not yet. "It wasn't like that. He was in some kind of trouble, I know it. He was upset because the wolves had been killed, and he ran away when you came. I promised to help him!"

Father's mouth set in a thin line. "That's enough, Alexandra."

Alex pulled free of her mother's loose hold and faced her father defiantly. "But we have to find him. I promised."

"Honey, it's better if we let Granddad take care of it."

"Your mother's right," Granddad said. "I'll look around for this boy tomorrow. Maybe he came from the reservation. If I find him, I'll make sure he's all right."

They didn't really believe her. Alex knew it, caught the way her mother looked at Granddad. But they had to believe, and she had to keep her promise. . . .

"Come on, honey," Mother said, tugging her away from the scene of death. "You need rest. When we're home, this will all seem like a bad dream."

A bad dream. It was much worse than that, because it was real. The boy needed help, Shadow was being hunted by a terrible man, and the sense of dread that had been hanging over Alex all day had only grown worse.

"I can't go, Mother—"

"This is your doing," Father hissed to Granddad. "You put these crazy ideas in her head and let her wander out here alone. Eve went through hell today because of it." He breathed out heavily. "I think Alexandra has gotten too old to be coming up here every year."

Alex looked up in horror.

"Now, William . . ." There was real concern in Granddad's voice. Even Mother looked as if she agreed with Father. Father could make sure Alex never came back here again—to her grandparents, to these woods, to Shadow and the boy who needed her help. . . .

"Please," Alex begged. "I won't cause any more trouble." She felt tears slide down her cheeks. "Mother, please let me come back."

Mother only pulled her close to her side and kept walking. Father and Granddad dropped behind, arguing in harsh whispers.

I have to come back, Alex thought fiercely, scrubbing at her face. She had to find Shadow again, make sure he'd escaped. And now there was another reason as well. Even if Granddad kept his promise and looked for the boy, Alex wouldn't be here to help as *she'd* promised, or find out who he was, or why he had called to her with the sorrow in his eyes.

Until she saw them both, Shadow and the boy, it wouldn't be right again. That certainty hung in Alex's mind like a terrible prophecy.

She moved a little ahead of her mother, taking the first step away from what she must leave behind. She didn't even look back at the wolves. There was nothing she could do about them now. But as she walked she made a silent prayer.

Be safe, Shadow. Wait for me. And if you meet Kieran Holt, tell him I'll never forget my promise.

1

Maheengun County, Minnesota, 1996

Alex unlocked the cabin door with a strange, nearly painful feeling of déjà vu.

As she stepped into the living room, the tightness in her throat grew almost unbearable. She stood very still for several moments, eyes closed, remembering, imagining familiar smells perfectly preserved over all these years. The lilac perfume her grandmother had favored; a hint of the tobacco Granddad had used in his pipe. And a thousand scents less easily defined.

Your imagination, Alex, she thought. Granddad had been gone a very long time, Grandmother as well. They'd willed the cabin to her when they passed away thirteen years ago. Caretakers and renters had kept the place running; the last tenant had moved out before winter, but the cabin had yet to be reclaimed by its rightful owner. Her grandparents' things were boxed away just like her memories, waiting to be released again.

She'd wondered how much the memories would hurt. But the ache was already fading, impossible to sustain. The last hurdle had been passed.

Alex let out her breath and watched it plume. The air was cold; she'd need to get the stove going. Late February in Minnesota wasn't like California's mild winters. But she hadn't been back to California in a very long time.

She tossed her bags down on the old plaid sofabed and walked into the smaller bedroom at the rear of the cabin. *Her* bedroom now, as it had been when she was a child coming for summer visits. And her mother's before that. The white lace coverlet on the bed was the same, and so was the antique furniture, though there were darker squares on the walls where old photos had once hung and been removed.

The bedsprings squeaked as she sat down. She smiled briefly, remembering how she'd loved to jump up and down just to see how much she could make them groan. And then she shrugged out of her backpack and pulled out her personal journal, balancing it on her lap. The pen shook a little in her fingers, just for an instant.

Dear Mother, she wrote carefully. *I'm home.*

Home. A real home after so many years of wandering. The place she'd dreamed of when she was out in the wilds of Alaska and Montana and Idaho, on her belly in the dirt or snow, tracking wolves. The one childhood fantasy she'd allowed herself. The single connection to the past she hadn't severed.

The last haven where she'd ever truly believed in miracles.

Alex set down the journal and went to the tiny closet. Boxes were stacked nearly to the ceiling. All the little things that had belonged to her grandparents, packed away by someone she'd never met.

Hers now. She pulled one box from the stack and pried open the dusty cardboard flaps.

There was no rhyme or reason to what lay in the box. Granddad's pipe was wrapped in several layers of yellowing tissue; she put it against her nose. The faded, earthy scent almost brought tears to her eyes. Under the pipe was a floral print box, stacked with Grandmother's pressed flowers. And pushed into the corner . . .

Alex lifted out the stuffed animal and held it to her chest. The fake fur was matted, though the toy wolf had hardly been played with at all. Granddad had given it to her the summer after the accident, when she came out of the hospital for the first time. The summer she'd wanted so badly to find Shadow again, and the boy.

Of course she never had. She'd been too weak from the operations, too blind with grief, and Granddad had tried to console her with this.

She stared into the closet and stroked the stiff synthetic fur over and over. It wouldn't have made any difference even if Granddad hadn't died. She'd never have found Shadow or the boy again. And yet she could almost feel them here, as if that magical summer were only yesterday.

She didn't believe in magic anymore. And yet . . . and yet she almost had to struggle against an absurd desire to believe again. It was safe to do that here, enveloped in a cocoon of memories.

She tucked the stuffed animal back in the box, closed the closet doors, and reached for the journal.

You were always an optimist, Mother. You always thought things worked out for the best. You even told me that the day before you died.

Maybe you were right. Things do have a strange sort of pattern. I found my profession after I lost you and Granddad and everyone else. Now I'm in the perfect place to carry out my research, right in the middle of wolf territory. Exactly where I want to be.

She closed the journal and set it on the beside table. She retrieved her suitcases, unfolded her clothing and stacked flannel shirts and wool-lined pants neatly in the chest of drawers. There wasn't much to put away. She'd been traveling light for years. Everything she owned was practical and comfortable. Luxury was hardly essential in her line of work.

Essentials were really all that mattered.

Alex finished in the bedroom and hesitated in the short hallway, looking around the cabin. She had everything she could possibly need here, including privacy. Privacy and quiet and her work with no disruptions. Exactly what she wanted.

Out in the living room her own few boxes waited, the equipment she'd already half unpacked and books to occupy Granddad's empty shelves. Every book on wolves that had ever been published, including those Mother had bought her before the accident.

There were books of fairy tales, too—the ones she'd loved as a child. The ones Mother had passed down to her and Granddad had read to her so many times. All in one box, still sealed with the same tape she'd used to close them up the week after her graduation from college.

She was almost tempted to open the box again. Maybe it would be . . . okay to do it here. But not now. Now there was a restlessness in her that would not be denied.

She flipped back the handmade muslin curtains from the living room window and stared out at snow that stretched across the clearing in a carpet of white, marred only by the tracks of her truck along the buried gravel driveway. She needed supplies in town, but there was something else she needed more.

Something that was waiting for her. Out there.

She shivered. *Crazy, Alex. Nothing will be the same.* Still, there was no good reason she couldn't begin exploring the area this afternoon—and start her search for wolf sign. It was the middle of wolf mating season in Minnesota, and there'd be a few weeks at least before she'd meet the other members of the wolf research team; time enough to get familiar with the area again.

A flash of dark motion caught her gaze, vivid against the snow. She rubbed away the condensation of her breath on the glass. There it was again—a black blur too large to be a raven.

She'd seen that shape too many times to doubt it now. It was a wolf—a lone wolf, there one instant and gone the next. Right on her own front lawn.

She opened the door and stared out toward the edge of the woods. A bold animal, to be sure, coming so close to human habitation. Even Shadow had never been anywhere near the cabin. But it meant the wolves were very near, and she'd be able to track them, study them intimately as she longed to do again. Here, in her *own* place, where it had all started.

Mother would have said it was proof that things were going to work out. A burst of simple happiness caught Alex unawares. Maybe it wasn't asking too much, to let herself feel it here. Maybe . . .

"Hello!"

Alex started. It was no wolf this time but a person, crossing the clearing on snowshoes. North, from the direction of the reservation.

The woman was Ojibwe. Alex had seen Indians before as a child; Granddad had pointed out the rough boundary where his land butted up against the reservation's border. Mother had played with children from the rez when she was young. But Alex had never really talked to any of them during her summers here, not even in town.

"You're the wolf lady, aren't you?"

The voice was husky, pleasant, and devoid of mockery. Its owner was several inches shorter than Alex's modest height, stocky under a heavy coat, with straight dark hair cropped at chin level. Black eyes in a web of sun wrinkles fixed on Alex.

Run. That was always her first instinct, the one Alex hated and had fought the past seventeen years of her life. It could still catch her like a kick to the stomach when she wasn't prepared: run and hide away from strangers who would look at her face and judge, or ridicule, or pity.

That was the first instinct, but the second had been stronger since the day Father sent her to boarding school with only half her reconstructive surgery complete.

Stand your ground. Fight. Don't let them win.

Like a wolf defending its territory. She imagined herself a wolf as she'd done so many times: strong and beautiful and certain of her place in the scheme of things. She straightened and waited on the porch as the woman thrust out a mittened hand.

"Hi. Hope I didn't startle you. My name's Julie . . . Julie Wakanabo. Heard you were our new neighbor, so I came to introduce myself."

Julie wasn't conventionally pretty, but her smile was open and warm, as if she had never seen the ugliness in the world. Alex took her hand and squeezed it firmly, holding Julie's frank gaze.

"Alexandra Warrington," she said. The fragile image of herself as a wolf shattered; she was only Alex again, her terrible flaws reflected in the eyes of a stranger.

Look your fill. I know what you see.

Clouds of beautiful red hair—her mother's hair—framed a face that should have been equally beautiful. It still resembled Eve's enough that her father hadn't been able to bear looking at his daughter after the accident.

But her skin wasn't her mother's smooth, porcelain complexion. It was still a patchwork, puckered with striations from the original stitches, discolored where her fair skin had formed rough, leatherlike patches. The worst swath of scar tissue extended from her left temple to her jawbone.

She hadn't looked in a mirror for over a decade, but she knew what she looked like. She'd heard voices aplenty describing her. Children's, at the boarding schools. *Look at her! Gross.* Some soft, some in taunts and shouts. Later the voices of peers—those always in whispers. And the looks, full of pity and curiosity.

Over the years her face had improved, with surgery and time. But it had never been enough.

"I can't stand the sight of you." Father's last words to her, the day of her graduation from college. And Peter's: "Do you think you're going to find anyone else when I'm gone?" Voices that never quite went away. She'd stopped looking in mirrors long ago, but the voices told her what she was.

The bride of Frankenstein. Only she'd never be anyone's bride.

". . . just dropped by to welcome you, and ask you if . . ."

Alex snapped out of the past. This voice was in the here and now, and she was still clutching Julie's hand in a death grip. She let go quickly.

"I'm sorry. I didn't hear you."

Julie didn't react to her brusqueness. Her smile remained uncomfortably warm. "I'm sure you've got a lot to do, moving in and all. I didn't want to bother you. But I wanted to make sure it's okay if the kids wander onto your land sometimes." She made a wry face. "Sorry. I mean my nieces and nephews and brothers and sisters and their friends. You know the south border of the rez is only a couple miles from here, as the crow flies, and the kids—well, it's sort of their backyard, if you know what I mean. Didn't want you thinking we were trespassing or anything."

Alex quelled her instant reaction and wrapped her arms around her ribs. She'd already begun to think of this as her sanctuary, where she could be left alone to do her work. Already that modest hope was being taken away from her. Kids roaming all over her woods, scaring away the wildlife . . .

"They won't be any trouble," Julie said. Her expression was suddenly grave, and the serious look seemed somehow foreign to her round, pleasant face. "They won't interfere with your work, I'll make sure of that."

Alex forced herself to relax. Julie wasn't staring at all, wasn't challenging her. There was no threat here. It didn't make any sense to antagonize her neighbors.

"Do you . . . want to come in for coffee?" she asked awkwardly.

Julie shook her head. "I'm willing to bet you don't even have your coffee maker unpacked yet. Anyways, I'll want to bring the kids over so you can see they're not so bad." She grinned. "Pretty good kids, actually. And since your mom and mine used to play together—"

"Your mother knew mine?"

"Yeah. A long time ago. Knew your grandparents, too." Quick as summer lightning her expression sobered again. "We heard about your mom. I'm sorry."

Sorry. Sorry about something that had happened seventeen years ago. But Julie still wasn't staring at her face, and there was no pity in her eyes.

Alex looked away. "Thanks. About the kids . . ." She flexed her fingers on her arm. "No snowmobiles. No guns. It's important that the animals, the wolves, feel safe here."

"I understand. I'll keep them in line, and they won't come too far in. Thanks."

As simple as that. Alex ventured a smile and tested the unfamiliar feeling of satisfaction. Someone—another human being—had needed something from her and she'd given it. Such a small thing, really. It hadn't hurt at all.

"You sure you . . . won't come in?" she ventured.

"Can't. Got to get back to the rez. But listen—" Julie pushed her hand into the front pocket of her coat and searched it thoroughly before switching to the other. "Damn, I know it's here somewhere. Ah!" She grinned and pulled out a smudged, wrinkled card and held it out. "I'm Merritt's resident mechanic, by the by. You got a pretty nice truck there, but you never know. You bring her in if you need anything and the repairs will be on me."

Alex took the card. "That's very nice of you."

"It's nothing." Julie lifted one showshoe-clad foot and knocked caked snow from the bottom. "I'm sure we'll see each other in town. I'm there most days. You drop by my shop on Pine Street and we'll chat some more. I'd like to know about this work you're doing with the wolves." She met Alex's eyes. "We're Wolf Clan, you know."

Alex watched Julie make her way across the clearing and vanish among the trees. *Wolf Clan.* She went back inside and into her bedroom, hardly feeling the warmth of the fire she'd started in the stove. She opened her journal to the page she'd left.

Julie Wakanabo. I like her. But I'm afraid, Mother.

She paused, reminding herself that no one would ever see the words she wrote here. No one else would know how afraid she was.

I know what you'd say. Maybe I will talk to her again. But once I'm working, I won't have much time to socialize.

Socialize. The word sounded false and forced and alien. She hadn't had any friends in school. And long months in the field alone, tracking and studying wolves, hadn't added anything to her minimal expertise with people. Her work had given her every excuse to avoid them.

I know wolves better than I'll ever know people. And the wolves need me—here as much as in Montana and Idaho. No matter what else happens, I'll still have that.

She hesitated a very long time before she wrote the next line. *I was happy here once. Maybe I can be again.*

Happy, yes. Happy if she could just stay out here, alone with her wolves.

She ended the entry as she always did.

I'm sorry, Mother.

She closed the journal and put it back on the bed table. She couldn't put off going into town much longer. And she couldn't expect anyone else in Merritt to be like Julie Wakanabo.

She wondered if anyone would remember her at all, that beautiful and naive little girl who'd suddenly stopped coming so many years ago.

Alex shrugged into her coat and headed for the door, gathering her hair into a ponytail at the nape of her neck, pulling it smooth until her entire face was exposed.

"They'll have to get used to me sooner or later."

But she still felt the same way she had that first day at boarding school. Exactly the same.

Alex flexed her fingers into fists and strode out the door.

*S*he was the one.

He knew her scent as he knew his own. She was the lost one, the companion, whose words still lived within his mind.

He followed her as she scouted the woods each day, tracking the other wolves whose territory this was; watched from cover when she found his prints in the snow. She had seen him once or twice, when he'd been less than cautious, but there was no fear in her. That was as it should be. She had never been afraid in that time Before.

Before. The memories returned in images brief and blinding as sunlight striking snow crystals. Feelings he was only beginning to comprehend. Needs that were part of the other self he had almost forgotten.

He had heard her voice, and it was the same and different. *"I'll help you,"* she had said, Before. *"Don't go, don't be afraid, I'll help you. . . ."*

His other self remembered pain and loss. Time had no meaning to the wolf he was, but to the other it was terribly real. Time passing, and mysterious purposes left unfulfilled. He wanted to run from the new thoughts, but *she* held him here.

And there was something else that spoke to him, something that had emerged out of nowhere to speak inside his head. *Go back,* it said. *Remember what you are.*

The scents of mating came to him on the late-winter winds; he heard the nearest pack squabbling as they prepared for the season of new life. Only *he* ran alone. But there was a great urgency inside him, and it would not be laid to rest until he went to her as he had done in the time Before.

You must go back.

He flung new-fallen snow from his coat as she returned to her den, and thought of his empty belly. A hunt—long and arduous, because he always hunted alone—and then rest. His other self knew there was more, much more. Soon there would be an end to hiding. Soon he would go back. Soon they would be together again.

Soon.

He turned on his paws and melted into the shadows of the forest.

" *T*hose God-cursed wolves."

"A guy could die of old age before those government people get out here to do what they were hired to do."

"You got that right. Damned if I'll sit around and watch those wolves tear up another of my cows."

Alex paused behind the shelf of canned vegetables, her hand tightening around a jar of pickles. The small general store in Merritt was a favorite gathering place for the local farmers and anyone else in the mood for chewing the fat. It was also the place to hear the latest town gossip, and during the two weeks since her arrival Alex had taken advantage of that fact as often as the natives.

She made it a point to learn who her enemies were.

"What d'ya think, Sigurd? What do you say we take care of this ourselves?"

Silence followed, as if the other farmers were acknowledging the seriousness of the question. Alex set down the jar and moved along the aisle, crouching to keep the top of her head from rising above the boxes on the highest shelf.

"I don't know, Howie. I've seen that black wolf. He's big. If he's anything like the one a few years back—"

"The one old man Arnoux was after," Howie said, his voice heavy with significance. "Five years ago. The same time that girl was found torn apart near the reservation."

Alex waited tensely. There was a silence full of unspoken meaning. Boots shuffled on the wet floor.

Dutch, an older man Alex had always known to be reasonable and levelheaded, gave an inelegant snort. "Hey, now. The police said that was a man's work. No wolf—"

Howie rounded on the older man. "I saw the body. I don't give a damn what the cops say. I know what Arnoux believed, and no one knows more about wolf killings than he does. His own parents were killed by wolves up in Canada. He—"

"Is a recluse no one knows much about. Maybe even crazy . . . been out in the woods an awful long time. I for one intend to use my head. The chances that this is the same wolf, after five years—"

"Does it matter?" Howie demanded. "We can't just let it slaughter our livestock. Last time we never caught the killer. I'm through with waiting. The black took two prime turkeys just yesterday, and the cow last week. For all I know he'll go after a kid next."

"Now, Howie, you know that ain't legal anymore."

"*You* don't know shit. I've never had no use for those wolf lovers—"

"Look, if we just call the Animal Damage Control people, you'll get your compensation. They'll come out and take care of the livestock killer. They know what they're doing."

Howie spat. "Yeah, like they took care of that wolf five years ago? If I had my way, there'd be no wolves in Minnesota at all—"

Alex straightened and strode around the shelf.

"Excuse me, *gentlemen*," she said coldly.

The four farmers, ranging in age from firebrand Howie's mid-twenties to easygoing Dutch's eighth decade, stepped back hastily from the shelf. Alex ignored Howie's hostile stare and looked at each of the other three men, one by one. Sigurd Brown pulled his feed cap low over his eyes and shuffled off with a muttered excuse. Norm McCallister shook his head and shoved his hands in the pockets of his coat. Dutch gave her a wan smile.

"Didn't know you were there, Miss Alex," he said. Howie snarled a curse and stomped off; Dutch shrugged. "Hope you won't take it too seriously. It's hard when a man loses livestock, especially this time of year."

Alex nodded, keeping her expression carefully blank. Dutch was a decent man, even if there was pity in his eyes. And she needed his help.

She was hardly the first researcher to settle in the area, but opinions like Howie's were entrenched and hard to fight. Especially not in the way she wanted to fight them.

She expected men like Howie to reject her. The first time he saw her, two weeks ago, he'd made his disgust very plain. But she'd run the gauntlet of Merritt's opinions, and she wasn't above using people's reactions to get what she wanted from them. Like Dutch's pity or even Howie's spite.

Nothing was more important than the wolves. Her job

was much easier with the goodwill of the people of Merritt—however she could get it.

"I understand your feelings, Dutch," she said carefully. "That's what the ADC is for." She grabbed a package of macaroni from the shelf and tossed it in her basket. "I hope you'll report the incident. If there's a depredation problem, it's to everyone's benefit to deal with it the right way."

Dutch nodded, though he avoided her gaze. "You bet, Miss Alex. Now, if you'll excuse me—" He touched the brim of his feed cap and walked off to join his friends, gathered around the checkout counter.

Control, Alex. Control. She eased her tense muscles and watched the men narrowly. *You can think whatever you want about me, but leave my wolves alone.*

"That ugly bitch, spying on us," Howie said, loudly enough for Alex to hear. "She'd love to drive us all out and give this whole state back to the wolves. I—"

"You shut up, Howie," Dutch said. "Pay for your food and get out of here."

"I'll pay for it if Olsen ever shows up."

Alex stared around the store, wanting out, wanting to get back to her woods. Mr. Olsen, the proprietor, was barely visible in the last aisle, his voice raised as he spoke to someone hidden behind the shelves.

"I know what I saw. You put that candy back and get the hell out of my store."

A teenaged girl emerged from the aisle, Olsen at her heels. Her skin was flushed, dark eyes bright with unshed tears. Ojibwe, like Julie, with long glossy black hair and a round, pretty face. Alex felt a lurch in her stomach as she recognized the hopeless anger in the girl's expression. Humiliation, shame, the desperate need to fight back when the odds were stacked far too high.

Alex didn't think at all as she moved to the girl's side and took her arm. "You okay?"

The girl looked up at her blankly. "Who're you?"

"My name's Alex. What—"

"I told you to get out," Olsen snapped from behind the girl.

Alex turned on Olsen, heart pounding. "What's the problem here?"

Olsen's eyes flickered at her and away. "I caught her shoplifting. Damned In—" He stopped, but Alex completed the sentence in her mind, and the girl stiffened.

Damned Indians.

Wolf lover. Ugly bitch . . .

"I didn't steal anything!" the girl protested, clenching her fists. "He was following me around—"

"I believe you," Alex said, never dropping her gaze from Olsen's.

"And so do I, Deanna."

The girl turned toward the new voice. "Aunt Julie," she said, visibly struggling to keep her dignity.

Julie stood just within the doorway, hands on hips, sweeping the store with an impassive stare. Alex looked from the girl's face to Julie's, noted the resemblance, and let her breath out slowly.

"So this is one of your nieces," she said.

Julie grinned, as if they were alone in the store and not the objects of several hostile stares. "Yeah. Not the best place to introduce you, but—Deanna, this is my friend Alexandra Warrington. The wolf researcher I told you about. Alex, this is Deanna, my sister's eldest daughter."

Deanna swallowed. "Hi, Alex." But her expression was still taut with strain, and Alex felt the girl's misery as if it were her own, hating the familiarity of it.

"You didn't by any chance get my truck finished?" Alex asked Julie with feigned casualness.

"Matter of fact, I was coming to find you. Looks like I timed it perfectly."

"You did. I was done here." She set her basket deliberately down on the counter, leaving the groceries for Olsen to put away. "Why don't we get out of here?" she said to Deanna. She held the girl's arm firmly as the two of them walked to the door. One by one she met the men's gazes and saw them slide away from hers.

The three women emerged into the wan sunlight. Deanna kept her expression rigidly in check until they rounded the short block. Then the tears came. Alex let Deanna go, flexing her empty hand, and Julie hugged the girl close.

"Thanks for what you did in there," Julie said over Deanna's head.

"Those bastards," Alex burst out. "Those damned bastards—"

"Easy. Come on, let's all go to the garage where we can talk." She ruffled Deanna's hair and started across the street.

The day was growing gray and promising snow. It had been a mild winter; the old snow lay in dirty heaps along the sides of the street. The sidewalk was wet under their boots. People loaded up supplies in preparation for the season's last big storms, or stood on the street corners talking about the weather. Alex ignored the stares that followed them.

"Does that happen often?" she asked as they reached Pine Street. "What they said to Deanna—"

"Often enough." Julie shrugged. "You get used to it."

Alex gritted her teeth. Get used to it. Was that what Julie and her relatives had done when people let loose their ugly prejudices? Was it so easy for them?

She glanced at Deanna. No, not easy. Not for Deanna, made to feel like an outcast at the most vulnerable age, when every minor slight felt like a kick in the gut. Oh, yes, she remembered.

"I didn't say we liked it," Julie said, and Alex started. Julie had an uncomfortable knack for reading silences. It was an uncanny thing; once or twice Julie had jokingly referred to her ability as an inheritance from her grandmother, a medicine woman on the reservation. If such talents existed, Alex was grateful that few people possessed them.

Especially people like Howie Walsh, and Olsen, and all the others who could see only her face and nothing underneath.

"The way I look at it, they're the ones with the problem," Julie said.

Alex strode ahead and up the driveway of Julie's garage, looking for her Blazer. This wasn't a discussion she wanted to pursue. But Julie was right behind her, persistent as a wolf on the hunt.

"Take Howie, for instance." Julie slouched down and thrust out her lower jaw in a parody of the man. " 'It's unnatural, the thing that woman has for wolves,' " she growled. " 'God knows what she's really up to out there.' " She snorted.

Deanna giggled, and Alex felt suddenly ashamed. They—the Ojibwe—had endured far more than she had, and they could still laugh about it—laugh at people who held them in contempt and feared them for their differences. Alex had never learned that trick.

She flexed her hand on the cold metal of her truck. *If you knew about my father and Peter, would you tell me the problems were with them and not me?* But she could never tell Julie about those things. Julie was the only real friend she had in Merritt, and even that wasn't enough.

"What was the problem with the truck?" she asked quickly.

Julie flipped back her dark hair and grinned. "Just the fan belt. This old Blazer of yours is a good deal. You ever want to sell it—"

"I'll let you know," Alex finished, falling into the familiar routine. It was the closest she ever got to casual banter, but it released the knot of tension in her stomach.

Julie's mouth twisted ruefully. "I got more cars than I know what to do with, anyway." Her smile faded. "You're worried about your wolves, aren't you?"

Alex looked up. There was no danger in this subject.

"Yes." She let her control slip a little. "I think Howie meant business."

"Yeah, I know." Julie pushed her hands into the pockets of her oil-stained coat. "Howie's not above poaching to take care of his problems. Not the patient sort, our

Howie." She arched a thick dark brow. "You know, you can report him."

"Not when I've finally gotten settled in here, when I'm so close to really beginning my research. I can't afford to make enemies in Merritt, Julie."

Which was nothing but the truth, when the wolves needed all the support she could win for them. Despite the fact that she wasn't much of an ambassador for anything. Despite the notion she'd briefly entertained of planting her fist in Howie's face—and Olsen's for good measure.

"One of the men was talking about a black wolf five years ago. Does that mean anything to you?"

For a moment Julie's face lost all expression, and then she blinked. "Five years ago," she muttered. "They must have been talking about the lone wolf that did a lot of damage not far from here—killed five calves and quite a number of sheep and chickens. Everyone was up in arms, but the wolf was gone before anyone could hunt it down." She hesitated. "It happens sometimes."

"Yes." Alex studied her gloved fingers intently and clasped them together. "Not often, but it happens."

A black wolf. She'd seen a black wolf on her land several times during the past two weeks. A wolf that wasn't overly wary of human beings. Yet black wolves were hardly rare, if not as common as gray. "This wolf—could it be the same one as before?"

"You'd know better than I would. Don't wolves live only a few years in the wild?"

Alex hardly heard the question. Her thoughts had fled into the past. Shadow had been black with a white blaze on his chest. She could see him clearly in her mind, as if she could walk right out into the woods and find him waiting.

But he would be long dead now.

"Alex?"

She shivered out of her reverie and focused on Julie again. "No, it probably wouldn't be the same wolf." She began to rummage in her backpack for her checkbook. "The men also said something about a girl from the reservation being killed around the same time," she said carefully. "About some people thinking the wolf had done it."

Julie was silent a long time, and when Alex looked up the other woman's back was turned. "We didn't believe it was a wolf. But the cops never found a suspect." She shook her dark head, walling off any further discussion of that subject. "That isn't the issue now. What are you going to do?"

Alex almost smiled. In two weeks and a few meetings Julie already knew enough about her to realize she'd never let the matter rest. Alex tested the unfamiliar feeling of knowing someone else cared enough to try to understand. She hadn't expected it, not even after she decided to risk Julie's friendship.

It felt strange to be able to expect something *good*.

"I'll do some investigating on my own," she answered. "There's a right way to go about dealing with livestock depredation, and it wouldn't be the first time a wolf's kills were exaggerated." She began to write out a check; Julie's hand came down over hers.

"Forget that. I told you it was on the house this time."

Alex set her jaw and almost argued, but Julie's pleasant face hid a core of stubbornness equal to her own. Alex hadn't been in debt to anyone since she stopped taking her father's money the day of her graduation from college. The only safety lay in not owing anything to anyone.

Maybe Julie was different. Maybe she was safe.

"Thank you," Alex said, stuffing the checkbook in her backpack. She opened the Blazer's door. "One more thing—you know of a guy named Arnoux? Some sort of recluse who might be a wolf hunter?"

Julie frowned. "Arnoux. Yeah, I know the name. He doesn't come into town much. He lives pretty far out, works on and off as a guide for some of the excursion companies. I heard his land is all fenced in, that anyone who comes near his place is taking a big risk. Sort of our token crazy backwoodsman, I guess. But that's about all I know."

Alex shrugged. Something to keep in mind, if this

Arnoux was likely to be an ally to Howie and his bunch of wolf haters. "Would you let me know if you hear anything else about the wolf?"

"Yeah, of course." Julie stared at Alex, brows knitted. "Just don't take any chances, okay?"

"I never take chances. You don't have to worry about me."

"Yeah," Julie muttered. "Thanks again for what you did in the store."

"Thank you," Deanna echoed.

Alex nodded awkwardly and slid into the driver's seat. She didn't need thanks for what little she'd done for Deanna. The only creatures that had ever really needed her didn't speak in human language.

They needed her now. She'd sworn to make a difference the very first time she went into the field as a wolf researcher, to champion the wolves in every way she could. They had given her a purpose, a memory of contentment, a reason for being alive. That was a debt she could never repay.

Adrenaline pumped through her body when she thought about Howie's threats. She'd seen dead wolves before, in Montana and Idaho, killed by fearful ranchers who couldn't share their land. And there were the vague nightmare images from her childhood, a fairy tale gone terribly wrong and tangled with tragedy.

But not this time.

It was a matter of simple justice. Howie Walsh and his ilk would kill a wolf over her dead body.

𝒥 2

Alexandra stretched her legs and tested her snowshoes one final time. Her gear was packed and the fire banked in the stove, awaiting her return. She knew how to get to Howie's farm cross-country; she could make it there and back in a few hours if she moved quickly. Waiting until tomorrow wasn't an option.

There wasn't even time to write an entry in her journal. Alex hitched her pack over her shoulders and started away from the cabin at a brisk pace.

She had just passed the driveway when she saw the wolf tracks. She stopped and crouched in the snow. One glance confirmed that they were the same ones she'd found before, closer to her cabin than they'd ever been: the huge prints of the black wolf she'd briefly glimpsed several times over the past two weeks.

This wolf was alone; there were no other tracks to indicate a pack anywhere near, though she'd heard them howling.

"I've seen that black wolf," one of the farmers had said. *"He's big. . . ."*

Alex looked up, squinting through the bare branches of a nearby stand of aspens. The tracks were fresh. The likelihood of observing the wolf was small, but at least she had an opportunity to see where it was going, what its patterns of movement were. If this was the same wolf the farmers had been talking about, she'd just been given the chance she was hoping for.

I've got to find him first. . . .

She let herself experience the excitement and the challenge, savoring the brisk air and the rush of blood beneath her skin. The tracks were easy to follow. Alex kept her pace steady and rhythmic, listening to the sigh of wind in bare branches and the cautious rustles and peeps of birds. She loved this world, as she had loved it as a child.

How those men in town would mock her if they knew her most secret dream, her only fantasy: to run with a wild wolf pack, to become one of them, to know what it was to live in a world free of human cruelty.

Alex blew out a long trail of condensed breath and watched it drift skyward. She was as close now as she'd ever come to that dream. Even closer than she'd been during her undergrad work in Idaho and Yellowstone as part of the wolf reintroduction programs there.

And very late at night, when she lay in her bed on the edge of sleep, she imagined a bond with the wolves that let her see them as no one else could. She also imagined that they could see *her* . . .

She skidded to a halt as a great dark shape emerged from nowhere to block her path. Immense, black as night, yellow-eyed, the wolf regarded her with an utter lack of fear.

Alex met the slanted gaze and memory flooded back, washing away every other thought.

"Shadow," she whispered.

She shocked herself with the name; even the wolf twitched its ears, as if to confirm her own absurdity.

She knew this wolf wasn't Shadow. Her childhood companion would have died years ago. But this wolf was what the long-lost Shadow might have been, if she had seen him grown to adulthood. He even bore the same splash of white on his chest.

Perhaps he was Shadow's descendant. If some part of Shadow had lived on . . .

No time for fairy tales now. This wolf was bigger than Shadow had been, surely bigger than any wolf ever sighted in Minnesota. One hundred and fifty pounds at least. Probably more. Wolves near this size were occasionally seen in Alaska, or the far north of Canada. Never here.

And he stared at her with an aggressive, almost human intelligence.

Alex moistened her dry mouth. *Healthy wolves never attack human beings,* she reminded herself. No wolf had ever attacked *her.* But this wolf should be running, long gone by now. Minnesota wolves knew too much about human treachery. This wolf looked as if it might be exactly what the farmers had said he was.

Fearless, reckless, a beast that had lost its natural distrust of human beings. A lone wolf the weight of a fully-grown man. A creature of which she should have the good sense to be afraid.

But she wasn't. The wolf's beauty set her heart to thumping in a hard, ragged rhythm. She wanted to reach out and bury her fingers in his heavy black coat, test its depth and richness against her hands. She wanted to go on looking into his eyes for eternity. She wanted to be one with him, as once a child had been a soul mate with a black wolf pup.

The wolf started toward her with a lurching step and collapsed in the snow at her feet.

Alex cast off her strange paralysis and crouched just out of reach of the wolf's massive jaws. The animal's breathing was labored, and his legs twitched spasmodically. A whine vibrated deep in his throat. The golden eyes closed. There were no visible signs of injury, but the other symptoms were devastatingly clear.

"Damn them," she swore, her voice catching on the curse. "Damn them."

She'd been too late. Howie or one of the other men must have put out poisoned meat even before she'd confronted them in the store. The poison they would have used was invariably fatal. Yet the wolf must have traveled some distance from Howie's land, and he was still, miraculously, alive.

He had come to her as if he knew she wanted to save him.

Sickness rose in her, and she reached out to stroke the wolf's coat, offering the only comfort she could. The animal accepted her touch without so much as a shiver of fear.

"I'm sorry," Alex whispered. "I'm sorry."

His eyes opened and fixed on hers. He whined again, flattened his ears, and raked his great paws in the snow. With supreme courage, he heaved himself onto his hindquarters.

As if in a dream, Alex moved to help him. She didn't stop to question why she should risk her life for a dying, desperate animal that might turn on her at any moment. She didn't wonder at the wolf's incomprehensible purpose. His urgency worked its way through her, compelled her to lend her strength to his.

She could hardly lift his great weight, but the wolf somehow found his feet and began to walk, half-supported against her. Staggering, lurching, he retraced the trail Alex had broken through the snow.

Toward her home. Toward the cabin and its clearing that he had marked with his massive tracks.

Alex had heard tales of dying wolves that found their way to human habitation in their final hours, as if in that darkest moment they recognized a distant kinship man had rejected.

But Alex hadn't forgotten. "Yes. Come with me," she murmured. "I'll take care of you. You won't be alone."

*H*e let her guide him, lead him, his heart nearly bursting with his battle for each step. Snow sucked at his paws, and he stumbled, muzzle plunging into icy cold. He licked the moisture from his nose and lurched forward again, urged on by *her* hands and voice.

And her words. Words his other self remembered. "I'll

help you. Don't go, don't be afraid." So she had said once.
And now: "You won't be alone."

Even as his vision dimmed they reached the open
place that surrounded her den, pausing just behind the last
stand of trees. His instincts screamed to send him away on
legs that no longer supported him, to leave this man-place
behind and find some quiet refuge to die. But his other self
had claimed too much of him now, as *she* had.

And there was a command within him—not her, not
his other self. *Come back,* it told him. *You must always
come back.*

He began to drag himself forward again. Her gentle
touch propelled him up to the entrance of her den. His
muzzle touched the dead wood as it opened before him.

Human scent—*her* scent—poured over him, envelop-
ing him utterly. His other self knew that scent as welcome.
He tried to lift his head and failed.

"Shadow," she said. "Only a little farther." When she
set her body against his, he found a last measure of
strength to help her, tottered into the sun-warmth of her
den. He had no will left to fear the fire to which she led
him. The ground was warm against the fur of his aching
belly. He lay down, closing his eyes, giving himself to the
soothing caress of her hand on his fur and the soft repeti-
tion of his name.

"Shadow. Shadow. Shadow . . ."

The pain began to fade. Somewhere his other self
waited, rested, gained strength. He would sleep, and when
the time came . . .

Come back. Remember.

*A*lex shifted the pile of wood in her arms and
awkwardly grabbed the doorknob, wedging the door open
with her foot. Behind her the night woods were still and
silent; on the other side of the door was another kind of
silence. She dreaded facing its inevitability.

The wolf might be dead by now, or in a coma. She
hadn't wanted to leave him for even a moment, but her

stove was burning low, and it was very late. Once she'd been outside in the peaceful darkness, she'd almost been afraid to return.

But it had to be faced. She'd begun this, and she'd finish it. She closed her eyes and stepped through the door.

The wolf was sitting up in front of the stove, staring directly at her. For a moment she couldn't believe what she was seeing.

He was *alive*. Incredibly, he'd managed to overcome an almost certainly fatal dose of poison.

And he was more than merely alive. He seemed to be in perfect health, ears pricked and tongue lolling. His slanted yellow eyes were clear and fixed on hers with focused intensity, as if he wanted something of her. Just like yesterday.

But now he was no longer helpless. She had no fear of wolves, knew they almost never attacked people, but wolves were also wild animals and by nature unpredictable. Particularly one who might feel trapped.

The wolf made a low sound, and Alex realized she'd been staring into his eyes—challenging him and declaring herself his equal in the only language he could speak. She looked away quickly, down at the wood in her arms. The door was still half-open behind her; with another kick she could have it open all the way, leaving the wolf a clear path of escape.

And then the reality of the situation hit her. She hadn't expected the wolf to survive. He was almost certainly the animal who'd been raiding livestock. If she let him go free, nothing would be changed. He'd go back and raid again.

What other choice is there? Dart him and turn him over to the ADC after he's fought so hard to survive?

But that was exactly what she should do. Exactly what professionalism demanded.

She heard the click of the wolf's claws on the hardwood floor as he moved to the water bowl she'd left beside the stove. He moved stiffly and slowly—not completely recovered, then. Not capable of surviving on his own. Still in need of her help.

He needed her. The wolves were the only creatures who did.

"Shadow," she said.

He looked up, water drops suspended from his chin. Answering to the name as if it were his. Dangerous, dangerous to personalize the animal, become attached to him when there would only be another loss waiting at the end of it.

But she hadn't been able to hold on to detachment yesterday, and she couldn't now.

She crouched cautiously to set down the wood, alert to the wolf's reactions. He watched her a moment longer and eased himself to the braided rug before the stove, laying his head on his paws. Unafraid. Trusting her. Ancient history repeating itself.

No. That past was gone. Alex rose again and walked into the kitchen with slow, deliberate steps. The wolf never moved. She took a chunk of venison from the freezer, setting it out to thaw. She had no idea how well the wolf would be able to eat, or if he would accept food from her. Everything would have to be played by ear.

Her journal was on the kitchen table where she'd left it last night. She sat in the chair facing the door and opened the book to a new page.

He survived, Mother. And now I wonder if I made the right decision. Nothing like this ever happened in Idaho or Montana. I was so sure that my best work would be done in Minnesota, and already I'm being tested. A scientist isn't supposed to lose her objectivity, but after only two weeks here—

She couldn't complete the sentence. After a moment she slammed the cover shut and went back into the living room where Shadow waited.

He was on his feet again, standing by the door. She forgot her resolve not to stare. Magnificent was the only word for him, even as shaky as he was. He lifted one paw and scraped it against the door, turning to look at her in a way that couldn't be misunderstood.

He wanted out. Alex felt a sudden, inexplicable panic.

He wasn't ready. Only moments before she'd been debating what to do with him, and now her decision was being forced.

Once she opened that door he'd be gone, obeying instincts older and more powerful than the ephemeral trust he'd given her on the edge of death. In his weakened state, once back in the woods, he'd search out the easiest prey he could find.

Livestock. Man's possessions, lethally guarded by guns and poison.

Alex backed away, toward the hall closet where she kept her seldom-used dart gun. In Canada she and her fellow researchers had used guns like it to capture wolves for collaring and transfer to new homes in the northern United States. She hadn't expected to need it here.

Now she didn't have any choice. Shadow leaned against the wall patiently as she retrieved the gun and loaded it out of his sight. She tucked it into the loose waistband of her jeans, at the small of her back, and started toward the door.

Shadow wagged his tail. Only once, and slowly, but the simple gesture cut her to the heart. It was as if he saw her as another wolf. As if he recognized what she'd tried to do for him. She edged to the opposite side of the door and opened it.

Biting air swirled into the warmth of the cabin. Shadow stepped out, lifting his muzzle to the sky, breathing in a thousand subtle scents Alex couldn't begin to imagine.

She followed him and sat at the edge of the porch as he walked stiffly into the clearing. "What are you?" she murmured. "Were you captive once? Were you cut off from your own kind?"

He heard her, pausing in his business and pricking his ears. Golden eyes held answers she couldn't interpret with mere human senses.

"I know what you aren't, Shadow. You aren't meant to be anyone's pet. Or something to be kept in a cage and stared at. I wish to God I could let you go."

The wolf whuffed softly. He looked toward the forest, and Alex stiffened, reaching for the dart gun. But he turned back and came to her again, lifted his paw and set it very deliberately on her knee.

Needing her. Trusting her. Accepting. His huge paw felt warm and familiar, like a friend's touch.

Once she'd loved being touched. By her mother, by her grandparents—by Peter. She'd fought so hard to get over that need, that weakness.

Alex raised her hand and felt it tremble. She let her fingers brush the wolf's thick ruff, stroke down along his massive shoulder. Shadow sighed and closed his eyes to slits of contentment.

Oh, God. In a minute she'd be flinging her arms around his great shaggy neck. *Wrong, wrong.* He was a wolf, not a pet dog. She withdrew her hands and clasped them in her lap.

He nudged her hand. His eyes, amber and intelligent, regarded her without deception. Like no human eyes in the world.

"I won't let them kill you, Shadow," she said hoarsely. "No matter what you are, or what happens. I'll help you. I promise." She closed her eyes. "I've made promises I wasn't able to keep, but not this time. Not this time."

Promises. One to a strange, lost boy weeping over the bodies of two murdered wolves. A boy who, like the first Shadow, she'd never found again.

And another promise to her mother, who had died to save her.

The ghost of one had returned to her at last.

The wolf whined and patted her knee, his claws snagging on her jeans. A gentle snow began to fall, thick wet flakes that kissed Alex's cheeks with the sweetness of a lover. She turned her face up to the sky's caress. Shadow leaned against her heavily, his black pelt dusted with snowflakes.

If only I could go back, she thought. Back to the time when happiness had been such a simple thing, when a wolf could be a friend and fairy tales were real. She sank her fingers deeper into Shadow's fur.

If only—you were human. A man as loyal, as protective, as fundamentally honest as a wolf with its own. A man who could never exist in the real world. A fairy-tale hero, a prince ensorcelled.

She allowed herself a bitter smile. The exact opposite of Peter, in fact.

And you think you'd deserve such a man if he did exist?

She killed that line of thought before it could take hold, forcing her fingers to unclench from Shadow's fur. "What am I going to do, Shadow?" she said.

The wolf set his forepaws on the porch and heaved his body up, struggling to lift himself to the low platform. Alex watched his efforts with a last grasp at objectivity.

Now. Dart him now, and there will still be time to contact the ADC. She clawed at the dart gun and pulled it from her waistband.

But Shadow looked up at her in that precise moment, and she was lost. "I can't," she whispered. She let her arm go slack. The dart gun fell from her nerveless fingers, landing in the snow. She stared at it blindly.

Teeth that could rend and tear so efficiently closed with utmost gentleness around her empty hand. Shadow tugged until she had no choice but to look at him again.

She knew what he wanted. She hesitated only a moment before opening the door. Shadow padded into the cabin and found the place she had made for him by the stove, stretching out full length on the old braided rug, chin on paws.

"You've made it easy for me, haven't you?" she asked him, closing the door behind her. "You're trapped, and I can keep you here until . . . until I can figure out what to do with you."

The wolf gazed at her so steadily that she was almost certain that he'd known exactly what he was doing. She wanted to go to him and huddle close, feel the warmth of his great body and the sumptuous texture of his fur. But she had risked too much already. In the morning she'd have to reach a decision about him, and she knew how this would end—how it must end—sooner or later.

Shadow would be gone, and she'd be alone.

Feeling decades older than her twenty-seven years, Alex took her journal from the kitchen and retreated into the darkness of her bedroom. She paused at the door, her hand on the knob, and closed it with firm and deliberate pressure.

She stripped off her clothes and hung them neatly in the tiny closet, retrieving a clean pair of long underwear. The journal lay open on the old wooden bed table, waiting for the night's final entry.

It's ironic, Mother. I thought I'd become strong. Objective. I can't even succeed in this.

Her flannel bedsheets were cold; she drew the blankets up high around her chin, an old childhood habit she'd never shaken. Once it had made her feel safe, as if her mother's own hands had tucked her in. Now it only made her remember how false a comfort it truly was.

$\mathcal{I}$t was a long time before she slept. The sun was streaming through the curtains when she woke again. She lay very still, cherishing the ephemeral happiness that came to her at the very edge of waking.

She wasn't alone. There was warmth behind her on the bed, a familiar weight at her back that pulled down the mattress. The pressure of another body, masculine and solid.

Peter. She kept her eyes closed. It wasn't often that Peter slept the night through and was still beside her when she woke. And when he was . . .

His hand brushed her hip, hot through the knit fabric of her long underwear. When Peter was with her in the morning, it was because he wanted to make love. She gasped silently as his palm moved down to the upper edge of her thigh and then back up again, drawing the hem of her top up and up until he found skin.

Alex shuddered. It had been so long. Her belly tightened in anticipation. Peter wanted her. He *wanted* her. His fingers stroked along her ribs with delicate tenderness. They brushed the lower edge of her breast. Her nipples hardened almost painfully.

The arousal was a release, running hot in her blood. In a moment she would roll over and into his arms. In a moment she'd give herself up to the sex, to the searing intensity of physical closeness, seizing it for as long as it lasted.

But for now Peter was caressing her gently, without his usual impatience—taking time to make her ready, to feed her excitement—and she savored it. She wouldn't ruin the moment with words. Peter wasn't usually so silent. He liked talking before and after making love. About his plans, his ambitions. Their future.

All she could hear of him now was his breathing, sonorous and steady. His palm rested at the curve of her waist, the fingers making small circles on her skin.

His fingers. Callused fingers. She could feel their slight roughness. Blunt at the tips, not tapered. Big hands.

Big hands. Too big.

Wrongness washed through her in a wave of adrenaline. She snapped open her eyes and stared at the cracked face of the old-fashioned alarm clock beside the bed. Granddad's alarm clock. And beyond, the wood plank walls of the cabin.

Not the apartment. Her cabin. Not the king-size bed but her slightly sprung double.

The hand at her waist stilled.

Alex jerked her legs and found them trapped under an implacable weight. A guttural, groaning sigh sounded in her ear.

Very slowly she turned her head.

A man lay beside her, sprawled across the bed with one leg pinning the blankets over hers. A perfectly naked, magnificently muscled stranger. His body was curled toward her, head resting on one arm. His other hand was on her skin. Straight, thick black hair shadowed his face.

Alex did no more than tense her body, but that was enough. The man moved; the muscles of his torso and flat belly rippled as he stretched and lifted his head. Yellow eyes met her gaze through the veil of his hair.

Yellow eyes. Clear as sunlight, fathomless as ancient amber. Eyes that almost stopped her heart.

For an instant—one wayward, crazy instant—Alex *knew* him. And then that bizarre sensation passed to be replaced with far more pragmatic instincts. She twisted and bucked to free her legs and shoved him violently, knocking his hand from her body. His eyes widened as he rocked backward on the narrow bed, clawed at the sheets and rolled over the far edge.

Alex tore the covers away and leaped from the bed, remembering belatedly that she'd left the dart gun outside, and Granddad's old rifle was firmly locked away in the hall closet. She spun for the door just as the man scrambled to his feet, tossing the hair from his eyes. Her hand had barely touched the doorknob when he lunged across the bed and grabbed her wrist in an iron grip.

Treacherous terror surged in her. She lashed out, and he caught her other hand. She stared at the man with his strange, piercing eyes and remembered she was not truly alone.

A wolf slept just beyond her door. A wolf that had trusted and accepted her as if she were a member of his pack. A wolf that seemed to recognize the name she had given him.

"Shadow," she cried. It came out as a whisper. "Shadow!"

The man twitched. The muscles of his strong jaw stood out in sharp relief beneath tanned skin, and his fingers loosened around her wrists for one vital instant.

Alex didn't think. She ripped her arms free of his grasp, clasped her hands into a single fist and struck him with all her strength.

3

"Can you hear me?"

He understood her question. Her voice, familiar and low, drew him back into his body.

The shock hit him again before he could open his eyes. The hair rose along the back of his neck, his muscles tensed, and he flattened his ears against his skull.

But the dream had been real. His ears remained motionless, and a chill raced along his hairless spine. When he moved, his body responded without ease or grace, all overlong limbs and awkward shapes.

It had happened. He had felt the change coming, his other self struggling to break free. And now the other was here.

The other was *himself*—himself reborn, helpless as a newborn pup.

Human.

Terror clawed at the wolf within him, the beast that cringed at what it could not comprehend. He fought the fear, as he had fought for survival a hundred times, and looked up at the only thing that was certain and familiar.

The woman gazed back at him with eyes the color of a clear winter sky. Her hair was bright like trees before the snow, thick and tangled about her shoulders. Her scent filled his nostrils, made his heart pound in his chest, and summoned memories from the inmost part of his mind.

"What the hell are you doing in my cabin?" she demanded. "Who are you?"

He heard the way the words shook with emotion. *Words.* He worked out the sense of them, tracking and catching them one by one like mice in a field. Sounds lodged in his throat, rough and unfamiliar.

Who am I? The thought formed in his head to match her words, but he could not voice them. He sat up, struggling to make his altered muscles obey his will. She scrambled back, her hands raised to hold him at bay, as if he were an enemy.

Hands. His own hands had reached for her, held her before she'd called his name and made him remember. She had tried to run, and he had thought only of keeping her close, regaining the warmth and comfort that had drawn him to her sleeping place.

No. There was a word for it—*bed*. And she had driven him from it, rejecting him as she rejected him now, with her body crouched and ready for battle. He knew how to interpret her movement and the sounds she made and the scents of her body. The knowledge grew, became a more familiar part of him with every beat of his heart. He looked into her eyes and read the set of her face.

She was afraid of him. Afraid. Her fear cut into him and squeezed his heart like the steel jaws of a trap.

"I don't know how you got in here," she said, "or who you are, but I have a rifle, and I do know how to use it."

The warning in her voice was as explicit as a snarl. For the first time he saw the slim, bright tube of metal resting against the wall. *Rifle.* More words—and memories.

He struggled upward, finding his balance. The world spun. He took a step toward her, needing, driven by a single realization.

He had *found* her.

"Stop," she commanded. He took another step, and she retreated. Frustration coiled in his belly. He looked down at the ground so far beneath him and saw the flat, dark shape stretched out from his feet, moving as he moved, touching the woman as he could not.

A *shadow*. More than a word. It was a name, what she had given him. She had called him Shadow, but now she didn't know him. He didn't know himself.

He touched his face. The smooth contours were strange and familiar at once. It was like hers. *Human,* he told himself. *Human.* He fought to remember, to find the path that would take him across the great darkness separating him from his only link to sanity.

The woman's gaze moved up and down his body. She touched her lips with her tongue, and her teeth came together with an audible click.

"You must be cold," she said.

Between one heartbeat and the next the world receded, changed, pulled him to another place. Back—to the time Before.

"You must be cold," the girl said. "Here, take my coat."

He lay shivering on the ground—shivering not from the cold but from the smell of death all around him. Only she was life, with her gentle voice and hands. "Please, let me help you," she said. But answers were locked away in his mind, sundered by terror and sorrow. He could only stare at her, memorizing her face as the one sure haven in the midst of hell.

"Help me," he whispered.

She started—not the girl but the woman. He looked at her and knew they were the same. He remembered. He remembered her as she had been, her promise that had kept him living.

He had *found* her.

He recaptured the image of the girl who had helped him. Slim and gawky with adolescence, like a half-grown pup, but already beautiful. His understanding of human beauty came back to him in a rush; he recognized it when he looked at her now.

Changed and yet the same. Red hair and light blue eyes, long-legged and undeniably female. Her scent had changed as well, in a way that made his body feel strange and tight.

"You can speak," she said. "Who are you?"

She had asked that before—here, and in the dream-time of long ago. He searched within himself and found something else. Something he knew, as he knew her.

A voice. A voice that whispered mockery of his mute-ness, grew louder as he listened and felt the first stirrings of fear.

Who are you? the Voice echoed. *You are a monster.*

Monster. The meaning escaped him, but he felt the judgment behind it, disgust twisting inside him like the Voice, faceless and ringing with authority. Pulling him, dragging him into a place where he couldn't see, couldn't hear, couldn't breathe.

Come back, boy, the Voice said. *Come . . .*

"No," he rasped. The woman's startled face became a blur in his sight. He backed away until his legs hit the bed again. He shook his head violently, trying to rid himself of the thing that rode on his returning memory like a leech.

Panic raced along his nerves. He twisted and leaped up onto the bed, circling to stare at the walls that impris-oned him.

Walls. They closed in, ready to crush and suffocate. He was trapped. But his eyes found the woman again and looked beyond her.

There was a door. A way out. Only she stood between him and escape from the Voice. He had run from the Voice—he remembered that now. He had run, and run, and run. . . .

He jumped down, forgetting as he did the transforma-tion of his body. His miscalculation sent him crashing to his knees. He surged up again, flung himself at the door and hit it with his full weight. It refused to give. He clawed at the wood with his bare, useless fingers until they were raw with pain.

Warm, strong hands caught and held them. He turned on his captor, a snarl caught behind his teeth. The woman's eyes fixed on his. She challenged him, denying her own fear, with the implacable authority of a pack leader.

"Stop," she commanded. "Take it easy. You'll be all right." She tugged, pulling his hands away from the door. "Let me help you."

He shuddered, remembering those words. They had drawn him here. They drowned out the Voice of judgment, worked a powerful magic on his soul.

He turned his fingers in her hold and gripped her hands. Her body resisted. His nostrils drank in the scent of her as his skin absorbed her warmth.

Another name came to him. A name from the past—a gift the girl had given him so long ago. *Her* name.

Alexandra. He formed the word in his mind and shaped his lips to voice it.

"Alexandra," he said, lifting her hand to his mouth. He touched his tongue to her skin and raised his eyes to meet hers. "Alexandra."

*H*is voice was deep, husky, and perfectly comprehensible. He was at least half-crazy, and quite possibly dangerous. Rationally, logically, Alex knew she'd never seen him before.

But somehow he knew her name.

She shivered at the touch of his tongue on her hand. His gaze held hers with so potent an appeal that she was helpless to look away or pull her hands from his grip. Only moments before she'd been trying to calm him, still his frantic attempts to tear down the door. Now, with a touch and a glance, he almost made her believe she had met his golden gaze a hundred times.

During the past few minutes her emotions had undergone a series of overwhelming transformations. First the erotic half dream of Peter, then the shock of finding a naked man in her bed, the fear when he'd come after her—and then the anger.

Her counterattack had been instinctive, a primitive surge of violence at his trespass. He had been touching her, caressing her, making her *feel*. For a moment this strange, wild man had been the focus of all her inarticulate rage.

But when she saw him lying there, hardly able to speak, with that desperate, haunted look in his eyes, her anger had died. And when he began to claw at the door like an animal in a trap, she'd instantly responded as she'd have done with any panicked wild creature.

Until the man had spoken her name and shattered that brief illusion.

He still looked wild, with his burning golden eyes and shaggy hair and unselfconscious nudity. He didn't seem to be aware of his state at all, but he had made *her* aware. He had made her far too aware.

Alex wet her lips. She hadn't seen many naked men in her life, and only one intimately. This man was taller and bigger than Peter, and he was . . . She struggled for the right word.

She felt herself drifting into a strange, dreamlike state as his warm breath caressed her skin. It occurred to her what he most resembled: a prehistoric human from some old movie, hunting mammoths and saber-toothed tigers. Or a man raised by animals in the forest, come back to civilization.

His tongue stroked across her hand once more. The feel of it was incredibly erotic. Another sensation, more fundamental than emotion, coiled in the pit of her stomach.

The same sensation she had felt lying in bed, one she'd never expected to know again. The touch of a man's hands, a man's mouth on her body. She was suddenly, profoundly aware of the stranger's utter maleness, the clean and formidable and entirely unobscured lines of his body.

Magnificent. That was the word she'd wanted. Like a predator in his prime—magnificent with his broad shoulders, deep chest, long muscular arms. Taut, ridged belly, legs corded and powerful. Skin that smelled of pine and earth. Strong facial bones, clean and untainted by any dissipation, nearly perfect in their beauty. Black hair that fell almost to his shoulders, painted with an unusual streak of white at one temple.

Strong hands that had moved gently on her skin and held her prisoner. Eyes like none she'd ever seen, except in one other creature.

"Shadow," she murmured.

His eyes flickered and the spell they'd woven evaporated. Alex's reason returned. She jerked her hands free and reached for the rifle propped against the wall. Her fingers stopped just short of the barrel. The wild man stepped back, regarding her with hooded wariness.

"You know my name," she accused. It was all she could think to say, and she hardly knew what response to expect. He might be mentally disturbed, but he had passed up an obvious opportunity to attack her when she was asleep, and his first words had asked for her help.

Her *help*. She found her gaze straying down his body again and forced it back to his eyes. They were hardly less dangerous. He was utterly focused on her face; she almost lifted her hand to touch her scar.

She looked behind him, at the floor and around the room. No sign whatsoever of clothes he might have abandoned. He must have left them outside the room. And it wouldn't have been difficult for him to break into her cabin. He'd stripped and lain down beside her, like a lover expecting a welcome.

Alex slid her fingers carefully around the rifle and gripped the doorknob in her other hand. Shadow hadn't come when she called before. He wasn't a pet dog to run at her command. But if the wolf was waiting just beyond the door . . .

"It's cold in here," she said carefully. "I suggest we move into the living room. I'll need to get the fire going again."

He cocked his head. "Cold," he repeated, a look of intense concentration coming over his face. He folded his arms. "Fire?"

"Me Tarzan, you Jane," she muttered. Could it be that he had a limited understanding of English? Had he suffered brain damage of some kind? He looked healthy—altogether too healthy.

It wasn't enough to treat this man like a potentially dangerous wild animal. Being male, he couldn't be trusted. Being human, he was by nature unreliable and wouldn't play by nature's sensible rules. She pushed from her mind the fleeting thought that Shadow hadn't either.

The doorknob turned with a click. Alex maneuvered her body to pull the door inward, never taking her eyes from the wild man. She backed away down the short hall and into the living room.

"Shadow," she called.

The room was silent except for the muted pop of charred wood in the stove. She risked a glance at the old woven rug where Shadow had lain.

It was bare. Alex gripped the rifle in both hands. The door to the spare bedroom was closed, and she could see the kitchen from where she stood. The front door was still firmly shut and showed no signs of having been forced. Neither did any of the windows.

Shadow was gone. He had vanished as mysteriously as the wild man had appeared.

But she had no time to spare for worry. The man was emerging cautiously from the bedroom, nostrils flared, looking for all the world like a transplanted wolf being set free of its cage.

Alex choked on a harsh laugh. *Hysteria, Alex?* There was nothing remotely amusing about this. She'd lost any hope of barricading him in the bedroom.

As if he'd heard her stifled snort, the man looked straight at her. His brows met over narrowed eyes.

"Alexandra," he repeated solemnly. "Funny?"

His vocabulary is growing by leaps and bounds. "Not very," she mumbled, and then louder, "Can you understand what I'm saying?"

He seemed to weigh her question with great care and then nodded. The movement was rough and unsure, but it was recognizable. Dark hair, streaked with white, tumbled over one eye. "I . . . understand," he said. His voice still held a certain roughness, as if he hadn't used it in a very long time.

Maybe he hadn't, wherever he'd come from. She imagined a fantastic new scenario: he was a trapper from way up in the taiga across the Canadian border who'd spent so long alone that he'd forgotten how to talk; he'd wandered south and found a comfy cabin and a convenient woman. . . .

Alex backed closer to the front door. Crazy. This was the twentieth century, and he wasn't much older than she was.

"Are you thirsty? Hungry?" she said. Simple questions first, since he seemed cooperative.

His reaction was immediate. He licked his lips, making her stomach tighten with the memory of his tongue against her skin. Raking the room with his gaze, he fixed on the metal bowl she'd left for Shadow and went directly for it. Before she could stop him, he picked it up and drank the remaining water in one long swallow.

"Not finicky, are you?" Alex said. She reached behind her to touch the front door, testing the knob. It was still locked, just as it had appeared to be. Solving that mystery was not a high priority. She could be out the door in a second.

The wild man made a sharp noise eerily like a growl. Alex snapped her attention back to him. He was looking at her hand on the doorknob, as if he knew exactly what she was thinking.

In a few long strides he was before her, holding her gaze with his. "How long?"

"I don't understand you," she said, keeping her voice very low. "How long . . . what?"

He flung back his head in a gesture of eloquent frustration. Long, dark lashes shielded his eyes. "How . . . long . . . wolf?" he said deliberately.

Wolf. Alex thought immediately of Shadow. The man must have seen the wolf after all. But what was he asking?

"Did you . . . see the wolf when you came here?" she asked. "Where did he go?"

He gave her a very strange look, as if she were the crazy one. And then he groaned. His shoulders tensed and began to shake, and the rough noise he made hovered between a sob and a snarl.

She realized after a moment of frozen fascination that he was laughing. Laughing with a peculiar helplessness, with more than a touch of madness.

Alex thought about the door again, and the rifle in her hand. She'd been bluffing about the rifle anyway; she'd pulled it out of the closet while he was unconscious, but the thought of shooting him made her feel the way she had when she tried to dart Shadow.

"Listen," she said. At once his laughter stopped; he focused on her again, and she almost wished she'd let him stay in whatever shadowy inner world he'd been visiting. "You need clothes. Where did you put yours?"

Again that strange look, and a flash of pain. "Don't . . . know," he muttered.

It was worse than she'd thought. "Where did you come from?"

His dark brows drew together, and he looked away.

"How did you get to the cabin?"

"Walked. Ran."

"Why did you come here?"

He seemed to gather himself, staring at her with that unnerving directness.

"To . . . remember," he said. "To find you, Alexandra."

The way he said her name was like a caress, as if it were something he could taste and savor. Familiar. Intimate. He might as well have licked her again.

But he said he'd come to find *her.*

"You know me," she said. "Where have we met?"

An inward struggle passed visibly over the man's face. "Shadow," he said slowly. "*Me.* This—" He touched his chest, made a gesture that encompassed his entire body. "Don't remember . . . who."

She passed over the incomprehensible part about

Shadow, though he clearly knew the wolf's name. "You've lost your memory," she stated.

He nodded. "Who, why, how long . . ."

Wonderful. Memory loss might explain a great deal, but it made him no less unpredictable. She considered the weather outside—there'd been sun, so it would be cold but relatively easy to travel in. One way or another this man needed help she couldn't give him, help she could only find in town. She wanted no more to do with him than was absolutely necessary.

With slow, cautious steps she left the door and circled around him toward the kitchen.

"I've got clothes you can wear," she said. "Sweats. They might not fit too well—they belonged to my grandfather—but they'll keep you warm. And there's food in the kitchen."

She kept up a steady, soothing stream of one-sided conversation as she raided the closet for her grandfather's old sweats, realizing too late that she'd had her back to the wild man for a full two or three minutes. She turned around. He was watching her, and she had another full frontal glimpse of his beautifully formed body before she tossed the clothes at him in angry confusion.

He let the clothes fall at his feet and simply stared at them.

Deliberately she turned her back and strode into the kitchen, propping the rifle against the kitchen table. The venison she'd gotten out for Shadow was still taking up space in the small refrigerator. Fiercely ignoring her worry over the wolf, she put the chunk of thawed meat on the table and began to rummage through her cupboards.

She came up with a box of crackers and a can of soup. Some faint sound made her look toward the table; a tense moment passed before she realized that the venison was gone.

The rifle, however, was where she had left it. She grabbed it and stepped into the hall.

Her wild man was sitting on the rug before the stove,

still buck naked, tearing at the raw venison with strong white teeth.

Alex covered her mouth. If he'd been truly starving in the wilderness somewhere, she'd have thought little of his eating raw meat. But along with all his other peculiarities . . .

She looked past him to the door. In town she could go for the sheriff or possibly the doctor—someone who could take the man in for care and questioning. Alex hugged the rifle against her side and walked into the living room. Amber eyes flicked up at her and down again. She made her way to the door, maneuvering her hand behind her back to unlock it.

"No."

The word was a resonant, rumbling growl. Alex let her hand slide from the doorknob and turned.

The venison lay abandoned on the floor. The man stood drawn up to his full, imposing height, every muscle tensed and quivering.

"No . . . leave," the man ordered. There was no mistaking the command in his deep voice; his gaze fixed on hers with almost tangible force.

"I need to get firewood," she said calmly. She jerked a nod toward the stove. "It's out in the shed. I won't be gone long."

He took a single, ominous step, eyes narrowed. "With you," he said.

She didn't have much choice. It seemed he regarded her as a hostage after all. "You'll freeze out there."

For the first time he displayed all his teeth in an expression that passed for a grin but didn't seem to be one. "With you," he repeated.

Alex shrugged with feigned indifference and opened the door. Bitter wind, hardly touched by the noon sun, swirled past her. The man was right at her heels; he didn't so much as flinch, though his skin broke out in gooseflesh. She could feel the radiant heat from his body, burning through the heavy flannel shirt at her back.

Just as she'd told him, she went for the woodpile, though her attention was entirely on his movements behind her. She could hear the subtle crunch of his bare feet sinking into the snow. At one point he paused, turning his gaze toward the forest; she was ready for that moment of inattention.

She swung the rifle around and leveled it directly at his heart.

"I don't want to hurt you," she said. "But we're going to go back into the cabin now. You need help, and I—"

His amber eyes focused on the rifle and flashed to her face. He should have been shivering, hunched against the cold, but he stood as if he were in his element. "No," he growled. Alex could have sworn the hair on his head lifted.

She took a step toward him, the rifle firmly aimed. "Please . . . go back."

She was utterly unprepared for his next move. With a sudden lunge he batted the rifle from her hands. Alex tumbled into the snow and rolled, trying to put as much distance between herself and the man as possible. The rifle landed just out of her reach. She searched desperately for the wild man's position.

He was on his knees on the snow, exactly where he had been standing a moment before. His arms were stretched rigidly to the sides, and his body trembled with paroxysms as if he were in the midst of a terrible seizure. Even as Alex watched, horrified, his eyes rolled back beneath his lids, and his mouth opened in a cry of pain and despair.

A strangeness came over her vision then. She rubbed her eyes fiercely, struggling to focus on the impossible.

For the man was . . . blurring. The edges of his strong body melted, drifted into mist, and a dark cloud drew about him like a magical cloak. All Alex could see was the cloud, a black void against the snow. Until it began to solidify, take on a new form: four-legged and equally dark, the edges of it softened not by mist but by a heavy pelt of rich midnight fur.

The wolf crouched where the man had been, and his brilliant amber eyes looked directly into hers.

"Shadow," she croaked. For it was Shadow, and his eyes were the wild man's eyes.

There was no difference at all.

4

Alex sat back hard. Nausea kicked at her stomach; she rolled sideways in the snow and lay there, running it through her mind.

He had *changed*. The wild man—the man with Shadow's eyes, who could hardly speak and walked around stark naked and devoured raw meat—had turned into a wolf.

No. It can't be possible.

Once, long ago, Alex had believed in fairy tales. The magical summer with Shadow had proven all the stories Granddad and Mother had told her, snug by the fireside and wide-eyed with wonder. In time she'd replaced the stuff of dreams with the marvels of nature, and that had been enough.

But this went far beyond any wonder nature could produce.

Alex forced herself to look again. The black wolf lay in the snow with his slanted eyes tightly closed, panting heavily. He looked perfectly miserable.

Humanly so.

Since the accident, Alex had never had any occasion to doubt her sanity. Her mind was the one part of herself she was certain of. A scientist needed objectivity, a keen eye for observation, a superior ability for analysis. She'd never let her love for her subjects interfere with her studies.

Until Shadow had come to her.

Now Shadow was exactly where the man had been. Black with a white star on his chest. Alex thought of the white streak in the man's black hair, remembered the way he'd growled, his broken speech and eating of raw venison—and her speculation that he had been out in the woods far too long.

A silent laugh choked her. It all made a bizarre kind of sense in hindsight.

Sense? She got to her knees, staring at Shadow. She hardly noticed the way her hands were freezing, plunged to the wrists in snow.

I saw it happen, she thought. *I'm not crazy. I saw it.*

She was a scientist. If she couldn't believe what her own eyes told her—if she couldn't trust *herself*—she had nothing left to trust.

Fighting off the lingering nausea, Alex rocked back on her heels. The wolf's eyes opened. He whined again, a perfectly heartrending sound, and tried to stand. His legs gave out from under him; he looked like a clumsy puppy, and just as harmless.

Suddenly she understood. She couldn't afford to let these crippling self-doubts paralyze her for even a moment longer. It would all become clear if she could only touch Shadow, confirm his reality and her own reason.

She held to that thought as she began to crawl toward him. He made not a single sound; his ears lay flat to the sides. But when she came within a few feet of him his hackles rose and he scrambled back, paws scattering lumps of snow.

"Shadow," Alex whispered. Something beyond her conscious control drove her to pursue, casting aside every sensible precaution. She crawled closer; the wolf bared his teeth and trembled as she reached for the lush fur of his mane.

The moment her fingers touched him a shock coursed

through her body. It jarred her teeth and transmitted Shadow's trembling along the nerves of her arm, tying her to him with invisible bonds of energy. Her thoughts grew fuzzy, clouded with images she could make no sense of and hadn't the words to name.

With her fingers buried in Shadow's pelt, Alex stared into his golden eyes. She had no astonishment left to spare when he began to blur again, the soft edges of his fur growing softer still, the black coiling and shifting like smoke. She clenched her jaw as the bizarre, indescribable sensations engulfed her hand and spread outward, blanking her mind to semiconsciousness.

The next thing she saw were the wild man's eyes, and her own fingers clutched on his bare shoulder.

She knew then that it was real. She had felt it all the way to her bones.

Alex let her hand fall and rocked back, feeling as detached and pleasant as if she'd had several glasses of wine. Her mind didn't want to fight facts, but it didn't know what to do with the impossible.

The harsh sound of retching forced her gaze back to the man. He was doubled over, his arms wrapped around his middle and his black hair brushing the ground. Steam rose from the snow. When it was finished he lifted his head and turned away from her, covering the traces of sickness with slow deliberation.

Alex shook herself back to reality. What the hell was he? What kind of—creature could change from man to wolf and back again?

The answer was patently clear. Half the reference books on Alex's shelves had sections on the wolf in mythology and legend. There was a word for what she had just seen, a definition for this supposedly imaginary condition.

Werewolf. A slavering creature that made meals of human beings and changed by the light of a full moon.

The fairy tales were real.

Alex jumped to her feet. A few long strides would

carry her to the rifle. The man was fast, but he was still down in the snow.

Just as she began to move she looked back and knew it for a mistake the instant her glance met those golden Shadow-eyes. He struggled to his knees and held out his hand, palm up. The gesture was unmistakable.

"Don't be afraid," he said. "I won't hurt you."

He spoke distinctly now, with none of the fragmented quality of his earlier speech. It was as if, Alex thought numbly, his bizarre transformation had restored his faculties.

"You are Shadow," she said. Her voice emerged as a croak.

He smiled, his lips closed over his teeth. "Shadow. *Your* name."

The name she had given the wolf he'd been. *Was.*

Common sense urged her toward the rifle, but common sense held no power. Fascination was rapidly replacing disbelief. Now that he was able to communicate. . . .

"You are Shadow," she repeated. "What are— " She took another step away, rephrasing the question. "*Who* are you?"

His smile faded. There was bleakness in his eyes. "My name— " He sighed, brows knitted. "My name is Kieran. Kieran . . . Holt."

Two voices seemed to speak the words—one that of a man, rich and husky, and the other a boy's: a boy she'd met all too briefly many years ago.

Memories flooded back; all the little details, forgotten or dismissed, about that magical summer with the original Shadow. The last day, when she'd run looking for her wolf to say good-bye, and had found a boy instead.

A boy with black hair and yellow eyes, who'd claimed to know Shadow as she did. A boy who had lain weeping over a pair of murdered wolves, and then howled out his grief like one of them.

Exactly like a wolf.

And *Kieran* had known her name this morning, before

she realized what he was. Just as he'd known her name then.

Two identical wolves she'd named Shadow, seventeen years apart. She'd thought them merely related, because no wolf lived so long.

But a man did. And a man who was also a wolf . . .

"Oh my God." This couldn't be happening, and yet it was. The implications were overwhelming. She backed up, step by step, until her calves bumped the porch. Her rear hit damp, weathered wood with the solid comfort of reality.

Oh, yes. It made sense now. How he knew her name.

Ever since she'd begun her study of wolves, she'd puzzled over the first Shadow's trust for the child she'd been. Now it was all explained. Because Shadow had never been an ordinary wolf.

She grabbed the edge of the porch with both hands as if the ground itself might rise up underneath her.

Fairy tales were real.

Kieran's breath was a deep gust, pluming white mist that obscured his face. She could see the resemblance, comparing him to her memories. Boy become man. He'd been skinny then, all limbs, shy and strange. Unthreatening, though she'd been wary of him until the end.

Now he was a perfect specimen of masculinity. Handsome and powerful and utterly unpredictable. The animal she'd once loved was packaged in a magnificent body she had no reason to trust. A man's body.

Except he isn't human . . .

"You remember me," he said. "From before."

God help her. Before. For her, Before was the last time she'd been truly happy. That summer with Shadow. But she'd never known Kieran. She hadn't had a chance to know him, or learn what had become of him after that strange and tragic parting.

"You—" She found her voice again with difficulty. "It was always you."

He rose, testing his balance as if he wasn't yet used to

walking on two legs. "You do remember." His gaze fixed on her and he began to stalk forward, step by slow step.

If she looked only at his eyes she saw that the single contrast between wolf and man was in their shape. If he'd had a wolf's ears they'd be pricked forward, intent on his prey. His body would be low to the ground, ready to spring. There was no difference. No difference at all.

And she was the prey. It was there to read in every movement of his body, wolf or man. She had never been afraid of wolves. She was afraid now, and she loathed herself for it. She hated being afraid of anything—or anyone.

She pushed to her feet when he was only a yard away and braced herself.

"I remember that we were *friends*," she said.

He stopped. The fingers of his hands—the hands that had caressed her—curled into loose fists.

"Yes," he said. "Friends, Alexandra." The timbre of his voice was rough and sweet, like a wolf's call to one of its own. Ardent with intensity, but not threatening. "I *remember*." He emphasized the word almost fiercely.

Amnesic. He hadn't known who he was, or even how to form complete sentences before his change from man to wolf and back again before her eyes.

"I had to . . . come back," he said.

"Back?"

A muscle in his strong jaw worked. Alex stared in fascination at the play of skin across bone and tendon.

"Because of you," he said. "I came back to find what I've lost."

His memory.

"You remembered *me*," she repeated slowly.

He pinned her with his stare. "And your promise."

She'd thought herself numb to any new shock. *Her promise.* Heat and cold flashed through her body.

Now that she knew all her childhood fantasies had been real, every word, every thought returned with stunning clarity. Yes, she *had* promised, with ten-year-old earnestness, to help that strange and sorrowful boy.

"Don't be afraid. They were my friends, too. I'll help you. I promise, whatever's wrong, I'll help you—"

But the boy had run. She had never seen him or Shadow again. She'd searched in vain for them the following summer—her last visit to Minnesota. And then she'd had to give up the woods, her sanctuary, for a life of pain.

But the boy had found *her*. Here. And she'd made him another promise only yesterday, without knowing to whom she made it—a promise to the wolf who had survived against all the odds. *"No matter what you are, or what happens. I'll help you. I promise."*

No mere fairy tale, Alex thought. This was beginning to take on the proportions of an epic myth. A boy who was not a boy had remembered her offer of help and tracked her down all these years later, his past a mystery and his nature an impossibility. Because of that same meeting, she'd become a wolf researcher, returning to the very place they'd first met.

It was more than myth. It was a miracle. A miracle dropped in the lap of a woman who hadn't been a believer in a very long time.

Alex inhaled and fought down the panic. "What happened to you, Kieran Holt? How did you find me?" The questions sounded desperate, as if she could make a cage of them to trap fear and hold it at bay. "Were you here all along, waiting for me?"

He shook his head, tossing black hair dusted with melting snow. His voice changed, took on a harsher note like a growl. "I don't remember. It's all . . . dark." He passed his hand over his eyes. "I only know that you were there when—"

He broke off. Alex watched his face become a mask of pain and bewilderment, as if he had become that boy again—the boy who had mourned for murdered wolves.

Shadow's parents. Wolves that surely hadn't been wolves at all, but like him. *His* parents, murdered almost before his eyes. Alex hugged herself, seeing it all in her mind. And seeing another death, another time she'd bro-

ken a promise to save someone she had loved, too weak
and too afraid.

Mother. . . .

Warmth touched her. Kieran's hand, closing around
her arm, pulling her back to the present. His grip was gentle, but it trapped her completely. She went very still.

"I can't remember what happened," he rasped. "You
were there, Alexandra. You will help me."

Help me. The boy's last words to her—and the man's
first. She met his gaze. His eyes hadn't changed. They were
still Shadow's. She had stroked Shadow, touched him,
loved him. Yesterday and a thousand years ago.

"There is something I must understand," he said.
"Something I must find."

Had it been yesterday that she'd wished Shadow were
human with all the noble qualities of a wolf? Fairy tales
were real, and her wish had come true. Crazy, crazy wish.

"Alexandra," he said—a plea in that vibrant, unprac-
ticed voice.

His eyes. She must focus on his eyes and not the rest
of him, the human shape that overwhelmed her with too
many emotions, too many impossibilities. "How?" she
asked hoarsely. "How can I help you?"

He was silent for a long while, the struggle for memory
visible in his face. Incredibly open, that face. In an animal
feelings would show in tilt of ears and tail. Wolves always
broadcast their intentions to their fellow pack-mates; such
signals fostered peace and cooperation and reduced misunderstanding.

He's not a man. . . .

"I was a wolf when I came here," Kieran said. "I have
forgotten . . . how to be human."

Alex choked on a laugh. "You want me to teach you
how to be human?"

Abruptly he released her, looking away at something
only he could see. Something that hurt. "I must be a man
to remember. To understand."

*And you think being human will help you understand
anything?* Alex wrapped her arms around herself. That she,

of all people, should be asked to teach a wolf how to be a man . . .

"There is no one else."

No, it wasn't a plea. He had too much dignity for that, Shadow/Kieran. He spoke as Shadow would, as Shadow *had* with everything but human language.

He waited before her now, the boy she'd never had a chance to know or to help. Kieran Holt and Shadow. Wolf and not wolf, human and inhuman.

Her heartbeat began to accelerate. She had promised. She'd been given a chance to make good on that promise, and more.

It would be second-best to becoming a wolf herself— the impossible dream she'd clung to in the most hidden corners of her mind. To have the magic back again . . .

No. I don't want this. It's too late.

But it was already too late. She had given her promise.

She looked up at him. Shadow was in his eyes. The wolf was still there, inside him. *And as long as he's a wolf, I can understand him. As long as he's a wolf, I'll be safe.*

Alex knew then that she'd gone right over the edge.

" *Cheryl!*"

Julie came wide awake, shivering in a cold sweat. It was the same dream again. The first one had come two weeks ago, the very night after she'd met Alexandra Warrington.

She pushed up from the desk, knocking the pile of invoices to the floor. Outside the grimy office window the watery noon sun seemed somehow unreal; the dream still filled her mind, far more solid than the bills and records she'd been contemplating before she fell asleep on top of them.

Cheryl. Julie scraped damp hair away from her forehead and closed her eyes. Before she'd met Alex, Julie hadn't dreamed of her cousin for over a year. And those old, terrible dreams had been replays of the night of the murder, five years ago—the night Julie had found Cheryl's torn and mangled body just outside the reservation.

These dreams were very different. And none had been as clear as this one. None had felt so urgent.

Julie grabbed a scrap of paper and began to draw. The image was still sharp: a broken circle, with darkness all around. Cheryl within it—alive, as she'd once been. Beautiful and whole, as she'd once been. Waiting. Waiting with unearthly patience while she held a mirror turned toward the opening in the circle.

Outside the circle stood Alex, facing the darkness, as if she couldn't see Cheryl or anything else. And out of the darkness came a wolf. A black wolf that ran toward Alex and divided in two like water flowing around a rock. Each newly formed animal dashed again and again about the edge of the broken circle, so fast that they blurred like dark mist.

Julie dropped the pen, staring at the clumsy marks she'd made. If she'd dreamed only of Alex, it could have been easily explained. The first time she'd met Alex she felt a jolt of awareness, a feeling of affinity she hadn't tried to question. Since then they'd become friends, though Alex was still guarded and cautious, afraid of reliving some hurt she'd faced in her own past.

But with these new dreams Julie knew that whatever had drawn her to Alex was more than a response to pain and loneliness.

Julie rubbed her eyes. She thought she'd put Cheryl's death behind her, even though the murder had never been solved. Now she knew she'd been fooling herself. Even Alex had mentioned the murder yesterday. As if the coming of this new black wolf were an omen.

A broken circle. The spirits were telling her it wasn't over yet. Something still remained to be done, and the time had come to do it.

She stood up and walked to the doorway into the garage, staring at the truck she'd been working on that morning. Alex couldn't have anything directly to do with Cheryl's unsolved murder. Five years ago Alex hadn't even been near Merritt. She'd been somewhere to the west, doing graduate work with wolves.

But the dream said there was a connection. A connection between Cheryl and Alex, no matter how slight. And the wolves . . .

It was times like these when Julie wished she had Grandma's gifts. But medicine people were born, not made.

Julie shrugged into her coat. Maybe it was time to drop by Alex's cabin for a little visit. Maybe seeing her again would make it come a little clearer.

A broken circle. But broken circles could be mended, and Alexandra Warrington would have a hand in the mending.

"You're probably freezing," Alexandra said. "You'd better come inside."

Kieran turned to her, hearing the change in her voice. He drew in her scent and smelled the slight easing of her fear, the first sweet odor of acceptance.

He felt a profound and sudden sense of release, and the tension drained out of his body. He could not have let her drive him away. He'd tried to make her understand, but his ability to speak was still stiff and awkward, like a muscle long unused. Like the shape he now wore and must keep.

But now there would be no need to make her afraid again. He had despised the possibility of forcing her to help him, hated the compulsion that would drive him to it. When he thought instead of what it had been like to lie beside Alexandra—the softness of her skin, the sweet smell of her, the comfort of her closeness . . .

"Unless you plan to shift back to a wolf again," she added.

Her words cracked his reverie like a brittle eggshell. *Shift.* That was the word for what he'd done. Nauseating. Painful. Forbidden. To be denied at all costs.

"No," he growled.

She stiffened and raised her chin. "Then go on in. I'll be coming in a minute."

He wanted to trust her. He must trust her or have nothing at all. But he waited, watched her retrieve the rifle and lift it in her hands. His hackles rose, undeniable instincts blending with vague and terrible memories.

She turned and saw him. Her face stiffened, and he knew his expression was wrong. With an effort he stopped the growling deep in his chest.

"I won't hurt you," she said suddenly. She moved by him with slow, wary steps, the rifle held close in her arms.

"I know," he said.

She looked away and walked into the cabin. He followed; her warm scent enveloped him, easing his hatred of high walls. This was her world, her territory.

His, now. He went to the stove and the rug. The venison still lay there, and he felt both hungry and nauseated by the sight and smell of the raw meat.

Beast.

The single word cracked at him. He jerked up his head, staring at Alexandra. She was setting down the rifle, and he could clearly see her face.

Alexandra had not spoken. The word hadn't come from her, but another. It was the Voice—the Voice that had come before Alexandra had struck him down in fear.

The Voice that was inside him.

You're starting to remember, boy. . . .

Remember. He worked his fingers and stared at his raised hands. Not paws. Hands. *Not* a beast.

Alexandra was staring at him now. He watched her gaze sweep over him, lingering as if she judged him as another of her kind.

He looked down at himself. His body was fit and strong; it had been his before, and he was losing his awkwardness. He saw no flaws or weakness. But Alexandra stared. Her breathing quickened and her scent changed subtly, stirring him low in his belly.

Not a beast . . .

"What do you see, Alexandra?" he asked.

The pale skin of her face reddened. Abruptly she snatched a blanket from the back of the sofa and thrust it at him, anger in the twitch of her arm.

"Cover yourself," she snapped. "If you want to learn to be human—" She stopped and swallowed. "People don't go around naked."

Naked. A flash of realization raked at his gut like claws. He was naked, and among humans that was forbidden. Crazy. He had forgotten the shame.

Heat flushed his skin. He ignored the blanket and searched for the clothing she had given him earlier. He crouched and gathered up the pieces, sifting the fabric through his fingers, turning them over and over. The shape was familiar.

He snatched up one piece of clothing. *Pants.* They tangled in his hands like a living thing, all long flaps and openings. Balancing awkwardly on one leg, he struggled to push one foot through the widest opening. The other flopping leg curled around his ankle.

Alexandra was watching him, watching his clumsiness. With a snarl he yanked at the cloth and heard it groan and give under his curled fingers.

"Here. Let me help you."

Her hand stopped him, settling over his so lightly that he felt her warmth more than her touch. Averting her face from his nakedness, she held the pants until he found his way into them. She located the shirt and showed him how to put it on; when her fingers brushed his skin, he felt like flinging back his head and howling.

But humans didn't howl.

Alexandra stepped back. "Good," she said softly. "All right, then." She folded her arms. "You asked me before how long you'd been a wolf."

Kieran rolled his shoulders, adapting to the sensation of cloth stretched taut against his skin. "I don't remember."

"Damn." She looked around the room, her gaze fixing on the far wall. "Come over here, Kieran."

He followed her to the wall. A picture was hung

there—a silver-white wolf against a background of snow. Beneath it were rows of lines and markings.

Kieran touched the paper. Numbers. *Dates*.

"Do you remember calendars?" Alexandra asked.

"Yes." It was a victory. He stared at the calendar until it resolved into sense. "1996," he said slowly.

"You can read."

They were very close now, and he looked into her eyes. "I'm not stupid, Alexandra."

Her jaw tensed. "I never thought you were."

He glanced back at the wolf on the calendar and saw another image in its place: a woman, naked, against a bright red background. And below a different set of numbers.

"Five years," he said.

"What?"

"Five years ago. When I last saw a calendar." He closed his eyes to hold the memory. Nothing more would come.

"Have you been a wolf all the time since then?" she asked.

He looked down at his clenched fists. If he could, he would run—far and fast, beating out the anger in his blood, hunting the memories like prey. He turned to the wall and struck it with his fist. "I don't know."

Alexandra was very quiet. Kieran spread his fingers flat and listened to her walk away.

"It's a start," she said. "Maybe we should focus on what you *do* remember."

He put his back to the wall. His breathing steadied. She held the answers; they were in her eyes, in the shape of her mouth and the sweet huskiness of her voice.

"I remember coming to you," he said.

"When?"

"Yesterday. In the forest."

Her tongue touched her lips. "You were very sick."

Yes. He remembered the sickness, and knowing what he must do.

"Do you know how you came to be sick?" she asked.

"No."

She shook her head and rubbed her arms up and down. "You almost died, Kieran. You must remember something."

She tried to hide it, but he heard the tightness in her words, the frustration in her voice. Yesterday she had spoken to the wolf he'd been with gentleness, touched him without fear. Now he was human, and she pulled away, angry and afraid.

But this morning she hadn't been angry, when he had lain beside her. Her skin had been warm, and she had made sounds of pleasure that stirred him in ways he hadn't the words to name.

"I remember you, Alexandra," he said, pushing away from the wall. "Yesterday and before."

She avoided his eyes. "You were alone when we met in the woods yesterday. But when you were a boy—" She broke off and exhaled slowly.

"Tell me," he said.

"You said you remembered me—"

"Your face. Your voice. Being with you. But not who I was." He moved close enough to her that she was forced to look up. "You know."

"I only know what you *were,*" she said. "When I was a child I knew you as a wolf I called Shadow. A young wolf. We spent the summer together. And I met you as a boy, just before—"

"Something happened," he said. He closed the space between them and caught her hand before she could pull it back. "Blood. Everything changing." He shut his eyes, buffeted by emotion. Loss too terrible to be borne. The smells of violence and hatred; the horror and denial.

And the Voice. The Voice had been there, like Alexandra. Promising as she had promised. Commanding, pulling him away from death.

Her hand flexed in his and he released it, but she twisted her fingers to keep the contact.

"I'm sorry, Kieran," she whispered. "I didn't realize then. The wolves—they'd been with you when you were

Shadow. I guessed they were your parents. But when you were a boy, I didn't know you. I think you tried even then to explain that you were Shadow." Her throat worked. "We heard shots, and found the wolves killed by a poacher. You grieved terribly for them, but I didn't understand. I didn't know."

Her hand in his was all that grounded him. "I don't remember them. *I don't remember.*"

"I'm sorry," she repeated. "When my parents came to take me home, you'd run away. The next summer I couldn't find you, not Kieran or Shadow—"

"They were wolves." He focused on Alexandra, fighting past one realization to the next. "You called them my parents."

"I never saw them any other way," she said slowly. "But they weren't like any wolves I've ever seen. I think they must have been . . . like you."

Like him. He groped for some sense of rightness, some image of belonging, of not being alone. But something else lay waiting for him, releasing a flood of poison into his body. Disgust. Loathing. Contempt.

"Beasts," he said, echoing the Voice. "Animals."

Alexandra dropped his hand. He backed away from her, baring his teeth.

"What am I?" he demanded. "What *am* I?"

But he heard the reply in his mind. *You know, boy. You are a thing that should never have existed, an affront to nature. You are a monster . . .*

"Monster," he repeated. It was suddenly dark again; all around him, damp and cold and smelling of things that grow in the absence of light. A place called hell, where the punishment came. "I am . . . a monster."

The Voice approved. *The beast has corrupted you. You must fight it.*

The beast. The wolf was still there—Shadow, a black demon who snarled and lunged at the Voice, defying what tried to destroy it.

You must deny it, boy. It is not too late. . . .

Kieran hit the wall hard enough to shake him out of

the darkness. He pressed himself there to keep from falling.

"Kieran!" Alexandra said. "What are you saying?"

He thought she must know, that she could hear the Voice that labeled him for what he was. Her eyes were wide and wary; he could smell her unease, sense the quickening of her heartbeat. Wolf instincts that would not be driven out.

Now he recognized why she had reason to fear him. A creature neither man nor beast. A creature never meant to exist, bereft of memory.

Alone.

"Where did you hear that?" Only a slight catch revealed the fear she tried so hard to disguise. She came closer, holding his gaze. "Who told you—what you are?"

Again and again he was driven to the same replies. "I don't know. I don't remember." But the Voice was real. Some part of his past, cloaked in shadow.

Alexandra extended her hand and let it fall before her fingers brushed his arm. "Do you know the word *werewolf*?" she asked.

Kieran shuddered. He knew the word, though it had became familiar again only as she spoke it.

"Yes. A man who . . . changes into an animal."

"How do you change? How do you make it happen?"

He tried to answer her questions. He tried to remember how he had done it, change from wolf to man and back again. But all he could see in his mind was a dark fog; all he could feel was nausea and emotions too snarled to unravel.

"Could you do it now?" she asked.

Kieran shook his head sharply. "*No.* No." But when he forced himself to calm again and thought of changing, he could see no way to do it. It wasn't only that he must not—he *could* not.

He met Alexandra's gaze. "I can't make it happen," he admitted.

She frowned, though not with anger or disgust. "You certainly didn't need a full moon," she muttered, turning away to stare at the row of shelves against one wall. Shelves—with books. Memory came to Kieran, the sudden image of a book in his hand, smelling old and mildewed and infinitely precious. Only a single beam of light to read by, a beam of light on which he rode to freedom.

Alexandra was reading, her lips moving silently. He left the wall and went to her. Over her shoulder he could see the page, and the heading: *Werewolves*. And below that a picture, a drawing of an upright beast wearing tattered clothes and a slavering fanged grin.

The book snapped closed. Alexandra pushed it back into the gap on the shelf, blocking it from his sight with her body.

"You'll have to learn . . . not to sneak up on people like that," she said.

"The picture," he said. Stark pain lanced through him.

"That's not what you are," she said sharply. "And you're not a monster. Whoever told you that—" She took in a shuddering breath. "I don't pretend to understand exactly what you are, or what you can do. That's what we have to find out. But I've made a life of studying wolves, Kieran Holt. Fighting down all the myths about them. I don't believe in those kinds of labels, and by God I'm not going to hang one on you."

There was such fierceness in her, such strength and beauty. Her face was as luminous as the first sun of snowmelt. He could lose himself in it, make a new world out of the ardent promise in her eyes.

She looked down, clasping her hands. "I have the utmost respect for wolves. And you are . . . partly wolf."

She had touched and stroked him before he became a man. She accepted the wolf in him now. He reached for her instinctively, needing the reality of her warmth.

Her body resisted, but his need was too powerful, his wanting too potent. She was light and firm in his arms. He ran his hands over her back, shaping the curves and hollows through the cloth of her heavy shirt. She made a small sound in his ear; he lowered his mouth to her neck, where her skin was exposed, and ran his tongue lightly over it.

The taste of her, like her scent, only made him want her closer.

"Kieran," she gasped.

He knew she took pleasure in what he did; he sensed it as he'd sensed her fear before, somewhere far beyond thought. He wanted to make her feel good, to know the rightness he felt when he touched her.

Her hair was a thick mass in his hands. He nuzzled her cheek and traced the line of her jaw. Her eyes fluttered closed. Her lips were slightly parted; he was caught in the grip of another memory and acted on it without question, brushing his mouth over hers.

Alexandra wrenched violently free of his hold. Her eyes were open now, and her skin was flushed. She pulled her fingers across her mouth.

"If you want to remember how to be human," she bit out, "one of the first things you'll have to learn is that people don't touch that way."

It took several moments before Kieran understood her. He stepped back, knocking the bookshelf with his arm. A book fell to the floor with a sharp slap. The silence after was absolute.

Alexandra stared at the book and covered one side of her face with her hand.

"You liked it, Alexandra," he challenged softly.

Her head jerked up. The bright color fled her skin, leaving it nearly white. "No!" She swallowed. "No. I just didn't expect it. A man wouldn't do what you did. Not without permission."

Her fear was back. Fear of him. "*A* man *wouldn't do what you did.*"

Anger stirred in him, a chaos of yearning. He pivoted on his foot and looked toward the door. Beyond that wall was freedom. Freedom from the feelings he couldn't master, from the turmoil in his belly.

"Try to understand, Kieran," Alexandra said behind him. "I'm willing to help you, but you'll have to do what I tell you if you want to learn to be human. You may still have . . . instincts that seem right to you, that would be right for a wolf. But what you did . . . with me, the way you acted, is something other people wouldn't understand."

Other people. Human beings he must learn to face in order to become one of them. Deny the wolf or they would see what he was, turn him away, fear him. As she did.

"This is new to us both, Kieran," she continued stiffly. "We knew each other in another way before. Now we have to start over."

He looked back at her, the pulse heavy in his chest. "Yes," he said.

"I know how difficult this is for you. The sooner we bring back your memories, the less difficult it will be." With long, deliberate strides she walked to the sofa and sat down. "Do you agree?"

She seemed very far away with only the width of the room between them. "Yes," he repeated.

Still she wouldn't meet his gaze. "Let's go back to what we do know. You were human five years ago. You don't remember your time as a wolf since then, except in fragments, or even how you change. And we know that you were human seventeen years ago, when we met, so at some point you must have been . . ."

He lost the thread of her speech, hearing only the sound of the words, their sharp and urgent rhythm. She was making a wall with those words, a cage meant to keep him out. He walked to the rug by the stove and crouched with his arms around his knees.

". . . and you came back here again, wherever you were in between. There must be important keys to your memory in this area. Damn, I wish I knew more about amnesia. But your amnesia might not be typical." She sighed. "In any case, the calendar brought something back to you, and other objects might have the same effect. We'll begin in the cabin, and after that . . . Kieran?" She looked from him to the ground by his feet. "Are you hungry?"

He realized he'd been blindly staring at the chunk of venison that still lay there, oblivious to its pungent scent.

All at once he remembered the look in Alexandra's eyes when she'd seen him tearing at the meat.

Shock. Disgust.

He rose, snatched up the venison, and went to the door. Cold air slapped at his clothing. His bare feet slid on the thin layer of snow coating the porch. He flung the meat as far away as he could, just past the border of trees edging the clearing.

He shut the door carefully, denying his anger. And his shame.

"I will eat like a man," he said.

She was the first to drop her gaze. "I'm short on supplies, especially for . . . a man of your size. And Granddad's clothes aren't a very good fit, either." She inhaled slowly. "I'll have to go into town and pick up a few necessities."

"Wherever you go, I go."

"That would hardly be wise, given your situation. Not so soon—"

"Because you don't trust me," he said.

"You asked for my help, and you'll have to trust my judgment." He heard an edge of panic in her voice. "You can't just walk into town without your memory."

"Why?"

She pushed to her feet. "Because, dammit, we still don't know what you might—" She closed her mouth and flushed.

What you might do. "I go with you," he repeated, the hairs rising along the nape of his neck.

They stared at each other, fighting a silent battle for dominance. He couldn't let her out of his sight—that was the unshakable conviction that drove him, that rushed through him like the blood in his veins, and filled his senses.

As *she* did.

A sharp, blaring noise broke the silence. Kieran leaped and turned in midair to face the door. Alexandra strode past him, flipping back the curtain at the window.

"God. It's Julie," she muttered. She rubbed the side of

her face and looked back at him. "Kieran, you have to stay in the cabin. This won't take long."

"Who is she?"

"I'll explain later, and we'll talk—" There was a crunch of footsteps just outside the door. Alexandra opened it quickly, cast a final glance at Kieran, and went out.

Kieran hesitated only a moment. He heard voices through the door before he reached it.

". . . been wanting to talk to you, Alex."

"I appreciate your coming out here, but this isn't really a good time—"

He opened the door. A smiling woman stood close to Alexandra, dark haired and honey skinned. She looked toward him just as Alex did; her eyes, too, were dark, and they fixed on him intently.

"I think I see what you mean," the woman said. "I'm sorry if I interrupted."

Alexandra's expression revealed nothing, but her gaze was sharp with anger. "I didn't think you were quite up to coming outside yet, Kieran."

"I'm very well, Alexandra." He jumped down off the porch. "I wanted to meet your friend."

She showed her teeth, jaw set. "Of course. Julie, this is Kieran. A . . . colleague of mine."

"Oh yeah?" Julie tilted her head as she studied him, her smile not quite reaching her eyes. "Another wolf researcher, I guess?"

"I know wolves very well," he said.

"I'm not surprised. Not by that, anyway." She glanced at Alexandra. "Sorry, I'm being rude." She thrust her hand at him. "Julie Wakanabo, Merritt's resident mechanic."

He looked at her hand and remembered what the gesture meant. Her fingers were callused and cool in his. "Kieran Holt."

She was quiet a long while, holding his hand, looking directly into his eyes. Almost as if she knew him. He returned her scrutiny, searching for familiarity and finding only confusion. Not fear, but suspicion. Wariness that belied her grin and friendly words. And he knew she saw something in him that Alexandra did not.

Do you know me? he thought. But before he could phrase the question Alexandra all but came between them, forcing him to release Julie's hand. Julie flexed her fingers.

"Quite a grip, Kieran Holt," she said. "So you're visiting Alex?"

"As I said," Alexandra put in quickly, "Kieran's a wolf researcher. He's been staying in a cabin up near Sturgeon River. He was heading cross-country trailing a wolf pack and ran into some trouble with a particularly nasty wolverine. Had to leave most of his gear behind, but he remembered where I lived and made it to my place."

"Wolverine, huh? Good thing you weren't hurt."

"I wasn't—" Kieran began.

"He needed clothes and a place to stay for a few days," Alex interrupted. "Since I have the sofabed in the living room . . ."

"Sure." Julie looked at Alexandra, who flushed. "I just don't remember your mentioning Kieran before."

"I didn't expect to be working with him directly, at least not so soon. He's been . . . living pretty solitary for the past year."

"Yeah." Julie turned stubbornly back to Kieran. "You've been out in the woods a long time, I can tell."

Was there a challenge in her voice? Her eyes were full of questions. He knew that feeling, that need for answers.

"We tend to get that way," Alexandra said with false lightness. "You know how I am, Julie."

Julie smiled, but the wariness was still there. "One thing's for sure," she said to Kieran, "if you'd ever been around here before, people would've noticed. You haven't been into town yet?"

Kieran didn't look at Alexandra. "We were going into town now, Julie," he said. "For food, and clothes."

"Great. I'll follow you out, and we can talk, maybe over lunch. If that's okay with you, Alex?"

Alexandra's fingers flexed at her sides. "If you'll just

give us a minute—" She grabbed Kieran's arm, and he let her pull him onto the porch and into the cabin.

"Are you crazy?" she demanded when the door was closed.

"I don't know, Alexandra. Am I?"

"Damn." She released him abruptly and folded her arms, rubbing them up and down. "It would have happened sooner or later. If we'd had more time—"

"You can trust me," he said. He caught her hand and held it between his, feeling the shape of each small finger. "As I trust you."

Her emotion was like a bird startled from the brush, sudden and too swift to catch. She closed her eyes and shivered. "Damn," she whispered. "All right. But this time you're listening to me." Pulling her hand free, she walked across the cabin and disappeared into the bedroom. She returned a moment later with a leather pack. "I've told Julie you're a colleague, a wolf researcher, so don't say anything to contradict me. Keep quiet. Do what I do, and maybe we'll get through this."

But it seemed she spoke more to herself than to him.

5

"We're almost there," Alex said. "Just remember what I told you—observe, do what I do, try not to talk. Let them think you're a mystery."

And there's no deception in that, she thought, glancing at Kieran. He'd spent the ride sitting stiffly in the passenger's seat, arms braced at his sides, long fingers driving indentations in the leatherette. *The wolf in him,* she reminded herself, and that knowledge should have brought some comfort.

But she didn't feel comfortable. In the confinement of the truck she was all too aware of his size and strength and masculine beauty. She felt herself begin to tense as they approached town, matching Kieran muscle for muscle, her fists gripping the steering wheel.

She glanced in the rearview mirror. Julie was right behind them. The other woman's reaction to Kieran had been strange enough to make Alex sit up and take notice, and it was going to be worse in Merritt.

No one there had ever seen her with a man, unless it was when she exchanged a brief word with Dutch or the few other townsfolk she occasionally spoke to. She could imagine what piercing looks and gossip would follow her and Kieran the moment they set foot in town. Even if Kieran behaved with absolute discretion.

When they pulled up in the small parking lot of Olsen's Market and General Store, the first faces that swung their way told Alex that her fears had not been unjustified. The women leaving the store paused, took one long look at Kieran, and bent their heads together with hissing whispers.

Alex got out of the truck and turned her back to the women. Julie was just pulling up behind them as Kieran opened the passenger door, breathing in the chaotic scents of Merritt.

Julie left her motor running and leaned out the window of her truck.

"Too bad Olsen's is the only game in town for what you need," she said, her normally pleasant expression edged with dislike.

Alex grimaced. "After what happened with Deanna," she said, "I'd rather go just about anyplace else." And Olsen was a prime gossip himself. But there wasn't any viable alternative without driving all the way to Juneville, and that was the last thing Alex wanted—to be in close proximity to Kieran for another twenty miles.

"Well," Julie said, "I'm going to the garage for a bit. Say I meet you back here, and we'll have lunch at the Big Mouth." She smiled at Kieran, but the hint of strain hadn't left her face. It had been there ever since Alex introduced them. "I'd like to get to know your odd friend better."

And that was the problem. Julie saw too much, even if it was impossible that she'd guess Kieran's true nature. "Actually, we . . . we weren't staying—" Alex stammered.

"Ah, come on. You've got to treat Kieran to the Big Mouth at least once. And anyway"—her voice dropped to a stage whisper—"you know everyone is going to be talking about him. You can't shut people in this town up. So you might as well charge right in."

Alex flushed, painfully aware of how it made her scars

stand out in harsh relief. "It's not what you think," she muttered. "He's just a colleague."

"I believe you. I'm just saying don't give people any more to talk about."

Julie was right. Disarming the gossips early on would be wise. If they thought Kieran merely another odd wolf researcher stopping briefly in the area, they might not search any further.

And if they assumed he and Alex were lovers . . .

"You're not afraid he'll eat with his fingers, are you?" Julie said, grinning at Kieran to bring him in on the joke.

Kieran looked at Alex, yellow eyes intent. "I *am* hungry, Alexandra," he said.

Alex couldn't seem to think clearly or rationally. The way he gazed at her set her heart thumping loud enough to drown out all the warning bells in her mind. "All right. A short lunch . . . in an hour?"

"I'll be here." Julie waved at Kieran and pulled out of the parking lot.

Alex folded her arms and stared after her friend. She couldn't believe Julie had tried to manipulate her. It wasn't in her character. And as for Kieran, he wasn't sophisticated enough, not by a long shot.

She turned around. Kieran's back was to her, and he was watching a pair of men emerge from the bar three doors down from Olsen's. Men Alex recognized as among Howie Walsh's cronies.

"I remember," he said suddenly. His eyes had narrowed to slits, and he was poised on the balls of his feet. "People chasing me. With guns."

Oh God. Alex felt her heartbeat accelerate. She could almost see Shadow superimposed over Kieran, bristling and snarling. His memories were starting to return, but they were not the most welcome ones.

"Do you remember when, or why?"

He didn't reply, and she remembered how Shadow had come to her, weak with poison. Trespassing on man's property and suffering man's punishment.

"There are people here who don't like wolves," she

said. "It's a slow process, bringing them around. That's why we have to be cautious." Her words were as much for herself as Kieran; if she saw Howie after what he'd done to Shadow—and she'd no doubt he was behind the poisoning—she didn't know what she might do.

Control, Alex. Control.

Kieran looked at her. His jaw was set, muscles moving under the skin. "What right do humans have to hate what was here before they were born?"

Hate. He spoke the word as if he knew the full measure of what it meant. As if he had experienced its curse just as she had. For a moment she felt such a powerful kinship with him that her fears vanished, and she found herself almost touching him, almost wanting his touch. Almost.

"Hatred," she said softly, "isn't rational or logical. Animals don't hate. Only people do."

His eyes seemed to see straight through her, the way Julie's did, but with far greater intimacy. He didn't need to touch her at all. She moved away and started toward the store. "Come on. Let's get this over with."

His fingers skimmed her elbow, drawing her back. "I don't fear these people," he said. "There is no need to run."

That final word held a wealth of anger, even contempt. For himself? He had called himself a monster with something very close to self-loathing. Did he remember running from men and feel shame because of it?

Shame was an all too human weakness. She pulled her arm close to her side. "You may know what to fear in the forest," she said tightly. "But since you don't remember your life as a man, you'd better leave the rest to me."

ᴀlex led Kieran into Olsen's, her back straight and stiff. He trailed behind her, like some massive shadow, into the men's clothing section. It was small and fitted out with the basics: jeans, warm shirts, jackets, socks, boots. And underwear.

For some reason the thought of underwear made Alex flash back to the first time she'd seen Kieran—buck naked and looking as though he'd never worn a stitch in his life. Unaccountably, she felt herself flush. This was an impersonal operation, after all. In human form he would need human clothing—all of it.

Brusquely she pointed out to Kieran the various items he would need. He fingered the garments, examining them carefully. Alex did a hasty estimate of his size and thrust a package of briefs into his arms. She picked out jeans and a shirt and explained the dressing room to him; he lowered his head and studied the blanketed room warily before going in.

This time she resisted the urge to help him dress, though she found herself imagining it all: his muscles flexing as he twisted out of the sweats, the impressive expanse of his naked body, the frown between his dark brows as he worked out the puzzle of zippers and buttons. She prayed he remembered that much. Occasionally she heard an unmistakable growl from behind the curtain, and she almost smiled.

"Help you, Miss Alex?"

She turned to find Mr. Olsen looking over her shoulder at the dressing room, brows raised. He took a toothpick from his mouth, examined it, and thrust it back between his teeth.

"Someone new, I see," Olsen commented in his flat, dry voice. "Don't remember him." He craned his neck, as if he could see through the blanket that rippled and swayed with Kieran's movements. "Friend of yours?"

Here it started. Alex bit her tongue to keep from snapping out a pointed warning for him to mind his own business. Deanna's tear-streaked face was still fresh in her memory. "An acquaintance. He got lost cross-country skiing out my way and needed help."

"Needed clothes too, I see. You have strange friends, Miss Alex." He smirked. "Well, that's—" He stopped as the blanket twitched aside and Kieran stepped through. Olsen's toothpick dropped from his mouth.

Alex turned to look. It wasn't that Kieran's appearance had radically changed. It was more subtle than that. In form-fitting jeans and plaid shirt, he looked . . . Alex swallowed. The faint ridiculousness of her Granddad's too-small sweats had vanished. Now Kieran seemed the pinnacle of masculinity—*human* masculinity—with a compelling edge of wildness.

He had brushed his hair back from his forehead and neatened it with his fingers. The shirt fit him, but did little to conceal the fine, long musculature of his body. Neither did the jeans. His bare feet made Alex's mouth go dry.

It was very hard to think of him as Shadow now.

Olsen cleared his throat. "Seems to fit, all right. But you'll need boots. Lost those too, did he?" Olsen studied Alex, but she ignored his comment. "I've got some good ones that ought to fit." He walked away and returned with a box. Alex noted that they were his most expensive boots, but she was in no mood to quibble now.

"Fine. We'll be up at the counter in a moment."

Olsen lingered, obviously eager for gossip. But Alex conspicuously ignored him, and at last he retreated.

"Is this enough?" Kieran said, plucking at his shirt. He seemed as unselfconscious of the impression he made now as he'd been in Granddad's sweats. Or naked, before she'd pointed out his indiscretion.

Alex quickly gathered up a second pair of jeans and two more shirts, socks, a jacket, and as an afterthought, flannel pajamas. Tonight, at least, he would not be sleeping in her bed, or anywhere near it.

She took Kieran into the adjoining small grocery. After a pause, he walked ahead and led her straight to the meat section. He examined the packages doubtfully, picked one up and made an expression of disgust.

"Old meat," he said. "You eat this?"

Shadow was back. Alex quelled an unexpected smile. "Sometimes. Not raw, though." She hesitated. "Will *you* eat it?"

He set down the wrapped beef. "I am a man," he said. "I'll eat what you eat."

She avoided his gaze and tossed several hefty cuts of beef into the cart, following up with a quick trip down the other aisles for vegetables, soup, bread, and the food she usually bought, in considerably larger quantities. Only time would tell if he could or would eat what a normal human did, and in what volumes. Kieran paused frequently to examine various items, perusing the wrappers and frowning as if the words describing ingredients and calorie content were somehow profound.

To him, bereft of memory, perhaps they were.

Kieran followed her to the counter and she paid for the items with her credit card, mentally totaling the bill. Her simple lifestyle had left her with substantial savings, and helping Kieran wasn't likely to cost her an arm and a leg—moneywise, in any case.

Other costs she refused to contemplate.

Olsen seemed about to comment again, but satisfied himself with long, narrow looks at Kieran. It wasn't until they turned to leave that he called after them.

"Hope you enjoy your stay here, mister," he said. Alex was well aware that Kieran's presence would be known all over town within the hour. At least he hadn't done anything strange; in fact, he'd been downright quiet.

But everyone in Merritt would be wondering why the hunk was with the scarred, bitchy wolf-woman.

"You don't like that man, Alexandra," Kieran said.

Surprise made her unwary. "Not much."

"Why? Did he hurt you?"

She stopped at the tone of his voice. There was an edge to it, an alertness that caught her full attention. He looked like nothing so much as a wolf on the hunt.

"I'm not stupid," he'd told her at the cabin. No. He was far from that. Somehow he'd sensed her hostility toward Olsen, veiled as it was, and reached a conclusion that startled her.

Don't be ridiculous. He has no reason to be protective of you.

No one ever defended her, hadn't since she was ten

years old. She didn't need defending. "It's a long story," she said. "I'll explain later."

She felt his gaze on her for a long time after she started walking again. Her neck prickled. She longed to escape, back to the safety of the cabin where she would be in control. But Julie was already crossing the street, coming toward them with a purposeful stride.

"You guys ready to eat?"

Julie seemed back to her normal self now, grinning and merry-eyed, one hand still smudged with oil. She pulled a handkerchief out of one capacious jacket pocket and wiped the stain away as Alex dropped the groceries off in her truck.

Ready as I'll ever be, Alex thought grimly.

Kieran looked from her to Julie and nodded.

"Then let's go. You're in for a treat, Kieran." Julie started off without waiting to see if they followed. Alex considered a hundred warnings to give Kieran then, but every one of them died a quick death when he looked at her.

"Well, come on," she said, striding after Julie. She stopped at the café door and looked through the big windows at the rows of booths and the counter along the open kitchen. The place was packed. Kieran paused beside her. Now, at last, he showed unease. His head lowered. She could almost see him bristling.

"We can still leave," she whispered as Julie opened the door and went inside. "I can make excuses—"

"You're afraid, Alexandra," he said.

Her gaze flew up to his. "What?"

He touched her arm, stroked down its length in a caress. "I feel it. Why?"

She was paralyzed by the ease with which he read her. "I'm not afraid of anything," she said hoarsely. "I'm not the one who's lost my memory."

"I'll protect you."

"I can take care of myself." But the ache had come back to her chest, and it had nothing to do with fear. "It's you we have to worry about."

Kieran's voice dropped intimately low. "Are you . . . worried about me, Alexandra?"

She was the first to look away, preceding him quickly into the café. Julie waved to them from a small booth in the very back. Kieran reached for Alex's hand, lacing his fingers through hers. She almost jerked free. They would all assume—

She stopped herself. Let them assume. No one, *no one* was going to dictate what she did or stand in judgment over her. She'd committed herself to this, given her promise; she wasn't going to turn coward now.

Kieran's gaze swept from side to side as they passed down the aisle, his stride more of a stalk. Faces turned up and eyes tracked their progress to the booth. A wave of hushed conversation surged under the thrum of some popular country tune on the jukebox.

"Here we go," Julie said, dropping onto the padded bench. "Privacy back here." She waved at an acquaintance across the café. Her gaze took in Kieran's grip on Alex's hand, but she forbore to mention it. Alex slid onto the seat opposite Julie, and Kieran, after a brief hesitation, sat beside Alex.

"Now, Kieran," Julie said with relish, "you've got to try their burgers. The best in Maheengun County."

Alex glanced at Kieran warily. Burgers seemed safe enough, if Kieran didn't remember how to use a knife and fork. "Fine by me."

Kieran was giving his silverware a cursory inspection. "Yes," he said. He grinned at Alex in a way she would have called conspiratorial if she hadn't known better. His smile alone still had the power to startle her.

"Hamburgers," he repeated. "With fries."

"I like a man who enjoys his food," Julie said, flagging down a waitress. The woman peered at Kieran over her bifocals all the while she took their order. When she'd left and returned with water, Kieran picked up his glass cautiously and held it to his nose.

Oh, God. Alex had a sudden image of Kieran lapping the water up like a wolf. She prepared to grab the glass from his hand just as he lifted it to his lips and drank. In a perfectly normal, human fashion.

"Thirsty, aren't you?" Julie commented. "I'm for a beer. Want one?"

Kieran licked his lips. Alex could almost see him thinking—remembering—as he'd obviously remembered burgers and fries. "No. Thanks."

Julie shrugged. "You *are* a strange one." She winked at Alex.

But Alex was staring at Kieran, watching his tongue catch the moisture on his lips. If he'd tried to lap the water, it would have been awkward—and a lot easier to remember he was Shadow.

She pulled her gaze away as the waitress returned with their orders. Kieran hesitated only a moment before picking up the burger with surprising delicacy and biting into it. In no time at all the burger and fries were gone.

Julie laughed. "You been starving the man, Alex?" She pushed her half-finished burger toward him. "Go ahead. I'm not that hungry."

He took her plate without demur as Julie rose and headed for the counter. A strange relief eased the tension from Alex's body. Wolves were opportunistic eaters—they'd gorge themselves after a kill, because there were no guarantees at all about the next meal.

Kieran's behavior was perfectly understandable—for a wolf. He'd probably eat until he couldn't move if she gave him a chance.

"You can have more if you need it, Kieran," she said, patting his arm. "But there will always be enough. You won't have to hunt your food from now on."

Comprehension sparked in his eyes, and the muscles of his jaw bunched. He pushed Julie's plate away. "I am a man, Alexandra."

Alex felt the full weight of his emotion, too complex to be mere anger. Shame. Pride. Pain. It was like looking into a mirror—a mirror that reflected not the outside but all the things that were hidden underneath. She dropped her gaze to her plate.

Julie reappeared to break the uneasy silence. "I asked Wanda if she could bring another burger—"

Kieran stood, skin flushed. He pushed his hands into his pockets. "I have no money, Julie."

"I do," Alex said, before Julie could offer to pay. She pulled a bill from her wallet. Kieran watched her, his expression taut.

In an ordinary man Alex would have called it masculine ego. She passed by that thought quickly. He clearly remembered money. Maybe this lunch hadn't been such a bad idea after all. It had jogged Kieran's memory about several essential things, with little prompting from her, and nothing had gone wrong. After the initial stares, everyone had safely ignored them.

"I think we'd better go, Julie," she said. "We can get a doggie bag for the burger."

Kieran stared at her, absolutely still. Her stomach knotted as she realized what she'd said and how Kieran had interpreted it.

She reached for him. "Kieran, it's not—"

But he had already turned away and was taking Julie's hand in a firm clasp. "I have enjoyed meeting you, Julie."

Julie looked up at him, her round face almost sober. "You too, Kieran." She glanced at Alex. "Listen, before you go I wanted to ask you—both of you—if you'll come to an early supper with my family tomorrow afternoon."

Alex started. "With your family?"

"Yeah. On the rez. You've never been there before, and, well, after what happened with Deanna, I wanted the rest of my family to meet you. And Kieran."

Supper with Julie's family. With Kieran. Alex pushed down a surge of panic and managed a smile.

"That's very nice of you, Julie—"

But Julie was already addressing Kieran again. "You'll like the spread my mom puts out, Kieran. My family's big, and we're big eaters." She grinned. "You won't starve there."

Kieran returned Julie's smile. "It sounds very good."

He looked at Alex. She knew challenge when she saw it—in a wolf or in a human being.

"Remember the work we were going to do, Kieran?" she said tightly. "The . . . urgent research you wanted me to help you with?"

"I haven't forgotten, Alexandra."

Veiled anger still hummed under the soft huskiness of his voice, triggered by her earlier words but touching on something far deeper. Something that came from his past. Alex felt control slipping out of her hands.

"You work too hard, Alex," Julie said. "You'll like my family. They're good people—no problems with *chimookomon*—whites." She grinned wryly to take the sting out of the label. "In fact, my grandma is sort of curious about all this wolf research business."

"We would like to come, Julie," Kieran said.

"Great!" Julie didn't even look to Alex for confirmation. She pulled a napkin out of the table dispenser and a grubby pen from her pocket. She began to sketch, tongue between her teeth. "Here's a map. It'll be fastest if you come cross-country. You just go straight across from your cabin, heading north, like this. Mom's house is here."

She shoved the makeshift map across the table to Alex, and then glanced at her watch. "Oh shit, look at the time. I got to go. Vern Mercado's truck is supposed to be finished by five." She started down the aisle and turned. "You two show up around two, okay? We'll eat around three or so. Just bring yourselves and a good appetite!"

As soon as she was out of earshot, Alex stood and made a grab for Kieran, swinging him around. "What the hell did you think you were doing?"

His expression was unreadable. "Accepting an invitation."

She balled her fists. "Great. Your memories are coming back, but you've been human less than a day. You aren't ready to deal on such close terms with strangers. You need more time."

"For what, Alexandra?" he asked. "Haven't I done well?" One corner of his mouth lifted in a smile she might have called mocking. "Haven't I behaved . . . like a human?"

"I asked you to follow my advice. This is the second time you've deliberately ignored me."

His smiled vanished. "No, Alexandra. I've never ignored you."

The feral yellow of his eyes held hers implacably. She shook her head to break the spell and noticed the curious faces turned their way. She slapped money on the table, slid from the booth, and strode down the aisle, Kieran a step behind her.

A draft of cold air swept into the room. Alex charged blindly for the door and nearly collided with someone entering the café.

"Hey, watch where you're going!"

The voice was all too familiar. Howie Walsh and a couple of his buddies blocked her only path of escape, looking her over slowly. Howie's contemptuous gaze lingered on her scar.

"What? Not out baby-sitting your cute little killers?" he asked with mocking exaggeration.

All the anger she'd been holding back broke loose. "What?" she echoed. "Not out poisoning wolves?"

Howie scowled at his friends and jammed his hands in his pockets. "Bitch," he muttered.

Out of the corner of her eye Alex saw Kieran move closer and fix his amber gaze on Howie.

The other two men exchanged uneasy glances. "Come on, Howie," one said.

Howie gave Kieran a belligerent stare. "Friend of yours, War-ring-ton?" he said.

Alex followed his look and forgot her rage. Kieran's eyes were lambent, his body drawn to its full, imposing height. The way he was focused on Howie left no doubt in her mind as to the current train of his thoughts. *"I'll protect you,"* he'd told her.

He looked like a wolf ready to defend one of his own.

Even Howie had the sense to size Kieran up and decide against direct confrontation. Like all bullies, he only attacked when the odds were in his favor. He let his friends tug him toward the rear of the café, but his next words were carefully calculated to be audible to everyone in the place.

"Didn't think she could get a man, ugly as she is."

The taunt still cut like a knife, even after all these years. "At least I can find better recreational activities than poisoning animals," she called after him. "Is that the best you can do for kicks, Howie?"

Howie turned around, but whatever retort he was gathering died before it reached his mouth. Kieran brushed past Alex and started down the aisle, shoulders hunched, growling in his throat.

Alex plunged after him while diners at booths and tables up and down the length of the café stood or craned their necks to witness the incipient confrontation. Alex managed to get between Kieran and Howie at the last minute.

She reached out to Kieran just as he began to blur. The strange mist was gathering around him, and she remembered what had happened when she last witnessed that eerie effect.

Kieran was about to *change*.

6

"*Kieran.*"

His name reached him through the pounding of blood behind his ears, through the rage that boiled in his blood and sizzled at the ends of his nerves.

Her voice stilled the primal need to attack, the preparation his body made for the shifting, every cell poised to take another shape, another identity.

Her touch, *her* voice held him back.

"Kieran, it's all right."

Her hand tightened on his arm, and part of him became her ally. *I am a man. A man. . . .*

"Kieran!"

His blurred vision focused on her. So beautiful, all light amid the shadows. The wolf remembered, and the man.

Kieran shivered violently. Between one moment and the next the shifting stopped. The rage fled to the place where it hid and waited for another chance. And he could *see*—see clearly, first Alexandra and then the men who watched him with open mouths and white faces.

"Jee-zus," one of them croaked. "He's crazy!"

"Did you see the way he growled?"

Sound resolved itself around him, voices raised in excited conversation. He turned his head. Faces, everywhere faces, staring. The walls were too close, the heat stifling.

"Alexandra," he rasped.

"Come on. Let's get out of here," she said, grabbing Kieran's hand. He went with her blindly, shaking and weak with reaction. When they burst into clean air and sunlight, it was all he could do to keep his feet. Alexandra pulled him around the corner, to some quiet protected place where no one could see.

The nausea came, and he doubled over, hands across his stomach. A cool hand stroked across his forehead, pushing back the hair that hung limp in his face.

"Are you all right, Kieran?"

He looked up. Her eyes were so blue, like endless sky and running water. Clean things he knew and understood and needed to live. His hand trembled as he wiped his mouth.

"All right," he echoed. But a second assault came on him then—memory, a vivid comprehension that made his knees give way. He crouched down against the brick wall of the building.

Alexandra knelt beside him. "It's okay. We're alone."

Alone. Safe. He opened his eyes and caught Alexandra's hands in his, taking care not to crush her delicate bones. She made no effort to pull away.

"What happened in there, Kieran?"

Wild laughter seared his chest. He drove it back. "I almost . . . changed," he said.

"Yes." Her mouth was taut with strain. "But it's all right. You didn't get far. You . . . stopped in time."

Kieran remembered the faces, the voices. "Did I?"

She gave him a stiff smile. "At worst they'll think you're odd, just like me. And I doubt Howie Walsh will come anywhere near me again."

Walsh. Kieran growled before he could stop himself. "He called you ugly."

Alexandra looked away. "You . . . don't remember Howie from anywhere else, do you?"

"No. I only knew that he was your enemy." Letting go her hand, Kieran touched her cheek with his fingertips. "But I didn't intend to change. I didn't think I *could,* until now." He hesitated, trying to put the new knowledge into words. "Now I remember that there was a reason I changed each time before."

"Of course," she said slowly. "You were angry. I turned the rifle on you, and you were angry."

"Emotion." Kieran looked away. "Anger. That is what makes me change. I couldn't control it." He bared his teeth. "I didn't want to."

Alexandra rose, her expression grim with concentration. "Can you remember other times when this happened? In the past, before you came to me?"

Kieran tried to fix in his mind how he knew so surely the source of his affliction. Pressing his hands flat against the wall, he pushed himself to his feet.

"Nothing. I only know it's true—I don't change unless I feel . . . strongly."

She looked at him, the blue of her eyes muddied like troubled water. "I *knew* it wasn't a case of waiting for a full moon," she said with a wan smile. It faded all too quickly. "We'd better get home."

*J*oseph Arnoux moved silently along the wall, keeping himself hidden as the woman and Kieran Holt crossed the street.

His hunch had been right. When the black wolf was sighted and the rumors began, he'd already been certain.

Kieran had returned. After five years the boy had come back, as Joseph had always known he must.

It was inevitable.

Howie and his friends burst out of the café, swearing and muttering. Joseph had no time to deal with Howie now. He slipped around the corner, his gaze still tracking the woman's truck as she pulled from the parking lot and headed out of town.

Another chance. Joseph closed his eyes. In the eleven

years since Kieran's escape from Joseph's guardianship, he'd returned to Minnesota only once. To kill, and escape again—this time as a wolf, elusive and swift, lost to Joseph far too long. But Joseph had known the time would come when the boy must be drawn back to the only place where he might find redemption.

Perhaps it was not too late. It had plagued Joseph, knowing his work was unfinished, his duty unfulfilled, and Kieran free with no one else to control him.

Joseph glanced once more at the subsiding commotion near the door of the café. The boy had nearly lost control, but in the end he had not. Joseph felt a strange regret; if the boy had changed, they'd all have known. It would no longer have been Joseph's secret—what others had called *his* madness, *his* superstition.

But that would be too easy. It was Joseph's to do. There was still some small hope for Kieran; that the boy had not succumbed was proof enough. Joseph knew his own weakness. Even now he could not kill the boy. Not yet.

And the woman . . . Joseph walked back to his truck, absently stroking the polished wolf's tooth that hung from the age-worn leather thong around his neck. He'd known about the woman, of course. He always kept track of the wolf researchers, on the chance that they could provide news of a certain black wolf for whom he had waited these five years.

But he had not thought the woman special, had paid her no more attention than the others of her kind. Why had the boy gone to her? When had he become human again? Did she know what he was?

She had been with the others in the café. But none of the others understood what they had witnessed. She had touched him when he stood on the brink, and he had remained human.

If she knew . . . Joseph felt the wolf's tooth bite into his palm. He dropped his hand. One thing at a time. First he must observe, and wait. At the very least the boy trusted the woman; he wouldn't run at once. There would be time to plan. Recapturing Kieran now would not be so easy as it had been when he was a grieving boy, numb with the shock of his parents' deaths.

The woman might be ally or enemy; in the long run it wouldn't matter. Joseph knew how to be patient.

"I can't let you go, boy," he said softly, though Kieran was long out of his sight. "I must finish this one way or another. If you can't be saved . . ." He shook his head and started the truck down the long road toward home.

"There must be an end," he muttered. "There must be an end at last."

"*It's* a beginning, Kieran," Alexandra said as the truck pulled into the gravel drive. "At least we have somewhere to start."

Kieran followed Alexandra to the door and into the sanctuary of her home. He was no longer uneasy within these walls; they kept him close to Alexandra, and bound him to his human nature. His rage was gone. The beast could not waken here.

Sudden exhaustion gripped him, the lingering after-effects of the near change. He found his place by the stove and settled there, eyes half-shut. He listened to Alexandra's quiet footsteps as she moved about the cabin, folding out a bed from the sofa and laying food out for him on the living room table.

Hours passed, uncounted. Several times he saw Alexandra writing in a book she kept very close, like something precious. He would have given much to know what she put on the pages. There was a distance in her, an inner silence he didn't know how to break.

She didn't trust him. He hadn't listened to her when she asked for his obedience. She had spoken to him as if he were not a man at all. His anger—his beast—had nearly betrayed them both.

Worse, he had failed to protect Alexandra from what she feared. And he wanted to protect her. That need was as fierce and compelling as his need to remember. And just as inexplicable.

When the light in the windows turned red with sunset Kieran rose from his dark thoughts and found Alexandra at the kitchen table, bent over her book. The remains of a small meal were scattered around her. She closed the book and put down her pen when she saw him, spreading her hands over the top of it as if it could fly away like a bird.

"Do you need something, Kieran?" she asked. The wariness was in her eyes.

He pulled the second chair out from the table and sat down with care, watching the way she tensed and stopped herself from drawing back.

The flaw was in himself, this inability to communicate, to speak the right words. He looked at the wall over her head.

"In the café," he began. "Why did the man call you ugly?"

She reached for the pen and curled her fingers around it. "Is that your idea of humor, Kieran?" she said hoarsely.

"I don't understand."

She stared at him, and he felt her disbelief. With a sharp movement she gathered up her thick red hair and pulled it away from her face. "You asked me once what I saw when I looked at you. What do *you* see?"

He looked as she bade him, at the clear blue of her eyes and the dark red lashes, gentle nose and full lips, delicate bones and stubborn jaw. "I see a memory," he said slowly. "A child I played with when I was young. My friend."

Her lips parted. "Is that . . . all?"

"No." He leaned forward, holding her gaze. "I see a woman who is also my friend." He hesitated, searching for the right words. "Hair like the leaves when they fall before the first snow. Eyes like the lake where it's too deep to see bottom. A beautiful woman. I remember what beauty is."

The pen slipped from her fingers and rolled across the table. She let her hair fall back around her face, the curls swinging forward like a shield. "Your memory isn't reliable, Kieran," she whispered.

Pain. He understood little else about Alexandra, but that he did. Like the fear. He hadn't been able to help her in the café, but here . . .

He rose and moved close to her. "That's why I need your help," he said. He brushed the tips of his fingers over her hair, taking care not to touch her the way he had done before, when she'd become so afraid. Not her mouth, though he remembered how sweet it had tasted, how good it had felt under his. Not her face. But he stroked her hair as she'd stroked him when he'd been a wolf. There could be no harm in that.

Alexandra didn't stop him. She sat very still, her eyes half closed. He should have felt contentment in touching her, being near her as he wanted to be—in knowing she accepted his nearness—but he was not. There was an ache in him, a heavy stirring in his groin that he had felt before, pleasure that was almost pain.

Part of him knew what it was, but the memories remained cloudy and half-formed. He drifted, imagining Alexandra stroking him where he ached most. Imagining her body against his as it had been that morning, the texture of her skin underneath her clothes. The supple curves so different from his own.

He remembered the way she'd looked at him before he put on the clothes she'd given him.

"You never told me, Alexandra," he said softly. "What *you* saw this morning when you looked at me."

She stirred with a slow, lingering motion, as if she had been far away. Her head turned. She inhaled sharply, scraping the chair across the floor as she stood up. With a sideways step she put the table between them.

"When I look at you?" she echoed. "I—" She wet her lips with her tongue. He could see the way she searched for words, just as he had, struggling to pull them up out of herself.

"I remember the boy I met once, long ago," she said, closing her eyes. "I see my friend from childhood. Strong and . . . graceful." She broke off. "I see Shadow."

She was hiding something. It was in her voice. The

answer was not what he wanted, though he didn't know what he did want. And she was afraid again.

"You were never afraid of Shadow," he said.

Her eyes opened. She circled the table and stood with her back against the counter. Her breasts rose and fell, pressing against her shirt in an irregular rhythm.

"It's late, Kieran," she said. "I'm really tired. It's been a long day, and we'll need to begin working on your memories tomorrow. I think we'll both be better for a good night's sleep."

Sleep. Had it only been hours since he returned to human form, lost and confused and barely capable of speech? It seemed like an eternity.

But part of that was because of Alexandra. He felt as if he'd been bound to her all his life.

"There're blankets folded up on the foot of the sofabed if you get cold," she said, edging away. "I put plenty of wood in the stove. If you want to read, help yourself to the books on the shelf. If you need anything else . . ." She didn't finish but retreated into the hall. He followed, and she stopped at the entrance to her bedroom, one hand on the doorknob.

"Good night, Kieran."

He turned on his heel before Alexandra closed the door, strode to the sofabed, and stared down at the white, sterile sheets.

Stiffly he undressed, examined the pajamas Alexandra had bought him, and tossed them aside with the blanket. His body—the body *she* saw as Shadow—had no need of them.

When he found it impossible to sleep he rose and went to the kitchen in search of food. Alexandra's notebook lay on the table where she had forgotten it.

He picked it up carefully. All day she had kept it close to her, as if it were a part of herself. Or as if she kept a part of herself inside it. He opened the cover.

Her writing was neat and precise and easy to read. His name was there.

In one day, Kieran has taken away any hope I had of peace here.

Peace. Maybe it was always asking too much. And I promised him—all that time ago, I promised to help him—and I'll never break a promise again. This is my chance to make good.

But if he weren't what he was—if he weren't Shadow—I don't think I could do this. Today proved I can't trust him to be human, that the wolf is still just under the surface. And yet that's the key, Mother.

As long as I remember he's not really a man at all, I can do what I have to do.

The rest of the words blurred into nonsense. Kieran shut the book and went back to the living room, past the bed and to the door.

The night called to him. He could smell it through the wood, through the glass. He opened the door and lifted his eyes toward a sky brilliant with stars.

Constellations. They had a sweet familiarity, and he knew he had gazed at those patterns a hundred times. Somewhere. The memory was of no use at all. He remembered the shapes and some of the names—heroes out of ancient tales, and creatures spun of myth. As he was himself.

A creature Alexandra wanted no part of and couldn't trust.

Kieran jumped from the porch and dug his bare toes into the crusty snow. He hardly felt the chill—a mark of his inhuman nature, the wolf in him.

She sees what you are.

The Voice. All the hairs rose on the back of his neck. He went very still, turning his senses inward.

Fight the Beast, boy. You must *be human. Only human, or you cannot be saved.*

He knew those words, as if he'd heard them a thousand times before, and not only in his mind. Bleak rage took hold of him. "Who are you?" he snarled.

The Voice began to fade, just as he willed it to become

clear, to give its true name. *Your only hope, boy. Your only hope . . .*

Kieran shivered. There was no hope within the Voice or anything it told him. He wanted to call it enemy, and yet there was no certainty even in that.

"Who are you?" he demanded again, spinning around. *"Who are you?"*

Kieran's cry finished as a howl. From the forest another call came—not the Voice, but the howl of a wolf, one and then another.

Wolves. They were very near, challenging him in the most ancient of ways. He listened, motionless, until their howls faded, until the stars had shifted in the sky and he could hear only the beat of his own heart.

But in the wake of that silence something else stirred— a profound familiarity, a sense of urgency that tugged at his most powerful instincts.

Kieran lifted his head and sifted the air. From north and west the call descended. A summons, though he didn't understand how he knew.

For an instant it was blindingly clear. This was the answer, this fragile thread that pulled him. North and west.

He began to cross the clearing and stopped. Slowly he looked back toward the cabin. The battle within him was brief.

He could not go where that summons called him. Not yet. Not while he understood so little about himself.

Not when the one certainty in his heart waited within those cabin walls.

Alexandra was still his only anchor, the only connection between his past and his future. She had promised to help him, and she would never break that promise.

He needed her.

Wrapped in utter silence, he walked back to the cabin.

*A*lex knelt by the closet door and hugged the stuffed wolf to her chest. It felt silky and cool against her hot cheek. She had gone straight to the closet and the box without thinking, desperate for distraction, and found her old toy—something she could touch that couldn't talk or assume or challenge with golden eyes.

"You were never afraid of Shadow," Kieran had said.

He was right. A stuffed animal was just about her speed at the moment.

Her thoughts were tangled and confused and nonsensical, her body hot and aching. Sleep was out of the question, had been since Kieran had spoken to her with such simple eloquence of things he couldn't possibly understand.

She listened for the sounds of his restless footsteps, as she had done since she left him at her door. Now, at last, he was silent, but the silence gave her no comfort.

She turned the stuffed animal's expressionless face toward her and touched the marble eyes. "I wish you could talk," she whispered, and laughed at herself. She'd made a similar wish only yesterday, and look where it had gotten her.

Her journal had always been enough before, enough to confide in and share her most private thoughts. But she'd left it on the kitchen table, and she wasn't prepared to risk finding Kieran awake.

Not now. Not until she got ahold of herself and figured out what to do.

With no clear idea of her purpose, Alex set down the wolf and looked at the unopened boxes in her closet. Methodically she unstacked them until she could reach the one at the very bottom.

The heaviest. The one filled to the brim with fairy tales.

She pried open the flaps, her hands not quite steady, and pulled out the top book. *The Sleeping Beauty.* One of the first she'd ever owned. She ran her fingers over the dogeared cover, stained with something she'd spilled on it as a child. She set it on the floor beside the wolf and reached for the next, flipping through each book more and more quickly, searching for . . . something.

For answers.

But no answers came until she reached the final book in the box. It was also the newest—the last her mother had given her before the accident. A lavishly illustrated version of *Cinderella*.

The inner cover was still inscribed with the words Mother had written in it: *Never forget to dream.*

But she had. She'd let herself forget for a very, very long time, forget the simple joys she'd known as a child. Even her love of nature had lost its innocence. She'd pushed the past away; now one of her banished memories had jumped out and bitten her, and she didn't know what to do with it.

Don't you, Alex?

She opened her eyes, opened the book to the first page and began to read, all the way to the happy ending. And after the last line was another inscription: *Never stop believing.*

But she wanted to believe. Desperately. Maybe Kieran's appearance was an unexpected gift, one she had to recognize for what it was—a key to her own past. Maybe she didn't have to be afraid of him, and could still find her way to safety. The child she'd been had never been afraid.

Maybe, just maybe she could steal a little of her childhood back again.

She left the stack of books on the floor and went to her bed, taking the stuffed wolf with her. It wasn't an answer, not completely, but she felt an easing in her heart. Perhaps, if she stopped fighting, the rest of the answer would come.

She smiled as she lay down and turned out the light, the wolf tucked in beside her. *Maybe I'm not a coward after all.*

Only in the last instant before sleep did she imagine that her counterfeit bedfellow was someone else.

The day was beautiful, with a clear blue arc of sky and weather warmer than any day she'd seen since her return to Minnesota—an omen that banished the last of

Alex's doubts. She sat on the porch and began to strap on her snowshoes.

"I think I know how we should get started on recovering your memories, Kieran," she said.

Kieran turned. He had been up before she was, well before dawn. After a hasty breakfast she'd found him standing quietly in the clearing, looking northwest. He was dressed in the second set of clothes she'd bought him, minus the jacket; even in human form he seemed immune to the weather. His boots and the hems of his jeans were already crusted with snow.

He came to join her. "I have also been thinking, Alexandra," he said.

His gaze was almost distant, half-hidden behind that perpetually stray lock of dark hair. She resisted a sudden desire to brush it out of his eyes and stood up instead, testing the buckles of her snowshoes with quick stamps.

Kieran looked toward the woods, his hands behind his back. "There's a place I want to find."

She stopped, alert and wary. "What place is that, Kieran?"

"Where you and I first met."

Alex relaxed. "We were thinking the same thing. Do you remember where it is?"

"I think I do."

"Can you find it?"

In response he turned and started out cross-country, breaking ground with no apparent effort. Alex hitched up her day pack and followed, making her own trail as Kieran headed unerringly in the right direction.

He ranged as a wolf would, sometimes ahead, sometimes briefly disappearing among the trees. Today he *was* Shadow. His steps were graceful and certain, finding purchase with his boots that she couldn't have done without her snowshoes. Each part of his body flowed with a wolf's grace, and when he turned to look at her his eyes were Shadow's eyes, clear and incapable of deception.

There was no denying he was a part of this world. This was where he belonged. Everything he'd done since the incident in the café proved he wasn't nearly ready to act as a man, but here, *here* he was safe. This was his territory. And hers.

Like the special place. She had passed by it several times since she returned to Minnesota, but she'd never stopped. Now, as they came upon it, she saw how it had changed. The skeletal remains of the fallen tree were still there, half collapsed after so many seasons of weather and insects. The shrunken hollow beneath was filled with snow—a hideout once big enough for a girl and a wolf.

Alex leaned against a tree and closed her eyes. For so many years she'd dismissed the memories of her time here with Shadow. They had hurt too much that summer after the accident when she'd gone searching for Shadow and hadn't found him. As she grew older, they had become only another kind of weakness, burned away in the crucible of reality.

Now the memories had a purpose again. She set them free tentatively, releasing them from captivity as she'd taken her old books out of the box last night. Tasting them cautiously, as if they could intoxicate with too deep a draft.

"Do you remember the time we met the skunk?" Kieran asked.

She opened her eyes. He knelt by the log, heedless of the wet soaking the knees of his jeans, and stared into the shadowed niche.

"Yes," she said. "Your fur smelled for days, and Grandma had to soak my clothes in tomato juice. . . ." She covered her mouth with her hand. "I *remember*."

He stood, gazing at her. "Tell me what it was like for you, Alexandra."

"It was magic," she whispered, hearing herself use a word she'd stop believing in. *Fairy tales are real.* "It was the happiest time of my life."

"And mine, Alexandra," he said softly. "It must have been."

She turned and pressed her cheek to the tree's cool bark. "So strange," she murmured. "Until now I'd never been completely sure how much of it was my imagination."

"It was real," he said.

Fairy tales . . . Alex swallowed and took hold of herself. She was in danger of becoming a quivering mass of sentimentality, and that was not to the purpose at all. *Remember why we're here.* She pushed away from the tree.

"You remember our times together," she said. "Does this place make the past any clearer in your mind?"

"A little."

"Do you know where you went from here when you left me each day?"

He tilted his head to the sky, black hair spilling over his shoulders. "The times when I wasn't with you are still dark." He looked at her with that focused intensity she could never quite get accustomed to. "You talked about the wolves you believed were my parents. The man who killed them. Who was he?"

"A poacher. I'd never seen him before." She folded her arms tightly and walked across the little clearing. "He was talking . . . about wanting to kill every last wolf in existence. I don't remember most of what he said. All I could think about was keeping Shadow safe from him."

Kieran was silent a long time. "Then I didn't die because I was with you."

She stiffened. *No.* The edge in his voice wasn't accusation. She'd been trying to help him, save him. "You'd come to me as a boy," she said, keeping her back to him. "To tell me what you were, I think . . . that you were Shadow. You said you'd left your parents to find me, that they'd be coming after you. And then there was a shot—"

Twigs cracked behind her, and she turned. Kieran gripped the bare branches of a sturdy birch sapling, breaking them one by one with chilling deliberation.

"What did this man look like?" he asked.

Alex tried to reconstruct the poacher's face in her mind. Hard green eyes, a severe mouth, cold and deliberate words that wouldn't quite come clear. She described what she could, watching the slow transformation of Kieran's expression.

It was just like when he'd shifted in the café: rigid jaw

and lifted lip, narrowed inhuman eyes, and a body preparing, muscle by muscle, for violence. His breathing came harsh enough for her to hear in the forest's stillness.

"Kieran?" She took a step toward him. "Do you know him?"

The branch in Kieran's hand cracked in two pieces. He let go of the hapless tree and closed his eyes. "It's gone," he said. "For a moment I felt— It's gone." He looked at her, his ferocity faded to bleak acceptance in the space of an instant.

"I'm sorry. Maybe—" She stared down at her feet. "It's possible there are things you aren't ready to remember."

She regretted the platitude as soon as she'd spoken it, but Kieran seemed not to have heard. He walked to the edge of the clearing, staring into the sun-dappled forest.

"You said you study wolves, Alexandra."

The non sequitur caught her off guard. "It's my life's work."

He looked back with an odd little half-smile. "It must have seemed ironic. That I came to you for help."

"No," she said slowly, joining him. "Not ironic at all. There's a kind of rightness to it. I became a wolf researcher because of you."

"Because of me," he repeated, his voice very low.

She picked up a fallen pine branch and brushed it back and forth like a broom, making shallow parallel grooves in the snow. "My fascination with wolves began here, with Shadow. With you. If I hadn't—"

He caught the branch as it passed in front of him, stopping it in midsweep. "They've been here, Alexandra," he said. He released the branch back to her and looked at the ground near his feet.

She followed his gaze and saw the tracks. Distracted as she'd been, she'd never even noticed them, but now she saw that they were everywhere.

Wolf tracks. She knelt awkwardly in her snowshoes, measuring the crisscrossed prints with her fingers. "I know

these prints. I've heard this pack but haven't had a chance
to track them—"

"They're very close," Kieran said. He crouched beside
her. "I smell them. Two males and three females."

"You can tell all that?" Excitement bubbled up in her,
unconstrained. "Do you realize what a researcher you
would make?"

But he was not there. She looked up just in time to see
him vanish among the trees.

His path was easy enough to follow. It paralleled the
wolf tracks through a dense stand of second-growth pines
and emerged into another clearing, bisected by a frozen
ribbon of creek.

On one side of the creek stood Kieran, and on the
other waited the wolves.

Alex froze. The pack was small, with three smaller
grays who were undoubtedly the females, a brindle yearling
male, and a big gray male in the lead. At any other time, in
any other circumstances she would have been stunned and
thrilled to find them so easily, so clearly visible for her to
observe.

But nothing about this was normal. Five pairs of lupine eyes were fixed on Kieran; not so much as an ear
twitched in Alex's direction. The pack should have been
running at the first sight and scent of her. She might as well
have not been there at all, so thoroughly did the wolves
ignore her. It was as if the very rules of nature had been
turned upside down.

Even as she watched, the lead wolf began to advance
on stiffened legs, his fur on end, tail straight out from his
body. Every aspect of his posture shouted challenge. The
other wolves followed the alpha male, radiating threat.

Kieran stared directly back at the alpha, yellow eyes
clashing with yellow. A growl rumbled from his belly.

Alex called on every ounce of the detached scientific
objectivity she'd spent the past years perfecting. The pack
was on the verge of attacking Kieran, as they would never
dare attack a human being. And he seemed to be doing his
best to provoke them.

He must have known the wolves were no threat to her. But he must have known equally well they were a very real threat to him.

Her paralysis shattered, and she stepped over into a realm beyond thought or the rules she thought she knew so well. She swallowed to ease her dry throat, cupped her hands around her mouth, and yelled for all she was worth.

Movement exploded in a flurry of earth and sun-bright crystals as the wolves scattered. When Alex opened her eyes they were gone, leaving only churned snow in their wake.

Kieran stared after them, chest heaving. Alex let her quivering knees give out and sank to the ground.

"Well, Kieran," she said shakily, "between the two of us, I think we've just set human-wolf relations back a decade."

He turned. She didn't know what she expected to see in his face; the same rage, perhaps, that he'd shown Howie in the café. But the stubborn defiance with which he'd faced the pack seemed burned away, leaving him strangely subdued.

"They wouldn't have hurt you, Alexandra," he said. "I wouldn't have risked your life."

She stripped off her mittens and scooped up a handful of snow to cool her hot skin. "I know. Wolves almost never attack humans. But they would have attacked you." She wavered between sudden rage and boneless relief. "What in hell were you trying to prove?"

Kieran crouched where he was, too far away to touch. "I was trying to show you—" He broke off, jaw set. "They wouldn't attack a human, Alexandra," he said softly. "What does that make me?"

She pushed her anger aside, hearing the hidden pain in his voice. "In their eyes—" She bunched her mittens in her fists. "Maybe they see you as a wolf, Kieran. Or smell, or sense in some way we don't comprehend. Wolves don't easily accept outsiders, and you are in territory they claim as their own."

"I'm not one of them," he said.

"But when you were in wolf form, you must have run into packs like this. Do you remember—"

"I was always alone," he said.

Alone. The word was so rife with sadness, so sharp with familiarity. Even if the wolves saw him as a wolf like themselves, he was still outcast.

God, she knew how that felt. Suddenly it was urgent that she break through that wall in his memory, help him find something, something that could make him smile the way he'd smiled in the café when he remembered hamburgers. She stood up, brushing off her pants.

"Let's walk, Kieran."

He rose without a word. She chose the path this time, avoiding the wolf tracks, and he stayed by her side. *It's up to you, Alex.*

"There's something I've wanted to ask you," she said.

He looked at her, a spark back in his eyes. "Ask."

"What did it feel like, when you were in wolf form? What was it like being Shadow?"

His lips parted. A faint line creased his brow. "Sometimes . . ." He hesitated, as if remembering even as he spoke. "Sometimes it felt like . . . freedom. No worry, because tomorrow doesn't exist. No fear, because death is only a part of life. Part of the balance. Everything fits together."

She listened, rapt. His words were searching, uncertain, yet there was eloquence in their very simplicity.

"Is that what a wolf knows?"

"It was what I knew. For a time."

What he *had* known, but no longer. Her heart suddenly felt very full. "Even though I've devoted my life to studying wolves, I could never be inside them, feel what they feel, know what they know. But you can."

His gaze sought hers. "Do you find that an admirable thing, Alexandra?"

She almost laughed. "Admirable? It's a miracle. To me, wolves are the perfect creatures." She paused, wanting, anxious for him to understand. "It's true they can be ferocious in defending their territory, but other wolves recognize the warning signals. They're fundamentally honest. They seldom play games, and when they do everyone knows the rules. They deceive their prey, but almost never each other. And they're absolutely devoted to their own. Their loyalty is legendary."

"And they take only one mate," Kieran put in.

She blinked at the interruption. Kieran was studying her with a quizzical expression, one dark eyebrow raised. "That's somewhat more complex than we once believed," she said, picking up the thread of her monologue. "But there are many cases where a mated pair are faithful solely to each other until one or the other dies. Wolves are phenomenal parents. The rest of the pack will often help care for the alpha's pups . . ."

She trailed off, remembering those rare times she'd actually seen wolf families at rest or play. How she'd envied them that perfect sense of belonging, that trust, that unstinting devotion. *Love,* she'd called it, knowing such a word had no part in scientific detachment. And not giving a damn.

Because part of her had to keep believing that kind of unshakable love existed somewhere.

"I respect and admire wolves, Kieran," she said at last, "but nature as a whole is clean and sensible. Balanced, as you put it." She started walking again, hands clasped at her back. "The same can't be said of people," she muttered.

He caught up to her. "Why, Alexandra?"

She'd forgotten how acute his hearing was. *You don't know—after what happened when you were a boy, what you saw in the café?* "It's pretty obvious. Greed, hatred, arrogance, war, prejudice against anyone different, anything that can't be understood. I could go on and on."

Kieran stepped neatly in front of her, giving her just enough time to stop before she collided with him.

"Is that all there is to being human?"

She found herself inexplicably mute, with nowhere to look but Kieran's eyes. He gazed at her as if she were all he could see, as if the rest of the world had vanished around them. "In two days I've seen . . . admirable things in people, Alexandra," he said. "Julie—"

"Julie is an exception. She's unusually—"

"Your own kindness," he persisted.

Her legs felt a little shaky. She brushed the snow off an old stump and sat down. "I don't think I'm particularly kind. It isn't the first quality people would attribute to me."

"Because they don't know you. They don't know your courage, your strength."

Her skin burned. Several times he'd accused her of being afraid, and now he praised her courage? He knew nothing about her. Nothing.

"Your certainty of who you are."

She stood up abruptly. "And that's exactly what we need to find for you," she said. "Certainty of who you are."

He looked away, sparing her too late. "Is that even possible?"

Her discomfort withered into chagrin. She was not the one with the mountain to climb, the emptiness of not knowing what lay on the other side. "It's possible," she said. "More than possible. We'll do it, Kieran. I promise you we'll do it."

But his face was so still, so bleak. *Damn* her clumsiness. She looked around, desperate to find some way to break through his melancholy.

In the special place, before they met the wolves, he'd been remembering good things about their times together as children. They'd been communicating so well. To recapture that . . .

To recapture that, as with her own childhood, meant taking risks. Letting go.

She knelt and began to unbuckle her snowshoes. "I've been thinking, Kieran," she said, "that you and I never got to play in the snow."

She felt more than saw him turn, a dark shape against the sun. She hesitated only an instant. It wouldn't be so hard, so strange, not if she thought of herself as the old Alex. She plunged her hand into the snow and gripped a chunk between her fingers, molding it to fit in the curve of her palm.

Something firm and cold bounced against the back of her head, trickling wetness under the collar of her jacket. She spun around on her knees.

Kieran crouched a few feet away, grinning at her. *Grinning.* He'd beaten her to it, as if he'd read her mind.

Suddenly, just like that, the rest was easy. She finished making her snowball and threw as hard as she could. The missile shattered on Kieran's thigh, leaving a round wet spot on the denim.

Alex laughed. She heard herself with wonder—the unexpected sound of joy in such a simple thing. She let herself laugh again, as loud as she could.

With a mock growl, Kieran stalked toward her. A very small but well-packed snowball promptly caught her square on the shoulder.

Alex let herself fall backward into the snow. Kieran stood over her, teeth showing. "Who's alpha now, Alexandra?"

She rolled to her knees, coated in crystals that were rapidly melting with her body heat. He remembered! That had been one of her favorite games with Shadow. "I always beat you before," she said.

"Because I let you." He smiled, and the little knot of joy she felt was mirrored in his eyes.

"Oh, yeah?" She glared up at him and began to form another snowball behind her back. "I'm not a clumsy kid anymore, my friend!"

He went very still for a moment, his expression arrested. "No," he said, and then shook himself like a wolf shedding water from its fur. "Now we are evenly matched. Can you beat me, Alexandra?"

She bared her teeth back at him. "Just watch me!"

The battle was joined in earnest then. Alex abandoned herself, scooping up snow and running and laughing while Kieran chased her with soft little mock snarls. It wasn't Kieran she saw, but Shadow; her eyes were fixed in a child's vision. It was Shadow's voice she heard; her own was raised in high-pitched squeals.

There was nothing left of the Alex who had forgotten how to play, who had become isolated by the looks of pity and her own unhappiness in those lonely years after the accident. It was as if she'd gone so far back in time that even her scars had vanished.

"Shadow," she cried gleefully, forming a huge snow-ball with both hands, "watch out for this one!" She stood up, squinted at his dark shape haloed by sunlight, and began to run toward him.

A buried branch snagged at her toes. She gave a little squeak as she pitched forward, arms pinwheeling as she lost her grip on the snowball. She fell into solid and famil-iar warmth.

"Shadow," she said, giggling. They rolled over and over in the snow, and she didn't mind the cold that inched down her neck. When they came to a stop she lay flat on her back, and Kieran crouched over her, blotting out the sun.

Kieran. Not Shadow. Her vision cleared and her mouth went too dry for laughter.

Not Shadow. His golden gaze held something that had never existed in the eyes of a wolf. She couldn't look away from his eyes, so beautiful, so mesmerizing.

"Alexandra," he said. "Alexandra."

Her own name was something he used to caress her as he pinned her there, his arms to either side of her shoul-ders, his thighs embracing hers. The ends of his hair brushed her cheek, the most delicate of touches that started a trembling she couldn't control.

"You . . . win," she whispered, trying to make a joke of it. But it was too late. This was no game. She wasn't a little girl with a young wolf for a playmate.

His body felt hard and warm along the length of hers. A man's body. A shape her own body identified with the truest of instincts.

Her flesh remembered what her intellect had tried to forget: the powerful stirring in blood and nerves at the caress of a man's hands. The memory of Kieran's hands touching her in bed that first morning, when she'd thought he was Peter. And woke as she realized Peter had never touched her so gently.

She stared at his mouth. His lips were slightly parted, a man's lips, that had brushed hers once before. The muscles of his arms pushed against his shirt as he braced himself, and she remembered the security of being held in a man's arms, of knowing she belonged there. The wild, urgently physical and emotional need she thought she would never face again.

"A passionate woman," Peter had called her once. He had made her believe it, skilled as he was. Made her believe he could really want her.

But he hadn't. He'd taught her a lesson she'd never forget, put her beyond any risk of responding to a man again. And yet now her body responded to Kieran. Impossibly, against her will, her body betrayed her just as Peter had done.

She tried to fight it, but she couldn't think. Her head was filled with light, and her heart was beating too hard and fast for her to hear her own thoughts. The heat of Kieran's body melted her, made her throb and yearn and shudder.

Kieran bent closer, impossibly closer. "Alexandra," he said again. His hair formed a veil that hid them from the world. She forgot to flinch when his fingers brushed her cheek and passed over the scar.

It was a dream. His jaw slid along hers, a gentle nuzzling; his breath puffed against her heated skin. The tip of his tongue stroked her eyelid. Strong arms lifted her from the snow, away from even the memory of cold.

There was a kind of wonder in his eyes as he touched his lips to hers.

7

Her mouth gentled under Kieran's for a single miraculous moment. He should have been content with that, content to feel her so pliant in his arms, ready to accept his touch. It was all he wanted, to be close to her.

But it wasn't enough. Not when he heard and felt the changes in her body that so closely echoed those in himself. Not when he felt how perfectly her softness fit against him, as if they were two halves of one creature.

Not when a new need came on him—to be inside her, to mingle with her very essence. To taste her more thoroughly than he ever had before.

Memory guided him, too compelling to be questioned. He slid his mouth along her lips with greater pressure, probed with his tongue, asked entrance to her body.

He had almost no warning before her knee thrust between them and caught the most sensitive, aching part of him. He stiffened with a startled grunt and bounded clear of her. Alex rolled over and scrambled to her feet.

"Damn you!" Her words came out as a thin, grating cry. "What the hell did you think you were doing?"

Her blow had struck hard, but her words were far more painful. His sweat chilled to ice as he watched her.

There was no joy in her now, no desire to play. Only anger—and fear.

Of him. Again. Because he hadn't thought, and then only of what he wanted.

She stared at him, breathing so hard that he couldn't see her face behind the plume of condensation. He tried to find words, but he was only beginning to understand what had happened, and the understanding was as shattering as her reaction.

Alexandra shook her head wildly and marched in the direction of her abandoned snowshoes. She sat down hard in the snow and buckled them on with sharp, brittle motions. One snowshoe was still only half-fastened when she stood and began to retrace their path back toward the cabin, heedless of snow-laden branches that whipped in her face and incautious steps that almost sent her sprawling.

Kieran caught up to her, taking her by the elbow with just enough force to halt her headlong flight. The feel of her sent a stab of sensation right to the pit of his belly.

She wrenched free. "Don't touch me," she gasped.

He sidestepped to block her path when she tried to barrel past him. "Don't run away from me, Alexandra."

"I'm not running, dammit. I—" She met his gaze, flushed a deep red and looked away. "I'm *not* running." As if to prove her point she planted her feet and crossed her arms. "In fact I . . . think we need to have a serious talk."

"I agree."

She started and hid her reaction behind a scowl, her fear behind belligerence. "Good. Then you can start by answering my question. What did you think you were doing?"

He found an answer, though it was only another way to hold her there. "Kissing you," he said.

Her eyes widened, and he realized she thought he was mocking her. "I only just remembered what it was," he added, cursing his own clumsiness.

She laughed—a strained croak, so unlike the happy

sounds she'd made when they were playing. "You only just remembered? How convenient." She hugged her arms closer to her chest. "What about yesterday? Or have you already forgotten everything I said to you then?"

Yesterday. Holding her . . . and kissing her, but only with the briefest touch before she'd pushed him away. As she'd done again.

"I told you," she said, her voice a little calmer, "that what you'd done wasn't . . . right for two people unless they knew each other very well." She broke off. "Didn't you hear anything I said?"

This time he flushed. He couldn't admit his ignorance to her, that he hadn't comprehended the nature of his need then. That he'd only now become human enough to see the full scope of it.

She searched his face, her expression softening. "No. Maybe you really didn't understand."

"Then you'd better explain it again, Alexandra," he said. "It seems I still have much to learn."

She didn't seem to hear the self-mockery in his voice. "Maybe I'm not a very good teacher," she admitted quietly. "When we were playing back there, it was so much like old times. I wasn't concentrating on the things I should have been. I may have . . . overreacted, because *I* forgot what I told you yesterday."

Kieran crouched and picked up a dead branch. It was brittle in his hands. "You told me that it's natural for wolves to show affection openly."

Her eyes were bright and earnest and didn't see him at all. "That's right. When we were young, Shadow was always that way with me. You only did what came naturally to you."

Kieran broke off the end of the branch. "As a wolf."

"Exactly." She sighed and smiled with a rueful twist of her mouth. "I shouldn't have expected you to just . . . toss that away. I apologize, Kieran."

He snapped off another segment. "Then you aren't angry that I showed affection for you."

She was quiet for a long time. Kieran held the branch still, waiting.

"No," she said in a small voice.

It was a tiny victory. He upended the branch and thrust it into the snow.

"Today," he said, "you said you admire wolves because of their honesty and loyalty. Yet you don't admire people because they aren't like wolves."

She said nothing. Her skin was slightly tinged with pink.

"If I'm a wolf," he persisted, "it's natural for me to show . . . affection. But yesterday you told me that people, unlike wolves, are not allowed to show what they feel. Is this the dishonesty you don't like in humans?"

She kept her face averted, but he saw the tension in her jaw. "People pretend to feel what they don't feel," she whispered. "They deceive—"

"I wasn't deceiving you, Alexandra."

She looked at him. "The human world sets up limits," she said in a tone devoid of inflection. "In human society, there are certain ways to show emotion, certain rules. Some emotions have to be controlled."

"As you control yours?"

Anger flashed in her eyes, quickly suppressed. "There are laws of survival—" She broke off. "There are customs we follow. They hold civilization together, for all its flaws."

"And people always follow these . . . laws."

She seemed to pull into herself, into a place he couldn't follow. "No," she whispered. "Not always. But when they don't, everything falls apart."

Pain. He sensed her pain though he didn't know its source, felt it as he felt his own. He wanted only to hold her then, with no more thought than to ease her sadness.

But she came back to herself, looking at him as if she had never been gone. "People need to follow certain standards of behavior, even when they care about each other."

Kieran rose. "You care about me, Alexandra," he said.

"Of course I care about you." She smiled stiffly. "We were friends. We still are. But there are levels of caring.

Friends, even good friends, don't kiss each other." Her gaze slid away from his. "Not that way."

"What way?"

"When two people kiss . . . that way, it usually means they are committed to each other." She hesitated, her profile as uncertain and fragile as ice in spring. "It means they feel more than just friendship."

"More than friendship," Kieran echoed.

"They feel what we call love."

"I know what love is."

She turned to look at him, lips parted. "Do you remember, Kieran?"

No. Nothing so concrete as memory. Only sensation, and the ghost of happiness from a time long gone. Enough.

"Do wolves feel love, Alexandra?" he countered.

She blinked. "We don't know. We know they can be extremely devoted to their mates and pack members."

"Wolves mate for life," he said. "Do humans?"

Her gaze dropped. "No. Not always."

"And you?" He moved closer to her, step by cautious step. "Have you ever taken a mate?"

She hesitated a moment too long. "People don't have to mate to be whole. Many of us are . . . happy being alone."

He knew what cynicism was, but still it came to him as a stranger. "I don't enjoy being alone."

"Of course you don't. Wolves are social anima—"

"I am not a wolf."

"Why do you fight it so much, Kieran?" she asked earnestly. "Why do you deny that part of yourself?"

The Voice was there without warning, mocking Alexandra's questions. *Fight it, boy. Deny it. You must be human. . . .*

Alexandra moved toward him, her hand extended in appeal. "Listen to me, Kieran. I know someone told you once that there was something wrong with you. It's not true."

Monster, the Voice reminded him. "Isn't it?" Kieran asked hoarsely.

"No. Dammit, *no*. You have to accept everything you are, both parts of yourself, or we won't get anywhere. You know that you haven't been able to throw off your wolf instincts, no matter how much you fight them. They're too much a part of you."

"The café . . ."

"We shouldn't have gone into town when we did, Kieran," she said. "But that's exactly my point. You couldn't control your shifting. Or your emotions."

"Control," he echoed.

"That's what you have to learn. Don't you see?" Her face became animated, alight, everything it hadn't been after he kissed her. "Your memory improved each time you shifted. Maybe the key to regaining your memory is controlling your shifting. And maybe the key to your shifting is to accept everything you are."

He laughed, though the sound emerged as a growl. "As you accept me?"

"Yes."

"Even this half of me?" He walked toward her. "You prefer the wolf side to the human," he challenged. "*This* body makes you afraid. But this is also what I am."

Her breath quickened, but she held his gaze. "Yes. And that's why I . . . trust you. Why I'm accepting Julie's invitation to supper this afternoon."

He had almost forgotten. "You were going to leave me behind?"

"I thought about canceling," she admitted, lifting her chin. "But you're right, Kieran. You can't learn without being around other people." She spoke with calm distance, but there was still fear in her, and not only of him.

"I promise to be a tame wolf," he said.

She smiled. For a moment her eyes lit as they'd done when she and Kieran played in the snow, and then the somber wariness returned. She pulled her sleeve up to look at her watch.

"All right. Julie wanted us there at three. We'll be walking cross-country to her place on the reservation, so we should get back to the cabin and wash up."

He nodded, but she had already turned away. He trailed her, watching the steady, strong movements of her body. Remembering how it had felt against his own.

She trusted him. It was a small concession, so little compared to what he had wanted to win from her.

Even now his maleness reacted to the memory of Alexandra's response, her brief but sweet surrender. Images tumbled through his mind, tangling past and present. Flesh on flesh, whispers, the erotic scents of what people called making love.

He had made love in that other, forgotten life. He could not remember details. The vague memories were enough to reveal the nature of his need.

Alexandra wanted him to be a wolf, one of the creatures she admired and understood so well. She could accept Shadow as she couldn't accept Kieran Holt.

All he had was patience. That was one thing wolf and man shared in equal measure.

The patience of a hunter.

*J*ulie and the children were waiting where Alex's land met the border of the reservation.

There was nothing different about the countryside here from the land on which her cabin lay. The snowbound woods were identical to the little patch of wilderness Alex claimed as hers. But beyond that invisible border were a people Alex had never taken the time to know.

Four of those people greeted her now. Julie stood to the fore with Deanna just behind her, two indistinguishable dark-eyed little girls clasping the teenager's hands on either side.

Julie gave a brief salute. "Hi, you two. Good timing. We're here to escort you to my Mom's house."

Alex heard Kieran come up beside her. She knew exactly when Deanna first saw him; her eyes widened and fixed on him with open fascination. The two little girls were less particular in their attentions and considerably less shy. As one they released Deanna's hands and marched directly up to Alex.

"I'm Tracy and that's Liz" one of them announced.

Alex almost laughed. Awkwardly she knelt to the children's level. "I'm Alex. And this is—"

"Kieran." With a whisper of footsteps he walked past her. He towered above the girls, who regarded him with none of Deanna's apparent awe.

"That's a funny name," the other twin remarked.

"Liz!" Deanna dropped her gaze from Kieran's face. "That's not a nice thing to say." She stepped forward, pulling the girls back into the circle of her arms.

Alex glanced at Kieran. He was looking at the trio with a strange, almost wistful smile. "It's all right," he said.

"I don't think it's a funny name at all," Deanna said, and blushed furiously. Alex felt a sharp stab of sympathy.

"Kids," Julie said with a shrug. "Guess you pass the test if the twins accept you and you don't run screaming in the other direction. You ready to go?"

Alex bit the inside of her lip. "Lead on."

She was grateful an escort had turned up, and not because she couldn't find her own way. Julie's map was still tucked in her pocket, and her sense of direction had always been excellent.

But all the way here Alex had been obsessed with crazy, useless thoughts of what had happened that morning. The kiss and its confusing aftermath. Kieran's dangerous insights, his devastating candor, the piercing questions that seemed so naive on the surface.

His kiss had been anything but naive.

I only just remembered, he'd said. She hadn't asked him what he meant. The wondering had tormented her ever since. And his words: *This body makes you afraid.*

The same masculine, powerful body that walked beside her. Alex stared straight ahead at the girls laughing and teasing each other as they retraced their path among the trees. Now she had something else to occupy her thoughts, though this visit wasn't what she'd have chosen.

She hadn't been to any sort of family gathering since

before Mother died. In boarding school and college, she'd been the student who stayed on and studied during most holidays and vacations. The times she'd gone home to Father had been worse than loneliness.

She watched Tracy and Liz, squabbling one minute in high, childish voices and walking hand in hand the next. She saw Deanna's affection for her younger sisters, the way the teenager tugged at their stubby braids and scolded them indulgently. And the way Julie looked on like the benevolent aunt she was.

Julie's family. Belonging to one like it had been a dream for Alex in those years after her mother's death. She'd watched television in the school dormitory and daydreamed about the people she saw on the screen—perfect families who resolved every problem. And loved unconditionally.

When things were going well with Peter, she'd altered her dream to one of making a new family, with her own children—several of them, so they'd never be lonely as she'd been. A chance to start over.

A chance long since passed by.

They were a half mile in from the border when they reached the edge of the residential housing projects Julie had told her to expect. They passed a gas station, general store, bar, and post office, all the staples of any small town. There were clusters of houses grouped together by decade, each built very much like its neighbor.

After another half mile Julie led them to a small, compact home backed by woods. A gravel driveway led behind the house, partially cleared of snow. Someone had begun and abandoned a snowman in the front yard; a large mixed-breed dog idly sniffed the base of it. Just visible behind the house were several half-rusted vehicles fenderdeep in snow.

"Here we are," Julie said. "Not so much to look at, maybe, but it's home. Mom's home, that is." She studied Alex for an uncomfortably long moment. "You're welcome here," she added softly.

Alex had no chance to reply. The twins and Deanna

were already barreling past Julie and into the house. A cacophony of human voices washed over them as Julie ushered her and Kieran in after; Alex had barely registered an image of several faces turning her way when a little boy, just past toddler stage, ran smack into her legs. Instinctively she reached down to steady the child, who grinned up at her with an expression almost identical to Julie's.

"Hi!" he said, and promptly flung himself at Julie's knees. "Joo-ee!"

"Hey, Bobby!" Julie hoisted the boy up in the air and over her head. "Prepare yourself. This is only the second wave."

Alex swallowed, looking sideways at Kieran. He, too, had paused, head lifted, as if some new memory had been awakened by the cheerful chaos awaiting them.

"Come on. You'll get used to it, I promise." Julie set Bobby down and wedged herself between Alex and Kieran. "Hey, everybody, our guests have arrived!"

The small living room was overflowing with people. The twins were already bouncing enthusiastically on a worn sofa, and a boy in his late teens sat on the carpet, engrossed by a television in the corner. A woman near Julie's age fussed over a baby. A small dog of indeterminate breed yapped at Kieran and darted away.

The hullabaloo faded just long enough to permit a general welcome and a series of introductions. Julie's mother was a plump, merry-eyed woman who briefly emerged from the kitchen to greet them and vanished again. The woman with the baby was identified as Julie's sister, Brenda. She had a serene reserve very different from Julie's natural ebullience.

"You'll notice Brenda's quieter than me. Two of us would have been too much, even in this family." Brenda made a face and Julie laughed. "These are mostly Brenda's kids," she said, gesturing around the room. "Bobby, here. And that's baby Tim, plus the twins and Deanna you've already met. Brenda's husband Toby drives truck and he's away right now."

Alex shook hands and smiled, well aware that she and

Kieran were being carefully studied in spite of the casual atmosphere. Kieran followed her lead, accepting the curious stares without any sign of unease.

Julie walked across the room and tapped the teenaged boy on the shoulder. "This here is Mike, he's my youngest brother. Don't mind him. He's not as bad as he looks."

Mike muttered a friendly insult, looked briefly but narrowly at Kieran, and returned to his television. Julie shrugged. "Kids. There's one other person I really want you to meet. Just a second. Uh—sit anywhere. Liz, Tracy, let Kieran and Alex sit on the sofa, please." She walked through the doorway into the kitchen, leaving Alex to face the twins, who hopped off the sofa with energetic glee.

One of the girls patted the sofa. "You want to sit down?"

"Thank you." Alex sat and was immediately joined by a child on either side. "Which one of you is Liz and which is Tracy?"

One girl made a moue of disgust. "Can't you tell? I'm Liz. That's Tracy." Two sets of brown eyes studied Alex intently. "What's that funny mark on your face?"

Alex fought back her instant reaction. *They're only kids. They don't mean any harm.* "It's a scar, Liz. I was burned when I was young."

"Oh." Liz looked across at her sister. "That's too bad. Do you know any stories?"

Just like that her deformity was dismissed. Alex blinked, disarmed. She'd almost forgotten how accepting young children could be.

Accepting. Only last night Kieran had looked directly at her and called her beautiful. Touched her as if her skin was smooth and unblemished.

A small hand brushed hers. "It's all right if you don't know any good stories," Tracy said. "Grandma will tell us one after supper." As one, the twins scooted off the sofa and dashed into the kitchen.

"They can be a handful sometimes. Hope they weren't bothering you too much."

Brenda sat down in the place vacated by Liz, the baby

in her arms. She gave Alex a friendly nod, a trace of Julie's wry humor in her eyes.

"Not at all. They're . . . very cute kids," Alex said awkwardly.

"Thanks. They take after Toby, my husband." She smiled, and her plain face lit up. "He's due home any day now."

The tone of her voice made Alex's skin prickle. It was love—Brenda's love and desire for the man coming back to her, the father of her children. Alex stared at the baby's tiny brown face peeking out from among the blankets, chubby and haloed by wispy black hair.

"You've got a good-looking man over there," Brenda said, nodding in Kieran's direction.

It took Alex a moment to find Kieran. He crouched in front of the television, staring at the screen as fixedly as Julie's brother, with whom he exchanged occasional brief comments. He looked entirely at home, and almost as if he'd forgotten Alex existed.

"He . . . Kieran isn't . . . he's just a friend," Alex stammered. "A fellow researcher."

"Oh. Sorry. Julie said—" Brenda shifted the baby in her arms and held the bundle out toward Alex. "Would you hold him for me? I'll go check on supper."

Any desire to protest died as Alex felt the tiny warm life settle against her heart.

The baby was perfect. Alex stroked the velvet cheek with the back of her finger, biting back the absurd endearments that gathered in her throat. A tiny rosebud mouth opened in a toothless yawn.

"Beautiful," Alex dared to whisper, touching Tim's dimpled knuckles as if they were as fragile as glass. "You're just beautiful."

"I'll bet you'd make a great mother, Alex."

Alex's brief contentment unraveled as Julie's words penetrated. She looked up with a brittle smile. "Lately it seems people know more about me than I know about myself."

Julie's eyebrow arched. "That goes on a lot around here," she said. "Don't take it too personally."

Alex rose and handed the baby to his aunt. "I'll try to remember that."

"Good, because there's someone else I want you to meet, and she tends to be a little on the blunt side."

"It seems to be a family trait."

Alex immediately regretted the words, but Julie seemed not to mind. Brenda reappeared, and Julie transferred the baby to his mother's arms. "What about Kieran? He's glued to that set as if he'd never seen one before."

"Maybe he hasn't," a new voice said.

8

The voice was female and slightly rough, honed with age and experience. Alex looked around. An elderly woman, well into her seventies, walked gingerly into the room from the kitchen and stopped in front of Alex, leaning on a cane.

The force of her presence struck Alex so unexpectedly that it was several moments before she saw the old woman's strong family resemblance to Julie. She wore a loose print blouse and knit pants and wire-rimmed glasses low on her nose. Her thick salt-and-pepper hair was pulled back in a wide, heavy braid. Keen eyes focused on Alex with uncomfortable frankness.

"Grandma, this is Alex," Julie said gravely. "Alex, my grandmother, Mary."

The elderly woman nodded perfunctorily and sat down on the sofa. She stretched out her legs with a sigh. "I've heard about you. The *chimookamon* who runs with the wolves."

Alex felt unable to move under that ebony gaze. It had the potency of Kieran's, but different; Alex felt less like prey being stalked than a defendant being examined by a judge.

And then she remembered: this was the grandmother Julie had mentioned before, the one from whom she'd supposedly inherited her "intuition." "I've heard about you, too, ma'am," she said.

"Ha!" Mary tapped her cane on the floor. "My daughter's daughter never could keep quiet about much of anything." She gave Julie a keen sideways glance. "But you were right, Granddaughter. There's more to this one than meets the eye."

Julie opened her mouth to reply, but Alex beat her to it. "I do my best," she retorted.

Mary studied her. "You try, but you don't always see what it is," she said cryptically. Her gaze shifted to Kieran. "What about your boyfriend over there?"

The temptation to snap back was almost more than Alex could stand. "I think Julie may have given you the wrong impression, ma'am. Kieran is—"

"Different." Mary frowned, adding new lines to her deeply seamed face. "Yes, you were right, Granddaughter. I want to talk to that young man for a while. Then we'll eat."

As if he'd heard the conversation, Kieran turned away from the television. He looked directly at Mary, rose and came to join them. Old woman and young man stared at each other in silence.

"Yes. I see," Mary muttered. She waved at Kieran. "Do me a favor and sit down. I can't keep looking up at you."

Kieran glanced at Alex and settled into a crouch at Mary's feet. "My name is Kieran Holt."

"And mine is Mary. So tell me, Kieran Holt—what's troubling you?"

His muscles bunched, and he relaxed with a visible effort.

"That bad, eh?" Mary muttered.

"There's nothing wrong with Kieran," Alex said quickly.

"No?" Mary bent over her cane. "That true, young

man? Don't worry, I don't bite. And I don't think you'll bite me, either."

Kieran smiled—an oddly open, wistful expression. "No, Grandmother. I won't bite."

Mary nodded and leaned back. "Tell me about yourself, Kieran Holt."

Before Alex could think of a way to intervene, Julie took her elbow. "Dinner won't be ready for a half-hour or so. The day's nice . . . let's go outside."

Alex closed her mouth on a protest. Any objection would make it look as though she and Kieran had something to hide. But Kieran would be totally on his own, with a woman who saw too much. . . .

She cast a final glance toward Kieran and followed Julie out the door. "Would you mind telling me what all that was about?"

"I told you my grandma wanted to meet you," Julie said. She leaned against the wall of the house and met Alex's gaze with implacable calm.

"But it was Kieran—" She stopped herself, struggling to match Julie's composure. "You told me once that your grandmother was a medicine woman."

"That's right."

"And she thinks there's . . . something wrong with Kieran."

"Those were *your* words, Alex. Is there?"

Julie was dead serious. Alex had never seen her look so grave—except the first time she'd met Kieran at the cabin. Suddenly Alex felt manipulated. Manipulated by Julie, whom she wouldn't have believed capable of it.

"There's nothing wrong with him," she protested. "He's a little idiosyncratic, but—"

"What's really going on between you and Kieran?" Julie interrupted.

"I don't know what you mean."

Julie walked across the cement porch, scuffing her boot over the edge. "He's not just another wolf researcher, is he?"

Alex hugged herself. She'd thought Julie was her

friend, as close a friend as she could hope to have. Even now she felt horribly tempted to confide in the other woman. And that was out of the question. But to admit a little of the truth was better than trying to hide all of it. "We knew each other as children," she said.

"Ah." Hunching her shoulders, Julie stared down at her feet. "I knew there was a link between you."

"Why does it matter to you?"

Julie's eyes were utterly bleak, as if their usual merriment was only camouflage for some hidden sorrow. "I can't help what I see," she said. "Grandma—"

Adrenaline pumped through Alex. "What does a medicine woman do?"

"It's a very rare gift," Julie said. "There aren't many real ones left. They aren't doctors in the usual sense."

It wasn't an answer at all. *Be rational, Alex.* Julie couldn't know anything about Kieran's true nature. Neither could her grandmother, whatever supposed abilities she might possess. *He'll be all right. He's got to be . . .*

"What are you trying to hide, Alex?"

"It's . . . there's nothing—"

"Do you consider me a friend?"

The blunt question left Alex floundering. "Of course I do."

"I always sort of figured that friends help each other. Like you helped Deanna."

"You have helped me, Julie."

"Then if I asked you something important, would you trust me?"

Alex breathed in and out deliberately and met Julie's gaze. "I would try," she whispered.

Julie's eyes warmed. "That's all I ask. For now—"

In a burst of noise and motion Tracy and Liz plunged out the door, arguing furiously over a toy, and inside the house baby Tim began to wail. Julie's mother poked her head out, wiping her hands on her apron. "Where is everybody? It's suppertime."

"Good. I'm starved." Julie took Alex's elbow and

steered her back into the house, yelling over her shoulder. "Come on, you kids."

Alex looked for Kieran as they stopped in the living room. He was standing, Mary on his arm. There was no sign of alarm in him, no worry. His eyes sought and held Alex's without a trace of hesitation.

"All right," Julie's mother said. "Alex, you and Kieran sit in the dining room with Grandma, Julie, Brenda, and me. Mike, set up the TV trays for the kids."

Chaos resolved into a surprisingly orderly routine as the family members found their accustomed places for the meal. Julie took her grandmother's arm while Kieran joined Alex. She tried to convey her questions with her eyes, but Kieran only gazed back at her in unnerving silence.

What did you say to her, Kieran? she thought. *What do they know?* Her own conversation with Julie kept running through her mind. But animated voices flowed thick and fast around Alex and Kieran, English and Ojibwe words intermingled, and every face was friendly. It was almost like being in the middle of a gentle hurricane.

Beside her, Kieran set to his portion with a will, handling himself without a trace of awkwardness. Alex tasted her food and found she had an appetite. The wild rice, potatoes, venison, and frybread were delicious. Just for a moment she pretended this was her own family, that she belonged to them. It wasn't so terrible a self-indulgence to let herself believe it was possible.

By the time the meal ended, the children had already insinuated themselves in among the adults. Kieran vanished before Alex's offer to help with the dishes was cheerfully refused. She found him sitting on the sofa with the twins on his knees and Bobby halfway into his lap, giggling. His face was absorbed and open in its wonder, just as it had been when he and Alex played in the snow.

And when he kissed her.

Her heart began to hammer. He'd looked natural and right in the wilderness, but he looked just as right here, with children crawling all over him. Gentle, patient, attentive. Perfect father material.

Perfect father wolf, she thought. But it rang false. Utterly false.

Kieran looked up as she came near, and his expression changed—subtly, intimately. Drawing her in to the golden vortex of his eyes.

"He likes kids, doesn't he?"

Alex cleared her throat. Deanna stood just behind her, hands clasped at her back. She smiled hesitantly at Alex.

"Yes," Alex murmured. "I guess he does."

Deanna scuffed the carpet with her sneakers. "He's a wolf researcher, like you, right?"

Alex was almost relieved to turn away from Kieran and focus on Deanna. "He knows a lot about wolves." She cast about for a change of subject. "Do wolves interest you, Deanna?"

"Yeah." She looked at the space between her feet. "Would you mind—could you tell me how you got started? Studying wolves, I mean?"

Alex relaxed. She found it easy, almost comfortable, to talk to the girl; this was Alex's element, her passion, and the one thing she'd never had any trouble sharing with anyone who could be persuaded to listen.

Deanna needed no persuading. They found a relatively quiet corner of the room, where Deanna sat cross-legged at Alex's feet, like a disciple before a master. She seemed fascinated even by the heavily edited version of Alex's early years in Minnesota, and how her love of wolves had come from that.

"For a while, while I was growing up, I . . . had different plans," she told Deanna. "But eventually I went to the university and got a degree in wildlife biology. After I graduated I started working in Montana and Yellowstone as part of the wolf reintroduction programs there."

"Reintroduction?" Deanna echoed.

Alex warmed to her subject. "Except for Minnesota, there are very few wolves south of the Canadian border. I worked with other researchers to trap packs and transport them to this side, establish them in the states they'd previously inhabited." She sighed. "It wasn't easy. Many people are opposed to having the wolves return."

"I know people like that," Deanna said.

"Yes. People who don't understand, who're afraid wolves will take away their stock, their livelihood. Studies have shown that those problems can be dealt with just as they have been here in Minnesota, with programs like Animal Damage Control, but some people try to take matters into their own hands—"

"By poisoning and hunting," Kieran interjected. He appeared at Alex's shoulder; his eyes seemed very dark, and his expression was tense as it hadn't been all through the visit. Was he remembering being poisoned, as yesterday he'd remembered being hunted? She'd put out of her mind that he almost certainly was the livestock killer the farmers were after. Until now that small fact had been the least of her worries.

Now was certainly not the time to bring it up.

"You said you trapped wolves, Alexandra," he said.

She hadn't imagined the edge to his voice. "Yes. I never enjoyed it, but it was necessary. For the wolves. To save them, to bring them back where they belong."

"To save them." Kieran looked right through her. "For their own good."

Alex smiled deliberately at Deanna, who was regarding Kieran in silent bewilderment. "We're always working on better ways to do it, Deanna. A leading researcher has already developed a new kind of radio collar that makes repeated trapping unnecessary once the wolves are relocated. It's called a capture collar—"

"Collar."

Something in the way Kieran repeated the word brought her up short. He was standing perfectly still, eyes half-closed. Remembering. Alex was certain of it.

"Of course it's not ideal," she continued slowly, looking back at Deanna, "but it's much safer for the animal than continually using darts or traps. The collars allow us to monitor movement, capture the wolves with minimal trauma in order to take samples, and . . ."

She lost the thread of her words. Kieran had begun to breathe very deeply. "Collared," he rasped. "Trapped. Couldn't live that way. Had to run . . ."

"Is he . . . is he all right?" Deanna whispered.

Alex touched Deanna's arm, thinking quickly. "He has bad dreams sometimes. Kieran? Maybe you need a little fresh air."

He gave a strange, almost wild look and brushed past her, striding to the door.

Deanna folded her arms across her chest. "I'm sorry he got upset. What was he talking about?"

"I wish I knew," she muttered. "Deanna, I'd be happy to talk more with you about wolves, but I—"

"You have to go," Deanna said. She gnawed her lower lip. "Before you leave, I—I wanted to give you something." Abruptly she turned, darted into the hall, and returned to thrust a tube of rolled art paper at Alex.

Alex unrolled it carefully. It was a drawing, awkward and heartfelt—a drawing of a woman running with a wolf. The woman had red hair in a cloud about her face, and the wolf was silver gray with a long, flowing tail.

"I'm taking art classes," Deanna said in a rush. "Our last assignment was to draw something from our imagination. So I—I just thought . . ."

Alex cradled the drawing carefully in her hands. "It's beautiful, Deanna." She swallowed. "I've never had anything like it before."

Deanna seemed emboldened by Alex's praise. "If it's not too much trouble . . . could we talk about wolves again sometime?"

"I'd be happy to. Maybe we can get together when I'm a little more settled in—"

"Hey, Dee," Julie said, strolling up to join them. "Don't forget you promised to take the little monsters out to the pond before it gets too late."

The "little monsters," Tracy and Liz, chorused in with enthusiastic agreement, tugging at Deanna's shirt. Deanna rolled her eyes at Alex and went to get the twins' coats.

Julie grinned indulgently. "Kids. Too much for Kieran, I see."

"No, not at all. I apologize for him. He's just . . . wolf researchers do tend to be solitary . . ." She trailed off, feeling awkward. "We've had a great time, Julie. Thanks."

Julie shrugged. "You're welcome." They watched while Deanna took the twins outside, trailing scarves and giggles. "Hey, you got Deanna to talk. She seems to have developed a case of hero worship."

Alex laughed. "For me?"

"Kids can be funny that way," Julie said. "They can see things pretty clearly sometimes."

Alex was spared a reply when Kieran came back into the house, his eyes untroubled and his face relaxed. He rejoined them in silence, and without any further comment Julie took Alex and Kieran on a round of good-byes and thanks. Julie's grandmother had disappeared, and Alex was frankly relieved.

Everything had turned out all right.

"*You* were remembering back there, weren't you?" Alex asked.

Kieran had said very little since they left Julie's house. There were about a hundred questions she wanted to ask him, such as what Julie's grandmother had said to him, and what he'd thought of the visit and Julie's family. But this one seemed the one most likely to break through Kieran's silence.

She was right. He looked up, a deep crease between his dark brows.

"When you were talking about trapping wolves," he said. There was little inflection in his voice, no echo of his earlier distress. "I had an . . . image of something. A cage. Being confined."

"As a wolf?" Alex quickened her pace to match his. "Were you trapped once?"

He gave her a long, unreadable look. "I don't know. I hated it, and I escaped."

His reaction told her it had been a bad memory. It would only be natural for him to block memories like that. She knew all too well. But she couldn't let him take the easy way out.

"Think, Kieran. When did this happen? Where? There must be something more you can remember."

His stride broke and resumed, uneven. "Close," he muttered. "Sometimes I feel it—"

"Feel what?"

But he was not looking at her. He came to a sudden halt and lifted his head as she had seen him do several times before, as if to test the air. When she would have touched him he raised his hand sharply, forestalling her.

"Listen," he commanded.

She did. For a moment she heard only the faint rustling of pine boughs, and then—very faint—a cry, high-pitched and wavering.

Kieran sprang away in a single long leap and was running before Alex could blink. She cursed under her breath and followed, floundering along in her snowshoes. The cry sounded again.

A child's voice, growing more distinct. Alex's stomach knotted. She struggled to set her feet in the widely spaced tracks Kieran had made, hating her human limitations.

After a quarter mile she recognized a cluster of boulders that she knew were close to the reservation's border. Behind it lay a pond with which Alex was familiar—a large one with a boggy edge, fed by a small spring. The spring's current made the ice thin and particularly chancy, and the weather had been unusually warm for February.

Julie had asked Deanna to take the twins out to the pond. If it were *this* pond, if the children had been out walking on it, believing it to be solidly frozen . . .

Another scream came, and Alex threw the last of her energy into a final dash around the boulders. She skidded onto a patch of icy ground that crackled under her feet.

The pond was just ahead; Deanna huddled on the bank with Liz. The two girls stared out into the center of the ice.

"Deanna!" Alex cried. Deanna turned, lurched up, and pitched into Alex's arms.

"Tracy!" the girl gasped. "She fell through the ice on the pond. We can't get her out!" Deanna grabbed at Alex, her hair sticking to her tear-streaked face. "It's my fault!"

Alex had no time to comfort Deanna. She set the girl aside and stumbled to the very edge of the ice. Where was Kieran? The sick feeling in her stomach redoubled.

And then she saw everything, an image silent and frozen and dark as if in an old photograph. The hole in the ice was a blemish marring the expanse of white, haloed with jagged cracks. A small figure lay half submerged, her upper body sprawled across the solid surface. Above her crouched a dark shape, furred and four-legged, the girl's sodden jacket hood clutched in powerful jaws.

Shadow. Kieran had shifted.

"Oh, God," Alex said. "Oh, my God."

Liz and Deanna clutched each other. Their very silence was unnatural, yet they were not screaming in terror that a huge black wolf should be trying to save their sister. Alex dropped to her knees beside them, tugging her pack from her shoulders.

"Listen to me, girls. I want you to run back home and get your family."

Deanna shook her head, whipping dark hair around her face. "I won't leave her—"

Alex spun and grabbed her by the shoulders. "You can't do anything here. Go. *Now.* Tracy is going to need help. You have to bring dry clothes and warm blankets and something hot for her to drink." She kicked off her snowshoes. "I promise she'll be all right."

All at once Deanna seemed to snap out of her hysteria. She grabbed Liz and flung herself homeward, desperation turned to a single driving purpose.

Alex turned back to stare across the pond. Shadow had braced himself on the fragile ice. His claws scrabbling for purchase. He tugged back with short, sharp jerks, dragging Tracy toward him. The soaked fabric of her hood seemed to give; Alex thought she heard it rip, and Shadow's teeth flashed as he sought a new grip.

Alex forced herself to breathe one heartbeat at a time, preparing to crawl out after them. But the ice gave suddenly, a long crack spearing out from beneath Shadow's hind paws. He never once stopped his tugging. A sob echoed across the pond, and Tracy reached up to clutch at the fur on Shadow's chest.

Shadow yelped. The girl lost her grip and began to slip back. He sprang after her, his forepaws almost plunging into the black water. His jaws fastened on the back of her jacket.

Alex jumped to her feet, remembering prayers she hadn't used since childhood. Shadow performed a strange maneuver, snapping his head to the side. The girl lurched up out of the water, skidding belly-down on the cracked ice, and lay there sobbing. Crouching low, Shadow nudged her. His tongue flicked her face, and his whine reached Alex's straining ears.

"Come on, Tracy!" Alex yelled, unzipping her jacket. "You can do it. Come to me, honey!"

The girl looked up, her face a pale blur. She began to crawl toward the bank. Shadow stood where he was, ears pricked, following the girl's progress only with his brilliant amber eyes.

Tracy had just reached the safe edge of the pond when the ice beneath Shadow gave way.

His yelp of surprise was utterly human. Alex grabbed Tracy and wrapped her jacket around the shivering girl. "Hang in there, sweetheart. I'll be right back." Without another thought Alex flung herself down, slid onto the ice and propelled herself the way Tracy had come.

Shadow's head bobbed above the water. His claws scrabbled at the edge of the hole. He heaved up and fell back again. Alex flung her arm out. The ice crackled. Her hand clutched at air, muscles straining.

Sodden fur brushed the tips of her fingers. She

reached a fraction of an inch farther and closed them on his pelt, then around the solidity of a foreleg.

Shadow helped her. She pulled, and he took advantage of the leverage she gave him. Desperation gifted her with more strength than she had ever possessed. His upper body slid up beside her own; ice cracked again. She buried both hands in the thick ruff of his shoulder and heaved one last time.

Panting, eyes slitted, Shadow lay beside her.

"We can't wait, Shadow," she whispered. "The ice may give any time. You've got to follow me."

He looked directly into her eyes with perfect understanding. His body heaved, and he rested his wet muzzle against the back of her hand. His tongue touched her skin.

Alex scooted around on the ice until she faced Shadow and began to shimmy backward, tugging him as he'd tugged the girl.

Somehow the ice held. By the time they reached the bank, she was exhausted, and Shadow was shivering under the weight of his waterlogged pelt.

Tracy watched, wide-eyed. "The w-wolf," she said through chattering teeth.

"It's okay." Alex pulled the girl close, warming her as best she could. "Your family will be here soon. I sent Liz and Deanna to get them. It's all right."

Tracy pressed her face to Alex's shoulder. Alex closed her eyes in silent thanksgiving and then looked for Shadow.

He was gone.

There was nothing to do but wait, and the waiting was torment. Then a whine of a motor pulsed in the heavy stillness—a snowmobile, coming ever closer. It sounded to Alex like a heavenly chorus. In another few moments the vehicle burst out of the woods, Julie driving and Brenda perched precariously behind her on the snowmobile's seat.

Alex stood, cradling Tracy in her arms. Brenda jumped down almost before the snowmobile stopped, her face stricken; she grabbed Tracy in a bear-hug.

"You'll be all right now, honey," Alex said, touching

Tracy's icy cheek. "There's something I have to do, and then we'll be right after you."

She caught a glimpse of Julie's mouth open on a question as Tracy's family closed around her, and then Alex was away, following the prints of a running wolf.

He hadn't gone far. She found him on his knees, naked, hunched over against sickness and the cold. Abandoned clothing lay scattered around him.

"Kieran," she whispered. She dashed for the shirt he'd left tangled on the ground and snatched it up. The buttons were torn away and it was stiff with cold. She fell to her knees beside him and wrapped the shirt around his shoulders with clumsy hands.

He shuddered. His breath fanned her cheek in hot puffs. "Tracy," he rasped.

"She's okay. You saved her." Alex pulled the torn edges of the shirt across his chest, trying to make them meet. "You did it, Kieran. You made yourself shift. And you saved her."

"I . . . had no choice."

She gulped, fighting down a wave of dizziness that was far more profound than mere relief. "How did it happen?"

He closed his eyes. "I got to the pond and saw . . . Tracy struggling. I tried to go to her. But then I could feel—" He shuddered again. "I don't remember anything after that."

"You don't remember?"

"It all goes dark." He looked at her, an edge of fear in his eyes. "I didn't know I'd changed until I came out of it again, here. I had no control."

"But you *did*," Alex protested. "Even if you weren't consciously aware of the transformation, you changed when you needed to, when it was necessary. You were afraid for a child." She slapped her hand on the snow. "Emotion, Kieran. Emotion makes you change."

"I know I ran into the trees. They saw me run, thought I'd abandoned them. . . ."

Shame. She *felt* his shame even more than she heard it

in his voice. She spread her hand flat on his back, rubbing the damp cloth.

"You couldn't let them see you," she said. "It was instinct."

He looked at her through the dark veil of his hair, yellow burning beneath the black. "Something in me still remembered what I had to do."

"So you went out onto the ice in the only way you could. As a wolf."

She relived it all, down to the paralysis of her muscles and the fear burning in her stomach. She smiled and brushed the hair away from his eyes. "You were very brave, Kieran."

His smile was twisted with self-mockery. "Not brave. It was only instinct, wasn't it?" His smile faded. "But you—*you* were afraid."

She gathered her legs under her. "Of course I was afraid."

"Afraid for me." He moved to get up, and she scrambled back. The torn shirt slid from his shoulders, and he stood before her in all his naked perfection—taut muscles, long clean limbs, innate grace, and inhuman beauty. No longer vulnerable but overwhelming.

Memories of the kiss raced through her mind. She thought she'd put it behind her. Only moments before, he'd been Shadow; she should have been able to look at Kieran as she'd study a wolf in the wild—a magnificent specimen of his kind.

It wasn't working. It wasn't working at all.

"Of course," she said thickly. "You could have died out there."

She felt rather than saw his movement, the lift of his hand, fingers spread to brush her cheek. Her own body locked against the desperate urge to fling her arms around him, hold him close, know he was alive and safe.

But she didn't give in. She made a pretense of looking around for his clothes—found his jeans still intact, his boots wearable though the laces had broken in Kieran's haste to undress before his shift. She gathered the clothing in a bundle and drew in the scent of him, mingled with pine and earth and all the things she loved.

There was something terribly intimate about watching him pull his jeans over those long legs, shrug the ragged shirt over his broad shoulders . . . Alex folded her arms and stared up through the leafless branches of aspen and birch, the dense green of pine and spruce. After a moment she remembered she had an excellent excuse for moving away.

"Let me just get my snowshoes, and we'll go back to Julie's to check on Tracy." She hesitated. "If you'd rather stay here—"

"No." Kieran rose, regarding her steadily. "I want to see that she's all right. And find some way of explaining why I ran."

"Kieran, they won't think—"

He only looked at her, and she was effectively silenced. What would they think? A man running away from a child's danger, in the opposite direction of the rez. And there was the question of Tracy's subsequent rescue by a great black wolf . . .

"Okay," she said. "We'll find a way to deal with it, one way or another. And no matter what comes of this, Tracy is safe." She took a step toward him. "She might not be, except for you and your abilities. If you can't control them yet, you can still learn control. What happened proves that you shouldn't, you *can't* deny your wolf side."

He didn't respond but remained bent over his boots, tugging at the broken laces. When he stood, he gave no acknowledgment of her statement. "Let's go," he said.

She gave up the argument as they began to walk back to the reservation. She realized suddenly that she was exhausted, and Kieran must be doubly so. He was alive, and Tracy as well; that was enough for today.

More than enough.

*J*ulie gave a final wave from the doorway as Mike backed her truck down the drive, Kieran and Alex in the seat beside him. Alex's face was a pale blur through the window; Kieran's was a mask, as unreadable as it had been ever since the two of them came back to check up on Tracy.

She turned from the door and met Grandma's gaze. "Well?"

Grandma folded her hands over the handle of her cane and rested her chin atop them. "I think you were right, Granddaughter. Right about Alex and especially about the young man."

Julie crossed the room and sat at her grandmother's feet. "I still can't figure what they had to do with Cheryl's murder. I know they couldn't have been directly involved. My dreams won't come clear. But somehow—"

"Somehow there's a connection," Grandma finished. "The spirits don't always make it easy, but they don't lay false trails either." She sighed and rolled her neck. "What did you think of Kieran's explanation for running?"

Julie knotted her fingers. "I can't see it. Running the wrong way for help, or running because he was afraid. It doesn't fit. But it's part of all this."

"Yes. That's what I got from my talk with him. He wouldn't be the kind to run that way." She leaned forward. "And the wolf?"

The wolf. The wolf that had helped save Tracy, who now lay exhausted but recovering in a warm bed, Brenda by her side.

"It's too strange. And it's no coincidence," she concluded.

Grandma scratched her chin. "No." She gestured Julie closer. "I know Cheryl's death was never resolved for you. We all grieved. But it's still a broken circle in your heart. That's why this is coming clear to you now."

"And do you think there's a chance to close the circle, Grandma?"

Grandma was silent a long time, rocking, her eyes half-shut. "There's more to this than even your dreams are telling you. Tonight I'll pray and burn the cedar. We'll talk tomorrow. I think the spirits will be ready to give us the rest of the story."

Julie helped Grandma to her feet, and the two of them went to check on Tracy one more time. The little girl had gone back to sleep, her small form bundled under blankets, motionless in the healing rest of an exhausted child.

Julie stood in the bedroom doorway long after Grandma and Brenda left. Tracy hadn't been afraid of the wolf that rescued her. She'd said something about wanting to thank him before she drifted off.

Maybe you'll get your chance, Trace, Julie thought. *Cheryl is gone, but you're alive. It's part of the circle. Alex and Kieran are part of it, too—the circle that hasn't closed.*

But something told Julie that it would be. Very soon.

9

The sun was sinking below the tops of the trees, limning their uppermost edges with a subtle halo of fading light. Alex leaned over the porch railing and smiled. This was one of her favorite times in the woods; everything seemed at peace, hushed and waiting, ready to reveal the answers to all her unspoken questions.

Contentment had stolen up on her with no warning over the handful of days since Tracy's rescue, like the most subtle of predators. It was a contentment that came with the unspoken truce between herself and Kieran—an agreement to let things flow as they would, with the timeless serenity of the forest. No demands, no pressure, no intimacy.

There was companionship. They shared meals, even quiet walks in the forest, but Kieran seemed careful not to intrude on any part of her privacy. He ranged far in the woods, returning without explanation when he was ready. She demanded no explanations. Kieran didn't push for her help in learning more of his past; she didn't push him to remember.

She hadn't forgotten her promise to him. This peace couldn't last. Alex knew she couldn't live with any man indefinitely; sooner or later they'd have to resume the lessons, and Kieran would go on to whatever fate awaited him.

But she didn't let herself think of that inevitable future. Now was enough. This was what she had hoped for when she returned to Minnesota. She'd have peace again when Kieran was gone. He wasn't the cause of it, only a temporary alteration in the untroubled course of the life she'd planned.

She was about to turn back into the cabin when Kieran emerged from the woods. Her heart chose that moment to skip a few beats. It didn't mean anything, of course, except that he was still a magnificent sight by any standards. Deliberately she jumped down from the porch and went to meet him.

"How was your run today?" she asked casually.

His eyes caught a last flare of light as he looked at her. "Good." He glanced down the drive to where it turned a bend through the woods. "Your visitor hasn't arrived yet?"

"Visitor?"

"I heard a truck," he said, and as if to illustrate his words high beams splashed into the clearing, accompanied by the growl of an engine.

"It's probably Julie—" she began. But it wasn't. The truck was unfamiliar, and there was enough light to see that it had rental plates from Duluth.

Alex didn't know why her chest tightened or her breath suddenly came short. She felt Kieran move closer to her when the truck door swung open; a tall figure, clearly male, stepped out.

He took a few steps forward and the truck's headlights washed over the man's features, turning them golden and as distinct as a statue's. Blond hair, stylishly cut; finely chiseled features, pale eyes.

Familiar. Handsome. Almost unchanged over the years.

Alex would never have believed seeing him again could still hurt so much.

"Peter," she whispered.

*T*he name she spoke held a wealth of hidden meaning, and her voice a lifetime of hurt.

Kieran watched the intruder with narrowed eyes and searched his memory of the past two days. The man was unfamiliar, not one of those from the town, from the store or café. Yet Alexandra knew his name.

Every instinct told Kieran she knew far more than that. And the stranger—the intruder—clearly knew her. He stared at Alexandra, smoothing a palm over impeccably groomed hair.

"Who is he?" Kieran asked softly.

She looked right through Kieran for a moment, her gaze unfocused. "Peter," she repeated. "He's . . . someone I used to know."

More than that. Far more. Kieran let his senses take him, those wolf senses Alexandra wanted so badly to encourage. Something was definitely wrong. "Why is he here?"

She blinked, flexing her small hands into fists. "I don't know. I haven't seen him in . . ." She trailed off, shaking her head. Kieran had no need to rely on the subtle shifts in her scent and posture to recognize what she felt. He could no more shut off his ability to feel her emotions than he could shift his shape on a whim.

She did not want to see this man, whoever he was. *"Someone I used to know,"* she'd said. Someone who had shared some part of Alexandra's past.

A part of her past Kieran knew nothing of. A part she didn't want back.

Kieran's stomach clenched. Until Alexandra saw the intruder, she had been happy. She'd looked at Kieran without fear, accepted his friendship. For a few days there had been only harmony between them. And hope.

He knew what he felt now was not rational. It was the beast in him, still close to the surface after his shifting when he'd rescued Tracy. It was the beast who looked on another male and saw a rival.

Deny it.

He breathed deeply and pushed his hands into his pockets. Peter came closer, and Kieran stared into the man's eyes—a lighter color than Alexandra's brilliant blue—that wouldn't meet Kieran's own. Peter was almost as tall as he was, but more lightly built. There was poise in his movements, a certain pride in the way he held himself. In a fight he would be—

"Alex?"

Peter's greeting severed Kieran's dangerous train of thought.

"Peter," Alexandra acknowledged. Her voice was not quite steady.

"It's been a long time, Alex," Peter said.

Alexandra's body jerked, as if she were laughing without sound, or crying without tears. "What are you doing here, Peter?"

"I guess that's the only welcome I deserve, isn't it?" He dropped his gaze. "Alex—"

"How did you know where to find me?"

Peter lifted his hand toward Alexandra as if he wished to touch her. Kieran moved closer to Alexandra and let his arm brush hers. Her warmth sent the blood singing through his veins.

Curling his fingers, Peter let his hand fall again.

"It wasn't easy, Alex. I've been hunting you down for the past two weeks. I came out here as soon as I arrived in town."

Silence hung between them, heavy with emotion. "You're staying in Merritt?" she asked. All at once the uncertainty was gone from her voice. She threw up walls against this man from her past, keeping him out. Just as she had done with Kieran.

Peter glanced at Kieran, a brief flicker of his eyes that hinted of calculation. "Yes. I've come because it's important. I wouldn't . . . disturb you otherwise."

"It *must* be important to bring you to this part of the world. This"—she gestured at the woods around them—"isn't exactly your milieu, is it?" She touched Kieran's arm. "But I'm remiss. Peter, this is my friend, Kieran Holt.

Kieran, this is Peter Schaeffer. We knew each other as children."

"A little longer than that, Alex," Peter said. He smiled with a charm even Kieran felt, his gaze resting on Alexandra's hand. "I wish my visit were only to renew old friendships."

"I doubt that would be possible."

Old friendships. Kieran shifted, and Alex tightened her grip on his hand.

"Alex, please," Peter said. "We need to talk."

"It's getting late. Maybe tomorrow—"

"It can't wait."

Kieran felt her weighing Peter's words, warring within herself. He understood that battle; his body tensed in sympathy. Instinct and rationality struggled for dominance of his own emotions.

Alexandra had wanted him to be a wolf. Wolves defended their territory from unwanted intruders. This was *her* place. And his.

"Alexandra," he said. "I can send him away."

She looked at him, resolve in her eyes. "No," she muttered, low enough so that only he could hear. "I can't. This is something I have to face." Her mouth crooked in a smile. "I think for once in his life Peter is going to be a little out of his depth."

Kieran felt her words on a level more profound than any mere string of sounds. He heard old anger and new courage, something in which he had no right to interfere. He let the wolf retreat, prepared to watch and wait.

Alexandra turned back to Peter. "All right," she said. "You can come in and tell me this urgent news."

Her body took on an almost insolent sway as she strode toward the door. Kieran hung back, waiting for Peter as he turned off his truck's headlights.

"Kieran, is it?" Peter said. "A pleasure to meet you." He glanced around at the darkened clearing. "I don't blame you for being cautious with strangers out here. But you can relax. I *am* an old friend."

An old friend. This Peter Schaeffer was no true friend

to Alexandra, whatever he claimed. But Kieran only nodded and let Peter precede him, keeping his thoughts to himself. Peter hesitated, as if uneasy with Kieran's silence, and broke into a rapid walk toward the cabin's open door. Kieran was only a step behind.

Alexandra waited for them, arms folded. She circled the room as if she needed to remind herself of its familiarity and reclaim it as her own. Peter paused just inside the door.

"May I sit down, Alex?"

She gestured to the sofa. Deliberately Kieran put his back to the wall where he could watch every move Peter made—watch and listen and learn.

Alexandra went to stand before Peter. "You said you had something urgent to tell me. I'm listening."

Perched on the edge of the sofa with his hands clasped between his knees, Peter sighed again. "I think perhaps you'd better sit down, Alex."

"I prefer to stand."

"Alex . . . it's about your father."

Her reaction was immediate. The defenses she'd raised surged higher still; her hands knotted into fists and her jaw tensed as silent emotion beat in the air like frantic wings. Kieran kept himself from going to her by a sheer act of will.

"What about my father?"

Peter looked over his shoulder at Kieran. "I think we should have privacy, Alex."

She stared into space. "Kieran, would you mind waiting here while I speak to Peter in my room? It will only be a few minutes."

The dullness in her voice disturbed Kieran almost as much as Peter's presence. "Alexandra—"

"Please, Kieran."

He let her go, watched her lead Peter into her bedroom. The moment the door was closed he stationed himself in front of it. His hearing was acute; no mere slab of wood could keep him from knowing all that passed behind it. He crouched and listened to Peter's smooth, self-assured voice.

"Alex, I don't know how to tell you this."

"What about my father?"

Silence. "Your father . . . Alex, your father passed away two weeks ago."

*A*lex sat down hard on the bed, the air rushing out of her lungs in a single long, harsh gust.

"I'm sorry, Alex," Peter said. "So sorry."

Even within the shock of the moment, she felt a part of herself thinking that Peter was probably sincere. After all, his family had known hers for a long time, and her father had been fond of Peter. She heard the creak of the bedsprings as Peter settled beside her, carefully looping his arm behind her back without quite touching.

Peter shook his head, and immediately smoothed back a few strands of his hair that had fallen out of place with the motion. "I wish there'd been some better way to tell you. The hospital and William's lawyers tried to find you when it happened, but they were having trouble locating you, so I offered to do it. I thought you should hear it from someone you know."

Alex wondered why, at a time like this, her senses seemed more acute than ever before. Why Peter's tasteful cologne seemed so overwhelming, and the perfect, cultured modulation of his voice seemed almost too affected. *Father is dead,* she thought, but there was no reality in it.

"How did it happen?" she whispered.

"A heart attack. He didn't suffer, Alex. I know this is a shock, and it'll take time to . . . sort it out."

Time. Time that should have healed all the old wounds and hadn't. All the time that had passed since she last saw her father, so long ago that it felt like another life.

"So you came out here to tell me," Alexandra said. Her voice was remote and strange, as if she felt nothing, when in truth she felt too much. "You stayed in touch with my father. When you took over Schaeffer Industries—"

"It was more than business." Peter moved closer, but she had no will or strength to put any distance between them. "We stayed in touch because I hoped you'd eventually come back to San Francisco. Even your father . . ."

She looked at him for the first time, amazed that her heart was still sensitive enough to feel this kind of pain. "My father," she echoed dully.

"It's true, Alex. Whatever happened between you—"

"You know what happened between us."

"Yes." Peter looked down at his manicured fingernails. "Just as I know that he—he wouldn't have wanted it to end the way it did."

Sickness twisted her stomach in a knot. Reconciliation. Was that what Peter meant? That her father would have wanted a reconciliation, after the things he'd said to her?

But now he was dead. And she hadn't seen him since the day of her graduation from college. Time had run out.

"I know it's hard for you to deal with right now. But I have papers here . . ." He reached into an inside pocket of his shearling jacket and produced an envelope. "When you're ready to look at them. The will."

The will. So her father had left her something after all, when he'd withheld himself? *As much your fault, Alex, for never giving him another chance . . .*

She curled her fists against the mattress so tightly that her blunt nails cut her palms. "He never tried to find me, Peter. Never."

"God, Alex. I wish I could say something to—"

"You don't need to say anything." She could feel her breath coming too short, shock giving way to feelings she wouldn't be able to control. And anger. Anger to block out the pain, anger that needed an object to turn on.

"I need to think about this," she said, pushing away from the bed. Her knees were a little unsteady, but she made them function. She heard Peter stand up behind her.

"Of course. Time is what you need. But I don't want you to be alone right now, Alex."

Anger. Anger to keep the grief and guilt away. "I'm not alone."

"You mean your friend out there."

She placed her hands flat on the old dresser and pressed her forehead against her knuckles. "Does it surprise you that I've found friends, Peter?"

"And exactly who *is* this friend of yours? What is he to you?"

He spoke casually, but she could tell he wanted an answer. Part of her wanted to tell him that Kieran was her lover, to prove to him that she'd been found desirable to other men. But she'd never been good at lying.

"He's a fellow researcher. Why does it matter?"

"Because you need more than some . . . colleague with you at a time like this."

"You don't need to trouble yourself—"

"Is that what you think it is? Trouble?" The floorboards vibrated with Peter's footsteps. "You have every reason to despise me, Alex. I was incredibly stupid back then. I've regretted the way it happened every day of my life—"

"Now is not the time, Peter."

"You need someone with you now, someone who shared what we did. Alex . . ." He touched her arm, very gently. Incongruously she remembered that dream of Peter that had ended with the discovery of Kieran in her bed. Some bizarre premonition. She felt wildly like laughing and caught hold of herself with every scrap of sanity she had.

"I may be a poor excuse for comfort right now, and I would have given the world to see you again under other circumstances—"

She turned on him. "You never came to find me, either."

Peter blinked. Stray hair had fallen over his forehead again, but as if to prove his earnestness he left it untidy. "I made some mistakes. I did some things I'm not proud of. But I'm here now, and I care about you. I never stopped caring."

Was he right? Was he right about her father, too? That he would have welcomed her back if she'd gone home? Accepted her? Loved her?

You never wanted to see Father again, she thought. *Now you have your wish.*

"That's why I'm staying in town," Peter continued. "I want to be here for you."

She looked at him—through him, a detached part of herself still separated from anger and grief. So breathtakingly handsome, Peter, with his blond hair and perfect tan and even white teeth, a body honed by swimming and tennis and carefully regulated workouts in his private gym.

It had been so easy to fall in love with him; he was the opposite of everything she hated in herself. Perfect where she was flawed; accepted where she was rejected, utterly certain of himself.

He still had that certainty, and she was lost.

"Have you forgiven me, Alex?" he said.

In a few seconds she relived that last terrible argument, the parting that had taught Alex her own worth in Peter's eyes. Right after she'd heard her father's damning words.

You can't ever talk to your father again, she told herself. *Never. You can't ever undo it. But Peter's here. . .*

"You married," she said. "You found the life you wanted. We—" Her throat closed. "We made our choices."

Choices. Peter's priorities had always been clear; at least he'd been honest about that in the end. It had been Alex's choice to abandon the plans she and Peter made after the parting with her father. *Her* decision that had forced Peter to shatter her illusions.

Peter looked away. "Some of them were the wrong choices, Alex. Terribly wrong. It didn't work out with Bev."

Bev Del Valle. The woman he had finally married, who'd had the money to shore up the faltering Schaeffer Industries, and perfect beauty to match. But now Peter's voice was so sincere, so filled with regret.

"We . . . divorced, Alex," Peter continued. His fingers covered hers. "I couldn't stop loving you. I thought I'd convinced myself, but—"

"You convinced me," she whispered.

"I know I deserve that. I was so obsessed with taking over Dad's work, getting the company running again . . . it blinded me, Alex. I couldn't see what really mattered. By the time I did see, it was too late. You'd left, and I'd married Bev. But it wasn't right. Not for either one of us." He touched Alex's hair. "It took me a while to work things out with her. But when your father died, I knew I had to come."

Alex couldn't move, even when he began to stroke her hair with a tenderness she didn't remember in him. "Peter—"

"Alex, I know this is a lot for you to absorb. I just want to be here for you. Let me help you get through this."

"Peter, I don't think I—" Her voice caught and broke. "You'd better go. Please."

"All right." He held up the envelope she'd almost forgotten and set it on the dresser. "I'll leave the letter here. I'm staying at the Merritt Motor Inn." Still he didn't walk away; Alex felt a weakness flooding her body, a weight grinding her down.

"Let me help you, Alex," Peter murmured. "At least let me do that." And he took her into his arms.

She let him hold her. She didn't have the will to summon a protest. Her head felt too heavy to hold up, and when Peter cradled it against his shoulder she didn't resist.

A second later the bedroom door swung open. Kieran walked into the room, looked at them, and froze.

"Kieran," she croaked.

He said nothing, only stared at her, his face expressionless. Peter held her a little tighter, and suddenly she felt trapped. Trapped and desperate and thoroughly unable to cope.

With a jerk she pulled free of Peter's embrace and backed away until her legs hit the bed. Kieran started after her just as Peter did. She stopped them both with upflung hands.

"I need to be alone," she said. "Please. Both of you, just leave me alone."

Peter smoothed his hair carefully back above his forehead. "All right, Alex," he said. He threw a long look at Kieran. "You know where I'll be. Please . . . think about what I said. I meant every word." He hesitated only a moment longer and strode to the door. Kieran made no move to follow. In the silence Alex could hear the front door close and the rumble of the truck's engine as it pulled away.

"Alexandra."

She looked through him, as she'd looked through Peter earlier. "Go. Please go." She squeezed her eyes shut, willing him to obey.

His breathing was soft, but in the silence it filled the room. "I can't, Alexandra. You need me."

The same way Peter insisted she needed *him*. Seeming devotion she could no more deal with than the anger and guilt and grief she had never expected to feel.

"You're hurting," Kieran told her, moving closer. She wondered if she could yell at him, if she could bring herself to say something hurtful enough to drive him away. But she knew that was impossible the moment she met his gaze.

"Your father is dead," he said. So baldly, with no finesse at all. "I'm sorry, Alexandra."

She turned to the window. "You heard everything, didn't you?" she said wearily. She flipped the curtain back, though there was little for human eyes to see in the darkness.

"You've never spoken about your parents," he said. He moved along the perimeter of the room, granting her at least a little distance. "I don't remember mine. Not the way I should. But I still think I know what you must feel."

She shuddered, fingers clenched on the curtain. Of course he did. He'd lost as much, or more, than she ever had.

"My father and I—we were never close," she said. She heard the curtain's old muslin protest and begin to tear in her grasp. She let go. "I hadn't seen him in many years."

"But you still grieve," Kieran said.

Do I? She rested her forehead against the cold glass. "My mother died when I was a child," she said, her voice flat and emotionless. "There was an accident. My father and I survived. But my mother's death didn't bring us closer. It had the opposite effect."

She expected him to ask more about the accident, to mention the scar at last. But he only leaned against the wall and watched her with those deep, steady eyes, urging her to talk with his very silence. So unlike Peter, with his endless questioning.

Alex moved away from the window. It wasn't as hard as she'd thought to simply . . . not feel anything, to talk about these things to one who'd had no part in them.

"My father didn't enjoy being a parent," she said. "He sent me away to boarding school most of the time, and wasn't around when I came home for the summers. It was as if . . ."

He were dead too. But now that was a fact, and too close to the edge of pain.

"I never lacked for anything," she continued. "We were wealthy. He gave me all the money I wanted. Especially when I stayed away. I went to one of the best colleges in the country. The day I graduated he actually came, but we had a terrible argument." She swallowed thickly. "I never saw him again. Now it's too late."

She knew how close Kieran was to touching her, holding her as Peter had done. He took a single step and braced his feet against the floor, as if he could lock himself in place there.

"The argument," he said softly. "What was it about?"

No. She wasn't getting into this. Not now, and not ever.

"I don't want to discuss it, Kieran. It's pointless." She struggled to regain her fragile calm.

"And Peter?"

His question was ambiguous, devoid of intonation or any hint of what he was truly asking. She remembered the blankness of his expression when he'd walked in on her and Peter.

"I told you we used to know each other. He came all the way out here from the West Coast to tell me about my father. To help." She turned to face Kieran. "I need to talk to him—"

"But you didn't want to see him."

Alex closed her eyes. "I know I gave that impression. Seeing him again—and the news he brought . . ." She faltered. "I don't know what I want anymore."

Even that admission was too much. Kieran was coming toward her, earnest in his desire to comfort her, and if she let go one more time she'd have nothing left to fight with.

"I know what I want, Alexandra," he said.

She waited for the touch of his big hands, torn between anger and helplessness and need, just as she'd been with Peter. But this was different. Different because Kieran came to her without the burdens of her past. Because he could understand exactly how she felt.

Would it be so terrible to accept what he was willing to give, even for a moment?

His touch never came. When she opened her eyes again, he was gone—without warning, as he had come.

She was alone then. Exactly as she'd wanted. Alone to sort through feelings she didn't understand. Feelings like grief, which should have been normal and cleansing.

Nothing could ever be that simple.

She lay down on the bed, staring at the ceiling with dry and burning eyes.

And when at last she slept it was not of loss she dreamed, but of a great black wolf who led her on a search for something wondrous that lay on the other side of pain.

*J*oseph found Peter Schaeffer easily enough. The outsider had the best room in Merritt's motel, a luxury model with its own kitchen and a king-size bed.

But Schaeffer seemed far from pleased with the world when he answered the door to Joseph's knock. He looked at Joseph with pinched mouth and narrowed eyes.

"Who the hell are you?" he asked.

Joseph smiled. Ill mannered, this boy, as ill mannered as all those of his generation who had forgotten the virtue of respect for their elders. Joseph pulled off his knitted cap and clutched it between his hands.

"You don't know me, Mr. Schaeffer, but I believe we have something in common."

Schaeffer was capable of great charm when he felt so inclined. Joseph had watched him since his arrival in Merritt the day before—had listened and followed, unseen, as the city man inquired about Alexandra Warrington and gave the gossips fuel to chatter about his purpose in Merritt. That he didn't belong here was apparent, with his polished city ways and arrogance; but his generosity in the bar and his quick smile had loosened the tongues of many who were more than willing to talk about Ms. Warrington and her odd guest.

Schaeffer had no charm to spare now. He looked Joseph up and down, hardly deigning to hide a sneer behind his smile. "I doubt we have much in common, Mr.—"

"Arnoux," Joseph supplied.

"Arnoux," Schaeffer repeated, mangling the pronunciation. "Do you have any idea what time it is? If you don't mind—"

"The wind is cold on these old bones, Mr. Schaeffer. Perhaps I could come inside?"

He could see the young man debating closing the door in his face. *What do you see, boy? An old, worthless back-woodsman? Someone far beneath your notice?*

"Whatever you're selling, I don't need it," Schaeffer said. Joseph moved his foot against the door and stopped its forward motion. He continued to smile at the young man until Schaeffer dropped his hand from the doorknob.

"I'm not selling anything, Mr. Schaeffer. I can see a man such as yourself needs very little in the way of worldly goods. It's something else you want, is it not?"

Schaeffer stared at him as if he were crazy. But so had many people. All those who didn't understand.

But I understand you, Schaeffer. I know what you want,

because your arrogance makes you announce your intentions to the world.

"You've come to town for the woman. Alexandra Warrington."

Schaeffer blinked, taken aback. "You don't know anything about my business here."

Joseph chuckled softly. "I know as much as anyone in town. What you've said yourself to anyone who will listen—that you had important news for the woman. A woman you once knew well, whom you've come a long way to find."

"So?"

"And you had more in mind than merely delivering your news. You went courting, did you not, Mr. Schaeffer? And your courting did not go as well as you planned."

Schaeffer eyed him, his expression caught between outrage and suspicion.

"How do you know all that?"

"I have eyes. And ears," Joseph said. "Anyone will tell you that Old Man Arnoux knows everything." *And I was there, outside the cabin, when you stormed out Alexandra Warrington's door, looking ready to commit murder.* He shrugged. "News spreads quickly in a small town. But perhaps you're not overly familiar with small towns, Mr. Schaeffer."

The young man all but shuddered. A man used to fine things, Schaeffer, and unaccustomed to meeting any resistance to his plans.

"You do want the woman, Mr. Schaeffer. That is why you're here, isn't it?"

He'd read his man well. For a moment Schaeffer hovered between slamming the door and opening it wider. In the end his fundamental greed won out.

"What if it is?" he said. "What does that have to do with you?"

Joseph took a step forward and Schaeffer fell back, allowing him just enough grudging space to enter the room.

"You see, Mr. Schaeffer, I know how matters may have

become complicated for you. I know about the man who is staying with Miss Warrington." He paused. "The man who would be your rival."

Schaeffer choked on a laugh, but Joseph saw the precise moment when the young man became interested. "Rival?" he echoed incredulously. "That big, stupid redneck I saw her with?"

Ah. Joseph shook his head mentally. *You are as guilty as I was, boy, of underestimating your enemy.*

"She said he was just a fellow researcher. A friend," Schaeffer said, striding across the room. He jerked out one of the two chairs by the small table and sat down, legs sprawled. "He doesn't mean anything to her."

"Are you certain of that, Mr. Schaeffer? The two of them alone in that cabin . . ."

"Of course I'm certain. I know Alexandra. She'd never—" He broke off, frowning. "What's the point of all this? Why are you here?"

"To help you achieve your goal."

Schaeffer was silent, his blue eyes calculating. *You want more than just the woman, boy,* Joseph thought, *but I don't care what it is. As long as you do what I need you to do . . .*

"I don't need your help, old—" He cut himself off, though without any trace of embarrassment. "I can handle Alexandra and this 'friend' of hers without any trouble."

"Your confidence is admirable," Joseph said. "But I know more about Kieran Holt than you do, more than your Miss Warrington does."

Schaeffer sat up straight in his chair. "What do you know about him?" he demanded.

Joseph studied the handsome, petulant face. *Even your confidence can be shaken.* "I know he is dangerous. Possibly mad."

With a sharp movement Schaeffer rose, crossed the room again, and turned. "He might be stupid and strange, but crazy?"

"You have only to ask around. Surely you've already heard some hint of this. Holt's sudden arrival in town, his behavior in the café." Joseph sighed. "Your Miss Warrington was very adamant in defending him."

The seeds of doubt had been planted. Whatever Schaeffer's certainty about his superiority and his ability to win Miss Warrington, he was not a complete fool. If he saw any way to use this knowledge to his advantage, he would take it. He was willing and ready to believe.

"Who is he, then? Is he a wolf researcher, as he claims?"

"In a manner of speaking. But he has had a . . . troubled past."

Schaeffer touched his hair lightly, as if to smooth a nonexistent imperfection. "Is Alex in danger? Should we call the police?"

"No! No. That would be a mistake." Joseph calmed himself, found a chair, and sat down heavily. "His madness is unpredictable. He must be approached carefully, kept at ease. I believe he has a certain affection for Miss Warrington that should make him more malleable."

Schaeffer stroked the faint lines bracketing his mouth. "Why are you interested in all this? In 'helping' me?"

"Isn't my concern for Miss Warrington enough?"

But Schaeffer's lip lifted, and Joseph was reminded once again that he was far from a complete fool.

"Very well, Mr. Schaeffer. The reason is simple. I have a score to settle with Kieran Holt."

"What kind of score?"

"My own business, Mr. Schaeffer. But I will say that he has done harm in the past that must be atoned for, and I am the only one who can bring him to justice."

Schaeffer shook his head. "I won't get involved in any kind of . . . vigilante justice."

"Such haste, my friend. I have no intention of harming Kieran Holt. But he is a danger to Miss Warrington as long as he stays with her. And as long as he stays with her I can't get to him, see that he is kept from being a threat to her or anyone else."

Schaeffer came to stand over him, his composure restored. "And what do you think you can do to help me?"

"Help each *other,* Mr. Schaeffer. Holt is a problem for you, whether you admit it or not. We both want him away from Miss Warrington. If you perform that task, I will see to it that he no longer stands in your way."

It seemed that Schaeffer wavered, nagged by doubts or even a touch of conscience. His pride, too, was touched. But at last he nodded, and smiled—a smile as icy as the wind outside the door.

"How do you suggest I go about removing Holt from Alex's cabin?"

Joseph rose slowly, ignoring the ache in his bones. "I know you to be an intelligent man, Mr. Schaeffer. You have more experience in these matters than an old backwoodsman." He smiled, as if joking at his own expense. "All you need to do is convince Holt to leave the cabin for a period of a day or two, longer if possible. But you must be careful not to set him off. Be mild and cautious. I have seen what he can do when he is . . . disturbed. But he can be manipulated. I think you're good at such games, Mr. Schaeffer."

The young man might have been offended, but he merely looked at Joseph with unshakable superiority. "I'll take care of it."

"And I will do my part," Joseph said. He rose and extended his hand. "To our alliance, Mr. Schaeffer."

Schaeffer looked down at Joseph's thick, callused hand, hesitated, and brushed it briefly with his own. "Allies," he said. "Until we both have what we want."

10

Alexandra had gone into town without him.

Kieran smoothed out the crumpled paper and let it fall to the kitchen table. He'd spent the night and morning roaming the woods near the cabin, his mind in turmoil. And when he came back, he had found the note.

There was no real explanation of why she'd gone. He knew she was hurting over her father, rattled by Peter's appearance, though she refused to share her troubles.

She'd gone to talk to Julie, she said. Checking up on Tracy again, and making sure the family had really accepted Kieran's account of why he'd run, as they seemed to—that they didn't think him the coward he'd appeared to be.

They would have no way of guessing the nature of the wolf who'd saved Tracy. Yet Kieran had felt at ease among them, even with Mary. He almost believed he could tell Julie and her people the truth. If he knew what the truth was.

But he did know the real reason Alexandra had gone into town. The last line of the note was underlined, emphasizing the command: *Wait for me at the cabin.*

Kieran leaned over the table, closing his eyes. It was

already noon. He could spend the rest of the day waiting for Alexandra to return. Passively, obediently. Refusing to force himself on her—retreating, as he'd done last night, even when he knew she'd needed him. Proving to himself that he was controlled, rational. Human.

While she was with Peter Schaeffer, listening to his smooth words. A man who shared her past and claimed to love her and wanted her back. Who could offer comfort out of knowledge of who and what she was.

Kieran pushed away from the table with such force that the chair beside him crashed to the floor. He left it where it was and strode into the living room. His boots were under the coffee table; he strung the shoelaces through the belt loops of his jeans and tied them together.

He smiled grimly. It was human to wear shoes but easier to run without them. His clothing had loosened and softened with wear, and no longer impeded his movements. He remembered the way to town as if he'd run it a thousand times.

His feet found purchase on the snowy ground even without benefit of leather pads and claws. The blood beat fast and hard in his veins. For the first mile he ran wildly, surrendering to the chaos of emotion. Then he settled into the sensible rhythm his body demanded and gave himself up to the uncomplicated joy of being, of sucking cold air into his lungs and smelling the wind and feeling the faint burn in his muscles.

By the time he reached the outskirts of Merritt he was almost tranquil. He crouched behind the cover of a thicket and pulled on his boots. A few faces turned his way as he walked into Merritt, but he ignored them. He sifted the odor-heavy air for the one scent he needed to locate.

Julie's garage was the first place he found, closed and locked up. Alexandra had been here and passed on. Kieran had crossed the entire length of Merritt and started back again when a different scent assaulted him. He stopped in midstep and lifted his head. The hairs rose at the nape of his neck.

Peter. And he was very close.

Kieran hesitated only a moment. He needed to know more about Peter. Much more. For Alexandra's sake. The scent trail led him to a door open to the sidewalk, music and hoarse voices and acrid odors.

Memory came without warning. It broke over him like a wave, pushing him against the grimy cement wall. He looked up at the sign over the door.

Lenny's, it read. He knew this place—or one so like it as to make no difference. A bar. A place where people gathered to drink, and to forget. Perspiring bodies, the harsh bite of alcohol, constant noise that made it impossible to fear the shadows. A place of utter anonymity.

How many times had he been in bars like this one? A hundred, a thousand—the memories all fused together, indistinct but undeniable. Like a single star visible in a cloudy sky, he could see one vivid image of his past: himself sitting at a long and pitted wooden counter, a glass in his hand, indifferent to the world.

It almost felt as if he'd come home. He knew what he would find if he stepped through the door. The bar would be as dark and confining as a cage, and yet he wouldn't be uneasy. There would be strangers on every side, and yet he would belong among them. His senses would dull, his vision blur, and he would forget what he was.

Kieran barked a laugh. He had gone to these places to forget, and they were all he could remember when he'd forgotten too much.

He pushed away from the wall, pausing on the threshold. A figure emerged against the frame of darkness. His telltale scent preceded him, trailed by the dense odors of the bar.

"Kieran! We meet again."

Peter Schaeffer smiled and held out his hand. Kieran stared at it, working his way through a ferment of emotion. Irrational emotion. His muscles twitched, but he returned Peter's smile and took Peter's hand in his own. The other man's fingers were narrow, his palm smooth. They tested each others' grips briefly and let go by unspoken agreement.

"Glad I ran into you, Kieran," Peter remarked. "We weren't properly acquainted the first time."

There were no undercurrents in his bland, handsome face, or in his equally pleasant voice. His bearing projected confidence and ease, self-acceptance of his natural superiority over lesser creatures. Including Kieran.

"Where is Alexandra?" Kieran asked.

"You don't know?" His pale eyes were sharp and watchful, belying his smile.

"I will," Kieran said. "Soon."

Peter's gaze swept from Kieran's feet back to his face. "I haven't seen her today. Yet. But I'm glad you came into town, Kieran. I'd been hoping to talk to you about Alex, and what she's going through."

Kieran let his teeth show. "You mean your arrival here and the news you brought," he said.

Peter's smile slipped a little. "It was rough on her, and I didn't like telling her." He cleared his throat. "I thought you might be able to fill me in about Alex's life here. She told me you're a fellow researcher." He arched a brow. "You seem to be a native of this area."

The way he spoke the final sentence suggested a vague condescension. Kieran smoothed down the hair that had risen along the back of his neck. "In a manner of speaking," he said.

"Excellent." Peter drew two fingers precisely over the neatly cut hair above his forehead, correcting a nonexistent flaw. "Come on inside, Kieran. I think we have a few things to discuss. Let me buy you a drink."

A drink. Two words that sounded vastly appealing at the moment. He nodded to Peter, who gestured him into the bar. "I suppose you haven't known Alex a very long time," Peter said pleasantly. "I know she hasn't been in this area more than a month. Plenty of gossip in town about what she's been doing with her research." He flicked a glance at Kieran. "Heard a few things about you, too, Kieran."

Kieran kept a tight rein on his distrust and pulled up a stool at the long counter. "People like to talk," he said.

Peter flagged down the bartender, a plump man with heavy folds of skin under his eyes. "Two Scotch on the rocks, please," Peter said. He glanced at Kieran. "Make his a double. So, Kieran, where do you live?"

Kieran put his elbows on the bar. The smells were more intense now. They wove around him in a muffling cocoon. "I'm staying with Alex."

"Ah," Peter murmured. "I did hear you'd had some sort of mishap with some wild animal or other. I'm not surprised Alex took you in. She's always been softhearted about animals and those . . . less fortunate."

The bartender put Kieran's drink down before him and he reached for it without conscious thought. His hands cradled the glass, fitting around it as if he'd done it a hundred times.

The alcohol burned into his nostrils long before he put the glass to his lips. For a moment he hesitated. The amber liquid was poison. A flash of memory revealed an image of himself bent over a toilet, heaving until his stomach was empty.

But the lure was too strong, too blessedly familiar when so little else was.

He drank. Peter leaned forward on his elbows, toying with his own glass. "I guess you know that Alex and I have known each other for a very long time. We grew up together, in fact."

Kieran finished the drink and wiped his mouth with the back of his hand. Warmth spread through him, a feeling of detachment that fulfilled the promise of his memories. "She mentioned it," he said.

"She told you we were going to be married."

Married. Mated in the way people did, joined by a ceremony that was seldom truly for life. Peter had said something to Alexandra about being divorced from the woman he *had* married.

And that he wanted Alexandra back.

Kieran's mouth twitched. "She told me it was over a long time ago."

Peter glanced away. "Did she? I'm surprised she'd

confide that to . . . someone who doesn't know her intimately. It's true, we had a misunderstanding and went our separate ways. For a while."

But not forever. Peter didn't need to speak the words. Kieran swiveled around on the stool. "I know Alexandra very well," he said. "We're friends."

"Friends," Peter echoed. He took a shallow sip of his drink. "I am glad she's had a friend here. This isn't ordinarily the kind of place where she'd find people who . . . share her background. Are you from this area originally, Kieran?"

Kieran stared into his empty glass. "I'm from many places."

"Alex's family was one of the most well respected in San Francisco. Money, influence, impeccable style." Peter looked around the bar. "Strange to think she'd ever want to settle in a place like this." But when he looked back at Kieran, it was as if his words were not about places but people.

Kieran straightened on his stool. "We knew each other as children. Here in Minnesota."

"Really. She never mentioned you." Peter touched his glass to his lips and put it down again. "But I do remember that she came here every summer as a child. Until the accident. And then her grandfather died—"

"The accident," Kieran interrupted. "What happened to her?"

Peter stroked the corner of his lip. "It should be obvious." He paused. "Didn't she tell you?"

There was that faint edge of mockery to Peter's question, at odds with the subject of Alexandra's suffering. Kieran set his jaw and gripped his glass more tightly.

But Peter read his silence easily enough. "I'm not surprised she didn't talk about it. She doesn't reveal herself to many people."

Anger eddied through Kieran's growing numbness. "I know that she and her father were estranged."

"Yes. A very sad and unfortunate thing. I tried at the time to bring them back together, but—" He shrugged with an air of regret. "Alex is very much like her father was. Stubborn and passionate."

He gave the last word a wealth of innuendo that hinted at personal knowledge. Very personal knowledge. Kieran pushed his empty glass aside and swung to face Peter.

"What do you want?"

Peter signaled to the bartender, who replaced Kieran's empty glass with a full one. "I want what's best for Alex. I always have. I know she needs to have a connection to what's she's lost. That's why I'm here." He rested his hand on Kieran's shoulder. "That's why I wanted to talk to you, Kieran. If you're her friend, you want to help her, right?"

With an effort Kieran stopped himself from throwing off Peter's hand. "Yes."

Peter slapped his shoulder. "Good. Believe me, I know what Alex needs." He grew serious. "And right now what she needs is privacy. Time to herself. She's always been that way when things get rough."

Kieran drained his glass and set it down with careful deliberation. "And?"

"To be blunt . . ." Peter leaned back on his stool. "To be blunt, I think you should move out for a while, give her some space. I'm sure a resourceful fellow such as yourself can find somewhere else to stay. As it is, with you living in such close quarters . . ."

"You said you wanted to see her yourself," Kieran said softly.

"But I'm not intruding on her space, am I? I want Alex free to work through her feelings, make her own choices. I'm sure when she has her privacy again, without feeling . . . obligated to deal with a guest, she'll be able to get through this."

Kieran stared at Peter through blurred vision. *Space.* He understood that need. He hated enclosed places. Was Alexandra the same? Was he making things worse for her by burdening her with obligations she had never wanted? Offering comfort she wouldn't accept?

His eyelids were heavy, his thoughts becoming as sluggish as ice breaking up on a river. Even Peter's scent was dulled, but Kieran distrusted it. Distrusted and disliked everything about Peter Schaeffer that made him fully human and certain of what he was.

"She doesn't . . . want to see you," he said at last.

Peter's mouth twitched and relaxed into a smile. "What she wants and doesn't want is her own choice. I don't think you can speak for her." He leaned forward, radiating earnestness. "Take it from me, Kieran. Alex and I come from the same background. We understand each other. If you're her friend, follow my advice. It's the best thing you can do for her."

"For her," Kieran repeated. His own voice sounded slow and strange. Somehow another drink found its way into his hands. He could hardly taste it now, but he had no desire to stop.

He didn't like Peter. He didn't trust him. Something Peter had done in the past had hurt Alex. But she had known him well, had nearly taken him as her mate . . .

"Good man," Peter said. "I knew you'd see things the right way." He scooted his stool away from the bar. "I'd be happy to give you a hand if you have any trouble finding a place to stay." He tossed a wad of bills on the counter and gestured to the bartender. "The drinks are on me. I'll be seeing you again."

Kieran hardly heard him go. He pushed his empty glass in slow circles on the counter until the bartender came by and refilled it.

He swirled the liquid around and around, mesmerized by the motion. He had come to town for a reason. To find Alexandra. He hadn't found her, and his meeting with Peter had been—less than satisfactory.

Maybe Peter was right. What did Kieran really know about Alexandra? How much of her life had he shared? A few days, and that time so long ago when they were children.

Maybe she would be better off if he left her alone. Took away the problems he'd dumped in her lap. *"I don't know what I want,"* she'd said last night. Maybe he could make it easier for her to decide.

With an effort Kieran planted his feet on the floor, working the numbness out of them. One more time. He'd find her, talk to her one more time, and then he'd know. . . .

"Lookee here. If it ain't the wolf-man."

Kieran turned his head. Someone was right beside him, too close, one arm across the counter. He recognized the scent just as the arm knocked his half-empty glass over, spilling the Scotch on the pitted counter.

"He sure can't hold his liquor, can he, boys?"

Howie Walsh gave a forced laugh, and others followed his lead. Kieran turned his head. There were four of them, one of whom had been with Howie in the Big Mouth Café. Four men with ugly, twisted faces and no friendly intentions.

Kieran braced himself against the counter and put his back to it. He grinned, showing his teeth.

"We weren't . . . properly acquainted last time," he said with exaggerated mockery of Peter's earlier words. "My *name* is Kieran Holt."

Walsh widened his eyes at his friends. "So formal! We been hearing about you, haven't we, boys? About you running away when a little girl was drowning."

Kieran hid his flinch. So they knew. He wouldn't believe that Julie's family had spoken of it, but somehow word had gotten out. And spread.

"Sure, it was only the Indian kid," Howie continued, "but it's all over town. How wolfie boy here took one look at that little pond and turned tail." He snickered and looked sideways at Kieran. "Scared of water, wolfie boy?"

Numbed though he was, Kieran felt the hostility in the room like a living presence. He bristled and began to relax his hold on the anger he'd held in check. There were consequences to letting go, but he couldn't seem to remember what they were. He pushed away from the counter. "What are *you* afraid of, Howie?"

Howie retreated as far as he could without actually

taking a step back. "You hear a threat, boys?" he said. He turned his head and spat, narrowly missing Kieran's foot. "I heard you was screwing the bitch." He laughed. "Wolf-man and wolf-bitch. Makes sense!"

But Kieran hardly heard the last few words. His vision blurred again, but not from the alcohol he'd consumed.

The rage came, just as it had done before in the café— the rage he had not allowed himself to feel in Peter's presence. Now he encouraged it, welcomed it. And as it surged like fire through his body, he remembered what it was he *should* fear.

The changing. Strong emotion triggered it. He could feel the shifting begin, his body preparing to alter, bone and muscle and flesh down to the last cell.

There was no fear. He *wanted* this. He gloried in the rage, because it was freedom and forgetfulness. In a few moments he would become a creature these petty humans could not face or defeat. He would finish what he'd begun in the café. Who then would be afraid?

But he knew within seconds it wasn't working. Now that he wanted the change it refused to come. His body spasmed but held its human shape. Nausea sent bile into his throat. He flung back his head, blind and paralyzed.

"I think he's having some kind of fit!"

Walsh spoke from a great distance. "Well then, boys, we'd better help him out. Take him someplace where he can . . . recover." Ugly laughter.

Hands grabbed Kieran from every direction. He tried to fling them off; a blow caught Kieran at the angle of his jaw, slamming his teeth together. His arms were wrenched behind him.

"You come with us, wolf-man. We'll take good care of you—"

"Hold it."

Not Walsh's voice, or any of his friends. Muttered protests and curses sounded close to Kieran's ears, and faded; restraining hands let go. Kieran swayed, reaching for the nearest support.

It was not the counter but human flesh he touched. He

snapped his hand away, staggered, and felt himself steadied by a hard grip at his elbow.

"Easy," the stranger said. Kieran tried to clear his vision, but it remained stubbornly dim. The man who stood beside him was tall, Kieran's own height, and he smelled—strange. Familiar and unfamiliar at once. He hadn't been here before.

"Sit down," the man ordered. A bar stool bumped Kieran's hip, and he obeyed without thinking. His head spun and his body ached. Dimly he heard the stranger walk away. A brief argument went on somewhere behind him, and the stranger was the last to speak.

Kieran thought carefully about getting up, but his legs had no feeling in them. He planted his feet and concentrated on the ground. It wasn't really spinning. . . .

"Kieran."

This voice he knew.

"Alexandra," he croaked. Suddenly he wanted another drink; he reached out across the counter, searching for a glass.

"Dutch said he'd seen you come in here," she said. "I told you to stay at the cabin." Her hand closed on his, her scent washing over him as she leaned close.

"My God. You're drunk." Censure. Disgust. "We need to get out of here. Can you walk?"

Walk. Of course he could walk. He shuffled his feet on the floor and pushed up. The counter tilted.

"Let me give you a hand," the stranger said.

Kieran blinked and cocked his head. "Who—"

"Concentrate on walking," the man said. Command laced his words . . . like the Voice, but completely different. There was no condemnation in it, no mockery. "*Maudite boisson*. This stuff is poison."

"I'll second that," Alexandra muttered. "Thanks."

Alexandra took one of Kieran's arms and the stranger the other, hauling him up. Kieran found himself face to face with the man.

Dark hair, shorter than Kieran's and peppered with

shades of white and gray. A hard, experienced face. And that haunting sense of familiarity, just out of reach.

Do I know you? Kieran tried to ask. *Are you from my past?* But it was all he could do to shuffle along between them, let them guide him into the painful light of day and Alexandra's truck parked at the curb.

"Get in, Kieran," Alexandra said, opening the passenger door. "Wait for me."

He did what she asked and slumped in the seat, letting the numbness claim him again.

*A*lexandra slammed the door and turned back to the stranger. "Thanks for your help," she said. "I've never seen Kieran do this before."

"My pleasure," the man said. "I could see he was getting into trouble."

Alex laughed. "Trouble," she echoed. "He seems to have a way of finding it." She caught herself and studied the stranger again in the light of day. He was ruggedly handsome, with a hard cast to his face and yellow-green eyes that—she started at the comparison that came to mind. His eyes were very much like Kieran's.

She realized that she'd been staring and thrust out her hand to cover her confusion. "My name is Alex. Alex Warrington."

"Luke Gévaudan," the stranger returned, taking her hand. He met her gaze the same direct way Kieran did.

A small crowd had gathered on the sidewalk. Howie's bunch was not among them, but their whispers and gestures stretched Alex's feigned calm to the limit.

Luke Gévaudan released her hand and glanced at the bystanders with a cynical twist of his mouth. "If you'll excuse me a moment." He turned and stalked toward the spectators. There was a brief silence, a ripple of uneasy glances, and all at once the crowd broke up, some retreating back into the bar and others walking away. Even Gévaudan disappeared.

Only one man was left, slim and handsome in an expensive and impeccable fur-lined coat.

"Alex," he said. "I was hoping I'd see you."

"This isn't a good time, Peter."

He raised an eyebrow and looked past her to the truck. "Your . . . *friend* doesn't hold his liquor very well, does he?" he said. But his smile had an edge to it.

Alex glanced over her shoulder. Kieran was slumped in the seat, eyes closed. "He doesn't drink much. I want to get him home."

Peter's smile gave way to a look of convincingly wistful sincerity. He extended his hand toward her. "You can't spare even a few minutes for me, Alex?"

She stared at his hand. Oh, he was so certain. So certain she would fall for him again as she'd done so long ago, when he was the only one who'd seemed to accept her for what she was.

So certain he could mold her to suit himself.

She pushed away from the truck and circled to the far side of it, putting its bulk between her and any observers in the bar. Better to have it out here. She didn't want him at the cabin again.

"I read the letter," she said without preamble.

He followed her. "Then you know—"

"That I'm wealthy?" She smiled at him, not bothering to hide her bitterness. "That Father left me his entire fortune?"

Peter shook his head in a parody of sorrowful exasperation. "That he cared about you, Alex. At the end, he wanted to make it right. He always—"

"Loved me?" Alex stared at the finely formed cleft in Peter's chin. "The money proves it, of course."

"It counts for something."

"Money always counts. But then you know that, don't you?"

He stared at her, and she saw the faintest flicker of unease in his eyes. Peter, uneasy. It was an oxymoron. He was desperate indeed.

"I know what you're thinking, Alex," he said at last.

"Do you?"

"Jesus, Alex. I know how it looks." He forgot himself so far as to disarrange his neatly groomed hair with a nervous sweep of his fingers. "I knew about the money, but that isn't why I came. I wanted to start over. To prove to you that things can change."

Here it came. More penitent protestations of undying love, impassioned pleas for another chance. He had to be badly off; Schaeffer Industries must be sinking fast. Had he spent all of Bev's money? Maybe she'd kicked him out. And even though he'd stayed in contact with William Warrington, the association obviously hadn't paid off for him.

Until now. He'd probably taken one look at her simple cabin, and her face, and convinced himself she was more than ready for his "comfort." Kieran's presence might have thrown a wrench in his plans, but it wouldn't have been in Peter's nature to consider a man like Kieran any kind of rival.

What a sacrifice it must be for you, Peter, to contemplate giving up your high standards in exchange for my money. Just like before.

"Alex! Listen to me, for God's sake. I love you."

Peter's touch brought her out of her thoughts. By the time she came back to herself he was already holding her loosely in the circle of his arms, his face a mask of desperate passion.

"You're trying to shut me out, Alex. Damn it, don't do this to me!"

He must have seen the look in her eyes. He muttered a curse very much unlike him. "I don't know how I'm going to make you believe me. But if you'll just give me time, if we can just talk, get to know each other again . . ."

She'd thought it might be difficult to finish this business with Peter. It wasn't going to be hard at all. She couldn't believe she'd wavered for even a moment yesterday.

"Is it him?" Peter gestured at the truck with a disdainful flick of his hand. "Have you heard what they're saying about him, Alex?" He gave a disbelieving laugh. "No. You have better taste than that. Alex——" His grip on her arms became a caress, the sort he'd always been so expert at. "What kind of life is this, here in this backwater town? With rednecks like him for company?" He lowered his voice to a whisper. "I want to make it up to you. Let me, Alex. Come home."

She focused on him slowly. "You never did understand, Peter."

"I understand that you ran away from everything you could have had, and you're still running."

Alex looked over his shoulder into the truck. Kieran's gaze met hers—fully awake, lucid. And dangerous. Just as he had looked in the café.

"Alex, listen to me——"

"Let me go, Peter."

"Oh, Alex." His eyes held the illusion of yearning tenderness. He lifted his hand and gently, deliberately touched her scarred cheek.

It was as if he'd pulled the trigger of a gun. She froze. The truck's passenger door swung open.

"Get your hands off her," Kieran snarled.

Kieran wasn't drunk now; he was in deadly earnest. His face was all harsh lines and bared teeth. The gentle man he'd been at Julie's, the vulnerable boy struggling to make sense of his life was gone. He was a force of nature, a wolf on the hunt, a man pushed to his limit.

Peter dropped his hand from Alex's cheek but didn't release her. He half turned toward Kieran, eyes narrowed. "Call off your dog, Alex," he said contemptuously.

Kieran had circled the truck and stood mere feet from Peter. He lifted clenched fists.

"Let—her—go!"

Peter never had another chance. Suddenly he was sprawled on the street, an expression of astonishment on his face. Kieran stood over him. Though he hardly moved, made no threatening gestures at all, Kieran radiated stark and absolute hatred.

Peter gathered himself to his knees. "You son of a bitch," he hissed.

Alex forced her legs to function and plunged between them. "Stop it!" She put her back to Kieran and stared down at Peter, breathing hard. "I want you out of here *now*. This isn't going any further."

Peter was no coward. He managed to hold Kieran's inhuman gaze, flexing his hands with angry jerks. "He started it."

"And I'm ending it! You've said what you wanted to say, Peter."

He barked an incredulous laugh. "You're not taking his side, Alex? This Neanderthal lunatic?"

"Bastard," Kieran snarled. "You—"

"Shut up, both of you!" Alex yelled. Kieran and Peter were backing her into a corner. Between the two of them, they'd destroyed whatever peace she'd made for herself. In that moment she hated them both.

Peter scrambled to his feet without dropping his guard and drew close to Alex. "All right. I don't want more trouble for you, Alex." He reached out. "But you haven't given me a chance to prove—"

"If you touch her again, I'll kill you."

The impact of Kieran's words was unmistakable. From any other man they would have been a meaningless, over-heated threat. But not from Kieran Holt. Even Peter sensed it; his jaw dropped in astonished comprehension.

"That's enough."

The terrible moment shattered. Peter stepped back, his head swinging toward the voice. Alex could see Luke Gévaudan over the top of the truck, his expression set and grim. Two loiterers from the bar stood behind him, staring in avid fascination.

"I think you should leave, Mr. Schaeffer," Gévaudan said. He gave Peter a long look. Without so much as a mutter of protest or another glance at Alex, Peter turned and walked away.

Gévaudan turned to Kieran, who met his impenetrable stare. Alex remembered when Kieran had faced the wolf pack; the silent confrontation had exactly the same quality.

Alex stepped between them. "It seems I owe you thanks again, Mr. Gévaudan."

He turned his attention to her. "Do you need help getting him home, Ms. Warrington?"

That was help she *didn't* need. She managed a smile and shook her head. "I don't think so. But thanks, anyway."

He gave her a brief nod. "I'm in town for a few days," he said. "I've heard you're a wolf researcher, Ms. Warrington. As it happens, I'm here to visit the International Wolf Center in Ely. I'm from British Columbia, and wolves are a special interest of mine."

Alex felt her smile become strained. "I see. That's . . . very nice, Mr. Gévaudan."

Gévaudan's mouth quirked, as if he sensed her desire to be gone. "I'd like to have a chance to talk with you further. I'm staying at a cabin just up Bigtooth Road. I don't have a phone there, but I check in frequently at the store. I'd be very pleased if you and your friend would accept an invitation to dinner, at your convenience."

Alex shifted from one foot to the other. "That's a very kind offer. I don't know if I—if Kieran . . ."

"Please think about it," Gévaudan said. "I hope to be talking to you soon." He glanced at Kieran, nodded to her a final time, and moved onto the sidewalk. Alex hesitated a moment longer.

"Thanks again."

"Glad to help," he said. He raised his hand in salute, and Alex turned to look for Kieran.

He was walking away—unsteadily, with none of his usual grace. Walking toward the edge of town.

"Damn," she said under her breath, and started after him. She grabbed his arm and hauled him to a stop.

"Just where do you think you're going?" she demanded.

He grinned at her with a lopsided lack of humor. "For a walk in the woods."

"You're drunk," she said. "You couldn't walk to the end of the block."

He started to shake her off, but for once she had the greater strength of will. He let himself be pulled back to the truck and pushed into the passenger seat. When she looked past Kieran and out the window, Luke Gévaudan was gone.

The fool. The bloody, arrogant fool.

Withdrawing into the doorway of the gun shop, Joseph watched Alexandra Warrington drive away.

Schaeffer had failed him. He was weak, a tool that broke under pressure, a rifle that misfired at first use. And Kieran Holt had gone with Alexandra Warrington once again, leaving Schaeffer in the dust. Back to shelter, where Joseph could not reach him.

Not until he had devised a new plan.

Arnoux examined the racks of rifles along the wall for a third time, ignoring the avaricious shopkeeper. Hefting one of the two weapons he'd selected, he sighted down the barrel.

A new plan. It would come to him in time, when he had a chance to think, to be alone and out in his woods, free of the noise and stupidity of people.

Perhaps he had made a mistake in not keeping a better watch on the Indians. They might provide the key that Schaeffer had not. Alexandra and Kieran had been on their lands, had often spoken to the Indian mechanic. Arnoux felt a shiver of unease when he thought of Julie Wakanabo, and shook it off with a grimace of anger. He had no belief in barbarous superstitions or Indian mystics.

Arnoux stalked back to the counter and paid for the rifle, earning an obsequious grin from the dealer. It would be best if Kieran Holt appeared to vanish completely—so completely, and with such good reason, that no one would think to look for him in the area, far less on Joseph's land behind the high walls that had once held Kieran captive.

But the woman was still a problem. Too involved with the boy, too close. And stubborn. Something must be done about her.

Carefully, Joseph. Patience. It will come to you.

He left the store behind him, the new purchase tucked under his arm. The end was coming. He could feel it. Soon he would see the boy was locked away where he could never hurt anyone again, or spread his unnatural blood among humankind.

Until then . . . Joseph started his truck and waited for the old engine to sputter to life. Until then, Joseph would take communion in the wilderness. He would hunt, knowing the joy that came of filling his true place in the world.

The hunt and the kill; they were what he required, what he must have. He would quiet his impatience another day. Once again he would demonstrate human mastery over the lesser creatures, just as Providence had intended.

Only blood would answer now.

11

"What did you think you were doing?"

Hands on hips, Alex stood over Kieran, who sprawled on the sofa in an inebriated haze. "Do you know what could have happened?" she demanded. "You were fighting with Howie and his friends! In a bar, no less!"

Kieran looked at her without expression. "I wasn't . . . fighting," he said. "They—"

"What about Peter?" she asked, pacing furiously across the room. "If it hadn't been for Mr. Gévaudan, you could have . . . could have—"

"Hurt him?" he said, grinning crookedly. "Don't you trust me, Alexandra?"

Words failed her. She spun to face him, wishing she had the strength to haul him up bodily and shake him within an inch of his life.

"Maybe Peter did need your protection," Kieran drawled.

"I wasn't trying to protect *him*."

"But you went into town to see him."

Alex passed her hand over her eyes. "I told you I had to talk to him again, to clear things up with him. I told you

Peter was none of your concern. I had things under control . . ."

"Yes, Alexandra," he said. "You do have . . . great control."

Was he mocking her? Could he see how close she was to losing it completely? With an effort she calmed herself, molding her anger into something manageable.

"You thought you were trying to protect me, Kieran," she said carefully. "I recognize that. But you only made it worse—"

"For Peter," Kieran said. His grin was like a dull knife, its edge blunted with hard use. Suddenly Alex remembered the stunned look on Peter's face when he'd sprawled on the street, and felt a highly inappropriate desire to laugh.

"You looked like you could have killed him," she said severely. "Kieran, you put yourself in danger, and for no reason. I was fully capable of handling Peter on my own. He was part of *my* past."

"I know." Kieran sat up on the sofa, shedding any lingering sluggishness as a wolf shakes water from its pelt. "You almost married him."

For a moment she was silenced. "Another little tidbit you overheard during my supposedly private conversation with Peter?"

Kieran made a low sound like a choked laugh. "No. Peter told me himself. We had a very nice . . . talk in the bar."

Alex started. *Talk.* He and Peter had *talked.* "I can't imagine you and Peter having much to talk about."

Kieran's grin showed all his teeth. "You're right, Alexandra. We don't have much in common. He's handsome and rich. Knows who he is. Gets what he wants. But we did find a common interest." He examined his strong, blunt fingers, so different from Peter's fine-boned, manicured hand. "He wanted to know if I was willing to help you. He wanted to . . . make sure I didn't complicate your life any more, especially since he'd be here to comfort you himself. He made it clear that you wouldn't need me."

Alex was very careful not to show any emotion at all. "Peter asked you to leave?"

Kieran looked away.

"And you were ready to do what he wanted you to—walk away—even after you pitched him on his butt in the middle of Merritt?"

There was no humor on Kieran's face now. "He claimed to love you, Alexandra. The way he shows love is strange to me, but I'm not human. Maybe you can explain it to me."

Alexandra felt behind her for the armchair and sat down hard. "You're asking me to make sense of human behavior?" She laughed and hugged herself. "I don't even understand myself. How's that for a revelation?"

Kieran looked at her—not mockingly, not distantly, but with that direct stare that made her feel he saw straight through to her soul. "You loved him," he said softly.

She looked down at her hands. "Yes. I loved him. We grew up together. Our families were close, and both our fathers ran large, successful corporations. The Warringtons and Schaeffers were leading society families in San Francisco. Peter and I . . . naturally spent a lot of time together."

"Then he does know you as well as he claims," Kieran said.

"Is that what he claimed? I thought he did, once. Peter was always very ambitious. He expected to take over his father's business. His family and mine were pleased when we decided to marry. We—" She breathed deeply to calm her heart. "We planned the wedding right after I graduated from college. I'd already been studying wolves, but I was ready to give it up for Peter."

She sensed more than saw Kieran lean forward, almost reaching out to touch her. "And then the quarrel with your father."

"Yes." She worked her fingers into knots in her lap. "When I argued with my father on my graduation day, things were bad enough that I . . . cut myself off from him completely. Refused to take the money he would have given me to start a new life with Peter. That was money Peter had counted on for his business, money he needed. He was always honest about that." She leaned over her hands. "We went our separate ways. I resumed my studies, and Peter married someone else who could give him what he wanted. I didn't see him again until yesterday."

"And now, Alexandra?"

And now. And now what? She could never believe Peter again. She knew why he'd come to find her.

"You have money now," Kieran said, laying it out for her in cold, hard facts. "You could have whatever you want. He told me what your old life was like. You could have it back again."

"The way Peter thinks I should?" She laughed helplessly. "For him, money solves everything. Clean slate. Start over."

"Isn't that what you want?"

He saw too keenly, and she'd said too much. She pushed to her feet. "I love my work here, Kieran. It's my life. I'd never give it up. That money can go rot in an old tree trunk for all I care." *Except that it came from Father. And Mother. It's all I have left of what could have been, if I—*

She turned away from unbearable thoughts and met Kieran's gaze. "I don't miss what I used to have."

"Not even love, Alexandra?"

"Didn't we go through this before? I—"

But he would not be put off. He rose, towering over her as he always did, even though his walk was still unsteady. "You loved Peter once. Can you live without that now?"

"Live without it? I'm grateful I don't have any such complications in my life!"

"Then you choose to be alone."

"Yes. *I* choose. And what about your choices, Kieran?" she said, desperate to turn the subject. "*Your* past? What about your parents, your family? What happened after I met you as a boy? Isn't that what you came to me to find?"

He walked slowly to the window and gazed out. "Strange you should ask, Alexandra. Schaeffer helped me remember."

"What?"

He turned his head, just enough for her to see the strength of his profile against the fading light of evening. "You said I was drunk. It wasn't the first time."

His voice grew strange, and Alex had the eerie feeling that Kieran had left the room in all but body, as if he journeyed on inner paths she couldn't reach.

"You remembered . . . getting drunk?"

"I remembered," he said. "Places like the bar. Many of them."

"You remember being in places like that bar before?"

"A hundred times," he said, with a kind of weary resignation. "Wandering from place to place, one after another."

Alex stared at him. Was this the result of today's debacle—Kieran's remembering a past of barhopping?

"And fighting," he continued. His mouth curled up. "I remember that, too."

She sat down in the armchair. "You remember fighting. Were you acting out your memories today? Did you make a habit of this in your former life? Getting drunk and—and . . ."

He gave no reaction, only a tight, self-mocking smile. She fought down her anger. "So you remember going from place to place," she said at last.

"Running."

"From what?"

He turned away from her again. "I don't know," he said. "But I did discover something else, Alexandra. When Howie's men came for me, I tried to shift."

She sat bolt upright. "You *tried* to shift?"

"Yes." Again that almost cynical, too-knowing smile, so unlike him. "It didn't work."

Alex sprang up, pacing across the room.

"I think it would have worked," Kieran continued. "I was very angry. But the alcohol . . ."

The far wall stopped Alex, and she leaned her forehead against it.

"I remember now." His voice was so damnably indifferent. "Drinking did that. No matter how angry I got, I couldn't shift."

Of course. Alcohol blunted the senses. Couldn't it also hamper Kieran's unique abilities?

"And you didn't want to," she murmured. "You would have been glad to find a way not to change. Because you couldn't control it. Because you couldn't accept what you are."

"You should be pleased, Alexandra. You wanted me to control my changing. I found a way."

"I never told you to hide behind poison. Isn't it just another kind of running?"

He was silent. She pressed her cheek to the cool wood. *What did they do to you, Kieran? What happened to you, to make you hate your own nature? Running, you said. Maybe you were running away from yourself. Because if you got yourself nicely drunk and then looked for a good fight, maybe you could make yourself believe you were human.*

His face was as bleak as a gray winter sky. "Perhaps," he said with an odd, distant gentleness. "Maybe I should keep on running."

She met his gaze and saw no trace of the lost boy-man who'd been so desperate for her help, so willing to do whatever she asked. "Damn it, Kieran, I want to help you."

"No." He looked at his hands, turning them over as if he expected them to change before his eyes. "No. You don't need the complications. Because it has become complicated, Alexandra."

"I don't see—"

"What do you see? A wolf that's safe as long as he can be controlled and studied and understood?" His bleak smile returned. "What happens when I become something you can't control anymore?"

She shivered in spite of herself. "I *accept* what you are," she said, "even if I don't completely understand—"

He stepped forward, forcing her back a step. "I won't be the cause of your fear."

"Fear?" She thrust out her jaw. "I'm not afraid of you."

"Look at me, Alexandra," he demanded. "I'm not human, and yet I'm a man. In every way." He loomed over her, and she felt his words at the most visceral level, deep in the pit of her belly.

"If I'm a *man*," he said, "you fear me."

Her throat closed. She searched for a logical response and couldn't find it. "No," she whispered.

"You don't lie well, Alexandra."

She moved blindly across the room, putting the sofa between them. "I'm not lying."

"Then why are you running from me now?"

For the first time she truly comprehended what it must feel like to be prey, run to earth and exhausted and with no hope of escape. To walk away now would be to prove what he said was true. To walk away now would make her a liar, even to herself.

So she stood where she was as Kieran came closer, until she could see the rapid pulse beneath the skin in the hollow of his neck. She focused on that faint movement with desperate fascination, unable to move as he stalked past and behind her.

Then the last chance to run was gone.

His arms were gentle as they closed around her waist. His heat leaped like electricity directly into her body, shooting through every nerve and muscle. It was like the first time he had held her, but a thousand times more compelling.

She didn't fight as he held her sealed to him. She didn't resist as he turned her around and spread his hands across her back to draw her closer still, until she could feel every hard line and contour of his body from chest to thigh. She took in the heady masculine smell of him—pine and earth and perspiration and something nameless and erotic.

"Alexandra," he said, his voice rough and guttural. He

took her chin in his callused palm, and she had no choice but to meet his gaze.

It was almost as if she'd never seen his eyes before. They were lambent, rich with the promise of summer and green foliage and endless light. Brilliant was too tame a word for them. Liquid gold, that she would willingly drown in. Suns bringing life to the sterility of the universe. Perpetual fire that had burned from the dawn of time. . . .

Before she could think of another metaphor his breath touched her mouth and his lips came down on hers.

The kiss in the snow had been gentle, hesitant, tinged with uncertainty. She had pushed Kieran away then. This kiss robbed her of such choices as it robbed her of thought. There was desperation in it, sadness, newborn passion. He held her gaze until she was blind to everything but brilliant burning yellow, until his mouth parted her lips and his tongue pushed deep inside her.

His kiss drained away her anger, her fear, her confusion, and left a void only he could fill. Everything became simple, the world reduced to the taste of him, the strength of him, the need and hunger that consumed her with its incandescent power.

Kieran spanned her waist with his hands, lifting her from her feet. The heavy pressure of his arousal pushed at her belly. Sensual, unreasoning joy sparked within her, stirred to life where only the ashes of old dreams had remained. Parts of her body that had lain dormant for so long came awake with heat and fire.

She arched up into him, gripped his taut shoulders, caressed the perfect symmetry of muscle and bone. The beauty of him, the scent of him, the feel of him was familiar to the depths of her soul.

"Kieran," she whispered before his mouth silenced her again. His hands slid beneath her shirt. His fingers left a burning trail as they pushed cloth up along her ribs and reached the barrier of her breasts.

She remembered. She remembered that first morning

in her bed, half-awake, feeling Kieran's innocent caresses and dreaming of Peter.

But Kieran's caresses were anything but innocent now, and Peter . . .

"No," she whispered.

She might have shouted. Kieran let her go instantly, leaving only a cold void where the heat of his body had been. She looked up, saw his eyes, saw them change like the sun gone dim and strange.

"Complications, Alexandra," he murmured, and touched her face with the back of his hand. And then he walked away from her. Turned his back and walked away, and all she could think was that she had almost lost herself. Almost let herself believe. Almost let her body come fully awake after she'd learned to let it settle into quiet acceptance. Almost let herself feel again what she'd once felt for Peter, when she'd thought loving was worth the risk.

She had come that close.

"Kieran," she said. But she couldn't think of a single word to explain, to call him back.

He'd been right. She was afraid.

She closed her eyes as cold outside wind rushed into the room, stirring her hair. The cabin door closed with a whisper of sound.

For a long while she stood there, her arms wrapped around herself. *Her* fault. All her fault. *She'd* let things get out of hand. Let Kieran too close. Not only today, but all the times before when she'd begun to feel so at ease with him. Thinking of him as Shadow. Someone who would never judge her.

She had been afraid to be honest with him. About Peter, about everything. And then she'd let him hold her, kiss her, forgetting her admonishments to him, to herself. Only to push him away. Not able to tell him that it wasn't *what* he was she rejected.

She'd responded to him as a man. Not as Shadow, or the boy she'd met so long ago, or a miraculous creature of legend, but a man.

Her fault. *Her* weakness. *She* was the one who'd

slipped, who'd forgotten every lesson she'd ever learned. And Kieran had solved her problem by walking out the door.

She put her hands flat on the wall and pushed away. Her legs were not quite steady. She made her way to the bedroom and pulled her journal from the bedtable's single drawer.

She opened her journal and wrote, ruthlessly recording everything that had happened since she left for town that morning, leaving herself no escape. Except the one Kieran had given her.

It was late when she finished. She stared down at her own words. The pen slid out of her nerveless fingers. She closed the journal and sat on the bed until she felt almost calm, almost normal. She noted that it was already getting dark outside; through force of habit she refilled the stove and began heating a can of soup in the kitchen.

She looked out the window only once. The woods seemed darker, more alien and impenetrable than she had ever seen them. Very much like her own heart.

Where are you, Kieran?

She wondered if she'd ever have the courage to find out.

$\mathcal{T}$he stalking began.

He tracked Alexandra, virgin snow sweet as spring grass under his feet. The woods grew silent at his passing, for every creature knew he was on the hunt.

She was close, very close; soon he would find her. Every one of his senses was alive, pulsing with joy; this time when he found her she would be his. *Only* his.

Her footprints seared the ground with her scent. Excitement stirred his loins; he could already imagine what it would be like when she was beneath him, nothing between them but passion.

He imagined her naked. Sweet curves and full, firm breasts, rounded thighs opening for him, the scent and taste of her arousal. She would gasp and writhe as he marked her for his own. . . .

"Kieran!" she cried. Just beyond the next cluster of trees, laughing, hiding. She wanted him. Her voice held a world of invitation, of yearning. His heart drove the blood through his body in time to the rhythm of his running feet.

She was where he knew she would be, no longer trying to run. Her skin was flushed, her eyes bright; she flung back her hair and laughed again.

"Catch me, Kieran," she said. "If you catch me, I'm yours."

And so he did. He sprang, one long clean leap, and trapped her in his arms. She put up a mock struggle, flailing with fists as her breasts pushed against his ribs. The gentle indentation between her thighs rubbed his arousal again and again.

He wanted her. He needed to be inside her. After that nothing could separate them, nothing keep them apart.

My mate, he thought fiercely. *Mine.* And while she hesitated, he captured her mouth.

It was like before, only now she welcomed him. Just as she had promised. Her promise was solid, certain, as real as the ground they stood on. Her lips parted, invited his tongue to explore and caress. She tasted of flowers and honey and sweet, clear water.

Kieran's body responded, growing hard and tight. Lust, unashamed and overwhelming, coursed along with his blood. Need and desire spun into a hot core of emotion more powerful than any he had ever known. As Alexandra laced her fingers through his hair, he felt the shifting begin.

His mind would not acknowledge the threat. Even when his fingers cramped and his jaw ached with the incipient change, he refused to accept. He thrust his tongue into Alexandra's mouth, thinking only of thrusting elsewhere.

Until she stiffened in his arms, and he saw himself reflected in the wide blue of her eyes.

The face he saw was hideous. *His* face. He raised his

hand from her shoulder and found it coated with coarse, dark hair.

Neither man nor beast. A monster. . . .

No! He tried to make the sound, and it emerged as a grotesque howl.

Alexandra screamed. She staggered back, and ran with the wild abandon of terror.

"Alexandra!" His mouth was awkward, as if even his lips didn't dare form her name. "You accepted me—"

But still she ran. Straight into the arms of another, a tall and pale-eyed man who shone with golden perfection.

A human being, as Kieran was not. Peter. He opened his arms and swung her up into them. Their lips met. And the desire in Kieran's heart burned to ashes.

The Voice howled in his mind: *What did you expect?*

Kieran dropped to the ground, to four black paws, his transformation complete. Alexandra and Peter were suddenly gone, but he knew how to find them.

A different lust held him now. Blood-lust drove him, and he never questioned it. This was life, the only reality, the one truth—this need for revenge.

This need to kill.

The woman he trailed was oblivious. She had dismissed him from her heart, but she walked alone now. Easy prey. He found her standing before her cabin, blurred to his eyes but vivid in her scent.

He knew when she saw him. She stiffened and held her hands before her face, as if warding off a demon. But Kieran did not glory in her fear. He swung his head to left and right, scenting for the other. And found him.

Peter smiled as he saw Kieran, flashed his perfect white teeth in a grin of contempt. "No success, eh, my friend? Don't worry. I'll take good care of her for you."

But his mockery went no further. Kieran was already stalking toward him, head low, ears cocked to catch every nuance of Peter's movements, his quickened breathing. Only at the end did Peter recognize his danger. He turned to flee, prepared to leave Alexandra behind undefended. Too late.

Kieran's muscles bunched to spring.

*A*t almost exactly 10 a.m., the morning after a long and sleepless night, someone knocked on the cabin door.

Alex pushed her chair back from the kitchen table, abandoning the bowl of cold oatmeal she'd been trying to eat. She forced herself to move slowly as the rapping started again; cool logic replaced the first wild surmise that had sent her heart into somersaults.

It wouldn't be Kieran. He wouldn't bother to knock.

She walked to the door with measured steps. Very few people ever came to her cabin. The most likely possibility was Julie, who hadn't come to town yesterday. Alex almost hoped it was. She desperately needed to talk to someone with clear sight and a calm heart.

She braced herself and opened the door. A stranger stood there, grimly impersonal in a neatly pressed uniform. Alex froze with her hand on the knob.

He wasn't really a stranger. Merritt was a small town, and you ran into everyone sooner or later. But she'd never had any reason to speak to a member of Merritt's tiny police force.

Her heart lodged firmly in her throat.

"Alexandra Warrington? I'm Officer Claybourne. May I have a word with you?"

Alex stepped back and gestured him into the cabin, feeling her way to the sofa. The officer followed, shutting the door behind him.

"I understand you knew a man named Peter Schaeffer, Ms. Warrington."

She could feel every thread in the rough weave of the sofa's upholstery under her palm. "Yes. I . . . know him."

He moved up beside her and took her elbow. "Here. Why don't you sit down, Ms. Warrington."

She sat because her legs gave her no other choice. "What's happened, Officer?"

"Ms. Warrington, Peter Schaeffer was found dead early this morning in the woods just behind the motor lodge."

She felt nothing at first, not even shock. She looked at Claybourne, around the cabin, down at the sofa to a threadbare patch next to her hand. Then the disbelief came, and the horror, and the sickness.

She doubled over. *No. God, no.*

"I'm sorry, ma'am. Truly sorry."

The air wouldn't seem to move in and out of her lungs. She concentrated on that simple, necessary act. "How?" she croaked.

The floor squeaked as the officer moved away. "I wish I didn't have to bother you, Ms. Warrington, but we may need your help. You've had a guest staying here with you— a Kieran Holt."

It was a nightmare. It had to be. She looked up at the officer blankly. All she could manage were words of one syllable. "Why?"

He sighed, shifting his hat on his head. "When did you last see him, ma'am?"

She couldn't think. The possibilities flooded her mind with wave after wave of horror. She doubled over again.

"He was . . . here," she gasped. "With me."

"Until when, ma'am?" He moved away again, his footsteps receding toward the bedroom, pausing and returning. "I don't see him here now. Do you know where he is?"

"I don't—I don't know. Please." She heaved, and it was only partly deception. "Please—"

"It's all right, ma'am." He hesitated. "We can talk to you later if you'll just stay here where we can reach you. We have other witnesses who heard Kieran Holt threaten the deceased yesterday afternoon."

Threaten. Kieran had threatened Peter in front of the bar. She had heard it, and Luke Gévaudan, and others.

"Here's my card, ma'am. If Mr. Holt returns, if you see him, please contact me immediately."

She took the card automatically and stared at the plain block lettering. Her vision blurred, running white card and black letters into a mass of gray.

"You think," she said, swallowing the sour taste of sickness. "You think Kieran—"

"I'm sorry, Ms. Warrington. But we have reason to believe it was murder."

12

His mouth tasted foul when he woke.

Kieran brushed the dead leaves from his hair, un-curling from the nest he'd made under the old log. The snow hadn't reached into this haven; he'd felt almost comfortable here last night, wrapped in ancient memories of a time when he and Alexandra had still been innocent.

But any sense of peace fled the moment he came fully awake. Because then the newer memories returned, un-purged by sleep, reinforced by the nightmare that left him tasting the acrid sweetness of blood.

The nightmare. Kieran rolled over onto his back, fill-ing the narrow space. He tried to focus on the fading im-ages that had survived the coming of dawn.

In the dream, he had hunted as a wolf.

Kieran's stomach twisted, though he knew it had long since emptied its contents. The dream had been so real. Stalking. Glorying in the hunt. Alexandra had been in it, and Peter. There was more, but when Kieran tried to make the images come clear his mind rebelled. He came up against a wall, a cage that held the beast in darkness.

A nightmare. A warning. He'd had all the warnings he needed now, and a surfeit of bitter truth.

He had been . . . an animal, last night as well as in the dream. Drink and anger and Peter's words had driven him to ignore Alexandra's pain over her loss of her father, the problems she faced even without his contributions. He'd been driven by some insanity to prove he was human, to act out what he had never dared believe possible.

That Alexandra could be his. That he could make her want him as a man, when he knew it could never be.

He'd almost succeeded. Alexandra had been in his arms, responding as she'd never responded before, as if she were accepting him as her mate. But in the end . . .

It was better this way, for both of them. Whatever Alexandra chose to do with her life—with Peter, and with her newfound wealth—she could do it freely. No more obligations. No more promises.

Kieran clenched his fists, welcoming the pain in his hands. They were scraped and raw, though he didn't remember how they'd come to be so. There'd been little rationality in anything he did last night. He looked out of the hollow, noting the angle of the sun. Already it was after noon, and he remembered nothing of the past hours but running, taking shelter . . . and the dream.

No. There *was* something else. Kieran pulled into a crouch, breathing in the late winter air. Something else had come to him this morning, while he slept. Or perhaps last night when he'd run himself into exhaustion with so little conscious thought.

It was not a physical thing he could touch or taste or smell. But it returned to him now: a revelation, memory brilliant as summer lightning.

A goal. A reason to go on.

He remembered feeling this compulsion once before, like a sweet voice calling. But other voices had filled his mind then: Alexandra's, and that unknown and familiar Voice inside himself that mocked and taunted.

No longer. Now no other purpose distracted him from the summons within him, could prevent him from following where it led. For it gave him a message as clear as speech, or the subtler languages of the forest. If he concentrated on the call, he had no need to think or feel.

North and west, it said. *Come. North and west.*

Kieran pushed out from under the log, stretching cramped muscles. He'd kicked his boots off sometime last night, shed his clothes and left them in a heap outside the hollow. They crackled when he shook them out.

North and west. It was so clear, so simple now that he let go. Into his mind came knowledge of a place, undefined by such mundane considerations as latitude and longitude.

A place. A destination. A sanctuary. A sense of safety and belonging that could neither be defined nor questioned.

Home. Kieran closed his eyes. The word hung in his mind. *Home.* North and west. If there were answers to what he was, if he had a past beyond the wandering he remembered, he would find them there.

Not with the woman he could never have.

Already he felt the drive to run again, put this place far behind him. Put *her* far behind him, where he couldn't touch her again.

A twig snapped. Kieran froze.

"Kieran!"

She walked into the clearing and stopped a safe distance away. He could still abandon his clothes and escape, before he could look into her eyes and hear her speak and remember every moment she had been in his arms.

"Kieran," she repeated. Her eyes were shadowed, her face pale and strained.

Too late. He breathed in her scent and was lost.

She took another step. "I was afraid I wouldn't find you. I've been . . . looking for hours."

Hours. For a moment his heart sped, and he wondered if there was hope after all. If he could be wrong. She had searched for him . . .

"What happened last night?" she asked.

He closed his eyes. He could never explain, never find the words to make sense of it. Not like Peter with his smooth, cultured tongue. He could not tell her that he wanted her. Wanted her desperately, with all the primitive instincts of the beast within his nightmare.

"You don't remember, Alexandra?"

She was silent for several heartbeats. "After," she said. "*After* you left the cabin."

It wasn't what he expected. He opened his eyes. She was crouched a few feet away, her arms wrapped around her knees. "Did you come here, Kieran?" she asked, her tone as expressionless as her face. "Were you here all night?"

He balled his jeans in his fists. "No."

She closed her eyes, as if she couldn't bear to look at him a moment longer. "Did you do it, Kieran?"

The jeans dropped to the snow as he rose. "Do what?"

Her face lost what little color it had. She shuddered uncontrollably. "Peter is dead, Kieran."

It took a moment for him to realize he had heard her right. "What?"

"They found him last night . . . torn—" Alex swallowed. "He was . . . mangled. As if—"

As if an animal had killed him. Kieran heard the words in his head, though she didn't finish the sentence.

"The police came to the cabin this morning to question me." She made a visible effort to continue. "People heard you . . . threaten Peter, Kieran. Yesterday at the bar." She met his gaze at last. "They think you killed him."

Nausea fisted in Kieran's belly. *The nightmare.* It had felt so real. The stalking, the hunting. Peter, running from him. And then the blood . . .

He had awakened this morning to the taste of blood.

Blinding pain filled the space behind his eyes. Peter. Alexandra's former lover. A man he'd come close to hating, whom he'd attacked in a drunken passion.

A man he would never have killed. Consciously.

His legs buckled. He began to fall, and suddenly Alexandra was in his way. He twisted and rolled in the opposite direction just as she reached for him.

"Stay back," he rasped.

She stopped with her hands outstretched. "No, Kieran."

"Stay where you are," he warned again. And when she kept coming, he snarled the words he had repeated a thousand times: *"I don't remember."*

That got through. She bit down on her lip until he could feel her pain.

"You came . . . you found me to ask if I killed Peter," he said. "You believe I could have done it."

The indifference slipped from her face like a discarded mask. "I *don't* believe it," she said hoarsely.

"You're a bad liar, Alexandra."

Her skin went pale, and he remembered when he'd said almost those same words last night. "What do you mean when you say you don't remember?" she demanded.

Despair warred with the need to drive her away. "The day I rescued Tracy," he said. "I told you I didn't remember changing. I didn't remember anything I did until after I'd changed back."

Comprehension widened her eyes. "And . . . last night . . ."

"I dreamed. Some kind of nightmare." A chill wind skimmed across the sweat that slicked his skin. "Last night I dreamed of Peter. Of hunting him." He choked on the words. "Of *killing*, Alexandra. I remember nothing else."

He saw her absorb his words, knew when she felt the full impact of them and drew the obvious conclusions. She hugged herself hard, rocking.

"No," she whispered. "No." Suddenly she burst into motion, striding around the clearing, studying the ground with fervent intensity. Gradually the color came back into her face. She came at last to stand before him, her eyes very bright.

"A dream isn't reality," she challenged.

"How do you know?" he countered. "I've already proven I can change without realizing it, without control—"

"But you remembered what you'd done afterward."

"That one time—"

"That one time when you saved a child from drowning!" She shook her head wildly. "I don't see any paw prints here. Or blood."

"I could have changed somewhere else, come back here as a man."

"Do you want to condemn yourself?" she shouted.

They stared at each other in stunned silence.

Kieran pushed his curled fingers into the snow. "Can you say there is no chance I did it?" he whispered.

"You would never—"

"Can you?"

She flinched but didn't reply.

"Why did you look for me?" he continued relentlessly. "You loved Peter once. If you thought I could have killed him, why would you come?"

Very slowly her expression changed. There was sorrow in it, but no fear. No anger.

"I . . . grieve for Peter," she said. "He—" She swallowed heavily. "I came because I knew you weren't capable of it, Kieran. The things I said yesterday, about your running from your past . . . I didn't believe them, either."

Kieran had to hold himself still to keep from touching her. She had answered her own question and his with a quiet conviction that humbled him, a certainty he could not refute.

But he had to try. "Belief isn't proof, Alexandra."

"Sometimes it's all we have."

He searched within himself for that same conviction. A man was dead, a man who had not deserved so terrible a fate. But when Kieran looked into Alexandra's eyes, the force of her belief flowed into him, as powerful as anything he had felt in the brief time of his memory.

It was all he had.

"Will the police *believe* also?" he asked.

She dropped her eyes, and the weight of sorrow fell over her like a mantle of snow. "No. They think a man did it, in spite of the wounds."

"Do they have other suspects?"

She shook her head. "They're going to want to question me further because they know you were staying with me, and I knew Peter." She lifted her eyes and looked in the direction of the cabin. "If they find you, they'll take you in for questioning, and—"

"I can't let them take me, Alexandra."

Strange how memories came, without rhyme or reason. When Alexandra had spoken of capture collars at the Wakanabos', he'd seen these same visions. Of walls and darkness and confinement that made death seem a welcome alternative.

That was what the police would do to him, lock him behind walls and bars like an animal. He drove the image from his mind. "I can't let them," he repeated.

"I know. I'm going to help you get away."

She was so near, so near that he could touch her without stretching his hand. "I don't need your help."

Her eyes flashed familiar anger. "Like hell you don't. You're the one who came to me, remember? You've done a damned poor job of taking my advice so far, but this time you're going to listen to me, Kieran Holt. You're my responsibility."

"You're not *responsible* for me."

"I am. I made myself responsible the day I took Shadow into the cabin." She laughed, a strange, lost sound. "No, long before that. I promised to help you, and by God I'm going to keep my promise if it's the last thing I do on this earth."

"I don't want your help," he told her harshly. "I don't need you. I know enough now to find my own way." He bared his teeth. "No more tame wolf, Alexandra."

Her eyes were dark as black ice, her skin pale as new-fallen snow. "I know you're not," she whispered. "I know—"

"Where I'm going you can't follow."

She blinked rapidly. "Where?"

"To find—" He stopped. Until now he'd had no need to put it into words. An image came into his mind, and he grasped it. "To find my own kind."

Astonishment transformed her face. "You remembered?" she said. "You know others like you exist?"

He couldn't tell her it was something within himself, something he could never explain to anyone. It had come with the distant call, and that he'd never spoken of. He was grateful for that now.

He bent to pick up his jeans and began to pull them on. "Go home, Alexandra. Tell the police whatever you choose, but don't follow me."

Her hand came down over his. He felt the prick of her blunt nails as they drove into his skin. "Damn you," she whispered. "I've invested too much in this. I've lost my Father, and Peter—" She made a little choking sound and bit down hard on her lip. "I'm not going to let it end this way." She glared up at him, her mouth mere inches from his. "If you run now, I'll follow you. No matter where you go, I'll find you."

He stared at her mouth, at the passion in her eyes, and trembled with the force of his desire. Desire, even now, amid so much tragedy and horror. He didn't even have the strength to pull his hand from hers.

"There's still no proof that I didn't kill Peter. And if I did kill him, I could do anything. I could turn on you, Alexandra."

"I'm not afraid of you," she said. "You would never hurt me." But her voice was no more steady than his heart.

He could still make her go. There was doubt in her, just enough to use. He could make her believe he was a mad beast capable of anything, at the mercy of a nature even he didn't understand. It might even be true.

And if there was a risk, any risk at all . . .

He twisted his hand to trap hers. "You should be afraid, Alexandra. It would be so easy to—"

"No more time for chitchat," someone said. "You've got to get a move on."

Julie walked into the clearing and regarded them both with grave intensity. Alexandra whirled to face her, breathing hard.

"Julie! What—"

"I'm going to help you two get out of here. And don't try to argue. You don't have any choice but to accept our help." She looked directly into Kieran's eyes. "My grandma and I have been talking, Kieran. My family owes you one. We know you saved Tracy's life."

$\mathcal{I}$t took a moment for Alex to realize exactly what Julie was implying. "What—what are you talking about?" she blurted.

"Don't bother," Julie said. "Your secret is safe with my family, and so are you." She put her hands on her hips. "Right now we've got to get Kieran onto the rez where we can hole him up for a bit."

It was all happening too fast. Impossible that Julie meant what she seemed to mean.

But nothing was impossible any longer. Alex had started down a path from which there'd be no returning, and it was fraught with shocks and revelations.

"Come on," Julie said, starting toward them. "I know you don't want to be caught. We've got to get going."

Kieran didn't move. His face had gone from hostile to unreadable. Alex folded her arms and held Julie's gaze. "Not until you explain—"

"I knew you weren't going to make this easy." Julie sighed. "Word's out that the police believe Kieran murdered your friend Peter Schaeffer."

"He didn't—"

"I know. If I thought he did, I wouldn't be taking you anywhere near my family." Her expression was grim. "The cops are going to be combing these woods once they figure out he's run, especially when you disappear with him. There's maybe one place they won't check right away, and that's the rez. Especially not my grandma's cottage."

Mary. The old medicine woman with her sharp tongue, cryptic comments, and too-knowing eyes. Who had been so intent on talking to Kieran.

"Your grandmother?" Alex repeated.

But Julie was looking at Kieran, and it was to him she

spoke. "I had a feeling the first time I met you. Grandma suspected. But when Tracy told us what happened by the pond, it all came together."

Brown eyes met yellow and held in silent communication. "You don't know what I am," Kieran said without inflection.

"We know enough."

He lowered his head and narrowed his eyes. "Don't get involved, Julie."

"Too late. We're already involved." Her voice dropped to a mutter. "In more ways than you know." She looked at Alex. "Have you made any plans about how to get him out of the area or where you're going to go?"

What little control Alex had gained over the situation was rapidly slipping out of her hands. "I didn't have the chance. Julie, listen to me—"

"No. You listen. Both of you." Every trace of Julie's usual good humor had vanished. There was something about her, a subtle authority and dignity that silenced all of Alex's questions. "I know trust doesn't come easily to either one of you. Maybe you've got good reasons. But right now you haven't got any choice, because you're going to need all the friends you can get. And my family's it. Now let's go."

Before Alex could summon up a reply Kieran had begun to move, head down and jaw set. Julie nodded once and turned toward the reservation.

"Wait," Alex said. "I left the cabin this morning with nothing. I wasn't thinking too clearly when I went to find Kieran. There are things I need—we need. Let me just go back—"

Julie gave a sharp sideways jerk of her head. "Wouldn't be a good idea."

"If it's because of the police—"

"Not only that. I went by your place after you'd already left." She glanced at Kieran, who was almost out of sight ahead of them, and shrugged out of her own backpack. "This is what I found."

The object she pulled out of her pack was black and

ratty and musty, the fur moth-eaten and old. Alex touched it.

A black wolf's fur. Some portion of a pelt, splashed with blood and pierced with a large hole.

"This was left on your doorstep with a stake planted through it," Julie said. "There was a message written in the snow. I'm not going to repeat it, so don't ask."

Alex let the scrap of pelt fall into the snow. "I don't understand."

"You don't want to. I sent Mike into town to check on the police and catch up on the latest news. Seems that the mood in town is ugly. Some folks are with the police, and believe a man did it."

"Kieran," Alex said hoarsely.

"Yeah. But there's a contingent, led by our friend Howie, who think it had to have been an animal. A wolf. The same black wolf, in fact, that was raiding livestock recently. The one you were defending."

Alex nudged the pelt with her foot. "So now they blame me."

"They need someone to blame. Peter was an outsider, but I guess he could make himself popular when he wanted to."

"Yes," Alex murmured. "Peter was that way."

"And you can't afford to mess with Howie's bunch now," Julie said. She sighed and closed her eyes. "There's another thing. Five years ago there was a similar murder near town. Same kinds of wounds. There was a black wolf around then, too. So both the cops and Howie's stooges see a connection from that other time. It's complicated, and it's no good for you or Kieran."

"Who . . . was killed before?"

Julie opened her eyes. They shone suspiciously bright. "A girl. A girl from the rez. My cousin."

Alex was silenced. Tragedy was everywhere, hemming them in like a thicket of thorns. "And yet you're helping us, when there could be a chance—"

"It's personal for my family, too. We want to find the

truth about this as much as anyone. But we know what the truth isn't." She met Alex's gaze. "Don't you, Alex?"

Alex had no answer. After a moment she said, "They didn't have any suspects before?"

"The cops never did have a solid lead, and the black wolf Howie's bunch suspected disappeared shortly after. Maybe this time . . ." She shook her head again and picked up the scrap of wolf's pelt. "No more time for talk now. Come on. Kieran's way ahead of us."

Alex looked up in alarm. Kieran could have run if he'd chosen to. But as they walked, she saw his footprints continuing at a slow, steady pace, directly toward the reservation.

"You'll need transportation and supplies to get out of town," Julie said, as if she were discussing an everyday event of no particular significance. "I've already got Deanna and some of her friends out scrounging stuff from town. You make a list of things you need from the cabin."

Alex hesitated. "There's a private journal I keep. I left it next to my bed. I'd really like to have that."

"Don't worry about it. I'll tell Deanna's bunch to get it and restrain their curiosity. Mike is still keeping an eye on Howie and the cops."

Alex swallowed. "Julie, I . . . don't know what to say."

"It's okay. I'll do enough talking for both of us." She grinned her old Julie grin, and Alex found it impossible to meet her friend's eyes. She fixed her attention on the ground instead, breaking trail through the deep snow.

She hardly noticed when they cut through the woods to Julie's mother's backyard. But when Julie stopped and Alex finally looked up, they were standing in front of a cottage well behind the main house, fenced in by a tangle of birch saplings. Kieran was waiting for them, staring toward the north.

"Grandma's place," Julie said. "You'll be safe here for the time being."

"You could get into trouble helping us," Alex protested. "If they find us here—"

Julie pushed her hands into her pockets. "Cops won't get anywhere near here for some time. I told you I had people working on this from every angle." She tilted her chin toward the cottage. "You two go in there and rest for a bit. Grandma's taking care of some stuff, and you're going to need to be ready for what's ahead of you."

While she spoke Kieran joined them. He gazed at Julie so long and intently that even the unshakable mechanic shifted a little under his stare.

"Thank you," he said softly.

Julie nodded. "You saved Tracy. And maybe you can help us again some day."

"If I can." Something passed between the two of them that Alex didn't understand. Kieran returned Julie's nod and started toward the cottage door without a single glance at Alex.

"You, too," Julie said. "Something tells me you've got a long road ahead of you."

Alex held her ground. "The same *thing* that told you what Kieran is?"

Julie smiled wryly. "You could say that. It isn't easy to explain."

"It can't be any harder than trying to explain a . . . shape-shifter."

Julie barked a laugh. "Yeah. I see your point." She sobered and touched Alex's arm. "It must have been tough keeping that to yourself. It explained a lot when we figured it out."

Alex shook her head. "I still can't believe you know. Or that you can accept it so easily. If I thought I could convince you that you were crazy . . ."

"You don't have to. I already know. I sensed the day I met Kieran that there was a difference about him."

"I remember. You acted strangely, and I couldn't figure out why."

"I told Grandma what I suspected, and she said I should bring you both over to meet her."

Alex exhaled slowly. "I always thought there was something going on during our visit."

Julie nodded. "When Grandma talked to him she saw a lot more than I could. She had her suspicions, but when that wolf saved Tracy at the pond—well, it wasn't that hard to figure out."

Not hard. Alex closed her eyes. "I wish it had been that easy for me."

Julie squeezed her arm. "We Ojibwe are like anyone else. We don't all think the same, or believe the same either. But some of us don't necessarily find these things as hard to believe as *chimookamon* do."

"You don't know the half of it," Alex said faintly.

"I grew up on Grandma's stories," Julie continued. "One of my favorites was the one about how the wolves taught Winabojo how to hunt. How he took the form of the wolves and followed their example. There are other stories like that, too. The idea isn't strange to us."

Incongruous, helpless laughter insisted on forcing its way past the tightness in Alex's chest. She choked it back. "Kieran should have gone to you for help instead of me."

Julie gazed at her intently. "Why did he need help, Alex?" she asked. "Why did he come to you?"

In for a penny, in for a pound, Alex thought. "I never told you about his loss of memory."

"So that's what it was," Julie interrupted. "The problem Grandma sensed."

"You mean besides his being a werewolf?" Alex quipped.

Julie took the question seriously. "What he is was not our worry. We knew you were helping him, but not how. You've been trying to help him get his memory back."

"And not succeeding," Alex said. "He remembers very little of his past. When he first came to me, he had been a wolf for five years."

"Five years." Julie's eyes grew distant. "You study wolves. Maybe he sensed that you'd accept him better than most . . ."

Alex tuned out the rest of Julie's words. *Accept.* She'd done as poor a job of that as everything else.

"But then you said you'd known each other as children, didn't you?"

"That's another very long story, Julie."

There was silence as they studied each other, each occupied with her own thoughts.

"However you came together, it's more than just helping him now, isn't it?" Julie asked.

"I made a promise."

"Yeah. But he needs more than just staying clear of the cops and getting his memory back."

Alex looked up. "What do you mean?"

"You know, or you wouldn't be ready to risk everything to go with him."

Once again Julie saw far too much. She'd assumed from the very first that Alex would be going with Kieran. Alex wiped her face of all expression. "Why are you so sure Kieran didn't kill Peter?" she asked abruptly.

Julie touched the region of her heart. "I know it here. The same way you do."

Alex found it difficult to meet Julie's gaze. "Yesterday I wanted to talk to you. I came to town to find you, but you weren't at the garage. Maybe if I'd told you about Peter, and Kieran . . ."

"I know enough." Julie's eyes were almost sad. "About your father dying and why Peter Schaeffer was up here." She hesitated. "I know you and Schaeffer had a past. Are you going to be all right, Alex? If you need to talk . . ."

Alex worked to keep the lump in her throat from expanding all the way through her body. If she opened her mouth she wouldn't be able to stop. If she took the comfort Julie offered, she wouldn't be worth a damn to Kieran or herself.

She had to be strong. It was all she had left. Chaos waited to claim her the moment she let go.

"How did you know Kieran would never let himself be taken in for questioning?" she asked.

"Because of what he is. You can't cage a wolf. They need freedom to survive." She held Alex's gaze. "Just like they need to belong. They're like people that way."

Alex looked toward the cottage. "So what happens now?"

Julie switched topics without blinking an eye. "Around the other side of the house is a truck, an old rusted heap that I finally got running but never had a reason to drive anywhere." Her grin had a feral edge. "No one's going to think to watch out for it for some time. I have a few more ideas to throw the cops off the scent. Which way are you planning to go?"

"I don't know. I've never been on the run." She remembered what Kieran had said: *"Where I'm going you can't follow."* "Kieran said something about—" *"Finding his own kind."* That was a revelation she couldn't take time to think about now. "He seemed to have a sense of where he wanted to go," she finished.

"Then trust him," Julie said. "Maybe his memory is pulling him, or the senses he has that we don't. Trust him, Alex."

Julie made it sound so simple. "Kieran can't run forever," Alex said bleakly. "Unless he becomes a wolf again and . . . stays that way."

"He won't have to." Julie hunched her shoulders. "This'll just buy time. While you're taking care of him, we're going to keep looking for the real killer."

Alex wished desperately for even a fraction of Julie's confidence. *You made your choice, Alex. . . .*

"You just concentrate on finding somewhere out of the way where the cops won't find you. We'll do what we can on this end. I've got a cousin who's a cop over in Baxter, and he'll pitch in too. I'll give you a number you can call for updates."

Silenced by the sheer scope of it, Alex swallowed several times, hard. "Without you, Julie . . ."

"Things have a way of coming together," Julie said. "There are patterns—" She broke off and gave Alex a sheepish grin. "Here I am going all mystical on you. It's simple. If you feel a powerful need to pay me back, you can finally sell me that Blazer of yours."

With a long, shaky sigh, Alex began to laugh.

13

When Joseph walked in on the meeting in the back of the bar, they all fell silent.

Even the loudest of them, Howie Walsh, looked at Joseph with respect. Joseph took it as his due. "Old Arnoux," they called him, but they knew his father had been one of the greatest wolf hunters in the north, and Joseph had followed in Jean-Baptiste's footsteps from a very young age. Until the wolf bounty had ended, and it became illegal to hunt wolves in Minnesota.

But the hunting had never really ended. The men gathered here wanted blood.

Howie got to his feet. "Glad to have you with us, Arnoux," he said. He puffed out his chest, gathering his compatriots in with his glance. "We knew you'd want to be part of this." He gestured to a chair and slapped Joseph on the back. "We were just talking about the rogue wolf five years ago, and how you went after it. This time the bastard won't get away."

Joseph took the offered seat and looked around the room. The men here were mainly of Howie's ilk—puppies who had no idea what they faced. They truly believed a mere wolf could have torn Peter Schaeffer's body into ribbons.

They waited for him to speak, but when he remained silent they resumed their rambling conference. Boasts and loud promises to bolster their courage against a man-killing monster.

No, they didn't understand what they faced. They worked themselves up into a killing frenzy, reducing the unknown to something easily faced. They were fools, most of them. They didn't possess the true hunter's spirit that understood and *became* the quarry in order to emerge victorious. But he needed their help. Alone, he couldn't watch on all fronts now that he knew Kieran had killed again and would be on the run.

"When we find that killer wolf," Howie was saying, "we'll take it straight to that bitch's house and hang it up over her door. Prove to all of them—"

"She wasn't at the cabin this morning," Norm McCallister said. "Maybe she's out trying to find the wolf to protect it."

There was a chorus of harsh laughter and protests. "She was screwing that bastard Holt," another man put in. "The cops think he did it. Heard they went to question her. She's probably holed up with him somewhere."

"Let the cops think whatever the hell they want," Howie snapped. "If Holt gets in trouble, great. But we still have a job to do. Kill that wolf and—"

"No."

The softness of Joseph's voice startled them to stillness. He got stiffly to his feet, meeting every set of eyes around the loose circle of chairs. "No. When you find the wolf, you must not kill it. You must bring it to me."

Men grumbled. Joseph had known there would be resistance. These men thought themselves great heroes. But he looked at the protesters and held their stares until they looked away.

"You all know my father was killed by a black wolf," he said. "You know I've hunted them, here and in Canada, much of my life. I know they are vermin, as you do. But I have a score to settle. I want this wolf."

The men looked at each other. Howie tilted his cap and scratched his head. "Dead is dead—"

"I want this wolf alive." He smiled grimly. "Are you afraid I'll be too merciful with the killer?" He held Howie's stare until the younger man dropped his, like the others. "I don't have a lot of money. But whoever brings the animal to me, alive, will have my gratitude."

They might have laughed. Old man Arnoux's gratitude might not seem worth much to most, who considered him a reclusive lunatic, living on the fringe of the wilderness. But these men, at least, understood something of his professed hatred.

Norm stood. "I'm willing. Arnoux kept after the wolf five years ago, longer than any of us. If it's the same wolf, he's earned it."

Joseph nodded his thanks. "You will still have your hunt. I only want the wolf alive, and not too close to death."

Mutters circled the room, but at last there were nods and shrugs. Howie had a rebellious light in his eye, but when he looked at Joseph there was a touch of unease.

Crazy old Arnoux. Yes, believe I'm crazy, boy, if it will make you obey me. Imagine what I will do to that wolf when I have it.

"All right," Howie said, too loudly, trying to regain control of the meeting. "You know what to do. It's too dark to start now, but you all have to start first thing tomorrow, from the places we planned. And if any of you find the wolf—" He glanced at Joseph, "bring it to my place. Alive."

The meeting broke up, a few of the men lingering over a beer while the others headed home. Joseph declined the one or two hesitant suggestions that he join the drinkers; they seemed glad enough to see him gone.

He drove the twenty miles to his property in the darkness of a near-moonless night. No one else ever ventured down the pitted gravel road that led to the fenced compound marking the barrier of his land. He threw open the high gate he'd constructed so long ago and locked it carefully behind him, exactly as if Kieran were still within these walls.

I failed, boy, he thought, standing in the silent vastness of the place he had built. His own mistake that he'd ever let Kieran run loose, even behind fences made to hold a creature not human; his own weakness that sympathy for the boy had led him to drop his guard.

Kieran had been twenty-one. The boy had just become a man when he tricked Joseph and ran. Joseph had known he'd return in time, and he had—five years ago, when he killed the girl from the reservation.

But I didn't catch you then. And still you returned, to kill again. This time I must not fail. My duty must be completed.

He walked into the cabin and sat heavily at the carved table in the corner of the room. He looked at the shelves that still held moldy books no hand but Kieran's had touched for eleven years.

But Joseph's Bible lay on the table, and he turned to the passage about Abraham and Isaac.

It gave him little comfort now.

I would have saved you if I could. But it would have been best if I'd killed you when I killed the other creatures. My heart was too soft. I thought you were young enough to redeem. I believed I could teach you, change you, make you human. I was wrong. Even when you were a child it was already too late.

Joseph closed the Bible and laid his hand on the ancient leather cover. He could have let the others kill Kieran if they found him as a wolf, but that would have been cowardice. *It's mine to do. Mine alone.*

You will not escape me again, my son.

Alexandra had no defenses against him now.

Kieran listened to her deep, even breathing as she lay curled toward the wall on Mary's bed, her arms against her chest and her knees drawn up like a child's. Her halo of red hair spread out across the patched pillowcase. Several wavy strands clung to the corner of her mouth; without thinking he brushed his finger across her cheek to smooth the hair away.

Her skin felt like—he didn't know the right words for the softness, the sweetness of it. Or the way her lips relaxed in sleep, the innocent sweep of her lashes.

While she slept he could dare to touch her. He traced the curve of her cheek, knowing he would never get another chance. Twice they'd shared moments of passion, and twice she'd pushed him away.

"Alexandra," he murmured. He ran his fingertip along the contour of her ear. The ache in him went beyond the pressure in his loins. He wanted to lie beside her, feel all of her under the layers of clothing, but he wanted more than the joining of their bodies. With Alexandra the two would be one. He would never taste either.

He leaned over her, the trailing ends of his hair mingling with hers. Her scent filled his nostrils, more potent than the alcohol he'd used to escape himself.

Closing his eyes, he let his tongue touch the lobe of her ear. Her body tensed, and he stopped, but she relaxed again. The taste of her skin he remembered from their kisses, but those other times had only left his hunger more potent. He curved his tongue around the soft flesh and pulled it by tiny increments into his mouth.

Alexandra made a low sound, but still she didn't waken. Not even when he touched his tongue to her brow, her eyelids, the corner of her mouth.

And yet she *felt*. He had always known when she was afraid. Now he knew some part of her enjoyed, wanted what he did. Asleep, her body lowered all the barriers her mind and heart erected against him.

Kieran closed his eyes and traced her lips, pressed his own gently against them. In his time with her he'd been only an obstacle to the life she'd chosen, a responsibility she didn't want. Now he was a danger. He'd never be allowed to give her what he wanted to give her. Or repay her for what she'd given him.

Slowly he pulled back, memorizing her face one last time. It was dark outside at last, after the long day of silent waiting; he knew Julie would be coming for them soon.

He turned for the door before he could delay again. He gripped the knob and opened it with exquisite care.

"Going somewhere?" Julie said.

He stepped through the door and closed it behind him. Julie moved back just enough, planting herself directly in his path.

She was not a tall woman, nor was she particularly big, but she regarded him with grave disapproval and hands on hips, as if these alone could turn him from his course.

"Let me pass, Julie," he said. She didn't move, and he braced himself for a confrontation he'd hoped to avoid. "You're a good friend to Alexandra. You should want what's best for her."

"And you, of course, know what that is." She shifted her stance, setting her feet wide apart.

"Yes." He met her gaze. "I won't put her in any more danger," he said heavily. "Or you."

Julie smiled without a trace of humor. "Very noble. So you're going to remove the danger by removing yourself. Well, if you wanted to keep me out of it, you saved the wrong kid. My family is pretty stubborn about repaying our debts."

"I don't want your gratitude."

She shrugged. "Too bad. And you're underestimating Alex if you think you could throw her off your trail by sneaking out in the middle of the night."

He bristled, showing his teeth. "Maybe you underestimate me."

"You think you're mighty dangerous, don't you?" she asked with calm dispassion.

"You don't know what I'm capable of," he said harshly. "And neither do I."

"Maybe no one does until they haven't got any choice." She studied him in silence. "Alex told me about your losing your memory. She also said you know where you're going."

"Yes." It didn't matter if she knew. "Northwest."

"Something is calling you that way, isn't it?"

He took a step toward her. "How do you know so much?"

"How do you know so little?"

He stiffened. Was she mocking his loss of memory? But there was no mockery in her voice, and only sadness in her eyes. Her eyes that saw so much.

With a sudden lunge he caught her arms. "Tell me what you see when you look at me," he rasped. "Tell me."

She didn't try to escape. "I see a blind man."

He tightened his grip. "Am I a danger to Alexandra?"

"You know the answer to that yourself."

Abruptly he let her go and backed away. "I know how Alexandra sees me."

"Do you, Kieran?" Julie said softly, rubbing her arms. "What are you really afraid of?"

He laughed briefly and bitterly. "You're very wise, Julie. Too wise for me."

"Not wise enough."

"I could still leave now—"

"Do you know what you'd be leaving Alex to face?" Julie snapped. "Not only Peter's murder and the cops, when she's been associated with you as a suspect, but Howie's bunch as well. They have it in for her now, since they think she was defending a wolf that's turned man-killer. They never needed much of an excuse."

"They think—"

"Yeah. Some of the townies think a wolf killed Alex's friend. So I'd advise you not to do any running around here as a wolf."

Kieran bared his teeth. "They'd never dare to hurt Alex."

"Maybe not. But are you going to run off and let her deal with whatever you leave behind?"

"Julie? Kieran? Is everything okay?"

Alexandra stood in the cottage doorway, rubbing her eyes. Kieran felt his heart lurch at the simple sight of her standing there, so beautiful and vulnerable and infinitely precious.

And even now the beast growled and paced and shivered with wanting her.

"Good you're up, Alex," Julie said, striding past him. "It's about time you were on your way. Everything's arranged. I've got the old rust heap ready—no one's gonna recognize that baby, it's been sitting in our yard so long— and enough food to tide you over for a while." She glanced at Kieran as if only the most ordinary conversation had passed between them. "I understand you're heading northwest."

"Northwest?" Alex said, her gaze seeking Kieran's.

"So Kieran says."

"That's not much of a destination," Alex commented. "You don't have any better idea of where you want to go, Kieran?"

"Maybe this will help." Julie pulled a battered and much-folded map from her coat pocket. She beckoned Alex and Kieran to join her within the faint yellow beam of the cottage's porch light.

"Take a look at this, Kieran," she said, pressing the map out flat against the wall. It covered Canada and the northern United States from Saskatchewan to British Columbia. "Anything seem familiar?"

Kieran looked. He studied the crisscrossed lines of a hundred roads, major and minor, and the vastness of Canada above the border. He traced the Trans-Canada Highway with his finger, felt a strange excitement sizzle at the ends of his nerves.

The names of towns small and large dotted the areas

close to the border, some of them hauntingly familiar. Places he had once passed through as a wanderer? He caught images of vast tracts of prairie, distant mountains, highways stretching to the horizon.

And a woman's face. Just for an instant—dark-haired, pretty, smiling at him. He put his hand flat over Saskatchewan and Manitoba, as if he could trap the image in place. But it vanished, and with it all familiarity.

"Some of this I think I recognize," he said to the women. "But I don't know the destination." He looked again, farther west into the mountainous, bent-L shape of British Columbia. "Here. That's all I can feel. Here."

Julie chewed her lower lip. "Okay. It's something. Why don't you choose a place to head for. I know it would make me feel a helluva lot better if I knew where you guys were going."

Alex nodded. "I agree." She stared hard at Kieran. "You choose, Kieran."

He shrugged. It didn't matter if he humored them in this. He studied the map of British Columbia and let his finger fall where it would.

"Kamloops," Alex murmured. She smiled crookedly. "Good a place as any, I suppose."

"It's always good to have a destination," Julie said. "Any idea of what you're going to do when you get there?"

Kieran met her gaze. "As much an idea as I have of my past," he said. "But maybe something will occur to me when we get there."

"I'm sure of it."

She refolded the map and passed it to Alex. "You keep this. I have another one." As Alex tucked the map in the breast of her jacket, Julie turned to Kieran, slapping her gloved hands.

"I have an idea of the best place for you to cross the border into Canada, at Manitoba. We've already cooked up an excuse for your absence here that should last until you get over the border, and hopefully beyond."

"I have another idea," Kieran put in. "The police will

look for a man and a woman, but they won't expect to see a woman and a wolf."

Alexandra studied Kieran with cool self-possession. "You mean to shift and cross the border that way?"

"Yes." He looked at Julie. "I won't change until we get out of this area. When we reach the border, Alexandra can cross alone. I'll go separately, and meet her on the other side."

"That's open country up there," Alexandra said. "No wolves, Kieran."

He smiled grimly. "No one will see me."

"You haven't learned to control your shifting," she protested.

"I *will* control it. I have no choice."

Her lips narrowed into a thin line, but he knew she had no argument to throw in his path. "You're right. It would be the best way."

Silence settled among them like a fourth ghostly presence. Julie coughed behind her hand. "It's still over two hundred miles to the northwestern border on the back roads. You'd better head out. The truck's parked just behind the house."

Alexandra gazed at Julie and swallowed. "Julie, I—" She moved suddenly into Julie's arms, and the two women embraced.

"Hey," Julie murmured, patting Alexandra on the back. "I know this has been a rough time for you. I just wish I could be there. But you won't be alone. Not if you don't want to be." She leaned close to Alexandra's ear. Kieran heard a faint whisper, just too low for him to decipher. Alexandra stiffened and pulled free of Julie's hold. Confusion washed over her face before she mastered it.

"Thank you. For everything you've done," she said to Julie. But she was looking pointedly away from her friend and Kieran both. "Come on, Kieran."

She started toward the main house, her strides long and reckless. Kieran watched her until she disappeared into the darkness. Julie moved up beside him.

"I've got one more piece of advice." There was a glaze over her eyes, moisture that gathered among her dark lashes like dew in summer grass. "Be sure you know what you're losing before you let it go."

She turned to follow Alexandra.

*I*n the chill of false dawn Alex waited a few hundred yards off a country road just over the Minnesota-Manitoba border, her truck parked behind a cluster of trees and her heart a leaden weight in her chest.

Kieran wasn't coming.

Alex worked her fingers convulsively and stared at the ancient, sputtering neon sign of the cheap motel along the highway. She'd stood here for hours, fighting exhaustion, remembering their parting at the border when he had shifted with such surprising ease. Reminding herself that Kieran had said he knew her scent better than anything in the world, that he could find her anywhere over a ten mile radius. She had never thought to question his conviction.

Now she questioned. She tried to stop the scenarios that played out in her mind: Kieran spotted and shot by a nervous farmer. Kieran losing control and shifting back in plain view of someone, or simply being recognized and captured as a fugitive.

She could call Julie; they'd made arrangements for Alex to call Julie's mother's house and leave a number at which Alex could be reached during their journey. Maybe Kieran had returned to Minnesota.

But Alex didn't really believe any of those possibilities. Her heart knew the truth.

Kieran wasn't coming because he'd chosen not to return to her.

Alex clenched her jaw and strode away from the truck for the thousandth time. It was prairie here: flat, open country dotted by farms and scattered clumps of trees planted as windbreaks. It was also a land almost empty of people, especially an hour before sunrise.

She walked to the edge of a frozen creek edged by a

fringe of dried grasses. Her flashlight beam danced along the ice, the sole point of illumination for a quarter mile in any direction. For a while there had been a kind of muffling in the darkness, a dreamlike unreality that kept her mental turmoil at bay.

That vague comfort was gone. Alex hugged herself, turning her face into the biting wind. Strange, how much she had taken for granted. For a time she had been the sole focus of Kieran's world. But she had failed him once too often—failed to accept him for all that he was. She had given him too little. Too late.

Now something was pulling him to the northwest. His own people, he'd said. British Columbia was the place they'd chosen. A good place for wolves, or remarkable beings that could take their shape.

Once it would have seemed another miracle to learn that others of Kieran's ability existed somewhere. She'd guessed it of his parents, but she had never truly thought beyond that. And Kieran had never spoken of it before the morning after the murder.

But if he found them, he wouldn't need her anymore, mere human that she was. Perhaps he had already realized that.

She remembered Julie's whispered words: *"Tell him, Alex. Tell him how you feel, or you'll lose him."*

Julie had recognized Alex's most terrible vulnerability without a word being said.

If he'd been Shadow in truth, and only a wolf, she could have spoken her heart as Julie had urged, as she'd done the first morning he awakened by her fireside.

But he was not a wolf. God help her, he was not.

She went back to the truck, turning to the one sure source of comfort she could always count on. Almost frantically she pulled her notebook from the backpack and opened the journal to the next blank page.

And realized that only one page remained.

With shaking fingers she stroked the lined white sheet. One more page and the notebook was full. Suddenly she was afraid. Somehow she knew if she filled this page, it would be over. The story would be finished. There would be no more chances.

Her father was gone forever. Peter had reentered her life and had paid a greater price for his duplicity than she'd ever wish on anyone.

And she had loved him once. She had loved them both.

Oh, Peter. I'm sorry. So sorry that it ended this way, that none of us had a chance to make it right. Not you, not my Father, not even myself. It will never be resolved. How much of this was my fault? I handled it all wrong, and I lost both of you. Just like—

But she cut off that line of thought. The only thing she had left of Father was the money she didn't want, didn't need in the simple life she'd chosen. She'd have to find something to do with it. The last connections to her old, privileged life had died with Peter.

She wrote a single line in the journal, closed it carefully and laid her cheek against the textured cover. "Kieran," she whispered. "They're all gone. I need you. Don't leave me . . ."

She didn't finish the plea. Stiff grasses rustled behind her. She turned as if in slow motion.

Kieran kept his distance, staring up at her with slitted yellow eyes that reddened in the beam of her flashlight. His black pelt was rimed with ice, and his ears lay at a low angle. Alex hardly noticed. He was safe. He'd come back, and she felt like shouting for joy.

"Kieran."

He backed away, turned smoothly, and leaped into the open door of the truck.

Her heart did a remarkable series of acrobatics that left her feeling breathless. She slid into the seat beside Kieran, holding her feelings in check. It wasn't the time for questions and confessions. Not yet.

"We're going to get a room at the motel for a few hours, check in with Julie, and get some rest," she told him, as if everything had happened exactly as she expected. "We may have to spend the day there. But Julie's family can't keep the authorities off our tail forever. We'll have to get some distance between us and Minnesota."

His ear twitched, and she knew he understood her. She prayed he couldn't hear the way her heart pounded at the prospect of spending a day trapped in the same tiny room with him. Or in the cramped truck, for days on end, heading for an unknown destination with a man to whom she could not yet reveal her heart.

The dam within herself was being held together with spit and twine and the frayed edges of willpower, but it was all she had.

As she put the truck in gear and headed for the motel, she spoke to him in the only way she dared.

Please stay, Kieran. Don't even think of running again.

But she knew he couldn't read her mind.

"*M*s. Wakanabo?"

Julie stopped in midstride. A man had stepped into her path on the Pine Street sidewalk—a man she'd never met before but knew about, as she knew through her family grapevine about all the outsiders who came to Merritt.

Especially now. And especially outsiders like this one.

"Mr. Gévaudan," she said, and held out her hand. "I've heard of you."

He arched a gray-shot dark brow. A handsome guy, tall and well muscled, with yellow-green eyes that seized and held her gaze as his fingers grasped hers.

"Perhaps through our mutual acquaintances, Alexandra Warrington and Kieran Holt?" he asked.

Julie stiffened. This one wasn't going to play games. She knew he'd talked once to Alex and Kieran, after the bar fight the afternoon before Peter's murder. She knew he'd been asking questions around town about Kieran since he and Alex had "disappeared."

His interest in them might not have been so strange if he'd been one of the townsfolk who suspected Kieran had committed the murder. But there was something else here, something Julie felt as he held her hand. Something very much like what she'd sensed when she first met Kieran Holt.

He released her fingers. "I've been concerned about what I've been hearing about Alexandra and Kieran," he said. "I didn't get a chance to know them well, but I'd hoped to learn more about their wolf research. I understand you're a friend of theirs."

Julie began to walk. She'd already talked to the police, dodged their questions with inscrutable smiles and nods, as had Grandma and the rest of the family. The cops had no real reason to suspect that her family had helped Kieran and Alex to leave the area, and still had no idea where the suspects might have gone.

But this one, this stranger—he was different. The back of Julie's neck prickled as she heard him follow.

"I realize you don't really know me, Ms. Wakanabo," he said. "But I've come to you because I want to help Alex and Kieran, and I believe you know where they are."

Julie forced herself to turn very slowly, to regard Gévaudan with an expressionless face. "What makes you think that?"

He smiled. It held a hint of charm, but it was also unyielding. "Call it intuition. Something you're not unfamiliar with, I think."

She planted her hands on her hips. "You don't know anything about me, Mr. Gévaudan. The whole town knows I don't believe this crap about Kieran killing Schaeffer. And Alex is my friend. Even if I knew something—which I don't—I don't think I'd tell you."

He grew sober. "I don't blame you for your caution. I'd do the same in your place."

"Glad you understand. And now I have stuff to take care of, so—"

"Are they by chance heading northwest?"

Julie dropped her hands and narrowly avoided letting her mouth hang open. "Now what makes you say that, Mr. Gévaudan?"

He held her gaze, unblinking. "An educated guess." He shifted his weight casually and hooked his thumbs in his beltloops. "I do have a suggestion as to their destination, and I'd ask you to pass it along to them next time you're in communication."

Julie stared at him with narrowed eyes. "Who *are* you?"

"Luke," he said. "Since we both want what's best for Kieran and Alexandra, we might as well be on a first-name basis."

Julie shaped her mouth into a humorless smile. "If we're going to get so cozy—Luke—we'd better go to my office."

She strode ahead once again, leaving him to catch up as she walked the rest of the way to the garage. He followed her into the cluttered office; she noticed the way he stood close to the doorway, his nostrils flaring with the heavy mingled scents of oil and metal.

"Okay," she said. "I want to know what you're talking about."

Luke leaned against the doorframe, eyes distant. "Then I was right. He's felt the call."

"What?"

Luke seemed to shake himself, and focused on her again. "I told you what you need to know. When Kieran gets in touch with you, tell him to go to Lovell. It's a small town in B.C., a hundred or so miles in from the Alberta border, northeast of Kamloops. He'll be able to find what he's looking for there."

Julie sat down in her chair, staring at Luke. "I don't know what you're talking about."

"I think you do. And I won't insult your intelligence by pretending otherwise." Luke straightened, and for a moment there was a silent battle between them, gaze locked on gaze.

Julie felt a vast compulsion to look away—look away or be drowned in eyes that held a subtle power. Eyes like Kieran's. Like . . .

"Why are you doing this?" she asked hoarsely. "How do I know this isn't some kind of trap?"

"You think I'm with the police?" He laughed softly.

"No. My interest is personal. But I assure you"—he moved closer, so close that she had to bend her neck to meet his eyes—"it's vital that you get this information to Kieran. It's the best chance he's got."

"For what?" Julie demanded. She got up, standing toe-to-toe with Luke.

Luke was silent a long moment. At last he sighed and gave his head a brief shake, as if he'd come to some decision. "For solving whatever problems he has because of what he is."

What he is. Julie stared, caught in a maelstrom of senses and feelings that clamored for attention. Without warning she caught his big hand between hers and clutched it with all her strength.

And she *knew*. She knew as she'd known with Kieran almost from the beginning, though she hadn't trusted her instincts at first. Now she did. She had no choice. She dropped his hand and tried to step back, trapped by the bulk of her chair.

"You're . . ."

Luke's eyes were inhumanly bright. "What, Julie?"

She refused to play his game, refused to put into words what she knew. What they both knew. Luke smiled, but his eyes were grim.

You knew there would be others. Grandma knew Kieran couldn't be the only one. And still the proof was startling. And dangerous.

"What is this place you . . . want Kieran to go?" she asked slowly.

He did her the favor of stepping away, leaving her room to breathe. And think. "I already told you," he said. "A place where he won't be alone. Where his problems can be dealt with."

"He isn't a killer."

"Your faith is admirable, Julie."

Julie folded her arms. "Do you think he did it?"

"I don't know," Luke said. His deep voice was stark. "I know about the state of the body. I know about the murder five years ago. I know the various theories, and how inadequate they are."

Five years ago, and an innocent girl savaged with wounds too terrible to be made by a human being, too calculated to have been the work of an animal. Still unsolved.

Julie swallowed. "You were in town when Peter was killed."

"So I was." Luke leaned against the doorway again, his pose all feigned relaxation. "But I had no motive."

"Someone did."

"Let me explain something to you, Julie. I have as much stake in learning the truth of this as anyone else. More. Because what happened here was something that never should have happened. I didn't come to Merritt expecting to find a murder, but now that I've found it, it involves me as much as anyone."

"Because of what you are?"

He didn't respond directly, but she knew. "There are responsibilities. Laws. Rules. Murder is a universal crime. It can't be allowed to go unpunished."

Julie leaned over her desk. She'd wanted Cheryl's murder solved, her murderer caught. And now, it seemed, this stranger wanted the same for reasons he wouldn't give.

She looked up. "Why should I trust anything you say?"

"I have no answers for you. All you have is your own judgment. But I think your judgment is sufficient. Look at me. Do you sense a lie, Julie? Do you think I'm something to fear?"

Julie closed her eyes, calling on the spirits for guidance. Nowhere within herself could she find either untruths or fear. Only a sense of rightness.

She opened her eyes again. "There's one more thing," she said. "Alex is with Kieran. This place you want him to go—is it a place she can go, too?"

He understood, and his expression was very serious. "It would be best if she came back and let him go on alone."

She was beginning to form a reply when she caught sight of a commotion outside the grimy window. A bunch of men were clumping down the street, huddled together and uncharacteristically silent. Howie, Julie recognized, and his band of wolf haters.

"I heard their hunt was unsuccessful," Luke commented. He watched the men recede, baring his teeth in a smile.

Julie joined him. "And what else did you hear?"

He looked at her, a glint of mischief in his eyes. "That they ran into a large gray wolf instead of the one they wanted to find. I hear they lost something of their dignity when the gray led them on a wild goose chase all the way out to the county line."

"I see. Amazing how quickly word spreads, considering they just got back."

"Yes. Amazing."

They exchanged a long look. "Lots of amazing things have been happening these days," she said. "Seems all a person can do is go with her gut." She extended her hand. "I hope my gut doesn't let me down, Luke Gévaudan."

*J*ulie's gut was still on full alert when she went to the pay phone at Merritt's gas station.

She dialed the number Alex had left at Mom's house and waited while it rang. Luke Gévaudan was gone, but the hair continued to prickle along the nape of her neck, and only Alex's voice pulled her out of the feeling that something wasn't quite right.

"We're about fifty miles west of the Saskatchewan border," Alex's voice said over the line. "At a gas station on the edge of a town called Falkirk. Kieran was insistent about stopping here, said he remembered something, but so far nothing has turned up."

Julie pulled the map from her pocket and began to unfold it one-handed. *Something's sure as hell happened here*, she thought.

"We made good time last night after we left the motel

in Manitoba." Alex continued. "We've been staying off the road for most of the daylight hours, but now that it's late afternoon we're getting ready to head out again."

Julie glanced at her watch—four P.M.—and at the map she held spread against the grimy Plexiglass of the phone booth. "You're still heading west on the expressway, right? Toward Kamloops? Does Kieran have any better idea of where he wants to go?"

"Not so far. He . . . hasn't really talked about it."

"Well, I've got a new suggestion. There's a town in the mountains northeast of Kamloops called Lovell. I think Kieran should make for that area."

She heard Alex's question in her mind before it came out in words. "Why, Julie? Have you learned something?"

Julie bit down on her lip. "You've trusted me before, Alex. I'm asking you to do it again. I really think . . . I sense Kieran should go on to Lovell. I think that whatever he's looking for, that's where he'll find it. Call it another of my 'feelings.' " She steeled herself for what would come next. "And I think you should come back, Alex."

Silence. Julie squeezed the receiver. "Alex?"

"I heard you. I'm sorry, Julie, I have no intention of leaving Kieran now. He still needs me, and I'm going to see this through, just as I told him." She paused. "You said you had a feeling. Is there more to this, Julie? More I should know?"

Julie fought a brief battle within herself. If she revealed what she suspected, what she *believed,* it was only going to make things more difficult for Alex. She didn't need any more complications right now. And Julie had sensed no danger from Luke Gévaudan. His warning about Alex had been subtle, not pointed.

But there was still time to ask for Grandma's help in this, find Luke and try to get more information.

"Just be careful, okay?," she said at last. "Keep checking in as often as you can, same arrangement. Especially when you get to B.C. Don't go to Lovell until you've called, in case I have more to tell you."

"I promise."

Julie sighed. "Good. We still have stuff under control on this end. The cops don't have any solid leads so far." She gave a brief, grim laugh. "Howie's bunch hasn't had much success in their hunt for the black wolf, either. How are things with you and Kieran?"

Another long silence. "Fine."

Yeah. Right. Julie had given Alex a lecture about hanging on to something good when she found it, and now . . .

Julie rubbed the back of her neck, feeling the roughness of goosebumps on her skin. "Alex, I—"

She broke off, arrested by something she'd glimpsed out of the corner of her eye. A shape—a man's silhouette, there one minute and gone the next, vanished around a corner of the nearest building several yards away.

"Listen, Alex, I've got to go. Call me again when you can. And be careful."

She hung up quickly and sprinted across the lot. The sky was dark and lowering, and the sidewalks were almost empty here near the edge of town. She looked around the corner of the building where she'd seen the man.

He was walking away, wrapped in a dark, somewhat ragged coat, a knitted cap pulled low over his head. Not Luke or Howie or anyone else she recognized right away.

Then she remembered when she'd seen that particular coat and cap before.

Old man Arnoux. The recluse she'd once mentioned to Alex. She knew he'd been in town lately. He'd been seen with Howie's bunch, undoubtedly after the same black wolf they'd been hunting. As he'd been five years ago. There'd been a few stories back then devoted to the odd old man's obsession with that black wolf, even when nearly everyone had been concentrating on Cheryl's murder.

Old man Arnoux. Julie shook her head. She hardly knew him, had never even spoken with him. He'd have no reason to listen in on her conversations—and even if he was trying to listen, he couldn't have heard a damned thing from that distance. Not even with the keenest hearing.

Julie turned back for the garage, wondering why that odd, shivery feeling refused to go away.

14

Kieran stared out across the prairie from his place beside the truck in the gas station parking lot, listening to the distant murmur of Alexandra's voice on the phone.

She was talking to Julie. Kieran didn't eavesdrop, though he could have. His hearing was good enough. But things had been tense between him and Alexandra during the hours they'd spent traveling, and they both needed their privacy now.

Everything was going as well as could be hoped. So far they'd been lucky—all last night and early this morning, following provincial routes paralleling the Trans-Canada Highway, they'd met only scant local traffic. They'd passed numerous tiny farm towns before pulling off the road to wait out the bulk of daylight hours, and hadn't once glimpsed the local law enforcement. No one had paid any attention to Julie's battered truck.

Yes, things were going as well as could be expected. As long as Kieran didn't let himself become aware of Alexandra sitting beside him in the claustrophobic confines of the truck—of her sweet scent and steady breathing; of the delicate lines of her profile and the lithe curves beneath her shirt and jeans; of the way his heart betrayed him when she met his glance.

As long as he didn't relive how it felt when she'd been in his arms. As long as he didn't imagine.

As long as he remembered he was only a responsibility to her, a duty to be performed, and no more.

He hunched his shoulders and stared northwest again. He'd asked Alexandra to stop here, at this little town in Saskatchewan. It was the place he'd seen on the map—a name that had pulled up a memory. Falkirk. But now they were there, on the outskirts, and he saw nothing to spark more memories.

I was here once, he thought. *Something happened here.* That certainty, and a woman's face, was all that remained. They'd lost valuable time and taken a risk because he'd acted on a scrap of memory.

Theirs was the only vehicle at the isolated gas station; flat, snowbound land stretched from horizon to horizon. The convenience store was empty except for the clerk, who was restocking shelves.

They were still safe, for the moment . . .

"Kieran Holt? Is it you?"

The familiar, hesitant voice was clearly audible in the lonely silence. Kieran froze, staring toward the store.

A woman stood just outside the door. Her hands rested on the shoulders of a child swathed in an oversized coat. She was petite, with short brown hair and dark eyes in a pinched, wary face that still showed traces of a worn, edged beauty. A too-thin jacket hung above black leggings and white rhinestoned cowboy boots.

Kieran exhaled as she began to walk toward him, the child close to her side. "Kieran, it is you. Oh, God—"

"Lori?"

Without warning the woman broke into a sprint, pulling the boy behind her. She hurled herself against Kieran, smelling of some musky perfume mingled with the scents of perspiration and cigarette smoke.

Kieran put his arms around her instinctively. And as he held her, he began to know her. The face that looked up at him was the one of his vague memories: pretty and thin, her brown eyes edged with dark lines and blue powder, her lips painted with fading color that made her generous mouth a slash of red against pale skin.

She pulled back. "You do remember me, Kieran?" And before he could reply she pulled his head down and kissed him full on the mouth with a desperate ferocity that startled him.

When she let him go he was able to speak.

"Lori," he said slowly. "Lori Carstens."

She smiled. "I never thought I'd see you again. After you ran—" She lowered her head and rubbed her hand over her eyes, further streaking the dark edging around them. "I was never sure what had happened to you. But you're all right." She looked up. "You're all right!"

After you ran, she said. Ran from whom, or what? From this town in the middle of nowhere? But this was what had compelled him to come to this place. This woman. He was certain of it. Kieran struggled to bring the memories clear.

"You haven't changed, Lori," he said.

Lori brushed at her ragged bangs and pulled the little boy close to her side again. The child regarded Kieran with eyes as dark as his mother's. "Six years," she said. "Six years since we were together."

"Six years," he repeated. *Together.* He and this woman.

The lines around her mouth—lines he hadn't noticed before—grew deeper as she frowned. With one hand she reached inside her ragged jacket and pulled out a cigarette pack. It was empty. She cursed under her breath, crumpled it into a ball and tossed it onto the pavement. Her face crumpled with it.

"Oh, Kieran. It's been so long." Her laugh was hoarse and hopeless. "I wish like hell I'd taken your advice and gone with you. Things would have been a lot different. They could have been so good." She caressed her little boy's hair with quick, nervous strokes. "Hardly a day went by that I didn't think of you, wonder what happened to you. I didn't ever expect to see you in this town again after . . ."

Kieran looked away, stalling for time to remember. "I've been moving around a lot."

"That was always your way, wasn't it?" Her hard smile returned, brittle with a wealth of pain. "I see you're traveling with someone now."

Kieran glanced toward the phone booth. He could no longer hear Alexandra's voice, and she had left the booth.

"I can't blame you," Lori continued. "You'd have been crazy to come back here after they drove you out. Crazy to come back to someone like me." She tossed back her hair. "But the two months you were here meant something to me. You understood better than anyone." She swallowed visibly. "I'm glad you made it, Kieran. I really am."

Made it. Kieran closed his eyes, trying to summon up the past. "How are things with you now, Lori?"

"You really want to know?" she asked, her voice bleak. "I wish I could tell you that things are different. That I'd been smart. But I wasn't." She shrugged. "You told me to go, but I didn't. And then I found out I was carrying Kevin. I didn't know what to do after the fight, after you left town. So I stayed." She looked at him through heavily caked lashes, eyes glistening. "But you don't need to hear my problems. You did what you could and got into trouble for it, and I didn't listen."

Kieran felt the memories begin to come. "I left you," he said heavily.

"You didn't have any choice." Lori held his gaze. "They were all Jerry's friends. They ran you out of town, and they would have killed you if they'd had the chance." She scrubbed her hand across her eyes again. "You made it. That's all that matters."

"What happened to you . . . when I was gone?"

She looked away quickly, and her hands gathered up the loose fabric of Kevin's jacket. Her little boy turned and hugged his mother's legs.

Without a word Kieran stepped toward Lori and touched her chin, drawing her gaze back to his.

"Jerry hurt you again."

"Yeah, you could say that." She leaned into his palm. "He was pissed off. And I was too scared to leave."

Jerry, Lori's husband. Images were filling Kieran's mind at last: this nondescript Saskatchewan town on the side of the road; a darkened bar, loud voices, violent conflict. Just like in Merritt. One of the places he'd remembered as a vague dream, a place he'd passed through on the way to nowhere.

But there had been someone here. Someone he'd known. Cared for. Someone to make him stay for a time.

And an enemy. Lori's husband, whom he'd fought because of her.

And failed. Somehow, he had failed.

Kieran dropped into a crouch before the solemn little boy. "This is your son."

"Kevin." All the harshness had left her voice. "I wanted to name him after you, but I knew Jerry would take it the wrong way."

Kieran felt his muscles clench. *I wanted to name him after you.* The child was about five years old, with black hair. A handsome little boy.

He offered his hand to the child. Kevin pushed back against his mother's legs, eyes still wide and wary.

"He's shy," Lori said. "Don't take it the wrong way."

Kieran looked up, his heart like a stone in his chest. "Is he mine?"

She was long in answering. In the brittle silence Kieran knew it was possible. More than possible. He had known Lori—well enough. Found in her an outsider like himself, an antidote to his own formless hunger. He'd lingered in this town, listened to her problems. Comforted her in the only ways he knew.

He might even have loved her . . .

"I wanted him to be," she whispered. "More than anything in my life."

Kieran dropped his hand between his knees and looked up at her. "Lori . . ."

"It's over now, isn't it?" she said suddenly, all the harsh bitterness back in place. "If you'd ever given a damn about me, you could have sent a letter. Something. But I guess that was too much to expect." She jerked her head toward the store. "You've got your life, and I've got mine. I've got plans now. I don't need your help anymore." She grabbed Kevin's hand and pulled him with her. "I was just on my way out anyway."

She began to walk rapidly across the parking lot. When she got to the edge of the highway she looked around almost wildly, swayed, and stumbled.

Kieran caught up to her in a second. She tossed him a look of shaky bravado. "Got a cigarette? I haven't had one in hours." She stared down the street. "My ride should be here any minute—"

"Lori." He caught her arm and held on. "What are you doing here? Where are you going?"

She laughed hoarsely. "Leaving town. A friend should be here any time to pick me up. I'm going to my sister's in Calgary—oh, damn it to hell." She dropped into an awkward crouch, pulling Kevin into her arms. "My ride never showed up. We've been here all day waiting. That bitch. I should never have trusted her." She covered her eyes with a trembling hand. "I finally decided to do it, Kieran. I'm leaving Jerry. And if I don't get out of here fast, I don't know what he's going to do." She looked up, dark streaks of mascara running from the corners of her eyes. "It's Kevin I'm worried about. If it was just me . . ."

He stopped her with a brush of his fingers across her lips. "You need a ride out of town? That's the way we're going."

Hope flickered in her eyes. "You offering me a ride, Kieran Holt?"

"Yes," he said. He touched her arm, and she turned to clasp his hand.

"And your girlfriend?"

He thought briefly of Alexandra, not bothering to correct Lori's assumption of their relationship. Alexandra would want to help. She had that kind of heart.

"She'll be glad to help you."

Lori's mouth twisted. "Yeah. I'll just bet she will." She sighed heavily. "I don't know why you showed up here when you did, Kieran. If you were alone, I'd call it fate. And I'd have . . . tried—" She touched his cheek. "We were good together, Kieran. And I've never stopped loving—"

"Kieran?"

He twisted around at the sound of Alexandra's voice. She stood a few feet away, red hair wind-tossed, her arms folded across her chest.

He met Alexandra's gaze and saw confusion in it. Confusion and that same wary distance she'd put between them since they'd left Minnesota.

Distance that protected them both.

"Alexandra," he said. Lori leaned against him, and he resisted the urge to push her gently away.

"Alexandra," he repeated, "this is Lori Carstens. An . . . old friend of mine."

She hesitated only a moment before extending her hand. "Glad to meet you, Lori."

Lori smiled, a compression of her red lips that thinned her gaunt face even further. She touched Alex's hand lightly and released it. "Hi." She swayed a little; a shudder ran through her body. "Sorry. I'm just a little tired. I haven't had much to eat today."

"I'm sorry," Alexandra said. She glanced at Kevin. "You don't look well. Maybe you should sit down. There's a bench in the lady's room—"

"Alexandra," Kieran said, "Lori needs our help. She was expecting a ride to Calgary, but it never showed up. She's stranded here. I told her since we were headed that way, we'd take her as far as we can."

Alexandra offered no protest, demanded no explanations. She moved to Lori's other side and took her arm. "Come on. You and your son can sit down in the back of the truck while Kieran and I take care of a few last minute things. Okay?"

Lori flung a glance at Kieran and nodded. "If it's really all right . . ."

"Of course it is." Alexandra said. She and Kieran guided Lori to the truck, and Alexandra made a comfortable spot in the back seat, smiling at Kevin and talking softly to Lori until both were settled. Only then did she turn back to Kieran, leading him away until the row of gas pumps was between them and the truck.

Her features were drawn, her eyes narrowed with weariness. All thoughts of Lori vanished from Kieran's mind. He wanted to touch Alexandra's face, to smooth the lines from between her brows, knowing that he had put them there.

But she made it almost easy for him not to touch her. If he looked at her too long, or moved too close, she always flinched away. And kept her distance, as she did now, standing before him with her hands clasped behind her back, walled off from him utterly.

"Who is she, Kieran?" she asked.

"I think she's the reason I needed to come to this place," he said. "She's a part of my past."

Alex wanted very badly to lean against the gasoline pump, to let the strength seep out and give up the attempt to hold herself together. But she straightened, aware of the woman and child behind her, and met Kieran's steady gaze.

"Then more of your memories are coming back."

"Not many." His eyes flicked away to the truck behind her. "I think when I decided to stop here, I was remembering Lori. But not clearly. Only that there was something here . . . part of something I hadn't finished."

Hadn't finished. A strange way of putting it. Alex thought of the woman who had appeared so suddenly out of the blue. She was pretty, in a hard-edged way; she wore heavy eye makeup, lipstick that was too vivid against her pale skin. Her nails were long and brilliant red. Her clothing smelled of cigarette smoke. Her overall appearance had a certain cheapness to it, as if—

Stop it, Alex. Just what are you trying to prove?

"How did you know her, Kieran?"

For the first time Kieran looked away. He didn't want to talk about it; she saw that in the tightly confined restlessness in his lithe body, like that of a wolf on the edge of flight.

"It's come back slowly, in fragments," he said with obvious reluctance. "I knew her six years ago, when I passed through this way before. You remember I told you I was a wanderer." He smiled without humor. "I don't know why I stopped in this town. I got some kind of work with a farmer. I spent my time off in the local bar."

A bar. Kieran had said he'd frequented bars. Alex shivered and hugged herself. "And that's where you met her."

He nodded, his smile fading into bleakness. "Somehow we got to talking. She started telling me about her life, and I listened. It wasn't a good life she had. Her husband . . . beat her up. Frequently."

Alex felt her face heat with shame for thinking a single uncharitable thought about Lori Carstens.

"I remember that I was angry about what she told me. I think I must have offered to take her away with me. She wouldn't come. I know I hated her husband for what he'd done to her"

And Kieran's hatred would be a formidable thing. Alex remembered when he'd confronted Howie in the café, and Peter in front of the bar in Merritt. In defense of someone he cared about . . .

She refused to think further. "Something happened, didn't it?" she asked softly. "What did you do, Kieran?"

Kieran no longer seemed to see her. "Lori didn't want me to talk to her husband. But she needed me. We kept meeting in the bar, and . . . other places, when we could. Her husband found out about it, and one night he came for her."

Alex could see the scene all too clearly. "You fought him," she said, praying that was all it had been.

"I warned him off," Kieran amended. "He wouldn't back down. He started hitting her, and I . . . attacked him."

Alex closed her eyes. "Did you—"

"I didn't change," Kieran said harshly. "I'd been drinking. But I injured him. Maybe I almost killed him. I don't remember. All I know is that I wanted him to suffer the way Lori had suffered. But then his friends came after me. There were too many of them. They took me out of the bar, and—" He broke off, and met her gaze again. "I ran, Alexandra. That's all I know. I left her there and ran—"

"Because they almost killed you," Lori said. "They would have if you'd stayed." She walked around the gas pumps and stood halfway between Alex and Kieran, but her eyes were all for him. "He's the last man who'd ever run from a fight." She glanced at Alex. "You'd know that."

"She knows it," Kieran said, his mouth a grim line. "Alexandra, Lori is leaving her husband. That's why she needs to get out of town."

"If it's not too much trouble," Lori put in. But there was no real reticence in her face or voice. She smiled at Kieran. "I don't know what I'd have done—"

"We'll be ready to leave in a minute," Alex said quickly. "You said you hadn't eaten all day. Here." She rummaged in her waist pack and pulled some bills out of one of the compartments. "Go get yourself and Kevin something to eat, for now. We have more stuff in the car."

Lori took the money, but it was to Kieran she looked again before she turned to go. Kieran's gaze followed her, a deep crease between his brows.

"Does she know what you are?" Alex asked.

His eyes flashed back to hers. "No," he said. "No one else has ever known."

Except me, she finished for him. *And Julie's family.* She felt the rekindling of warmth in her heart.

"There may be risks, Kieran."

"I don't care about risks," he said. "Not when someone . . . needs my help."

"You're obviously quite a hero to her," Alex said. "And with good reason. It sounds like you were the only one to ever defend her."

"I failed."

"You said you tried to get her to leave her husband, to go with you. It wasn't your fault that she chose not to."

"I forgot about her," he said bleakly.

"You forgot most of your *life*." She hesitated. "Do you think this is what's been pulling you northwest, Kieran?"

His brows came together in concentration. "No. It was something along the way, but . . " He paused, as if at a loss for words. "I still feel something there." He looked northwest. Toward British Columbia. Maybe toward the mysterious place Julie had told her about with so little explanation.

"Does the name Lovell mean anything to you?" she asked.

"No. Should it?"

She looked toward the store. Lori and Kevin were emerging, Kevin with his mouth half full of a sandwich. "Never mind. We'll have time to discuss it later, once we've taken care of Lori." She sighed. "Calgary is northwest, but it's still a good four hundred miles from here."

They stared at each other. Alex felt almost as if he were caressing her face with his eyes as he might with his hands. She jerked away. Her feet seemed bent on tripping over themselves as she went back to the truck.

"I want to thank you for this," Lori said, meeting her by the gas pumps. "You don't even know me, and—"

"No need," Alex said. "We're going that way ourselves. Plenty of room in back for both of you to get some rest while we drive."

Lori brushed her little boy's cheek. "He's drooping on his feet," she said. "It's hard on him. . . ."

Kieran appeared and scooped Kevin up into his arms. The boy didn't so much as whimper a protest at being handled by a stranger; he snuggled into Kieran's shoulder.

"You're good with him," Lori said.

Lori was right. Kieran looked complete with a child in his arms. Just as he had with Julie's nieces and nephews.

Alex turned her attention to the supplies that needed rearranging in the back of the truck. She was thinking crazy thoughts, none of which were helpful at the moment. "We'd probably better get going."

Lori accepted Kevin back from Kieran. The two of them shared a long look as they held the child between them; their hands brushed in the transfer. With visible reluctance Lori took Kevin and settled him in the back of the truck. After a moment she scooted back to the edge of the seat, worrying her lower lip between her teeth.

"Hey, Kieran," she said. "Did your friend ever catch up with you?"

Out of the corner of her eye Alex saw Kieran go very still. "My friend?"

"An older man. A month or so after you left town, he came by. He was asking around the bar, looking for you. He wasn't from around here, though. He said he'd known your parents."

The silence was almost tangible. Kieran looked at Alex, his face like a mask.

"What was his name?" Kieran asked.

"He never gave it."

Kieran stared northwest, withdrawing into himself. Alex frowned. A man who'd known Kieran's parents. There was something here she ought to understand, something teasing the back of her mind. "We can talk about this while we drive," she said. "Kieran—"

But he was already sliding into the passenger seat. The tension in his body seemed to vibrate through the truck. Alex took her own seat and glanced in the rearview mirror. At least Lori didn't seem concerned by Kieran's silence. Just as she couldn't be aware of the inhuman nature that drove him.

Alex was still the only person within five hundred miles who knew that secret.

"I heard on the radio that there may be bad weather

up ahead," she said briskly as she started the engine. "We'll drive as long as we can. Don't worry, Lori, we'll get you and Kevin safely to Calgary."

 $\mathscr{A}$ lex gunned the motor again as Kieran pushed the truck from behind, wind-driven snow whipping around them in a blinding mass of white.

"So much for four-wheel drives," Alex muttered. The truck settled back into the ditch, stubbornly uncooperative.

Kieran's head emerged next to her window. "We'll have to keep trying," he said. His hair was soaked with snow melted by his exertions, and his breath rolled away from his face in long, ragged plumes. "How are Lori and the boy?"

"Don't worry about us," Lori said from the back. "Kevin's still sleeping. It would take more than this to wake him up."

Lori was being very calm, Alex thought. It had been Alex's lapse in judgment that got them into the ditch, and Lori hadn't made a single complaint. Five hours of driving behind them, near midnight, freezing cold, and in the middle of nowhere, but Lori had probably suffered far worse.

And Kieran, at least, was immune to the weather. He stood in the middle of nature's worst and claimed it for his own like some elemental god, black hair lashing in the wind.

He was beautiful.

A handful of snow crystals blew through the gap in the window, bringing her back to reality. "All right," she said. "We'll try again."

Kieran nodded and circled back to the rear of the truck. Alex adjusted the rearview mirror to watch as he braced himself and prepared to push.

Light caught at the edge of her vision. The truck rocked once and stopped. Kieran vanished.

Headlights. She was seeing headlights, coming along the road from behind.

She shut off the engine and waited as the car drew up alongside them. Four letters were clearly stenciled on the side of the vehicle: RCMP. Royal Canadian Mounted Police. The provincial equivalent of local police and highway patrol.

Her heart performed the cliché of stopping for several seconds. She looked frantically in the mirror for Kieran, but he was still out of sight.

The officer made his way from his car to the truck, wielding a flashlight, hat pulled low and coat buttoned high. Alex pulled her own muffler farther up and rolled the window back down a crack.

"You okay, ma'am?" the officer said, peering into the car. The flashlight beam washed over Lori and Kevin and settled at the level of Alex's waist. "Looks like you got a bit stuck here."

"My fault," Alex quipped, managing a smile. "I'd hoped to make it to the next town and pushed a little too far for this kind of weather."

He nodded with a grimace of sympathy. "Happens to the best of us. You're from the States, are you?"

He'd have seen her plates, so there was no point in denying it. "Yes." She nodded toward Lori. "Visiting friends."

She waited for him to make some comment that would reveal he had suspicions, or recognized her, but he only nodded again and glanced back at his car. "Well, it's a good thing I came along. I'm just going home myself. I know there's a motel about four kilometers down the road. I'll get you out of here and take you by."

Alex clenched her teeth together to keep them from chattering. "I'd appreciate that, Officer."

"My pleasure, ma'am. Just let me get set up here." He touched the brim of his hat and walked back to his car.

Kieran, where are you? Alex leaned across the passenger's seat and stared out the window. He'd been right to hide, but Lori was sure to start wondering where he'd gone.

"What happened to Kieran?" Lori asked, leaning forward. "I don't see him."

Damn, and damn. "He's probably talking to the officer right now," she lied quickly, smiling at Lori. "We'll be out of here in no time."

Alex turned back to watching the officer, who was rummaging in his trunk. Thank God for the poor visibility. Alex couldn't see any farther than the near side of the Mountie's vehicle, and Kieran would be invisible only a few yards away. . . .

"Oh, my God," Lori gasped. "Oh, my God."

Alex whipped around in her seat. She caught only a glimpse of Kieran standing naked in the wind, his clothing pooled about his feet, before he began to blur. And shifted, in full view of Lori. For a moment he stood, blackness framed by white, and then dashed away.

Lori leaned back in her seat, face drained of color. Alex reached for her hand.

"Lori, listen to me. Are you all right?"

Her mouth worked. "I saw . . . I saw—"

Alex had no time to press further. The Mountie was coming back toward the truck, and she could only pray Lori was too shocked to make a scene.

Lousy timing, Kieran, she thought. Her eyes began to water. *I hope to God you can track us, because I can't wait for you now.*

~ 15

He stood shivering in front of the motel room door, naked and bathed in sweat. Very gently he set his knuckles against the wood, rapping once and then again.

The door revealed a slender crack of light. "Kieran?" Alexandra whispered. And then he had only a moment to step out of the way before she flung the door open and stepped over the threshold and into his arms.

"Kieran," she said shakily, "you scared the hell out of me."

The words were familiar and beloved. Her scent filled him like music. For a moment he simply held her, the blood singing in his veins, warming him beyond the need of any other heat. For a moment he allowed himself to believe that she came to him with more than relief, more than friendship defined by her stubborn sense of duty and the promise she had once made him.

For a moment he wondered if he could trust himself.

Alexandra stepped back. "For God's sake, come in!" She pulled him into the room, shut the door, and braced herself against it.

"What happened?" she demanded.

He hardly knew the answer himself. One moment he'd

been watching the officer, the next he'd been stripping off his clothes, blinded by images of capture and confinement. "I panicked," he admitted.

She closed her eyes and let out a long, heavy sigh. "I can understand that. I was pretty nervous myself." She pushed away from the door and sat on the edge of the bed. "It didn't take you long to find us."

Kieran glanced around the room. It was very spare and modest, with a single bed and two chairs and a table. Above the dresser was a mirror, draped awkwardly with Alexandra's coat and a sweatshirt, almost as if she had intended to cover the glass. She had already laid a spare set of his clothes over one of the chairs.

"I didn't lose all my reason," he said, tugging on his jeans. "As soon as you and the Mountie pulled out, I followed the road." *And your scent.* He shrugged into a plaid shirt and let it hang open, allowing his body to cool. "I left you to deal with the police alone," he said heavily.

She shrugged with indifference he knew she didn't feel. "It was better for you to be gone. The officer didn't seem to know or suspect anything. He dropped us off here and headed on home, so we're still safe." Her gaze dropped to her laced fingers. "But there is a problem."

"Lori," he said.

Alexandra looked up without meeting his eyes. "She saw you shift, Kieran."

He sat down in the nearest chair. "How did she react?"

"She was . . . pretty shocked, of course—" Alexandra broke off, swallowing. "I put her in the next room. She's been very quiet since it happened. She's obviously learned how to keep her feelings locked away. I think she believes what she saw, but she won't talk to me. She's terrified."

Of course she was terrified. Alexandra had been afraid of Kieran in the beginning, and she'd had some reason to accept that a creature such as himself could exist. Julie's family was another exception. But Lori would be like the rest of mankind, unable to look upon what he was with anything but fear and loathing.

And the Voice, which had been silent for so long, emerged to taunt him: *What will you do now, boy?*

He rose slowly. "I'll talk to her."

Alexandra shook her head. "I don't think that's wise, Kieran."

"I have to."

She hunched her shoulders in surrender. There was uncertainty in her eyes. "Maybe. . . She trusted you before, Kieran. You were the only one to stand up for her all those years ago. Maybe that will give her a way to accept."

"And Kevin?"

"He seems okay. Maybe he didn't see what happened."

Kieran's hands were a little shaky as he began to button up his shirt.

"Here. Let me." Alexandra finished for him, the tips of her fingers brushing his chest. He worked very hard to keep his body calm, though it was no longer entirely the prospect of facing Lori that affected him.

Alexandra handed him a key. "I got an extra one to Lori's room. Kieran . . . be careful."

He'd left his boots behind at the side of the road when he shifted, so it was on bare, noiseless feet that he went to Lori's room. No one responded to his knock. He used the key and eased the door open.

The room was identical to Alexandra's, unnaturally quiet. Lori lay on the bed, Kevin fast asleep at her side. She turned her head on the pillow and looked at him, blank-eyed, without recognition.

"Lori?"

She stirred. "Kieran?" She looked around the room as if he were invisible. "Kieran, is that you?"

He risked touching her then, hoping to penetrate her strange detachment. Her reaction stunned him. With a sharp gasp, she flung herself away and stumbled into the corner of the bed. Kevin opened his eyes and sat up.

"Mama?"

Lori scrambled across the bed, putting herself between Kieran and her son.

"Stay away!" she cried, her voice high and thin.

He kept himself perfectly still, washed in waves of sickness. Her brown eyes held accusation and trial and punishment, condemning what he was.

"Lori—"

"What *are* you?" she demanded hoarsely. She scooted closer to Kevin and wrapped him in her arms. "I saw you . . . you aren't human!"

He couldn't protest when she spoke only the truth. "I would never hurt you, Lori."

But she didn't hear him. She was as lost in her terror as he had been when he saw the Mountie, irrational with it, transformed by it. "You touched me," she said in a sickly whisper. "You're some kind of . . . monster. Oh, God—" She slid down against the wall. "Go away." Her voice rose to a shriek. "Go away!"

What now? he thought bitterly. Any further attempts to speak with Lori would be pointless. She was beyond the reach of words.

He looked at Kevin, searching for fear in the little boy's eyes. But Kevin regarded him with solemn puzzlement, glancing up at his mother's ravaged face as if trying to make sense of the bizarre exchange.

Kieran retreated, banging into a chair as he reached for the doorknob. Kevin continued to stare until the door was shut between them.

He leaned hard against the door and breathed in the clean air of freedom. The night was very tempting. The snow had stopped. Kieran looked up; a tiny patch of clear sky was visible through the clouds, dotted with stars.

Lori could not accept what she'd seen, what he was. No hope of making her understand. And there was always the risk that she'd go to the police.

He drove that thought from his mind, walked the few paces to Alexandra's room, and went in.

"It was bad, wasn't it?" she asked, rising from the bed.

He stayed by the door, as far from Alexandra as he

could get. "You were right. She would never accept. She thinks I'm some sort of monster."

Her footsteps were hesitant behind him. "You're not a monster, Kieran." She came close enough that he could feel the heat of her body, hear the slight catch in her breath." You helped Lori . . . before and tonight . . ."

"Did I?"

Her fingertips brushed his arm, and he closed his eyes at the miracle of that touch. "You tried." Her hand trembled. "Did you love her, Kieran?"

The question hung in the air like something tangible, weighted with unspoken words and emotions he couldn't name. He gave her what honesty he could.

"If I did," he said, "it's gone now."

"Because of what she said?"

He shook his head. "Long before."

She held his gaze. "Is Kevin your son?"

"No."

"But he could have been," she whispered.

For that he had no answer. Alexandra turned away. She sat down on the edge of the bed. "Funny thing about the past," she said in a monotone. "It comes back to haunt you, whether you remember it or not." She clasped her hands in her lap, twisting her fingers. "There are so many things we still don't know about your past. Lori is just a small part of it. Until we find the rest—"

"It doesn't matter," he said. "What happened with Lori is just . . . more proof. Like what happened in Merritt. I don't belong in the human world."

Suddenly all the old fire was in her eyes. "What happened to you that you can believe such things about yourself? Who told you that you were some kind of freak who shouldn't exist?"

He could still flinch at that, even now. He listened for the Voice. He had never told Alexandra about it, except what it had named him. *Monster.* Just as Lori had. But the Voice had no comment; even the call from the northwest was silent.

"You *helped* Lori," Alexandra said. "And back in

Merritt, you saved Tracy. There were probably others, many others." All at once she knelt before him, her hands lifting, reaching, catching his own hands like fire contained in flesh. She went very still, as if she were startled by her own impulsiveness.

"Lori—" She swallowed, and her voice dropped very low. "It's obvious that Lori loved you, Kieran."

Kieran eased his hands free of hers. "Maybe she did, in her way. But if she loved me," he said hoarsely, touching his chest, "it was only *this* part. Until she saw everything I am. Until she knew the truth."

"That isn't real love."

"Then what is?"

Alexandra blinked, shielding her eyes with her lashes, leaving her hands in midair where he'd abandoned them.

"Most of the world is like Lori," he said. "Isn't it, Alexandra?"

Once again she didn't argue. Not in words. But she brushed his hand with her slender fingers—hesitantly, gently, tenderly, so lightly that she had recaptured his hand before he could think to resist.

"You're not alone, Kieran."

His breath came thick and rough. He knew he should get up and walk away. They were too close. Once all he'd dreamed of was being able to touch her, have her touch him as she did now. Now he wanted more. Expected more than she would ever willingly give.

But he couldn't work his hand free; she'd twined her fingers between his and held on with tenacious strength. "You're not alone," she repeated. "You said yourself that you sensed others like you. Somewhere." She stared at their interlaced hands. "I promised to help you until you find all your answers. We *will* find them, Kieran."

His pulse stuttered and resumed a faster beat. "Alexandra," he sighed. He'd meant it as a warning, but it emerged an endearment.

Her eyes lifted back to his, startled and wary. But he found himself gazing at her lips, the curve of her cheek, the push of her breasts against her shirt. Her scent rose to him, warm and enticing.

It was no longer merely his heartbeat that reacted to her nearness. His groin stirred, filled, went rigid with the need to possess her. Possess, overwhelm, devour, consume utterly. His emotions were the beast within him, driving inevitably toward release.

The beast. He felt the change wake, responding to feelings he couldn't control.

Nausea pounded in his belly. Without warning he lifted Alexandra to her feet and thrust her back, letting her go when her legs hit the bed. She stared at him, anger and humiliation radiating from her like waves of shimmering heat.

And Kieran *knew,* with a blinding flash of insight, everything that was inside her. She thought herself rejected, her offer of help reviled.

She saw in *his* eyes what he'd seen in Lori's.

"Alexandra," he said, starting toward her. "Don't. It's not you. It's me." He struggled to find words that could reach her. "I—can't let you get too close. I don't trust myself."

Still she looked through him, her face pale and her body trembling. "Because you still think you might have killed Peter?" She laughed. "Do you want to know something, Kieran? *I* could have killed him." Her eyes grew dark with horror. "There was a moment when I was glad Peter was dead. When I saw him again, when I realized why he'd come back, that he was trying to make me believe he still loved me, I hated him. I *hated* him."

Kieran broke his paralysis and strode to her, taking her shoulders in his hands, touching her as much as he dared. He had thought only of himself, his own pain, and Alexandra had suffered far worse. Losing her father, and then her former lover, to a terrible death—forced to go on the run to fulfill her obligation to him . . .

"Alexandra," he said. "It wasn't your doing."

She raised her head. "I did love him once. Once he was the world to me, when he was the only one who didn't turn his back. He never deserved—" She swallowed several times, set herself stiff and straight on the bed. "You asked me after the murder . . . why I would warn Peter's possible killer." Her eyelids trembled. "I felt so little when he died. I still feel . . . numb. But it's as if my wish to make him go away did something, caused something. There's something wrong with me, that I can't feel *more*—"

"There is nothing wrong with you, Alexandra," he said harshly, shaking her. She flopped like a doll. He turned her around to face him. "Too much has happened. You need time."

But she seemed not to hear him at all. "It wasn't only Peter I hated," she whispered. "I hated my father, almost as much as he hated me. I *thought* he hated me. And now they're both dead. And my mother . . ."

Her mother. The one she spoke to in the journal she kept so close. Kieran damned the risk and pulled Alexandra to his chest, cradling her head against the hollow of his shoulder.

"It's all connected," she said into his shirt. "All the same. My fault. *My* hatred . . . it might as well have killed Peter. And my father. My mother died because of me."

"You didn't hate your mother," Kieran said, stroking her hair.

Her voice came muffled and small. "I loved her. But it was still my fault that she died." The words came halting and fragmented, pulled out of the very depths of her. "We were driving by the ocean that day. It was only a month after I'd come back from my grandparents'. My parents were arguing about whether I should come back to Minnesota. Father didn't want me to go again. I was begging Mother, and they were shouting . . ." Her fingers worked spasmodically at the cloth of Kieran's shirt. "I don't know how it happened. Father was yelling. He turned around to yell at me, and suddenly there was another car coming toward us, and we were swerving, and falling, rolling over and over."

Kieran stroked her hair. "Alexandra."

"Father was . . . thrown clear. I was trapped. Mother

was bleeding everywhere. She got me out, and then she told me to run, but she fell unconscious." Alexandra's fingers dug hard into Kieran's back. "I promised to save her. I tried to pull her out. But there was a fire, and I was afraid. I ran, and it exploded . . ."

Her pain was his, her horror. "I *promised* to save her," Alexandra whispered. "I couldn't do it."

And he understood, at last, her obsession with promises. Her stubborn determination to keep her promise to help *him*.

"Your father survived," he said softly. "And he blamed you for your mother's death."

Bald words, but he knew they must be true. She pulled back and looked up for the first time. Her face was strangely still, eyes unfocused, calm water over a turbulent current.

"That's why he never wanted me around, avoided me and sent me away when he could. I came to believe he was right. It seemed everyone and everything in my world changed, grew away from me. Only Peter . . . stayed the same. He was all I had, and I was grateful."

"Until the argument with your father," he said, remembering.

With careful deliberation Alexandra disentangled herself from Kieran's hold and walked with halting steps across the room.

"I told you my father came to my college graduation ceremony. I tried to talk to him. Too many feelings had built up for too long, and we argued. That was when he said—he told me—he hated the sight of me."

Her buried grief was so intense that Kieran wondered how any being could bear it. All these years this had tormented her, a history far worse for being remembered than his forgotten past could possibly be.

Her back was rigid. "He was right. He was right to hate me. The argument in the car, the accident that killed my mother. . . they were my fault. And I didn't keep my promise."

"You were only a child!"

"All my father knew was that my mother was gone, and I was still here. After that day, I . . . didn't want anything from my father. Not his money. I told him that. I thought Peter and I would marry and I could forget. But Peter—"

"Abandoned you because you wouldn't take your father's money any longer."

She shook her head, but not in denial. "He was honest, at least. I should have given him credit for that." She broke off, and her arms came up to hug herself, as if that were the only comfort she could ever expect. "I should have understood my father better. He lost so much, and I was only a reminder. I should have tried again. We were the only family left."

Kieran began moving toward her, as delicately as a stalking hunter. "I'm sorry, Alexandra."

Her head came up in a wild, sharp gesture. "I hated them both. And now they're dead." She turned to face him. "You think there's something wrong with you. Look at me!" Her eyes were fever-bright, unnaturally dry. "Peter . . . Father . . . they were right. *I'm* something that shouldn't exist."

He wasted no more time but closed the space between them, capturing her again. "You're wrong," he said fiercely. And then, when she only stared at him, he moved his hands to cup her face. "Alexandra. Oh, Alexandra."

She shuddered and closed her eyes. "Don't," she gasped.

He refused to accept her denial. She *needed* his touch, as he needed to touch her. He rested his thumb lightly on her cheekbone and stroked her skin with utmost gentleness.

Her eyes focused on his, filled with fear, wide with vulnerability. "My scar," she whispered. "Please, don't."

Kieran studied her face. The skin under his palm was slightly rough, different in texture from her other cheek. He had never thought anything of it, because it was part of her. "I don't understand."

"The explosion," she said harshly. "They couldn't fix

it all." She tossed her head from one side to the other, trying to shake him loose. "It's ugly. *I'm* ugly—"

He caught her face between his hands and pressed his lips to the roughened skin.

"You are beautiful, Alexandra. I never saw this scar."

Her face grew stiff and cold. "Don't lie to me, Kieran. Not you." She stared at his chest, unseeing. "Do you know what Peter told me, the day we had the argument about my father's money? He told me I was lucky to have him, that no other man would ever be able to overlook *this*." She put her hand to her face, fingers curled. "The ugliness—it's all . . . me . . ."

Kieran caught her hand and pulled it to her side, locked his arms around her and held her while she struggled like a frantic animal in a trap.

"Let me go! Damn you—" She flailed awkwardly, knocking her body against his. Gradually her movements weakened and slowed like a mechanical toy running down.

He smelled the tears before he heard the ragged change in her breathing. She tried to hold them back, leaning away from Kieran as if she could still escape.

"Stop it," she demanded in a whisper. He knew she was speaking to herself. "Stop it, stop it. I don't cry. I *never* cry."

But her protest dissolved into a long, low moan. She collapsed against him, boneless and limp, all defiance gone. Suddenly she was clinging to him as frantically as she had fought him moments before. She hugged his waist, fingers convulsing helplessly against his lower back.

As she wept, sucking air in long, racking sobs, Kieran felt a shifting between them, like the first subtle turning of winter to spring.

It was too tenuous, too new. He didn't dare hope. And yet he did; he hoped even as he told himself that nothing mattered but her happiness. He had no right to take comfort in her pain, in knowing that very pain made her turn to him at last.

Alexandra snuffled, smearing tears across his shoulder. When she looked up her gaze was stricken and unguarded.

Afraid of *his* condemnation. He barely stopped himself from kissing her trembling eyelids, licking the tears away. He could almost taste her on his tongue.

He curled his finger and brushed his knuckle across her cheek, catching moisture. She closed her eyes. "Please . . ."

"You believed what Peter and your father told you," he said, willing her to listen. "But they were wrong." Gently he turned her in his arms, half carried her to the mirror she had so awkwardly covered. Now he knew why she had done it.

He knocked the jacket aside. "Look, Alexandra."

"No—"

"Look."

And she obeyed, shaking, terrified. He held her from behind, cradling her jaw.

"See what you are, Alexandra."

She looked. He knew the very moment when she finally let herself *see*. Slowly, so slowly her expression changed from frozen expectation to amazement. She lifted one hand and touched her cheek.

"How long has it been since you looked in a mirror?" he asked.

"I . . . don't remember."

"Now you see. You aren't what you thought."

She ran her fingers over the slightly rough, slightly blotched skin of the scar. He saw it now through her eyes, saw how she had magnified it all out of proportion and punished herself with her belief in her own ugliness.

Her belief that no one could love her.

And he felt the release in her, felt the weight of years slip from her shoulders. She leaned back against him with complete trust, knowing he wouldn't let her fall.

"And . . . I'm the one you came to for help." She gave a rusty gurgle. "*Me*. Falling apart. So weak—"

"Strong," he corrected her, running his hands up and down her arms. "Stronger than you know." He looked over her head, at his own human face. "You've given me so much, Alexandra. If I'd been able to be with . . ."

She turned and looked up. And smiled, tremulously, with a warmth that made his heart stutter.

"In a way you were. My memories of Shadow kept me going. And even when I . . . put the dreams away, I still had my research. It gave me a purpose, something to care about. To love." She tugged gently at his shirt. "I owe that to you."

He closed his eyes. "You owe me nothing."

"I made a promise."

Her promise. Her damnable promise. The ache in his heart expanded to encompass his entire body.

She needed him. She turned to him at last, trusting. Yet still he wanted more, as if he didn't already have the world in his arms.

"Is that all that keeps you here?" he asked. "Your promise?"

She wedged her hands between them, her palms flat on his chest. Her gaze fled his. "I . . ."

He let her go and stepped back, but she caught his hand, digging her small, blunt nails into his skin. "Why did you leave that night at the cabin?" she whispered.

Now he was the one bereft of answers, but she wouldn't release him. "Why did you run when I let you have what you seemed to want?"

Was that how she saw it, a battle to be won or lost? And she'd thought him the victor.

He met her gaze. "Because I wanted you too much."

"You . . . wanted me?"

"Yes."

She let him go, as he'd known she would. "You . . . I know about your needing to touch, to have physical contact. I should have accepted that from the beginning. The wolf in you—"

"It isn't the wolf," he rasped. "It's the man. It was always the man." He strode away so she couldn't see his expression. "I should have left you when we first crossed the border, but I couldn't do it. I'm a coward, Alexandra. I couldn't leave you."

Her footsteps whispered behind him. "I'm glad, Kieran. So glad."

The tension in his body sang like a scream along his nerves. "Do you remember when I kissed you?"

"Yes." Her voice was so faint, so hesitant.

"Did you like any of it, Alexandra?"

She laughed, hardly more than a breath of air. "Like it? Oh, God."

He turned halfway, heart near the top of his throat. She took one step toward him, and then another, until she was facing him again. She lifted her hand, stroked the tips of her fingers along his jaw. "I fought it. I was terrified. Terrified by what was happening to *me*. Because when I started seeing you as a man, I was afraid you'd see—"

"See you as you are," he finished huskily. "But I always did, Alexandra."

Her gaze dropped. "I wanted something I didn't think I deserved," she whispered. "I wanted you, Kieran."

He went still, disbelieving. "Why? Why would you want a creature that isn't even human?"

She grabbed him by the shoulders and pulled him around to face the mirror's unwavering stare. "*Look.* See what I see. You're beautiful, Kieran." Her gaze met his in reflection, bright and clear and true. "You were right that night, when you said I was afraid of you. All the time I was trying to mold you into something safe, a creature I could control. And yet you were so much more than I imagined. I was scared that I was losing myself and the life I'd made. Scared of my past, and most of all myself. But I can't let my fears rule me anymore."

"Sometimes fears have a purpose," he said hoarsely.

"And sometimes they force us to look in the mirror." She turned to catch and hold his face between her small hands. "When I look at you, I see myself. Not myself as I've always thought I was. But . . . myself as I want to be."

Her voice was low with wonder, with joy, with emotions he could hardly compass. "You said before you were a coward because you couldn't leave me. Well, that makes two of us." She smiled crookedly. "It's damned lonely being a coward by yourself. I think we'd better stick together, Kieran. You and I."

Her eyes were brilliant with tears and courage and conviction. Her lips parted. And she reached up, buried her hands in his hair and pulled his mouth to hers.

Her kiss was almost wild, conveying all the turmoil he knew she felt. But it was real—achingly, deliriously real. Kieran wrapped his arms around her waist and lifted her, lost in his need and hers.

"If you . . . still want me . . ." She shivered and looked away. Even now, after all he'd said, she was afraid of rejection. From him.

"Yes," he said. "Yes, I want you."

She looked up, humbling him again with the naked emotion in her eyes. The need. The simple, gut-wrenching joy.

He lifted his hand and traced her lips with his finger, brushed her cheek with his knuckles, marveled in the sweet contours of her face. He touched the different texture of her scar, lingering deliberately on that part of herself she despised.

She flinched, but only for a moment. Her gazed fixed on his face with heartbreaking trust.

"Are you sure, Alexandra?"

"It's the only thing I *am* sure of."

"I don't deserve you," he murmured.

"The feeling is mutual," she said, covering his hand with her own. She bit her lip. "Are you going to . . . make me beg?"

"Never."

"Then love me, Kieran. Make love to me."

*H*is response was without pretense, tender and gentle and fierce all at once. Alex melted into him with a little flutter of surrender and release, let the last of her doubts slip away as he pulled her into his arms, lowered his head, and kissed her.

He explored her mouth as if it was the first time, hesitant at first, taking cues from her reaction. And when she parted her mouth, urging more, he accepted the invitation. His tongue slid along the inner rim of her lips, dipped inside, withdrew and thrust again.

Alex felt her body thrum, her nerves catch fire. She'd been envisioning this for days, even as she tried to ignore her own desire. But the reality far exceeded imagination. Or the memory of that night in the cabin.

This was what she'd been fighting so hard, this miracle: Kieran's heartbeat, the warmth of his skin, the gentle possessiveness of his embrace. He released her mouth and lifted her in his arms, holding her close, as if he could absorb her into himself. He nuzzled her neck, rubbed the slight roughness of his cheek against her jaw. She turned her head to kiss the corner of his mouth, and he groaned softly.

She knew what he needed as she knew herself. Skin on skin, the hard planes of his body fitted to hers. But he took only what she had offered him, leaving no part of her face and neck untouched: running his tongue along the curve of her ear, licking the hollow of her throat; worshiping her forehead and eyelids and chin with kisses, caressing the puckered skin of her scar without hesitation.

Alex responded with unbridled joy. She marveled at the textures of him, the hard planes so different from her own. She tasted the faint saltiness of his skin as he'd tasted her, using tongue and lips until his body quivered beneath her.

And there was another hardness, the blatant evidence of his desire for her pressed against her belly. It lay so close, nearly within her reach.

She hesitated for only an instant. Kieran drew back, taking her face between his hands. "If you're . . . ready . . ."

In answer she snared her fingers in his shirt and pulled him to his knees.

"I want to see you again, the way you first came to me," she said huskily. "All of you."

He dropped his hands and watched her, unmoving. She escaped his gaze by kissing the base of his throat, feeling his rapid pulse beneath her lips while she unbuttoned his shirt. And he began to tremble as she slid her palms against his chest, pushing the shirt aside and back along his shoulders, tangling her fingers in his dark dusting of hair.

Alex had never wanted to give or take so much. She gloried in Kieran's harsh gasp when she pressed her mouth to his bare skin and found his nipple with her tongue. He threw back his head, praising her with the intensity of his response.

He was beautiful beyond any beauty she'd ever known. Sleek and powerful and perfect. And he wanted *her.*

"Alexandra," he murmured. He trapped her hands and folded her fingers inward, carried her fists to her lap. "I want to see *you.* I've never . . . seen you."

Naked. He'd never seen her naked, had only touched her bare skin that first morning before he even knew what or who he was. Suddenly her mouth went dry, and she couldn't meet his eyes.

"I've dreamed of you," he said. "Let me see you."

She looked up again. There was quiet strength in his eyes that reached out to her, wrapped like a caress around her fear and gentled it like a frightened animal. He had seen the worst of her already, and accepted.

He *wanted* her.

Slowly, holding his gaze, she reached for the buttons of her shirt. The edges parted. Kieran pulled her shirt back as she'd done his. His breath caught and hung suspended.

She closed her eyes. She wanted this moment to last forever, ached with the anticipation of feeling his hands on her. His first light touch was no more than a grazing of his fingers across her breasts, but it unloosed a jolt of sheer erotic excitement unlike any she'd known could exist.

Instinctively she thrust against him. Yet he cupped her breasts with gentle reverence, as if she were a figurine made of porcelain, or a goddess to be worshiped. He ran his thumbs across her nipples, drawing them into taut, aching peaks.

He fit his hands to the shape of her, caressing and massaging until she whimpered with need. Need to feel his lips on her breasts, his tongue stroking her nipples, his mouth suckling with the same urgency that claimed her body.

"Kieran. Please."

He groaned and locked his hands around her waist. She felt herself lifted, felt his hot breath on her flesh an instant before he tasted her.

Nothing had prepared her for this. He pulled her into his mouth, rolled her nipple on his tongue. He arched her back across his arm, leaving her helpless and exposed to whatever he chose to take. And he took fully, granting no quarter to her vulnerability.

It was a vulnerability she had no wish to deny. His primitive male strength, his drive to claim her, only increased her excitement. Surrender to Kieran was more liberating than anger and denial had ever been. It was as if he suckled the very essence of herself, accepting back the courage she had taken from him.

Breast to chest, thigh to thigh, he kissed her again, laved her mouth and neck with long strokes of his tongue.

"The taste of you, Alexandra," he said. "I can't get enough."

Alex felt for the waistband of his jeans. "There's more, Kieran. So much more—"

The snap popped between her fingers, and Kieran went rigid as she slipped her fingers beneath. She followed the line of crisp hair that ran down from his chest, found him straining to be set free.

All at once it was reversed, and she held the power. The fundamental power of Kieran himself, hard and hot in her palm; the power of feeling his need and desire for her. The power of knowing she could make him feel what she felt.

The muscles of his torso stood out in hard relief when she stroked him, easing him from confinement. He accepted her caresses with naked pleasure, nostrils flared and lips parted. She caught his lower lip between her teeth and sucked in time to the movements of her hand.

Until he locked his fingers around her wrist and held her still.

"Not yet, Alexandra," he gasped. He slipped free and rose, stripping out of his jeans in one smooth motion, and she was faced with the full magnificence of him. Just as she'd first seen him in a time that seemed so long ago, unselfconscious in his nudity, flawless and undeniably virile.

Now she could revel in it. She reached for him again, but he stepped to the side and lifted her, growling as he took her lips. He thrust with his tongue as his fierce maleness pressed into her, and all she could think of was opening for him, laying herself bare until nothing remained hidden.

Kieran swept her up into his arms and carried her the few feet to the bed. Their fingers tangled around the zipper of her jeans; somehow she got free of her clothing. And then she was naked and beneath him as he knelt over her, devouring her with his eyes. He didn't so much as touch her with the tip of his finger, but she felt as if she had already been possessed.

Almost.

"I've dreamed, Alexandra," he whispered, "of touching your body like this." He placed his palms on either side of her face, drawing her hair out across the pillow with his fingers.

"Kieran," she sighed.

A kiss stilled her lips. He trailed others up the side of her face until every portion of the scar had been touched. She didn't protest, didn't deny what he told her in the most ancient of languages.

He caressed the delicate skin of her shoulders, followed the slope of her breasts. He ran his big hands over her, exploring every contour with focused concentration. He stroked her thighs with his knuckles until she was racked with shivers. She caught her lip between her teeth as his mouth traced the dip of her waist and the flare of her hips.

It was as if he had to know every part of her body, claim it as his own to make it real. He massaged the flatness of her belly. With fascination he discovered the red thicket of curls below. He stroked down with his finger, and Alex arched against him with a soft cry.

Pleasure. Pleasure such as she'd never known—that Peter had never even tried to give her. But Kieran drove all memories of Peter from her mind as he dipped deeper still, wet his fingers on her, massaged and stroked until she was flushed and gasping.

"The scent of you," he rasped. He lifted his fingers to his lips and tasted what she gave so freely. "The taste." Drawing away to kneel at the foot of the bed, he pulled her with him and set her legs to either side of his shoulders.

"Kieran." His name became a moan. He discovered with his tongue and lips the same territory his fingers had explored, but now the journey was one of ecstasy. He drank from her eagerly, greedily. Her breathing became labored and her hands worked into his hair, clutching and releasing again and again.

It was almost beyond bearing. She was ready for him, more than ready. Yet he tested her one last time, thrusting deep with his tongue as if he could consume every remaining drop.

Alex bucked against him, her hands dragging at his hair, pulling him up.

"Kieran . . . Now. Now . . ."

Bracing himself on his arms, he slid up the length of her. His eyes were liquid gold, hot and rich, gazing at her with naked desire. He was a force of nature: irresistible, potent, undeniable.

Her denials were long since vanished. He took her lips with sudden ferocity, positioning himself to thrust hard and hot into the center of her body.

And stopped. He went utterly still, head flung back, eyes squeezed shut. Sweat glistened on his forehead.

"Kieran?" Her fingers brushed his cheek, urgent and tender.

"I'm . . . afraid," he panted.

"Of what?"

"The beast is so close—"

Alex laced her fingers in his hair and pulled him down. "It's part of you, Kieran. I'm brave enough for both of us."

He groaned, a cry wrenched from his very heart, and plunged down, entering in one smooth stroke. She gasped and rose to meet him. And they danced: the mating dance, older than the forests and the prairies, the one instinct that made all creatures kin.

The joy drove out every shadow of the past. Her name came to her from his lips, transformed by his husky voice into something sublime. The name was beautiful. *She* was beautiful. With each thrust it was as if he left part of himself inside her, gave her his inherent perfection. Together they made a bond that went far beyond mere pleasure, far beyond dreams.

But the miracle wasn't finished. Not until Alex whimpered and arched against him one last time, her body convulsing around him, caressing him to his own climax. She held him tight as he rode out the last waves and lay panting above her.

He rolled onto his side and pulled her with him, cradling her with arms and legs and the steady exultation of his heartbeat.

Fairy tales are real, Alex thought, dazed with joy. She wanted to tell Kieran, but her throat was too filled up to make any sound.

So she let herself simply feel. All she wanted of the world was here. There was no yesterday, no tomorrow. Kieran had robbed her of her past and given her himself. That gift was worth any sacrifice.

Any sacrifice at all.

16

"I've talked to Lori, Kieran."

He turned away from the window, and she almost forgot what she was about to say. To look at him now, to feel freely and without denial, to see him look back without disgust, with hunger in his eyes—it was a miracle she'd never dreamed of having again. The light of early morning softened his features and glowed in his eyes, rivaling the sun itself.

"What did she say?" he asked. Calmly, now, with none of the self-recrimination he'd shown last night. As if their lovemaking had healed them both a little, somehow.

Alex went to him. "She won't travel any farther with us, Kieran. She's still too scared . . . not thinking clearly either, I suspect. She told me she'd called her sister in Calgary to come get her here, but her sister has to work and won't be able to make it until late evening. It looks as though it'll be another day's wait here, but"—she met his eyes—"I don't think we should leave until we know she's safely away with her sister."

She felt his caress, though he didn't touch her. "You're right. We must wait. I owe her that much." His gaze grew distant. "I wish I could help her . . ."

"I'm sorry, Kieran." She wrapped her arms around his waist and rested her head against his chest. "I'm afraid there's nothing you can do. She'll have to deal with this in her own way. At least her son seems all right. Children are pretty adaptable."

He stroked her hair, sending shivers down her back. "I should stay away from her, then," he said.

"I think that would be best. If you could find some safe place nearby to hide out until her sister comes, there would be less risk of Lori seeing you."

He set her back, smiling crookedly. "There are miles of prairie here. I think I can find some out-of-the-way place." Fire snapped in his eyes. "But if you came with me . . ."

"You know I can't. Someone needs to stay here with Lori. But I admit the prospect is tempting."

They indulged in a quick but thorough kiss. Last night had been no fantasy; it was the most real thing in the world.

"Well," she said at last, catching her breath, "we're running low on supplies, but you can take what's left, and my pack." She felt a sudden chill of foreboding. "I don't like the delay because of the police, but it can't be helped. At least I don't think anyone else saw you come to the motel last night. If you're careful, no one will see you leave. We'll have to hope luck is on our side." She grabbed his arms and shook him lightly. "For God's sake, Kieran, keep out of sight. And don't go too far. I don't think I could stand the worry."

Kieran said nothing. He didn't need to; his eloquent eyes spoke for him.

"There's still another problem," she said. She let him go and walked across the room, arms folded. "If Lori goes to the police with what she saw—"

"Would they believe her?"

"No." She turned again. "Not likely. I don't see that we have any choice except to hope no one would believe. It's possible she might hear that the police are after us, but—"

"It's a chance we'll have to take," he said simply.

Yes. It really was that simple. "One more thing," she said. "Do you remember when I mentioned a place called Lovell?"

He looked at her, one eyebrow lifted. "Yes. You asked me if it was familiar."

"Julie mentioned it on the phone yesterday. Said she'd gotten another one of her feelings, though I think she was holding something back. She told me she thought we should make for this particular town in British Columbia. She didn't say why."

Kieran frowned. "It's the right direction. And I trust Julie."

"So do I. Next time I talk to her I'll try to get more details about this feeling of hers." She gave him a lopsided grin. "I guess I'm still not used to all these . . . paranormal things that aren't so easily explained by science."

"Like werewolves?" he said, but there was no self-mockery in his tone. "After me, Julie should be easy to understand."

They gazed at each other until the slam of some other motel door snapped them out of it. Kieran glanced out the window one more time and let the curtain fall.

"I'll go, then," he said. He gathered up some small snacks and a few other items from the food box and filled her pack. "I'll stay away until just before dawn, to make sure Lori has left."

Alex wanted to argue, but maybe he was right. Better to avoid any potential complications.

"And I'll keep my eyes and ears open here." She thought quickly. "If you see a scrap of red material on the antenna of the truck, don't come back. It'll mean something's happened here, and it's not safe. I guess we'll have to play it by ear."

He smiled. "I do have very good hearing, Alexandra."

She managed a chuckle, but her smile faded as she watched him edge around the building and lope out onto the prairie, across the highway and away from the road.

The day dragged by. Once or twice Alex checked up on Lori, who regarded her with a barely concealed look of revulsion and suspicion. *Almost as if she expects me to sprout fangs,* Alex thought grimly. There was nothing else to do but listen to the tinny radio in her room and imagine scenarios that didn't bear thinking about.

Kieran's absence left her with an ache of yearning. She kept going over the previous night in her mind. Every touch, every whispered word, every moment of the miracle.

Only one revelation, one certainty, got her through the tense and tedious hours.

She loved him. Now she could say the words to herself, admit them fully. She opened her journal and wrote two brief lines, unable to keep the miracle to herself. *She loved him.* And if she had held back from speaking them aloud to Kieran, she knew it was only a matter of time.

Perhaps, one day, he could even return them. Alex dared to let herself hope: that there would be a future for them. That somehow the murders would be solved. That Kieran would find what he needed to find, and still have a place left for her.

Whatever happens, we'll be together.

She fell asleep repeating that litany of hope. When she woke again the clock on the bed table read after midnight; voices seeped through the wall between her room and Lori's. Two women—Lori's sister had come, then. Alex sat up in bed and listened. The words were indistinct, but one of the voices rose in agitation and gradually fell silent again. Minutes later Alex heard the door close.

She moved to the window. The beams of a car's headlights shone into the room, blinding her; she saw two figures get into the car, and with a faint screech of tires the car backed up and sped from the parking lot.

So. It was done. Alex pulled the curtains back together and sat in the chair next to the window. Now all she had to do was wait out the remaining hours until Kieran's return.

Their luck had been in after all. *It will be all right,* she told herself, closing her eyes. *It has to be.*

*J*oseph had passed through Falkirk over two hundred miles ago, and still there was no sign of them.

He'd cursed the foul weather that had slowed him through Manitoba and part of Saskatchewan, though he'd known it would delay his quarry as much as it had himself. By the time he reached Falkirk, the late winter storm had passed. He'd stopped in the town and asked about the ones he followed—at the local bar, at the tiny store, at the single gas station. And there he had had his first good fortune.

The attendant at the station had seen them. In an old, rusty truck of no particular color, with mud-splattered U.S. plates—a man, two women, and a child. Kieran fit the description the attendant had given him, and Alexandra Warrington one of the women. The other woman and the child had been locals. Why Kieran would take them on, Joseph didn't know, but it spurred him to greater urgency.

They could still be a full day ahead of him. All he had to go on were their direction, expected route, and destination—the information the Indian woman had revealed on the phone in Merritt.

They were heading for a town called Lovell in British Columbia. Joseph dared not wait that long to find Kieran. The boy might kill again.

So he drove. The coming dawn promised to be brilliantly clear, but he didn't notice. His clothing was rank with the smell of sweat, but he endured it, as he had endured so much else. His gaze swept the highway from side to side, noting all the places they might have stopped, the nondescript roadside towns. They had traveled into the storm heading west the night the attendant had seen them, and they couldn't have gone far then. But since—

He pressed down on the accelerator and almost missed the lone woman walking toward him on the opposite side of the road. His mind acknowledged her presence and almost dismissed it. Until, in the first breaking of sunlight over the horizon, he saw the shaggy dark hair, black leggings, and glittering white boots the gas station attendant had described.

There was no child with her, but surely this was the woman Kieran and the Warrington girl had picked up. She *must* be. Providence had given him aid at last.

Joseph drove another half mile, braked, and turned the truck in a careful U on the deserted expressway. He pulled up alongside the woman, rolled down his window, and leaned out.

"Where are you headed, miss?" Joseph asked, touching his cap. "It doesn't seem safe for you to be out here alone."

There was brief alarm on her pale face, in the eyes smudged all around with heavy makeup. But she smiled nervously, brushing at her hair and sniffling from the cold.

"I'm . . . just walking down to the bus stop at Redding," she said.

He returned her smile. "Could be I'm headed the same way."

She relaxed a little, though her eyes continued to shift from side to side, as if she feared pursuit. "I'm going to Falkirk."

Falkirk. He'd been right, then. Joseph closed his eyes in a brief prayer and smiled. "So happens I'm going that direction myself. I'd be more than happy to give you a ride as far as I can." He looked up and down the long stretch of highway. "No telling when the bus will be along."

She hesitated, long enough to make him wonder if perhaps she had seen him pass in the other direction. But there was something about her that hinted at desperation, of having few choices, and a certain worn cheapness in her look that made it unlikely she'd turn down any opportunity that offered itself.

"All right," she said. She got into the truck and closed the door, leaning away from him as he rolled onto the expressway again. A car passed, and she followed it with her gaze.

"What brings you out here on the road to Falkirk, miss?" he began. "Seems an unusual hour to be traveling."

She hunched against the window. "I had to," she muttered. "I had to." And then, as if she heard the strangeness of her own voice, she sat up and looked at him. "I just moved out of Falkirk last night, but my car broke down and I . . . forgot to pick up my last paycheck. I have to go back and get it."

The story was strained, but there was a ring of truth to some of it. "Perhaps we should go see to your car, then," he suggested. "I could lend you—"

"No." She hunched down again, clutching her thin jacket with long, chipped red fingernails. "All I need is my paycheck, and then I'll be okay."

He let her have silence for a while, a chance to realize he was no threat to her. "So you just moved out of Falkirk," he began. "Perhaps while you were there you ran into some friends of mine. A young man named Kieran, and a woman with red hair. Alexandra is her name."

She stiffened, and inwardly Joseph rejoiced. The trail was not so cold.

"I . . . may have seen someone like that," she said. "Why do you want to know?"

Panic laced her voice. Yet less than forty-eight hours ago she had been with Kieran and Alexandra—had gone with them willingly, according to what Joseph had understood from the gas station attendant.

"Oh," he said genially, "I'd hoped they'd still be in the area. I've been trying to locate them for some time. Old friends, you see. I have important news for them, but they move around, so—"

"I remember you," she said suddenly. "You were in town about six years ago, asking for—"

"Kieran, yes." He raised his brow and smiled. "You'll forgive me if I don't quite remember you, miss. At my age the memory starts to go." He leaned back in his seat. "I do remember being told Kieran had left town not long before I came. But I'd heard he'd been in the area again, so I thought I'd give it another try."

She stared a little longer and then turned away. "You don't want to find him," she muttered under her breath. "You don't."

He pretended not to notice her odd, almost trancelike tone. "I don't think I understand, miss."

"He's—" She broke off, tearing at a fingernail with her teeth.

"Something's wrong, isn't it?" he said gently. "You're frightened of something. What is it? How can I help?"

"Get me to Falkirk. Away from— Just get me back."

"But you know Kieran, don't you? Were you with him?"

She froze like a rabbit in a snare and stared at him. "I knew him. I—"

"If he's done something to hurt you—"

"Please!" She covered her ears with her hands. "Don't ask me anything. Please!"

Her voice rose to the edge of hysteria, as if she were a taut but weakened bowstring that had finally snapped.

"I only need to know where they are, miss. You'd be doing me a great favor."

She would not look at him again. "A mile west of here. There's a motel. That's where they were."

Joseph hid his exultation. He had been close, so close, and yet he might have passed them by if he hadn't found this girl.

"You were with them, then," he said.

She was silent, but from the corner of his eye he could see her shivering. "I think . . . if you could just drop me off at the bus stop," she whispered.

"I don't mind, miss. You'd be better off with me—"

"Please! Just let me out here!" She clawed at the door handle and almost opened it. Joseph braked and reached out to restrain her, steering one-handed. He felt the bones of her wrist compress in his grip.

"You know what he is, don't you?" he asked.

With a breathy cry she arched the fingers of her free hand and raked her nails across his face, struggling to break free. He felt the sting of the scratches but didn't let go, pulling her toward him with a rough jerk.

"Calm down, girl. You have nothing to fear from me. But I must know—"

She made a wordless keening sound, raked at his arm and pushed herself bodily against the passenger door. Joseph fought to keep control of the truck as he kept his grip on the girl, steering at last to the shoulder of the road. The truck bumped into a low ditch, and he let it roll to a stop.

The woman had begun to sob. Black rivulets of makeup tracked over her cheeks.

"Please. Just let me go." Her voice became a whimper. "I need my check, and to go to Calgary. That's all. I never wanted this. I just wanted Kevin safe. Let me go . . ."

"Of course," he said gently. He touched the side of her face. "You'll be fine. I want you to tell me all about Kieran and his friend, and where they were going."

But she only stared at him—stared and stared, as if she had gone mad. Or as if she looked upon a monster. Joseph spoke to her softly, and still she would not speak except to beg and whine.

Joseph knew himself to be a patient man. But he was wasting time, and the woman tried his patience. The scratches on his face wept tiny drops of blood and began to ache.

"Tell me what I must know, young lady," he said. "I don't like being angry. Tell me."

But she did nothing but babble. *Useless,* Joseph thought. *Useless.* He threw open his door and walked around to the passenger side.

"Get out," he said heavily. "You're useless to me."

Like a terrified rodent she crept from the truck, flinching away from him. Yes, exactly as if *he* were the monster, and not Kieran Holt.

None of them understood. None of them would ever know the truth.

He balled his fists. *No.* He had to make someone understand. If this woman knew what Kieran was, she would have to understand, and help him. It would be worth the effort.

"Wait, miss," he called. And as she turned, eyes wide, he smiled.

*I*n her dream, someone screamed.

Alex bolted out of the chair, staring around the room. The phone rang again—not a scream at all, but just as startling. Sleep-dazed, she stumbled for the phone on the bed-table and fumbled for the receiver.

"Hello?"

"Is this Alexandra? I'm Cass, Lori's sister. I haven't been able to get an answer from her room, so . . ."

Alex shook the cobwebs from her mind and glanced at the clock. It was already after eight in the morning. She'd overslept, fallen asleep right in that chair by the window after she'd seen Lori and her sister drive away.

Lori's sister. Trying to call Lori in her room? Alex grasped at the threads of conversation that seemed to make no sense.

"Lori's sister?" she repeated.

There was silence on the other end. "Yeah. I came by late last night, so you didn't see me. Lori told me all about what you'd done to get her and Kevin out of Falkirk." A pause. "I wanted to talk to her again before she goes back with you, but she's not answering her room phone. Finally figured I'd try your room. I want to tell her that Kevin's fine, and—"

Alex sat down on the bed, rubbing her eyes. "Lori said . . . she was going somewhere with me?"

There was an impatient sigh on the other end. "She told me her asshole of a boss wasn't willing to mail her last paycheck to my place in Calgary, so she had to go back today and pick it up. I guess she wasn't thinking too clearly when she left the other day, but she's pretty damned broke and needs that money. She just wanted to make sure Kevin was out of town first, so Jerry couldn't do anything." There was the sound of distant traffic through the line. "I couldn't take her to Falkirk—I couldn't miss any more work—but she said you'd give her a lift back. You know, she was acting pretty freaky last night, pretty weird. I just wanted to make sure she's okay."

Alex stared at the receiver. Lori hadn't gone with her sister last night? She'd stayed behind, and told her sister Alex was giving her a ride back to Falkirk? After what Lori had seen of Kieran, there wasn't much chance she'd ask any favors of Alex.

"I haven't spoken to Lori this morning," Alex said warily. "Let me go check her room. Maybe she's still asleep. Can you give me a number where you can be reached?"

She jotted the information down on the dogeared hotel stationery and dressed quickly, alarm spreading through her. It was well after sunrise, and Kieran wasn't back. And now this, with Lori God only knew where.

She hurried next door, pulling out the duplicate key. Inside, the room was silent, dark and empty. Nothing left in the bathroom or any of the drawers or the closets.

Gone. Lori had gone, but not with her sister. Alex went back to her room, staring out the window. That Lori hadn't been thinking clearly was a given. Had she tried to hitch a ride back to Falkirk, and told her sister otherwise to reassure her? Or maybe there was a bus somewhere.

If Lori chose to go back to pick up a paycheck, that was her business and her decision to make. But she could just as easily go to the police with stories about Kieran, and even if they didn't believe her, they might get enough of his description, and Alex's, to do plenty of damage.

Alex pushed her worries to the back of her mind and finished dressing and packing. At the last minute she pulled a knitted cap down over her forehead and wrapped a muffler around her neck so that it covered the lower part of her face. Sunglasses completed the camouflage.

She went outside and scanned the horizon in every direction. Kieran must be on his way back. He had promised to return before dawn. And now, with Lori disappeared . . .

Hunching her shoulders, she walked across the parking lot to the motel's greasy spoon. Someone there might know if Lori had been seen early that morning, or at least if there was a bus running into Falkirk from here. If Alex had to go chase Lori down, she'd be leaving Kieran behind. And even if she caught up to Lori, what would she do then?

She shivered as she heard the distant wail of sirens.

*K*ieran stood across the road from the motel where Alexandra waited, and knew that something was very wrong.

He lifted his face into the wind. It was past dawn, but still early—a time when the world seems hushed and every sense is at its peak. A wisp of scent came to him, and he inhaled deeply, testing it. Distinctive, yet faint; a shift in the air current might carry it away.

But it hung in the air as if to taunt him. His body stiffened, and he felt every hair stand on end.

He *knew* this scent. Not as he knew Alexandra's, or any of the myriad odors of nature. It wrapped around his disordered memories like chains, boxed them in like unscalable walls. It tormented him like hunger and thirst and loneliness. Like the Voice that sometimes spoke within his mind.

Once before he had caught this scent, in the woods near Alexandra's childhood hiding place. He had not remembered enough then, but now he did. It was the scent of a man. He knew it as he might know the face of an enemy.

He began to walk toward the scent, pulled like a puppet on a string. East—back the way they had come two nights ago. He and Alexandra and Lori and her son. But Lori would be gone now, and it was safe for him to return to Alexandra.

His steps slowed. Alexandra. The mere memory of her almost blotted out the scent, as he had tried to lose himself and keep her from his thoughts over the long day and night before.

Endless hours, because he had been apart from her. But now the taste and smell and sound of her filled his mind and senses, leaving no room for anything else.

Two nights ago, when he'd wanted Alexandra so much, he had felt the beast straining to break free, threatening to be released by the intensity of his emotions. With a few words and a touch Alexandra had accepted the beast and tamed it, accepted Kieran into her body and made him almost whole.

He stopped and almost turned back. She expected him now. In a few minutes he could be with her. In a few minutes she would be in his arms, feeding his hunger, filling him to completion.

But again the familiar scent came to him, and a growl started low in his chest. His body acted, beyond thought, propelling him into a run. Away, away from the motel.

Who are you? His pumping heart beat out the question.

He had run nearly a mile, behind the windbreaks and snowdrifts along the side of the road, when the second smell assaulted him.

Death. He stumbled and ran on. Blood, and death, mingled with the familiar scent and one other equally so. It sickened him, and still he ran, drawn inevitably to a circle of flattened snow a few yards from the highway's edge.

A body lay there, surrounded by footprints. She sprawled on her back, sightless eyes turned heavenward in silent supplication, her face still taut with terror. Bile rose in his throat.

Lori. He had no need to touch her to know she was dead. Her blood stained the snow and soaked the remnants of her torn clothing.

Kieran sank to his knees. The horror of death surrounded him, and yet he could not move, could not touch her even to close her eyes. The scent that had drawn him here was mingled with all the others, telling a tale of violence and pain and a cruel, tragic murder.

Murder. Like Peter's murder. Alexandra had told him. Body torn, as if by a crazed animal. Exactly the same. Here, a thousand miles from Merritt. It couldn't be, and yet it was. Inescapable. Undeniable.

And, like a predator from ambush, memory came.

"Look, boy. See what you've done!"

The Voice. It mocked him, invisible, in a place that reeked of blood and fear. A place he knew within his mind, wooded and steeped in emotion. Minnesota—

"Look!" the Voice said again. Kieran looked, as he had been commanded to do.

A body lay before him. Savaged and torn, throat ripped open, clothing rent to shreds by raking claws. A young Ojibwe woman's face forever locked in a grimace of terror.

Kieran retched until his stomach was empty. But still the Voice was there.

"How many others have you killed, boy, in all these years you've run from me?" The Voice beat him down as it had done a hundred times before. "And you think you can walk among men? You are a savage, a murderous butcher. You cannot control your evil. But if you obey me, if you come back, no one else will know what you've done. You may still be saved. . . ."

Memory. It was real. Kieran came back to himself with a lurch, the taste of vomit in his mouth.

He had not killed Peter. He had *known* it. Alexandra had believed it. But he had threatened Peter, had hated what he'd had with Alexandra, what he still might take. And Lori—Lori had seen him change, had been unable to accept, had reviled him for what he was.

And the girl, from the reservation in Minnesota—

"No!" Kieran leaped up, shaking violently. Peter, that Ojibwe girl, Lori. All bound by the same unspeakable deaths. All had come within his path.

He backed away. Last night. This morning. He had roamed, and slept, and dreamed. He did not remember his dreams. He had awakened after dawn, cramped and stiff from a makeshift bed of dry grasses and old hay.

He stared at his hands. They carried no marks. His

clothing was wrinkled but unstained by blood. But when he became a wolf, he discarded his clothes. No victim's blood would return with his humanity.

No. He threw back his head and denied it, denied it until the muscles in his throat ached with the unvoiced cry. Until he heard the distant wail of sirens. Until the deepest needs of self-preservation brought him back to himself, and he remembered Alexandra.

Alexandra, who had been with Lori. And Kevin.

With a howl of despair he turned and ran. Back to the motel, away from the sirens that pursued him like baying hounds. And when only the road lay between him and the place where Alexandra waited, he stopped.

He had to know she was all right. He must know.

Her hair and face were covered, but he recognized her when she stepped out of the motel room door. She raised her hand to shield her eyes against the glare of sun on snow and looked to the north and east and west. Searching, for him. She turned toward the south, and he knew she would see him in a moment.

He crouched nearly to the ground. Her gaze passed over him, and her hand dropped. Her body sagged. She began to walk across the parking lot, toward the café beside the motel.

She was safe. And Kevin—where was the boy? Alexandra would never let the child come to any harm.

The sirens had stopped. A mile down the highway lights flashed, and Kieran knew the police had found Lori.

He watched Alexandra disappear into the café, his body yearning toward her; his heart compressed in a vise. He would not go near Alexandra again. He could not take that risk, because he did not *know*. He might be what the Voice had called him. He might have killed, unaware, the memory purged from his conscious mind.

No, he could never go back to Alexandra. He'd been deceiving himself, certain her faith in him was enough.

But it wasn't. She trusted him, but he couldn't trust himself. Not as long as there was any chance that the Voice was right. Nothing was more important than Alexandra's safety, even if the cost was her faith in him. Even if he must abandon her forever, after last night, after she had given herself to him. He dared not even leave her a note. It was better this way—a severance quick and clean.

He looked east. If he went back, he could let the police take him. Let them do their tests. Then he would know. Then he would pay, if payment was required. And if he had killed, he would never kill again.

But he had no control over the wildness within him that would not let itself be confined by chains, by bars, by walls. It was no part of his humanity. It moved him to look northwest once again, as he had done so many times since Minnesota.

The silent call was more powerful than ever before. Alexandra had been his anchor, but he must cut her free. And run again, to a place he had never been. A place where there might be others like him. Others who would know what he was. Who would be his match. Whom he could not hurt if he were mad, who existed in a place where, in his deepest soul, he knew there would be an ending.

He would not change to wolf, not even to make his journey faster. But he could still run as a man. He would find the way.

He took one step, and then another, each longer than the last until he was running. Running northwest. Lovell, Alexandra had said. Still hundreds of miles away. But he never doubted he would find it.

In silence he ran, and in silence he mourned. For Peter, for Lori, for the unknown Ojibwe girl. For Alexandra, who had given him one night of wholeness.

They were lost forever.

⚘ 17

Alex pushed open the door of the café, assaulted by heat, the scents of bacon fat and strong coffee. A pair of truckers sat at the counter putting away platefuls of scrambled eggs, while the waitress talked to someone in the kitchen.

Alex found a booth out of the way and waited for the waitress to notice her. No point in calling attention to herself. The smell of food made her stomach churn, and even the idea of coffee was thoroughly unappealing.

Her gaze strayed to the window, across the road. Surely Kieran would turn up any moment. She had to be ready to leave when he did. They'd taken enough risks already, spending over thirty hours in this motel.

"Hey, didja hear the news?"

She looked up. A man had entered the coffee shop—skinny and middle-aged, a sheepskin coat hung over his lanky frame. He strode to the counter and pulled up a stool next to the truckers. The waitress hurried over to him, and the truckers put down their forks.

"I just caught it on my radio," the newcomer said. "They found a body down the road about a mile—girl, all torn to pieces. Seems someone reported it anonymously just after dawn, but didn't hang around until the cops showed up. I heard it's pretty godawful—"

Alex felt her body go numb with a wash of adrenaline.

"Do they know who it was?" one of the beefy truckers asked. "The girl, I mean?"

"No, but she wasn't from here. They think she may have been hitchhiking when it happened, and it wasn't more'n a few hours ago. Dark hair, white boots." His voice dropped to a dramatic whisper. "I heard the boots were covered with blood."

"Jeezus," the other trucker said. "Here?"

"I heard already that it almost looks like some kind of animal did it. But it would have to be the size of a bear, and there ain't nothing here that big, not that anyone's seen. They think it has to be murder."

Alex tried to push herself up from the table. The muscles in her arms gave out, and she sat down again.

"Hey, honey . . . you okay?" The waitress had finally arrived, at exactly the worst possible moment. "Can I get you something? Sorry I didn't notice you earlier, but—"

"I'm fine," Alex managed. "I . . . just feel a little queasy."

"No wonder, honey." A gentle hand touched Alex's shoulder. "Isn't it horrible? A young girl killed here . . . it just doesn't happen. Used to be you could go anywhere with anyone and not have any reason to be afraid. Lord, what's this world coming to?"

Alex got her legs to work and slid sideways from the booth. The waitress steadied her.

"Sure I can't help? Something to settle your stomach?"

"Thanks, but I think I'll be better if I just—" Alex gestured helplessly and walked out of the café as fast as she was able. The truckers had already abandoned their half-finished breakfasts and hurried to their trucks for more information. Alex nearly ran back to her room. She slammed the door closed and leaned against it, sliding down until she sat on the worn carpet.

No. Not again.

But she knew. She knew what the trucker had described was what she had seen when she identified Peter's body. She knew exactly how Lori would look. Because she knew it was Lori, and all she could do was fold her arms around her ribs and let the tears run down her cheeks until the mindless horror began to pass.

Then the thinking came. The cold, cruel logic that followed blind emotion.

Lori was dead. Had been murdered, just as Peter had been. Her body ripped and torn as if by an animal. An animal that no longer existed on this prairie—except now, and only in one distinct form.

And the murder had happened here, in this small, sleepy town. Here, where Lori had rejected Kieran, calling him a monster.

The body had been found just after dawn. And Kieran had not come back.

Alex stood. She walked carefully to the window and opened the curtains, letting the sun strike her face until the light brought new tears to her eyes. Gradually her heart began to function as more than a vessel for pumping blood. Slowly the ice began to thaw.

It had happened again. Again she faced what she'd faced in Minnesota. She had made this decision before. She'd believed herself certain then.

Certain that Kieran was not a killer, a beast, a monster. And now . . .

Alex closed the curtains and went to the bed. She stroked the faded bedspread. Two nights ago she'd given herself to Kieran. Not only her body, but her heart. And he had given her back all she'd lost of herself since her childhood. After so much wasted time she knew who she was.

And she knew who *he* was. *What* he was. He was good, and brave, and kind. He was her lover, who saw only beauty in her face. He had risked his own life to save that of a child. He was strong in the finest way—strong enough to battle his own demons and not let them destroy him. He was her beloved.

Kieran was not a killer.

But he had run. She was sure of it. He had not returned because he'd learned of the murder somehow, and would not have been able to absolve himself of the possibility, the terrible chance that he might have truly turned monster.

And you would not come near me again, would you? You'd fear for me. You'd never take the risk. How can I know you so well, Kieran, when for so long I didn't know myself?

He didn't have anywhere to run but the same place they'd been heading—British Columbia. She'd told him about Lovell, what little Julie had revealed. There was still a goal, and Kieran would let his instincts guide him when he had nothing else to believe in.

Alex caught up a handful of the bedspread and clutched it tight. *I'll believe for both of us, as you believed for me. As you saw the beauty in me. And I'll find you, Kieran. I'll find you, and together we'll discover the truth.*

The most obvious truth came over her as suddenly as an unexpected chill. Kieran hadn't killed Peter or Lori, but someone had. Someone who had the same pattern, who left the same marks on his victims. Someone who had chosen the very woman whom Kieran had tried to help.

Someone who had been in Minnesota, and now might be here.

Alex glanced at the clock. There was nothing more she could do for Lori. The police would connect Lori to the motel, and to her and Kieran, soon enough if they hadn't already. She couldn't talk to the police. Not yet. Not while Kieran was on the run.

But Lori's sister would have to know what had happened. And Kevin. Kevin had someone to look after him, but he had lost so much.

Alex mourned as she got into the truck and pulled onto the westbound expressway. She drove through a blur of tears until she found another gas station with a phone booth. She dialed Lori's sister's number and heard the drone of an answering machine's mechanical voice. In a monotone she left a message asking Cass to call the authorities in Saskatchewan and hung up, sick with sorrow.

Then she called the Wakanabo home. Julie answered. Julie, like a harbor in a storm, an island of sanity in a world gone mad.

"Something's happened, hasn't it?" Julie asked quietly.

Alex told the story between ragged gulps of air. When it was over, Julie was silent a long time.

"He didn't do it, Alex," she said at last.

"I know."

"You're still going after him, aren't you?"

"Yes."

"Don't, Alex. Come home."

Alex rubbed tears from her eyes with the back of her hand. "He needs me now, more than ever. I have to know he's all right. Julie—" she closed her eyes, "Julie, I love him. More than life."

Julie sighed, her breath shuddering with emotion. "I know. And I told you not to let him go. But there's something else. Kieran . . . he's not the only one of his kind."

"How do you—"

"It's true."

Alex was too numb to work through all the implications of Julie's certainty. "Another feeling, Julie?" she asked hoarsely.

"That's why you have to come back, Alex. It's too dangerous. Who knows what's out there committing these murders? Maybe someone like Kieran. And I believe that the answers will have to come from Kieran. Only he can find them."

"You're wrong, Julie. I have to be there, with him. I know he needs me, and as long as he needs me I'll never abandon him."

"Then know what you're getting into."

The voice was no longer Julie's. Alex recognized Julie's grandmother, imagined the deeply lined face and unfathomable dark eyes. She shivered and gripped the receiver as if it might fly from her hand.

"What Julie said is true," Mary said, "but even she

doesn't know all of it. A great darkness shadows you now. Kieran is a part of it. If the shadow touches you, you may never escape it. And it is right behind you."

Alex looked over her shoulder. The morning was clear and bright, the sky free of clouds. "Is it the real killer?" she asked with deliberate calm.

But it was the operator's voice she heard, demanding change she didn't have. She hung up and looked at her watch. The police could already be on her tail. She couldn't worry about shadows when Kieran was out there in need of her help.

She cleared her mind of all thoughts but one and began to drive. Northwest, toward a town called Lovell. *Find Kieran,* she chanted silently. *Find him, and the answers will come. For all of us.*

*J*oseph drove as if all the demons of hell snapped at his heels.

He drove with the sight of a young woman's torn body caught forever behind his eyes. He could hardly recall now what she'd looked like when she was alive—when he finally dropped her off, after she refused to listen. He'd gone on his way and then thought of how he had frightened her, thought of apologizing and making it right. But the place he returned to, where he'd left her, had been trampled and soaked with blood. She would never hear his apology. And now all he could remember was the terror on her face, terror of the last thing she'd seen before she died.

He had been too late. Kieran had killed again.

Joseph wept silently. *My son, my son. You must die. There is no other way.*

But not at the hands of police. No. Joseph had let the authorities know about the girl, but then he had left. There could be no more delays. He knew they were ahead of him again, Kieran and the woman. He had to reach them, stop them. Too many failures. Too many deaths because he had let a monster live.

Over three hundred miles to the border of British Columbia. Time enough. And if he didn't catch them by then, he knew where they were headed.

He drove through the day, leaving the prairie behind. The mountains took him in, whispering of secrets they had kept for a thousand years. And when dusk began to fall, he saw the red glow of taillights ahead and knew: *it might be them.*

It was only a matter of time.

$\mathcal{T}$he fourth time she nearly drove off the road, Alex knew she had to stop.

She had barely slept in forty-eight hours, counting the single night with Kieran. She hadn't eaten in longer than she could remember, except for a fruit roll and a handful of peanuts left over from the original travel supplies. Her mouth was dry as cotton. It might be only a matter of hours to Lovell, but without coffee she'd never be able to negotiate winding mountain roads or keep herself awake long enough to make it there, especially in the dark.

Her luck had held so far. Twice she'd seen RCMP vehicles on the road, and both times they'd passed by or been otherwise occupied. Only a few more hours was all she needed, all she asked of fickle good fortune.

At the next exit advertising food she pulled off the expressway. Another nondescript roadside café, but it would have coffee. Her hands trembled as she pulled on her cap and muffler. In and out; that was all it would have to be. A quick trip to the rest room and a few sips of caffeine, no more.

She walked stiffly into the coffee shop, relieved to see that she was only one of many travelers who'd stopped for a drink or a meal. Her stomach growled, but she ignored it. She ordered her coffee and took the steaming foam cup into the rest room, burning her tongue as she sipped.

The coffee was nearly half gone by the time she got back to the truck. She took one last, hasty glance at the map to be certain of her route. She was very near Kamloops now; Lovell was north and a little east from here. Sometime tonight she'd reach it. Kieran would either already be there—though he'd have to have hitched a ride—or she'd be waiting . . .

The hand that covered her mouth was big and very strong. That was the only thought she had time for as the cup of coffee was knocked from her hand and the man dragged her away from her truck and into the shadows.

She struggled, but she might as well have been a child. He held her easily, maneuvering her backward until her body hit something solid. Another vehicle, a dark truck of some kind.

His bare, callused hand slid over her mouth. "If you scream," he said softly, "I'll have to hit you."

She shook her head. He let his hand fall and opened the truck door one-handed, his arm locked around her throat. She couldn't have screamed; she could barely breathe.

He pushed her into the truck and slid in beside her. Her head bumped the window. She felt blindly for the door handle. Her captor caught her wrist and twisted it behind her; the pain brought tears to her eyes.

"Where is Kieran?"

For the first time she saw him, his face faintly illuminated by the light from the coffee shop. Fifty-five, she thought, or sixty; a face weathered with outdoor living, stubbled and gaunt with exhaustion. Iron-gray hair visible from under the hunter's cap he wore. Expressionless, almost—except for his eyes.

Green eyes, hard with purpose. Ageless eyes. They demanded something of her, and she felt if she looked long enough she would give this man whatever he asked.

"Where is he?" he repeated. He held her almost lightly now, his grip no longer painful. "I know he's been with you."

She kept her head, even though her body tightened in mindless fear. "Who are you?" she countered. "What do you want?"

He closed his eyes and sighed, as if annoyed by the

stubbornness of a recalcitrant child. "My name is Joseph Arnoux."

Arnoux. For a moment her mind went blank, and then she remembered. Julie had told her what little she knew of him—a backwoodsman, a recluse who'd been known as a wolf hater. A man Howie had mentioned in his tirade about killing the black wolf, before Kieran had come back into Alex's life.

But that had been back in Minnesota, over a thousand miles away.

"And you are Alexandra Warrington," he said. "I know all about you, and I've come a long way to find you."

A long way. A very long way. Julie's grandmother's words came back to her with all the force of prophecy fulfilled: *"A great darkness shadows you now. Kieran is a part of it. If the shadow touches you, you may never escape it. And it is right behind you."*

She knew the shadow had found her.

"It will be simplest if you tell me now," he said, almost gently. He glanced at the dashboard, and she saw the gun that lay there, within his easy reach but well beyond hers. "I don't want to hurt you. Is he here?"

She had no plan, almost no information, nothing to go on. But she knew if she forgot herself for even a moment, she would never have the chance to find out. With studied calm she met Arnoux's gaze. "I don't know."

His grip tightened on her wrist, but she didn't let him see the pain on her face. "No games," he said. "I have no time for them. He was with you in Saskatchewan."

"Not anymore."

She could have sworn then that Arnoux looked directly into her mind. His strange eyes searched hers while she struggled to keep her breathing even, her expression blank of all emotion.

Abruptly he released her wrist, and only by sheer act of will did she stop herself from rubbing the bruised skin. "He's gone on to Lovell, hasn't he?"

Her heart stopped. "I don't know what you're talking about."

He smiled. It was a weary smile, and it chilled her to the bone. "But I know, Miss Warrington. I heard your Indian friend tell you. Sooner or later I would have found him."

Alex looked toward the coffee shop. A couple came out and went to their car, never once glancing in her direction. "And why do you want to find him?"

"You know what he is, Miss Warrington."

She looked at him, revealing none of her shock. "I know very little."

He leaned back. "You are clever, Miss Warrington. But you can't protect him with words. I've hunted him too long. My duty is greater than your misplaced loyalty to a creature that isn't human."

He *knew*. Alex fought past the paralysis that tried to claim her. *Think. Think.* Inspiration struck amid the chaos of her thoughts.

"And all this time I thought I was the only one who understood what he was," she said. "All this time I've been studying him—"

"Studying?" he echoed. He stared at her, eyes narrowed.

"I'm a scientist, Mr. Arnoux." She folded her arms, trying for the perfect blend of wary unease and scientific detachment that might convince him. "You claim to know everything about me. When Kieran came to my door and showed me what he was, I knew I'd made the discovery of a lifetime." She shook her head. "But you don't care about that, do you? If you know he's gone to Lovell, you know as much as I do. He left me back in Saskatchewan, and I've been following ever since."

She knew then she'd caught him off guard, that somehow she'd found the right tack to take. He didn't believe her—not yet—but even the tiniest wedge of uncertainty was a beginning.

"Look, Mr. Arnoux," she said. "I don't know what you want with Kieran. All I can say is that he's not here, and I don't want to get in the middle of whatever is going on." She clasped her hands as if in supplication. "My whole purpose from the beginning has been scientific. By studying him, I—"

"*Studying?*" he exploded. She shrank back from the sudden violence in his face. "Studying a monster that has killed again and again? The beast that killed your lover?"

Peter. He meant Peter. And in his rage he revealed more of his motives than he had done with words. "*I have hunted him too long,*" he'd said. "*Monster,*" he said, and "*beast.*" His voice was filled with loathing for what he clearly believed Kieran to be.

What Kieran feared himself to be. Needles of ice pushed deep into Alex's heart. Some terrible knowledge crouched just at the edge of her memory.

She let her feigned coolness falter. "Peter?" she breathed. "He couldn't have killed Peter. I was watching him. He wasn't able to control his ability to change—"

Arnoux gave a harsh bark. "No. The beast controlled *him*. But I know how capable he is of murder."

"But there was . . . no evidence—"

"How cold-blooded you are," he said, his rage replaced with contempt. "To continue your 'study' after your lover's death, blinding yourself to the obvious truth." He leaned forward, and Alex smelled the old sweat on him, felt the heat of his breath. "But you are a scientist, and scientists require proof. What of the woman he killed in Saskatchewan—the woman you picked up in Falkirk? Did you ignore that as well?"

Alex fought harder than ever before to show nothing of what she felt. "Lori?" she whispered.

"He tore her to pieces, Miss Warrington. Just around dawn this morning. I saw her body."

"I don't believe you!"

"You can read it in the papers tomorrow. Or did you know all along? Was this part of your 'study'?"

"No!" she cried, jamming her hands over her ears. "I didn't know! Oh, God." She bent double, bringing back all the horror she'd felt when she first learned of Lori's death. It wasn't hard to do. "We picked her and her son up in Falkirk," she said, letting the words spill out. "Kieran said he'd known her once. But he was acting strangely, and we fought. We fought, and he . . . ran off, and I didn't see him after that. I thought he'd continued his journey here. Lori's sister came to get her son, and then Lori disappeared—"

"Isn't that proof enough?" Arnoux said heavily.

She stared at him through her tears. "He never . . . hurt me."

"You were lucky, Miss Warrington. You gave him what he wanted. But sooner or later, he would have turned on you." His fanatic's eyes took on a glaze of distance. "Just as he turned on me."

As Arnoux traveled to some place beyond her reach, Alex forced herself to be as cold-blooded as Arnoux had suggested, tallying the few facts she'd managed to gather. Arnoux was hunting Kieran, apparently believing him to be a murderer, and with full knowledge of what Kieran was. He knew all about her and Peter, and Lori. Somehow he'd overheard, from Julie, where they were bound. He had followed them all the way from Minnesota.

Followed them, like a dark shadow. He had been at each place where the murders had happened. Julie'd said he lived near Merritt. He could have been there five years ago when Julie's cousin had died the exact same way.

"You saw . . . Lori's body?" she croaked.

He focused on her again. "Yes. As I've seen the others he killed."

She covered her face with her hands. "I don't understand," she moaned. "I thought I'd . . . discovered a scientific wonder when Kieran came to me. But you're saying I . . . helped him when he'd . . . killed . . ."

Arnoux grasped her wrists and pulled her hands from her face. "Is there something human in you after all, Miss Warrington?"

"I'm no murderer!" she shrieked.

He slapped his hand over her mouth. "Quiet." When she nodded, eyes wide, he let her go again. "What has been done cannot be undone." He sighed. "Your error is almost understandable. I believe such creatures have great power to delude mortal men. They can look into your eyes and make you believe falsehoods, in the same manner as their Master. As Kieran deluded me."

Alex swallowed several times. Unbelievably enough, her act was working. "Then . . . what if I want to help you?"

His eyes narrowed again, and she hurried to keep her momentum. "If—" She sniffed and rubbed her nose with the back of her hand. "If I helped him kill people—if he killed Peter—then it's partly my fault." She met his gaze with the look of one who has reached a sudden but difficult decision. "I have to stop him. Isn't that why you've come—to stop him?"

"Yes." There was no hesitation in his reply, but he offered nothing more.

Alex sat up. "He was with me for over a week. I know his habits. I know how he thinks. I can help you."

"Then tell me why he came here."

"I don't know." *Stick close to the truth,* she told herself. She leaned forward, holding his hooded gaze. "Not entirely. Only that something was calling him here. I had to find out what it was."

"Why should I trust you?" he demanded with a strange gentleness.

"I only want to do what's right."

"Then tell me, Miss Warrington, did you let him mount you?"

She swallowed her shock. "What?"

"Was that part of your experiment?" His hand closed around her wrist with bruising force, belying the eerie softness of his voice. "Was he your lover?"

"No!" She let a look of utmost horror and disgust pass over her face. "He isn't human! He can change into a wolf. Do you think that I—that I—" She choked. *Forgive me, Kieran.* "He was a subject of study, that's all!" She made a visible effort to calm herself and lowered her voice. "He wanted to, but I held him off. That was why we fought, after we picked up Lori. I couldn't let him touch me. I had to pretend, to make excuses. And then he left."

She saw the subtle changes in Arnoux's expression that told her she had finally convinced him, that her story held together and matched whatever it was he believed of Kieran.

"You are fortunate that the beast didn't kill you for refusing him." He leaned back again, his body relaxing by increments. "He could never control his animal passions. It was my mistake to believe he could learn. Your refusing him undoubtedly drove him to kill that unfortunate girl." A hard light came into his eyes. "Maybe you can be of use to me."

"I said I want to help." She hesitated. "If I can help you find him—what will you do to him?"

Suspicion closed his features again. "What would you do, Miss Warrington?"

She lowered her eyes. "He's still an anomaly of nature, something that should be analyzed—"

"No. Make your choice, Miss Warrington. You will either help me hunt him down and kill him, or you are only a burden to me."

"And if I'm of no use?" She let terror edge into her voice. "What will you do to me?"

He stared at her. "I would like to believe you, Miss Warrington. I have looked for an ally for a very long time. You and I should be enemies, because you succor vermin just as you took in Kieran." He looked out the window. "No one has understood my duty, the curse that haunts me because once I was merciful. I can no longer afford mercy." He released her wrist and clenched his fist so tightly that the blue veins under the skin stood out in harsh relief. "Can you know what it's like to spend your life trying to undo a single mistake? Kieran was my great sin. And now I must atone."

Alex beat back her loathing and reached out to touch Arnoux's arm. Lightly, hesitantly, as if she wished to offer comfort but feared his reaction. "So, it seems, must I. How can I prove to you that I want to help in any way I can?"

Slowly he turned back, looked at her hand on his arm. The harsh lines of his face revealed nothing. "I'll give you a choice, Miss Warrington. Go back to your truck and leave here. Don't look back." He trapped her gaze. "Or you may hide your truck and come with me."

"You'd just . . . let me go?"

"No one will believe any tale you tell." His lip curled in disgust. "But if you want to atone for your part in the murders . . ."

"All right." She threw back her shoulders. "Where do you want me to go?"

"Drive west along the expressway until you find a place to hide your truck. I'll be right behind you."

She opened her pack and fumbled for her keys. He grabbed the backpack from her hand. "I'll keep this until we meet again."

She just barely kept herself from hesitating. Her wallet was in the backpack, but it wasn't the wallet she was worried about. Her diary was in the pack as well, and it contained incriminating statements that would tell Arnoux she was lying about her feelings for Kieran.

She slid out of the truck, half expecting him to attack her from behind. But he only watched with those strange, fanatic's eyes while she reached her truck, started the engine, and got back onto the expressway. Her damp palms slipped on the wheel, and cold sweat soaked the hair at her temples. She'd done it. She'd pulled it off. So far . . .

Very briefly she considered making a run for it. But that would gain her no more than an uncertain freedom and a few seconds' lead. He still knew where to go. He still intended to kill Kieran, whatever the reasons that drove him. And she was the only one who could learn his motives—and his weaknesses. She had to find a way to warn Kieran at the very least, stop Arnoux if she could.

And not only for Kieran's sake if the most terrifying, unthinkable possibility were true.

She watched him in the rearview mirror as she found a place to pull off the expressway, where the trees were thick and a fire road led into the forest. She pulled over and parked. Arnoux was already waiting for her, the gun tucked in his coat pocket.

"I'm glad you made the choice you did, Miss Warrington," he said. But his voice held nothing but glacial calm.

She knew then that he would have killed her if she'd tried to run. That for some reason he wouldn't risk letting her go free to talk, in spite of his seeming certainty that no one would believe anything she said.

But now he had reason to believe *her.*

She took the last box of supplies and her suitcase out of the truck and carried it to Arnoux's. This was it, then— the big gamble. Julie's grandmother had seen this trouble, but Alex still hadn't been prepared.

She tried to walk a fine line between normal unease and feigned confidence, hoping it would continue to convince Arnoux. He acted the gentleman, taking her luggage and loading it into his truck, then holding her door open for her. She almost choked on the irony of it. But he never stopped watching her.

They continued west toward Kamloops, and then took the provincial highway north and east deeper into the mountains. The night closed in around Alex. She was intently aware, every moment, of the man by her side. What drove him? Was he merely a man who sought what he seemed to think was justice, a fanatic, or something infinitely worse?

After a half hour of silence, she cleared her throat and looked at his set profile. "If we're going to be allies," she said, "we need to know more about each other."

He glanced at her. "Fair enough, Miss Warrington."

"Alex."

"Miss Alex," he said, with a certain stiffness, as if he didn't know how to share even so slight an intimacy as first names. "But I already know much about you. Your sympathy for vermin—"

"Wolves," she said evenly, "are not vermin."

She was taking a risk, guessing that he might respect her more if she didn't cower and bend easily to his will. He smiled, a grim set to his mouth, and nodded. "Now is not the time to convince you otherwise. But you want to know why I hunt Kieran Holt. Why I've made it my life's work to stop him."

"It would help," she said. "It seems you've known him for much longer than I have."

"Oh, yes. Much longer." He shifted gears to compensate for the road's steady ascent. "I knew him as a boy, before he was fully corrupted by his nature."

Alex reigned back the hundreds of questions she wanted to ask, filtering them for the most essential. "In Minnesota? Is that where you knew him?"

He gripped the wheel and stared ahead. "That was where I found him. Where I took him in, and tried to make him human. That was where I failed."

"And how did you find him? How did you come to realize . . . what he was?"

But he countered her question with another. "Did you know such creatures existed before he came to you, Miss Alex?"

This she could answer with complete honesty. "No. It was a fairy tale to me, and even after I saw it happen I questioned my own sanity."

"Yes. As so many have questioned mine. Crazy old Arnoux." He chuckled, a bitter, grating sound. "But I had reason to know the full truth of what he was long before I found him. I knew from my youth that such creatures are the hounds of Satan, the mortal enemies of mankind."

"Then—you saw others?"

His voice was low and icily calm. "I will tell you how I came to learn of the werewolf kind, Miss Alex." Once again he seemed to retreat from her in all but body, re-living some part of his past. "My father was one of the great wolf hunters in Ontario, in those years when they were known to be the vermin they are. Jean-Baptiste Arnoux. His name was legendary."

A wolf hunter. Alex suppressed a shudder, but Arnoux didn't notice. "The day it happened," he continued, "I was only sixteen, hardly more than a boy. My father had taught me to hunt and trap. One day I set out alone to hunt the wolves we had seen days before. They had been very bold, and my father had promised to take their pelts before the week was out.

"My pride was greater than my skill. I came home empty-handed. But in the cabin—in the cabin . . . " He clenched his fists around the steering wheel so hard that the truck jigged to the side. "I found them dead, my mother and my father. They were torn apart. The cabin was covered in blood. And when I ran out into the snow, wild with grief, I saw their murderer. A naked man, his fingers and mouth running red. As I watched, he shifted his shape. Changed into a wolf black as hell itself."

Alex closed her eyes. He could be crazy, or the story could be true. She had no way of knowing, no experience.

"I thought I was mad. Grief had addled my senses. But after I buried my parents with my own hands, I studied the tracks around the cabin. Wolf spoor and footprints intermingled. I prayed for guidance. The presence of inhuman evil had made itself known to me as to no other. I had been shown that such creatures existed. I knew I had to find my parents' killer at any cost.

"I took my father's inheritance and came to the States to study all the legends and stories of the creatures known as werewolves. I knew their kind had been hunted in Europe. But after years of fruitless search I still had not found what I sought, so I settled in Minnesota, where I could follow the studies of wolves, and hunt them when I could."

Before she could stop herself, Alex blurted, "But wolf hunting has been illegal in Minnesota since 1973—"

"Yes," he said simply. "A law made by men who never walked beyond their front doors. But it never stopped me. And my vigilance paid off in the end. Seventeen years ago I finally found my prey. It was sheer chance that I saw them change—a male and female with their young, skulking in the woods as wolves. I followed and observed them, until it was the right time."

Alex felt true sickness clench at her stomach. "Seventeen years ago," she repeated. "What year did you find them?"

"Nineteen-seventy-nine. I had waited so long, and the

male was black, like the monster that had killed my father and mother. I destroyed him, and his mate, while they ran as wolves. But their offspring, the boy, I could not bring myself to kill."

"Kieran," Alex whispered. Memory crystallized, punched through the tissue of years, drawing her back to childhood and a day when wolves had died at the hands of a cold-eyed poacher.

She looked at Arnoux with a new and terrible understanding. It was *him*. She saw it now, saw the same features she'd seen then, many years aged but marked with the same ruthless purpose. She had seen Kieran's parents die at his hands.

"Yes," he said, oblivious. "Yes. It was Kieran. With his sire and dam dead, I should have killed him as well. But he seemed young, almost helpless. Dazed with shock, whatever his kind are capable of feeling. It was a simple matter to get him to come with me. Something moved me, and I thought it was Providence demanding mercy. But now I know it was evil that pushed me to take him in, believing I could make him human."

And that's why I never saw Kieran again. Arnoux took him. "Then, in a way, you were studying him too."

He laughed without humor. "To learn how he might be redeemed. How he might be forced to expel the beast. I gave my life to that purpose. It was as if a madness gripped me, but I thought it was the will of heaven. So I persevered."

Alex couldn't quite keep the quiver from her voice. "What did you do to him?"

"I knew I needed solitude to carry out his salvation. I built a compound of my land, a place to keep him from all outside influence and from harming innocents. There I began his education. I became as a father to him. I taught him how he must deny the beast. When he faltered, I taught him the necessity of discipline. I forced him to accept the evil in himself that must be purged."

The evil. A part of Kieran had always believed there

was something terribly wrong with himself. Now she knew. Now she understood.

"And yet I failed," Arnoux said heavily. "Even when he learned to control the changing, he lost all will when he weakened with emotion and reverted to his true nature. But even in his weakness he retained the God-cursed abilities of his kind. When he had become a man, he deceived me and escaped."

"When?" she asked hoarsely.

"It was 1985. I tracked him for a time, but I knew it was fruitless. Eventually I knew he would come back. To me. I was all he had, all he had known for six years."

Six years. Six years of imprisonment. No wonder he feared walls and craved freedom. No wonder he'd driven such memories from his mind. What "discipline" had Arnoux used on him? What had he made Kieran believe of himself?

"Five years ago he did return," Arnoux said. He looked at Alexandra. "But he came with rage, to confront me. And in his rage he hunted down and slaughtered an innocent, an Indian girl who fell in his path."

An Indian girl. Julie's cousin. Alex forced herself to keep breathing. Arnoux had been *there* as well.

He sighed. "I confronted him with proof of his evil, the mangled body like those of my parents. But he gave himself over to the beast. Five more years he ran as a wolf, far to the north. I waited, and again he returned, as he always must. And he came to you." He looked at her. "Why?"

"I found him," she said. "As a wolf, poisoned, in the woods. After that he trusted me."

Arnoux's mouth set in a grim line. "Vermin," he grunted. He shifted his hands on the wheel. "I didn't know what his five years as a beast had done to him. I watched you both, and waited for the right time to act. I had learned so well how to wait. But in the end I delayed too long. He killed, and ran, and killed again.

"I was the one that let him loose on the world. My life's purpose now is to see that Kieran kills no more."

She wanted to scream at him, to tell him that Kieran was no killer, to rant and rail against the man who had warped Kieran's life. But she choked back the intemperate, possibly deadly words, and only nodded in sham agreement.

In silence they drove on. They reached Lovell after ten; only a few streetlamps lit the narrow main street. Just another small town, like Merritt, surrounded by woods that climbed up the steep slopes of the Canadian Rockies. Alex licked her lips and looked out the window for any source of help. A few inebriated men emerged from a bar and staggered down the street, arm in arm; the rest of the town had gone to sleep.

"What now?" she asked.

Arnoux drove through the town and out of it, following a potholed single-lane road that dwindled to dirt and gravel and then to frozen earth, virgin snow, and untamed wilderness.

He turned off into the woods and circled around, stopping the truck in a sheltered place well beyond the reach of any light from Lovell.

"We'll wait here until morning," he said. "And then we'll prepare our trap." He stared at her, as if weighing again the risk of trusting her. "You said he wanted you, Miss Alex. His sense of smell is remarkably keen, as you must know. If he is here, he'll find you sooner or later. I will disguise my own scent and watch while you lure him in."

Alex held his gaze. "It sounds reasonable."

"I know you'll find it reasonable if I keep watch from the truck during the night, Miss Alex." He gestured toward the rear of the truck. "There's food, a tube tent, down sleeping bag and heater in the back. I assume you know how to make your own camp?"

"Yes." The last thing she wanted was any personal help from him—and at least the wind wasn't blowing. With her own multiple layers of clothes and his supplies, she'd do well enough.

He dismissed her with a nod. "Make yourself comfortable. I'll do the rest."

She obeyed, keeping her thoughts focused on the practical motions of setting up a cold-weather camp, knowing she would spend the night trying to keep herself sane. Trying desperately to come up with a plan of her own.

Don't find me, Kieran, she begged. *For God's sake, don't find me until I can get free to warn you.*

But she knew he would come. And she was all that stood between him and death.

🍃 18

Kieran jumped down from the truck and turned to the driver. "Thanks for the ride."

"No problem. Glad of the company. Hope you find what you're looking for." The trucker hesitated, glancing at his watch, and shivered melodramatically. "You sure this is where you want to be let off? It's only six A.M., freezing as hell, and the nearest town a good five kilometers from here."

Kieran shook his head. "I don't want you going any farther out of your way. I can walk."

The driver shrugged. "Have it your way. Just follow the road from the junction, and you'll hit the town." He turned up the volume on his radio. "Back to the lonely road!"

Kieran saluted the trucker and stretched cramped muscles as the truck vanished into the predawn darkness. He'd been lucky to catch a ride so soon after crossing into Alberta; he'd run himself to exhaustion that morning, but the idea of trying to shift made the gorge rise in his throat. He wouldn't have risked coming close to any human being if he'd had any other way of reaching Lovell. That need was all he had left, all that let him hang on to sanity.

Now he was here. Here, so near the place that was calling him. He lifted his head, searching for some confirmation in the scents of unknown territory.

Nothing. The air was heavy and still and very cold, empty of messages.

He began to walk down the winding two-lane highway that the trucker had pointed out to him. So different from Minnesota or the prairie, with these snow-clad mountains on every side. Yet here was a true wilderness, a sense of sanctuary Kieran had never felt before.

Sanctuary. He set his jaw until it ached. If he was a murderer, he deserved no sanctuary. If he found no answers here, there would be none. And then . . .

There was no "then." No future or past. Only the present. He would have to live in the perpetual "now" as the wolves did. Anything else was intolerable.

He walked for a mile and then ran another three. The scents of gathered humanity came to him at last, and he could see the faint glow of man-made light. False dawn tinged the sky with an eerie glow.

He stopped before he reached the edge of town, turning his head in every direction. Alexandra had told him to come here, but this was not the source of whatever summoned him. It lay somewhere beyond . . .

"I was waiting for you."

Kieran turned, sinking into a crouch. A man walked out of the shadows, tall and lean and confident in his stride. He wore a heavy green plaid shirt, jeans and boots; a small backpack swung from one hand. As he came nearer Kieran saw his eyes: yellow-green, set into a chiseled face topped by a shock of hair mingled gray and black and white.

In the space of an instance Kieran knew who the man was. He straightened, his muscles still tense and ready for battle.

"You remember me," the man said. "From Merritt."

"Luke," Kieran said hoarsely. "Luke Gévaudan."

Gévaudan smiled, lips closed over teeth. "You weren't as far gone as you seemed at the time."

Drunk, he meant. He'd offered Alexandra help in getting Kieran out of the bar, and spoken to her afterward. Now he was *here*. Waiting.

"Why are you here?" Kieran said. He took a step forward, knotting his fists.

"I live here." Gévaudan's deep voice was mild, but his eyes were wary and alert as he dropped his pack. Kieran saw the same concealed readiness in his body that Kieran kept in his own. "I only flew back yesterday myself, but I knew you'd turn up."

He *knew*. Kieran judged the space between them and analyzed Gévaudan's size and weight in his mind. If it came down to a fight—

"I was the one who advised Julie Wakanabo to send you here," Gévaudan said. "I knew the call was summoning you, but I thought I'd make it simpler, given your circumstances."

Kieran kept himself from revealing his shock. "Explain," he demanded, advancing another step. "Tell me exactly what the hell you're talking about."

Gévaudan held his gaze. "I think the best explanation is in the showing."

Calmly and deliberately Gévaudan started to strip. When the first touch of gray mist formed around him, Kieran began to understand. And when the great gray wolf stood before him, ears pricked and tail high, Kieran knew.

"You," he whispered. "You're like me."

Within seconds Gévaudan was dressing again with the same efficient nonchalance he'd shown before. "Yes. As I've known you were one of us ever since I saw you in Merritt."

One of us. *Us*. Impossible, and real. Like himself. Kieran's mind raced, but he let none of his confusion show. "You're a werewolf," he said.

"We prefer the name *loup-garou*." Gévaudan finished buttoning his shirt and tossed back his hair with a jerk of his head. "You aren't the first outsider to come to us. How long have you been hearing the call, Kieran Holt?"

Kieran braced his feet firmly against the ground. "What is it?" he countered. "What is this place?"

"Not here." With fluid, unconscious grace Gévaudan settled onto his haunches. "Val Caché. A hidden valley, a village, and a sanctuary for our people. And now a source of gathering." He cocked his head. "Did you think you were the only one? You aren't the first to believe that, and you won't be the last."

Others. Others had been called here, just as he had. Others had believed themselves alone. "How many?" he asked.

"The call is erratic. A few more come to us every year, but how many exist outside Val Caché . . ." He shrugged, a gesture that belied the intensity in his eyes. "In Val Caché alone there are over fifty of us now."

Fifty. A village of people like himself. "Did you . . . come to Merritt to find me?"

"No. Not exactly." The yellow-green eyes had grew wary. "But as soon as I saw you I knew you were one of us. And I knew you were in trouble."

Trouble. Far too mild a word, but Kieran was in no mood to appreciate the irony. "What does that have to do with you?" he challenged.

Gévaudan rose slowly. "It has everything to do with me. With all of us. You need help, Kieran Holt, and we are the only ones who may be able to provide it."

Adrenaline pumped through Kieran's body. "What help?"

"I was there in Merritt. I know about the murder. I know why you ran, and what the police believe."

"And what do you believe, Gévaudan? That I murdered Schaeffer?"

"I don't know. Not yet."

Kieran backed away, shaking his head. "I don't remember. I lost my memory of my past. If I killed—" He choked on the word. "I don't remember."

Gévaudan sighed. "I suspected something like that. I didn't interfere in Merritt because I knew you'd come here when you ran. But I do know how the body looked. I did my own investigation before I left Minnesota." He shifted his stance with a subtle motion. "I know what could have killed him."

"A werewolf," Kieran supplied, hearing the bitterness in his own voice. "A monster."

"We aren't monsters," Gévaudan said sharply. "But it is possible that a few of us—some beyond our reach—could be sick or mentally ill, just as among humans. And if such a one killed Schaeffer, and the Indian girl five years ago—"

Kieran reeled with the memory of the image that had come to him when he saw Lori's body. Gévaudan hadn't mentioned that death. "Who could stop such a killer but one of his own kind?" he asked in a whisper.

Gévaudan nodded. "We have laws, and we live safely and in peace by obeying those laws. We don't kill humans, whatever myth claims." He took a step forward, raising his hand. "I know you don't believe you killed. With us, among your own kind, there may be a way to learn the truth. And isn't that why you're here, Kieran Holt—to learn the truth?"

"And if the truth is that I killed, then you'll make certain I never do it again."

Gévaudan said nothing, but his silence was answer enough. The only answer there could be.

"If you're innocent," Gévaudan said at last, "we can offer you a home, a place among your own kind where you'll be accepted. And needed. There are not many of us in the world. We welcome all who come. You'll have a purpose here."

Kieran met and held the other man's gaze. "I'll go with you to this Val Caché," he said.

He saw Gévaudan relax, so subtly that perhaps only another of his kind would have noticed the change. "Good. It's faster if we run as wolves—"

"No."

"Then we'll walk." He shrugged into his pack and started off into the woods, north and west on a route that would just skirt Lovell. "I'm taking the short route straight through the pass. I've got enough supplies that we can camp over a night if you're not up to it."

Kieran smiled humorlessly. "I think I'll be up to it."

Gévaudan gave him a sideways glance. "I saw Ms. Warrington camped just outside Lovell with the other man, so I assumed you split up for some reason and came separately. You'll have to leave them behind——"

Kieran came to a dead stop. "What?"

"When we're in Val Caché you can send a message to her. I'd strongly advise that you tell her to go home——"

"Alexandra is here?" he said.

"You didn't know?"

Alexandra, *here.* She had known where he was headed—she had told him about Lovell herself. In his anguish over Lori's death and his own searing flash of memory, he had thought only of leaving Alexandra safely behind. There had been no time for explanations, to make her see that she must let him go.

But he'd been blind to think she'd simply return to Minnesota, even though she'd surely heard of Lori's murder and would have been faced with all the same horrifying possibilities that had driven him away from her. He'd underestimated her courage and stubbornness, her own deliberate blindness.

Alexandra, here. His heart sped with mingled joy and dread. To see her once more, only from a distance, when he'd thought never to see her again. To know she was still safe . . .

And then he remembered Gévaudan's words, all of them: ". . . *camped outside Lovell with the other man.*"

"Who is with her?" he demanded.

Gévaudan's eyes narrowed to wary slits. "I don't know him. An older man. You didn't know she'd come here? You two left Merritt together——"

But Kieran was no longer listening. He didn't know this older man, or why he had joined Alexandra in her journey here. But he knew he would never go with Luke until he had seen Alexandra, spoken with her, assured himself she was safe. He would convince her that she must go back to Minnesota. He would not let her risk herself again.

She was more precious to him than life, and he could never tell her, because to speak such words would bind her to him irrevocably. He had to drive her away at any cost, now and forever.

He broke into a run. Gévaudan gave a soft grunt of surprise and caught up to him within a few strides.

"No, Kieran! Leave her where she is. It's better this way—"

Kieran brushed past him, and Gévaudan caught his arm. They skidded to a stop and faced each other, breathing hard.

"Whatever separated you is for the best," Gévaudan said urgently. "Her loyalty to you is admirable, but you don't know what you are. She's human, and vulnerable. Until you do—"

But Kieran had shut out every faculty, every sense, every need but one. He jerked free of the other man's hold and began to run again. He breathed in the mingled scents of the nearby town and forest, sifted through them, isolating the one he must track to its source.

Alexandra's.

He knew Gévaudan followed, and he welcomed the other man's trailing presence. If Kieran should be the killer, if he posed Alexandra any threat at all, another werewolf would be there to stop him.

*D*awn.

Alex sat shivering beside the small fire Arnoux had laid for her. He'd roused her just before daylight, though if she'd slept at all she hadn't been aware of it. His truck was parked just out of sight, so that he could watch from among the trees without being seen.

She'd smelled the stuff he rubbed on himself to disguise his scent. She prayed it wouldn't do him any good. *Kieran, for God's sake . . .* But she didn't complete the thought. For the past thirty minutes, in the feeble light, she'd been trying to locate something—anything—to use as a weapon against Arnoux. But he'd done a remarkable job of clearing away the snow and any potential objects, including the smallest sticks and stones.

One could say that he simply knew the proper way of making a woodland fire. Or it could mean he didn't trust her at all.

She knew he was watching. She felt his eyes like some malignant presence, scanning the forest. He made no sound, had given no indication of his presence since he left her there. "You know what to do," he'd told her.

But she didn't. God help her, she didn't. She'd gone along with Arnoux, hoping for some break that would allow her to escape once they'd reached Lovell, or some moment when he wasn't alert. Neither had come. She berated herself again and again. There must have been something she could have done, something she'd missed.

When the time came, she'd do whatever she could, no matter how desperate. That was the only plan she had left.

She thought of her backpack. Arnoux had failed to return it to her, and she hadn't dared appear anxious about it. But if he found her diary—

A single twig crackled behind her. She whirled around in a crouch. *No, Kieran!*

But it was Arnoux. She lost none of her wariness as he approached, surprised to see him come out in the open. *A slipup*, she thought hopefully. Maybe in his fanatic zeal he'd lost some part of his judgment.

"I thought you were staying out of sight," she said, feigning indifference. "You aren't going to lure him in this way."

Arnoux smiled his cold, hard smile. "I appreciate your concern for my mission, Miss Alex. But now that we're allies, I thought I should return this to you."

Her backpack dangled from one big, rawboned hand, his rifle from the other. She shrugged and reached out to accept the pack just as he flipped it out of her grasp.

"I'm sure you'll forgive me if I've already searched the

pack for weapons," he said mildly. "But all I found was this."

He crouched just out of her reach, unzipped the pack and pulled out the journal.

"Do you know, Miss Alex, for many years I also kept a diary. A record of my work with Kieran. In time I found the words were meaningless." He flipped open the cover and stroked the paper with roughened fingers. "To confine your life to these pages is to run from your destiny. Or destroy it."

Alex smiled thinly. "You'll forgive me if I disagree. I've found my journal to be very useful in my studies. Now, if you don't mind returning it to me . . ."

"It's private. Of course." But still Arnoux did not relinquish it. "Does this contain your observations of Kieran, perhaps? You promised to share them with me, Miss Alex." He began to thumb through it, skimming pages and passing on. Until suddenly he stopped, the weight of his concentration focused on her neatly handwritten lines.

" 'And after all that happened, Mother, I didn't want to fight anymore.' " Arnoux read in a flat voice. " 'I wanted him to kiss me. I wanted more, but I didn't dare take it. I knew I'd never earned that kind of happiness, that it could never work.' " Arnoux lifted his head, expressionless. "Fascinating research, Miss Alex." He jerked the book open to the final page. The page she'd left blank except for a single line. She clenched her fists, fighting off waves of panic.

Arnoux stared at her as he recited it aloud. " 'God help me, Mother. I love him.' "

Almost gently Arnoux closed the book and laid it on the ground between them. "I almost believed you," he said. "You were most convincing. You did lie with him, did you not?" He grabbed her wrist with the speed of a striking rattler and crushed her bones until she had to bite back a cry of pain. "Are you carrying his seed?"

But she had no time to respond, for Arnoux's head jerked up and his eyes focused on the woods directly behind her. Alex twisted in his grasp, just in time to see

Kieran, half-masked by the trees but well within range. Just in time to see Arnoux reach for his rifle and begin the motion of raising it to his shoulder.

"*Run, Kieran!*" she screamed, and in the same instant flung herself at Arnoux. He kicked her away without even looking, as if she were some species of lesser pest, and took aim.

"*Kieran!*" Alex screamed again.

A blur of motion was all she saw. Arnoux stepped back, his rifle wavering in his grasp. "Stop," he said harshly. The rifle swung down, the muzzle inches from Alex's head. "Stop now, or I'll kill your whore, Kieran Holt."

It became a perfect tableau. Kieran stood three yards from Arnoux, teeth bared, eyes narrowed, fingers curled into claws at his sides. Arnoux held the rifle on Alex, a strange and terrible smile on his face.

Kieran. Alex let herself look her fill, as if it were the last moment she would ever have. He was more beautiful than anything she'd ever seen in her life, more precious than anything in the world.

His eyes met hers. In that brief gaze he gave her more courage than she would ever need to make any sacrifice.

Then he looked again at Arnoux. "I don't care about this woman," he said, and took another step forward.

Arnoux laughed, a low rumble of bitter amusement. He pressed the muzzle of the rifle directly against Alex's temple. "No, my lost and damned son. No farther. You were never very good at lying." His smile vanished. "I will kill her. I've hunted you far too long, and nothing can stop me again. I'll let the woman live if you give yourself up to me."

Kieran stared at Arnoux, and Alex knew he didn't remember, didn't recognize the man before him. "Who are you?" Kieran grated.

Arnoux's expression changed. "How can you have forgotten your father, boy?" He shook his head in a travesty of weary resignation. "My name is Joseph Arnoux."

*K*ieran froze. *Joseph Arnoux.* The name seized his heart in a fist of pain and rage.

I know him.

The thought was not a rational one. It settled in his gut with instinctive certainty, fed by emotion that sprang directly from the beast within. It came with a wisp of scent covered over by some other stench, from the very look of the man: tall and broad shouldered in his heavy coat, cold green eyes in an aging, weathered face. And it came most of all from the sound of his voice.

The Voice. The voice he had heard in his mind when he'd thought himself so close to madness.

Joseph Arnoux.

And with the beginnings of recognition came rage. Rage that even Alexandra's presence had no power to temper. Violent sensations pumped through Kieran with each beat of his heart, emanated from the man before him in equal measure. Hatred was like a bond between them, a heavy chain forged in the fires of a past Kieran could not remember.

Kieran forced himself to look again at Alexandra. Her gaze was fixed on him—pleading, but not for her life. He knew her too well for that. Because Kieran had left her back in Saskatchewan, it had come to this. She was a madman's hostage, and still his memories would not come clear when he needed them most.

The forest was silent, as if every creature in it felt the deadly tension. "Let her go," he commanded.

Arnoux shook his head. "Can you remember so little, boy? So little of our last meeting, all our time together? I can fulfill my duty at last, atone for all my mistakes." He pushed at Alexandra with his rifle. "She's human. I don't want to hurt her. Perhaps there's nothing in you that would sacrifice yourself for another. Or is there, boy?"

"Kieran, no!" Alexandra lurched up onto her knees, her face flushed and her eyes bright with tears. "Don't listen to him! He followed us all the way from Merritt just to kill you!"

Kieran didn't look at her. He thought of Luke

Gévaudan, somewhere in the woods behind him. He would come soon, if he wasn't already here. If Kieran could stall for time . . .

"Why?" he asked, swallowing back the rage. "Why do you want me dead?"

Arnoux searched his eyes. "You truly don't remember. I see it in you." His hard mouth twisted. "My failure with you was great, boy. The evil could not be excised. It even exacted a price from your memory."

Kieran fought to think, to hold on to the rationality that was his only hope of finding answers. One by one Arnoux gave him clues, keys to unlock his past.

"But you didn't forget how to kill, did you, boy?" Arnoux continued, his voice bitter. "Was it the face of your own evil that drove you to the beast five years ago, after I showed you the body of the girl you'd slain—as you killed Peter Schaeffer and Lori Carstens?"

"Don't listen to him, Kieran!" Alexandra cried.

Arnoux never looked away from Kieran. "I held hope for too long because of my own misplaced mercy for the boy you were. I was a father to you." His voice softened. "I took you in, fed you, cared for you—"

"You're . . . not my father," Kieran choked.

"I was in every way but one. I tried to save you. God knows I tried."

The memories struggled to emerge, coaxed forth by Arnoux's low, intense words. But Kieran dared not lose himself to them, even when they were close enough to touch.

"You hunted me," he said. "All the time when I was with Alexandra—"

"I was watching. Waiting. I knew you'd come back, no matter how far you wandered." He lowered the rifle, almost as if he believed Kieran had no power to resist him. "And you haven't changed. Not from the day I took you into my home. But now the killing is over. You have been and will always be a monster, and I must end it."

Monster. The word lodged in Kieran's mind, and he

staggered as he felt memory smash into him without warning, grinding him down, blurring his vision.

He struggled to keep his feet. Cold green eyes had become the world, the world Arnoux had shaped, and Kieran could no longer see Alexandra or sense her presence.

Only memory remained.

19

Kieran remembered.

The long years vanished. He was a child again, and his parents were dead. They had warned him to stay close, but he had left them to find the girl. And when he returned . . .

Kieran staggered with the pain of it, unbearable pain, the severance of love and belonging. He lay between the wolves, sobbing, lost. And then the man had come.

"I will be your father, boy," he had said. "I will save you." And Kieran, dazed and blind with shock, had believed. The man had led him to a place of safety, a place of high walls and isolation.

But there was no safety, no belonging. And the place of high walls was where the lessons had begun.

"You are a monster," the man had said, the man who called himself Joseph Arnoux. "You must be human." Kieran had tried to please him. There was no one else but Arnoux in his world—Arnoux's voice, Arnoux's eyes. Kieran had fought the powerful instincts that urged him to run as a wolf, had tried to control the shifting, but he had been young and inexperienced.

When he failed to control the beast, he was punished.

Arnoux had found the worst punishment of all: to lock Kieran up in darkness, chained, like the animal he was.

Darkness. Isolation. Hell. Reality had been reduced to those simple words, and by another repeated again and again by the man who shaped Kieran's fate: monster. *Years passed, and Kieran grew to manhood. There came a time when he could almost control the beast, but emotion had been his undoing. The more he fought that part of himself, the more cunning it became in finding ways to be set free. The time came when anger or fear alone triggered the shifting.*

A madness had come over Kieran then. He had discovered a way out of the compound, waited with animal cunning, pretending abject defeat. Until one day he had turned on Arnoux, blind with rage too long suppressed, and escaped with nothing but hatred—of the man who ruled him, and of himself.

He wandered. Place to place, trying to forget, learning to survive in a world he barely remembered. Towns where no one knew him or of his affliction; people who accepted without asking questions, bound by a brotherhood of hopelessness.

Sometimes there would be someone he could reach out to. Like Lori. For a short time he would find companionship in sorrow and loneliness. For a while he would remember something gentler, something good, the boy who had known love and was capable of giving. But it always ended. And then the running once more, before he revealed his inner evil to the world.

No home. No people. Until he returned to the place where it had begun, to the burial site of parents he hardly remembered. There Arnoux had found him. There Arnoux had shown him the body of an innocent girl.

The blood. The blood, the taste and smell of it—the horror. Shifting, shifting back into the wolf, who would not remember. Because he was guilty, evil and guilty and cursed. . . .

"No!"

Memory splintered like shards of ice. Kieran's vision cleared.

"You remember," Arnoux said.

Kieran felt nothing. "You offered an exchange," he said flatly. "My life for hers. Let her go, and I won't try to escape."

Arnoux weighed Kieran's sincerity for a long, aching moment. Abruptly he lifted his rifle and jerked his head at Alexandra.

"Go," he commanded.

Alexandra scrambled to the side on hands and knees and jumped to her feet. She stood there, breathing fast and hard, the stubborn set of her jaw and the light in her eyes defying Arnoux with silent courage.

"Go!" Kieran repeated savagely. "I won't have your blood on my hands!"

Her expression revealed nothing as she began to back away. Kieran knew she would never run. But he still had a chance to throw Arnoux off balance, to do whatever was necessary to insure her safety. His own no longer mattered.

Kieran stepped forward until only a foot separated him from the business end of Arnoux's rifle. "Now you have me, Arnoux. Finish it."

A strange look passed over Arnoux's face. "Once I . . . cared for you, boy, in spite of your evil," he said softly. "Once you called me Father."

"Never," Kieran croaked. "You were never a father to me. You were my tormentor."

"For your salvation," Arnoux said. "It was necessary."

Kieran turned his head from the bizarre mingling of contempt and sadness and hatred in Arnoux's eyes. He caught a subtle flash of motion in the woods behind him. Not Alexandra; she had worked her way to a point a few yards behind Arnoux. A whiff of scent came to him, and he knew it was Gévaudan.

"I know Miss Warrington is behind me," Arnoux said. "Foolish." He sighed. "It is a great sadness to me that she must die when I'm finished with you."

Kieran almost leaped. The rifle's muzzle swung up.

"Your bestial emotion was always your undoing, my son. I follow reason. And reason tells me that you have almost certainly defiled Miss Warrington beyond any redemption."

Kieran snarled. "And you call me evil?"

Arnoux was unmoved. "How could she, a human woman, give herself to you?" His thin lip lifted in a grimace. "But she did, didn't she? She may even now be carrying your seed, and that I can't permit."

"Run, Alexandra!" Kieran begged, meeting her eyes across the chasm of space that yawned between them. But she only looked at him with a deep and infinite sadness.

"Her loyalty is almost admirable," Arnoux said. "She'll stay here to watch you die, and then—"

"No!" Kieran roared. He lunged at Arnoux. Light flashed on the barrel of the rifle as the dark eye of death aimed at Kieran's heart and then just as swiftly swung to a point just beyond his shoulder. Someone screamed a harsh battle cry that ended in a grunt of pain. Alexandra exploded into a run, barreling into Arnoux from behind. He batted Alexandra aside as if she were an insect. Kieran ripped the rifle from Arnoux's grip and tossed it into the brush.

For a split second everything froze. Kieran smelled blood mingled with Gévaudan's scent and knew that the other werewolf had been shot trying to intervene. The harsh sound of Luke's breathing in the silence proved he was still alive. Alexandra lay dazed on the ground, struggling to lever her arms under her body, hurt but conscious.

A wolf's howl shattered the moment—a deep, wild baying that seemed to carry within it all the chaotic emotion in Kieran's own heart. And then Arnoux was charging, slamming into Kieran with the full force of his greater weight. Kieran had just enough time to brace for Arnoux's attack. The two of them rolled in the snow. Arnoux pounded Kieran in the jaw with his bunched fist. Kieran bent his legs, shoved Arnoux in the belly and kicked. As Arnoux went flying, Kieran launched himself after his enemy.

Before Arnoux could scramble to his feet, Kieran was

on top of him. He pushed Arnoux down, hard, and stared into the unrelenting green eyes.

Something happened then, inexplicable and terrible beyond words. Kieran had no reference for it in memory or experience, and yet he knew it was real. Between one instant and the next it was as if his body had dissolved, his and Arnoux's both—and with it all barriers between them, leaving them battling with only mind and will. He felt himself slipping into the black pit that he knew was Arnoux's consciousness, Arnoux's vengeful soul.

It was as if a monster were devouring him alive.

He struggled against it, summoned up his own will, lashed out, until their very minds seemed to meet, to meld, to become one.

One.

Kieran reeled with shock. Arnoux's body had gone rigid, unresisting. They were inextricably bound, but not only by hatred. Not only by the revelation of Kieran's wretched past.

A howl burst in Kieran's mind, a greater rage than he had ever known. *Arnoux's* rage. *Arnoux's* denial. Arnoux dragged him down into madness, another seething cauldron of memory.

Five years ago. A body, and blood. The victim, a once-pretty girl from the reservation, face contorted in death. A figure rose from her mangled form. Clawed hands, coated in blood, reached for Kieran in supplication.

Arnoux's hands. Not Kieran's. Arnoux's.

Another victim. And there had been still more. Peter Schaeffer, dying in terror beneath tearing claws and fangs. Lori Carstens . . .

Kieran saw them through eyes not his own, through a mind twisted with violent fury and rapture.

Arnoux's eyes.

"Lies!" Arnoux screamed. He heaved under Kieran, throwing him off.

But Kieran *knew.* "You killed those people," he snarled. "I see it. *You* killed them."

Kieran was innocent. Innocent.

"*You* killed Schaeffer," he snarled. "And Lori."

Arnoux laughed. "Evil. You lie—"

Lies. Kieran sobbed for air. Truth itself had been twisted into something almost obscene. But there was yet another truth that leaped between them like a fatal current.

He and his enemy were the same. One breed, one kind.

Arnoux was not human.

"You're like me," Kieran said, staggering to his feet. "You are a—"

Arnoux screamed. He leaped straight up, twisting in midair and falling heavily to the ground. He began to claw at his clothing.

No—no—no—no— The crazed savagery of Arnoux's denial severed the bizarre mental link between them, setting Kieran free.

He searched desperately for Alexandra. She had worked her way to her knees and was trying to rise, but she was too weak. God, how he wanted to go to her.

Kieran backed away, putting more space between himself and Alexandra, watching Arnoux as he ripped off the last of his clothes and scrambled to his feet.

Kieran knew how this must end. It was clear in his mind, so recently joined with that of his pursuer and tormentor: what must be, the resolution of so many years lost to Arnoux's madness. There was only one way to stop the man who had never accepted his true nature and used it to kill.

Kieran began to strip. He gathered his hatred, his rage, his grief for all he had lost and spun it into unshakable purpose. Arnoux had murdered his parents. Arnoux had warped his life. Arnoux had killed innocents, and left their blood on Kieran's hands. Arnoux might have killed Alexandra . . .

"Arnoux," he snarled.

Kieran's enemy faced him with grotesque eagerness. His coat and cap, shirt and trousers and boots, lay scattered around him like the remnants of some terrible, bloodless battle. His body was lean and scarred and powerful for its age. His short gray hair stood on end like a wolf's bristling pelt. His eyes burned.

Even in Arnoux's madness he understood. He bared his teeth in a death's-head grin. "I'll send you to hell."

*A*lex tried to rise. She tried to move, to speak, but Arnoux's blow had robbed her of voice and strength. She could only watch as destiny played itself out in this silent, snowbound forest.

Arnoux had always been the killer. Alex knew it was true, though she understood almost nothing of what had passed between Arnoux and Kieran after she was struck. All she'd heard were Kieran's accusations, Arnoux's denial—and the raging madness in his voice that could only come of facing a truth too terrible to bear.

"You're like me," Kieran had said. The pieces had fallen into place. Arnoux had always been what Kieran was. Kieran's search for his own kind had led him back to the one man who had made him hate his own inhuman nature.

There was no humanity in the deadly, silent dance that began now before Alex's eyes.

Kieran moved like fire, like lightning burning the snow, his hair whipping about his face. And Arnoux—Arnoux had the strength of madness. In hatred they were equally matched.

They went at each other without quarter or mercy, hands curled into claws, teeth bared. Alex knew why they fought as they did, naked to the freezing air, and yet still they fought as men. Kieran could have shifted, had prepared to shift, and yet he controlled himself as he had never done before, now when the stakes were life and death.

And he was winning. It became clear after the first few minutes that something crippled Arnoux, far more than his greater age. His punches began to fall without strength, his movements to falter. Kieran beat Arnoux back ruthlessly, step by step. When the older man stumbled and fell the battle was already finished.

Kieran stood over Arnoux, feet braced wide. Every line of his body spat hatred. Arnoux didn't move. Great clouds of mist rose from his open mouth as he waited. Waited to die.

Alexandra's vision blurred. She found no pity in her heart for Arnoux. She wanted him punished, but not by Kieran's hand. Not in a way that would haunt Kieran for the rest of his life, as Arnoux had haunted his past.

As if he sensed her thoughts, Kieran turned his head. Amber eyes fixed unerringly on hers across the distance between them.

Don't do it, Kieran, she begged silently. *There must be another way.*

Arnoux roared and moved with terrifying speed, kicking Kieran's legs out from under him. He fell on Kieran and struck Kieran's face with his bunched fist, again and again, until Alex could see blood spattering the snow.

Her throat unlocked in a scream. Her body obeyed her will at last, and she pushed to her knees with desperate concentration.

But Kieran had already responded to her cry. He began to blur, the familiar mist forming around his body. Becoming a wolf at last. Arnoux's next blow never landed. Massive jaws closed on Arnoux's hand and bit down. The crunch of bone was audible. Arnoux staggered back as the great black Kieran-wolf scrambled to his feet and leaped.

This time there was no hesitation. Kieran straddled Arnoux, his forepaws pinning the older man's bare shoulders to the ground. He flung back his head and howled, a chilling cry of victory.

Alexandra crawled through the snow, sobbing for breath and strength. Kieran's muzzle drew back from his fangs. His head plunged down toward Arnoux's naked throat.

"No!" Alexandra hurled herself forward the last few feet, arms stretched, fingers reaching. Her hand brushed the wolf's shoulder as she landed on her belly. *"Kieran!"*

She threw her soul into the word, her being, the memory of all they had shared. She clutched a handful of his pelt, dug her fingers down to the skin as if she could reach his very heart.

"Kieran, you're not a killer. Listen to me! You're not what he taught you. You never were."

Kieran shuddered under her hand. She couldn't let go of him, not even long enough to wipe the blinding tears from her eyes.

"You're the best of what it is to be human and wolf, Kieran. You're a miracle. Don't throw that away."

His eyes turned to her, lambent and filled with pain.

"I love you, Kieran." She repeated the words she had never quite dared to say. *"I love you."*

She knew she had won when he closed his eyes, his ears dropping down in a gesture of surrender. She knew she had won, and gloried in that fragile victory.

But there was to be no moment of peace. From the woods wolves came, three of them, behaving with a boldness no ordinary wolf would dare in the presence of humans. Two men followed, lean and pale-eyed, supporting between them a limping comrade, his denim-clad thigh bound with blood-soaked cloth. Luke Gévaudan, last seen in Merritt.

Confused, she turned to Kieran. He had shifted back in the space of seconds, but he was not looking at Luke and the strangers. She followed his gaze to Arnoux's face.

It was no longer human.

"My God," she choked. "My God."

Kieran pulled her against him and dragged her free of Arnoux. They knelt together in the snow, staring at the man who had caused so much misery and pain.

Arnoux's eyes were the same shape and color as they had been before. They gazed back at Alexandra in wordless appeal, begging pity and absolution when once they had only condemned. But the face—the face was grotesque.

It was neither wolf nor man. A blunt muzzle pushed out from a high human forehead, covered in patches of hair. Ears grew halfway between the side and the top of the head. And below—below lay a twisted torso, misshapen, pelted in gray, the chest laboring with each fall and rise. His malformed mouth twisted in a parody of a smile, baring rows of pointed teeth.

"What . . . do you see?" he croaked. His hand flailed toward her, and she saw it was like the rest of him, a shape caught between one form and another, tipped with claws. "What am I?"

Alexandra couldn't answer, but Kieran never looked away from Arnoux's agonized gaze. "You know what you are," he said softly.

*A*rnoux arched up, breath rattling. The horror in the woman's eyes left him no path of escape. The truth in Kieran's words was torment beyond anything he had imagined could exist short of hell itself.

He had fought the harrowing revelation at first. Such a perversion could not be. Providence would not so mock him. But when the instincts had awakened, all the denials had done no good. From the moment his mind had met Kieran's in battle, he had known. And when the boy had shifted, Arnoux had been pulled into the shadows and emerged the abomination he was now.

Remembering everything. *Everything.*

"Yes," he whispered. He met Kieran's unblinking, oddly quiet gaze. "Kill me, boy."

Kieran glanced once at Alexandra. "No." His voice shook. "I'm not your executioner."

Arnoux laughed, the sound tearing up from his lungs like broken glass. "I would have been yours."

But he understood then. There would be no mercy. This was the beginning of atonement. For he was to be punished for his terrible sins, punished with the realization of what he was, this grotesque shape to which he had been condemned.

Only *she* was human.

He flexed his fingers, reaching out to her, needing to

touch, to explain. But there was something wrong with his tongue. He could not make it form the words of confession. The horror was too great. His vision began to blur strangely, and he blinked, disoriented and lost.

The woman bent over him, touching his face. Her brown hair was as he remembered it, pulled back from her plain, lined face. So gentle, her hands.

"Joseph," she said.

"Maman?"

"We are here, Joseph."

The second voice was grim and heavy. Papa had ever been a hard man. He stared down at Arnoux without pity.

"You remember what you did to us, boy."

Arnoux writhed. No. No. But he saw it all, like an ancient black-and-white film played out behind his eyes.

"The beast . . . killed you," he gasped.

"You killed me," Papa said.

"You killed us both, *mon fils,"* Maman echoed.

Maman's voice ached with sorrow. The last time he heard it, it had been raised in terror and accusation.

"I didn't want to, *Maman,"* he said. "But you wouldn't understand that Papa tried to kill *me."*

"I tried to destroy a wolf," Papa said harshly.

"It was me, Papa." He tried to sit up, but his limbs were strangely heavy. "I didn't want to be a wolf. I didn't know what was happening. When I saw you, I tried to change back. But I couldn't. And you tried to kill me. . . ."

"You brought his body back to me, and then you became a monster," *Maman* said, so sadly.

"I was afraid when you screamed. I didn't mean to hurt you."

"You denied your own evil," Papa said. "You buried us unconsecrated and convinced yourself some other creature had killed us. But it was you. Always you."

"Papa," Arnoux sobbed. "Forgive me."

"It is not only for us to forgive," *Maman* said. "There were others. Innocents. You blamed another for their deaths." She stroked his forehead. "It is almost time for you to come to us again, but first you must go back. Go back and make your confession."

Go back. He didn't want to. There was a tight band around his ribs, and his body was leaden. *I am dying.* But the thought brought only a great release. Now he could speak.

When he opened his eyes *Maman* was gone. He gripped another woman's hand. His fingers were human in hers.

His vision was blurred, but he could see Alexandra, and Kieran, and the others. They would hear his confession, and *Maman* would still be waiting.

"I confess my sins," he whispered. "I killed." And he began to recite the names of those who had died by his hand, beginning with his parents; the girl in Minnesota five years ago, her death used to convince Kieran that *he* was the murderer; Peter Schaeffer, victim of Arnoux's bloodlust and frustration; Lori Carstens, innocent of any offense. All savaged under the fangs of a monster.

Himself.

He looked at Kieran one last time. His hatred was gone. "I laid my guilt upon you," he said, his voice fading. "Now we are both free."

Alexandra leaned over him again, and he heard fragments of words: ". . . doctor . . . hang on . . ."

He tried to shake his head. *"Maman* is waiting," he said, and closed his eyes. She was still there, as she had promised.

"The beast has gone away, hasn't it, *Maman*?"

Tears ran down her face and fell on their joined hands. "It will go away, Joseph."

"Can I come with you now, *Maman*?"

Maman looked up at something Joseph couldn't see. A veil fell over his eyes. His ears closed. The ground fell away from beneath him.

"Maman! Don't let me go!"

"I won't, Joseph. I promise—"

"Maman . . . the beast . . ."

It was coming back for him. He could feel it in his heart, filling him up with hate and the need for blood.

Never again. He fought it, felt his body begin to twist inside, bones and organs and skin stretching and contracting. Fur rippled across his skin and vanished again. Wolf and man, back and forth, battling for mastery.

"*Maman!*" he screamed. "Hold me!"

And she held him through the convulsions, one upon another as he gave a last push and drove the beast from his body. His life went with it, but he gave it willingly, gratefully.

"Come, Joseph," *Maman* said from very far away. "You are free."

20

Arnoux was human again, as he'd begun.

Alex held his hand until she knew the last life was gone. It was Kieran who eased the man's fingers from her own, who shut the staring green eyes with a gentle brush of his palm.

So quiet. Alex scrubbed her face and gazed around at a world that seemed unreal. Kieran seemed very far away, as if he, too, had been pulled into Arnoux's final madness and hadn't yet found his way back.

Luke stood over them with his companions, silent and still. She knew what he was, what he had to be. He and the wolves at his side.

"Alexandra," Kieran said. He reached for her blindly, brushed her arm and cheek with a fleeting touch. "Are you all right?"

"Yes," she said, swallowing hard. "We're both all right now."

"He was going to kill you." His voice shook, the rage muted to a smothered flame as if all the fuel that fed it had been burned away.

"But he didn't." She rested her hand on his shoulder, almost expecting him to flinch away. "It's over, Kieran."

His gaze held hers clearly for an instant and then turned inward. "He killed his own parents. He couldn't . . . accept what he was."

That was the terrible tragedy that had twisted Arnoux's life, and Kieran's, and even her own. But her suffering was nothing to theirs. She could pity Arnoux at last, but he was beyond any need for it.

Kieran had his memories to live with. Memories he would have to work through and integrate into himself.

"My parents," he said. "I remember them now." His eyes saw something far beyond her vision. "They loved me."

As I love you. She wanted desperately to hold him, to be held by him, but he was so remote. She couldn't expect so much of him. She had no right to.

She stood up slowly, her body stiff and heavy with more than mere pain.

"Alexandra Warrington."

Luke Gévaudan's voice. She remembered it from their brief meeting in Merritt. He and the two men who supported him had moved off a little, as if to grant Kieran privacy. Alex joined them.

"Luke," she acknowledged wearily. "We meet again." She glanced at his leg. "Arnoux shot you."

Luke smiled with one side of his mouth. "I'm sorry I wasn't able to intervene in a more timely manner."

"You should see a doctor."

"In time. We heal quickly."

We. She nodded without surprise. "I heard a howl after the gunshot. You . . . called the others, didn't you?" She hugged herself. "Kieran was right all along. He believed there were others like him."

"Yes. We are Kieran's people. We call ourselves *loup-garou.*" He bent his head toward the man on his right. "My cousin, Philippe. And Gaston." He followed her gaze to the wolves who had gathered around Kieran. "Kinfolk. There are many others."

Many others. Kieran had never truly been alone. Just

as he wasn't now. "Kieran was driven to come this way," she said. "He could never explain it."

"It's not easily explained. It's a call that wakes in our kind and draws them here—to Val Caché, the village our people founded a hundred years ago. As it woke in Kieran."

"But when you were in Merritt—"

"I knew that he was one of us," Luke said. "That was why I offered my help. And why I told your friend Julie to send you to Lovell. It's the closest human town to our village."

Alex remembered the way Julie had avoided explaining why she urged them to make for this particular town in British Columbia. "Then Julie knew what you were, just as she knew about Kieran."

"Only after you left Merritt," he said. "We had an understanding." He shifted his weight with a grimace. "Very few humans know about us, and we prefer to keep it that way. We choose carefully."

Alex shivered from more than the cold that so easily penetrated her flannel shirt and sweater. "There's still a lot I don't understand, and I don't think I know how to begin asking." She looked at Arnoux's body, and beyond. Kieran was standing now, gazing off into the forest. "Did you know about all this? About Arnoux and what he was?"

"No." Luke's expression grew bleak. "I knew about the killings in Merritt. Our people are not murderers, Alexandra. I had no choice but to suspect Kieran of aberrant behavior. I believed only his kind could help him, and I knew he would come to us. But I never suspected Arnoux, even when you arrived here with him." He shook his head. "We can usually recognize one of our own, but Arnoux had denied what he was so powerfully that he blocked himself from my senses. And Kieran didn't know how to recognize me."

Alex braced her legs to keep from swaying. "You were waiting here for us."

"I was waiting for Kieran."

"Then you sent Kieran to look for me."

"I did everything I could to keep him from going to you. He'd already made the decision to come with me to Val Caché. I thought it was for the best, that he had to be among his own people to learn the truth."

Among his own people. For the first time Alex felt a strange, dull shock run through her body, a brutal new understanding she had been pushing into the back of her mind.

"You didn't think I'd be able to help him," she said, her tone devoid of emotion. "Because I'm not . . . one of you."

Luke was silent for a long time. "It was here we learned the truth," he said at last. "You did help him, Alexandra."

"I put him in danger, believing I could—" She looked away. *Believing I could help. That I could somehow stop Arnoux and warn Kieran. If I hadn't followed him when he ran from me in Saskatchewan, he wouldn't have had me to worry about. He left me for a reason.*

He left me because he knew I couldn't help him anymore. But I made myself believe that one night together could solve everything . . .

Alex passed her hand over her eyes. "I have a . . . lot to think about," she whispered. "And Kieran has even more."

"There's time for that now," Luke said. "The hunt is over. Arnoux is finished. Kieran has found what he was looking for." He held Alex's gaze with grave intensity. "And we have found him. There are so few of us in the world. Now he's come home."

Home. Alex swallowed again. A home among his own. A home to make up for the travesty of it he'd shared with Arnoux. A future to replace the past he had lost. A chance to start over.

As if to echo her thoughts, a howl rose on the wind. Men and women drifted into the clearing, moving like graceful shadows. Even from a distance she could see their eyes: wolves' eyes, yellow-green and yellow-gray and amber and emerald and every shade in between. They made unerringly for Kieran.

Alex caught a glimpse of his expression as he saw them: it was as if the light shone full on his face and through him, a mingling of hope and slow amazement. The three wolves that had come with Luke blurred into mist and became men almost as beautiful as he was. They and the newcomers surrounded Kieran—touching his arm, smiling, speaking in soft voices of welcome, accepting him among them until she could no longer see Kieran at all.

Even Luke had left her to join the others, limping between his kinfolk. Alex felt the terrible pain of joy for Kieran, knowing what he must feel. No longer rejected, no longer bound to hide his nature. Belonging as he had never belonged before. Oh, she knew how wonderful that felt, and how precious a gift it was.

She could not be a part of it.

She hardly knew when she turned to go, blindly, floundering in the deep snow with no direction in mind but away. The cold reached deep inside her, numbing her heart as it chilled her skin. Still she blundered on, past trees that all looked identical, over creeks as ice-bound as her thoughts.

And right into a solid, warm wall of flesh and bone and muscle.

"Alexandra," Kieran said.

She stumbled back. "Kieran. I thought—"

"That I'd abandoned you?"

She backed against the nearest tree trunk and wrapped her arms around herself. He was dressed now, in snug cords and a loose shirt. Not the same torn clothing he'd worn before the fight; perhaps Luke had given these to him. But there was more change in him than that. It was in the way he stood—a kind of unconscious pride, a self-acceptance, a charisma that she'd always seen in the wolves she loved.

Arnoux had not destroyed him. Everything he'd endured had made him stronger. He had become so much more than human.

This is what he was meant to be, she thought. Pride and love tightened her chest. She remembered when he'd first come to her—so vulnerable, so confused. He had needed her so much then. Now he resembled in every way the true miracle he was, free at last of the chains of his past.

"You're all right, Kieran," she said, just to fill the silence.

"Are you?" he countered softly.

She looked into his eyes. They were so clear, like a mountain lake dyed by the setting sun. They seemed to hold wisdom that no adversity could ever take away again.

Some of that wisdom had rubbed off on her. She smiled crookedly. "Just a little cold."

He held out a bundle to her. "Your coat. Thank you."

She took it from him, careful not to let their hands touch in the transfer. "What about the . . . others?" she asked.

"Luke is having Arnoux's body taken care of. He knows the local doctor." He searched her eyes. "So much has happened, Alexandra, and I haven't been able to explain—"

"You don't need to." She maintained her smile with an effort. "I think I'm beginning to understand. Luke told me some of it. How he knew what you were and told Julie to send us here. About your people and their village. Kieran, it's everything you were searching for."

"Is it?"

She held his gaze. "Look at you," she said. "I can see it. The peace inside you. Because you know who you are. Because you've come home."

He took a step toward her. "Is that what you see?"

She willed him to keep his distance. "Yes. And I'm so glad." Her throat closed, and she thought better of saying more.

Kieran stopped. "People have died to bring this peace." He spoke without bitterness, an infinite sadness in his eyes. "Peter. Lori. The girl from the reservation."

She looked down, blinking back tears. "That wasn't

your fault, Kieran. You didn't know. And you stopped Arnoux in the end. You faced your past and defeated it, without killing."

"Arnoux defeated himself," Kieran said. "Something happened during the fight. Somehow Arnoux and I . . . linked minds. That was how I learned what he was and what he'd done. Luke told me that such things are possible among the *loup-garou*." He exhaled heavily. "Arnoux saw his own reflection. He couldn't live with it."

"But even he found some kind of peace when he confessed the truth. I hope Lori and Peter and Julie's cousin have found theirs, somehow." She twisted her coat between her hands. "I've been thinking . . . all that money I inherited from my father. I want to put some of it in an account for Lori's son, for his education. He's lost so much, and . . . it's a way of giving some of it back."

She felt rather than heard him move closer. "Thank you, Alexandra."

With a sharp motion she shook out her coat and pulled it on. "I'll go see Lori's sister as soon as I can. Kevin's father might want the boy back, and I want to help her with any custody hearings. He needs a good parent, a safe home to grow up in. And don't thank me again. You'd do the same."

Kieran's dark hair lifted and stirred around his shoulders. "You make it very hard for me to tell you what a good person you are," he said softly.

She shook her head, cooling the heat in her face. "I'm grateful for whatever I can do to help."

"As you helped me."

"As you and I helped each *other*." She met his gaze. "I promised to help you find out who you are, rediscover your past. Now you have those things. And you . . . you've taught me how to face myself."

She touched her scarred cheek. The rough skin felt natural to her now, as much a part of what she was as the wolf was part of Kieran. She no longer wanted to make it disappear.

"You gave me back myself," she said. "I've let go of

the old stuff I was dragging around for so long. I can never thank you enough for that."

"And now it's over."

To hear him say the words was more painful than she could have believed. "Arnoux is gone. You have nothing to fear in yourself anymore. You've found your people." She looked back the way she had come, knowing the were-wolves would still be waiting for him to return. "I saw the way they accepted you, welcomed you—"

"Is that why you ran away?"

She jerked up her chin and glared at him. "Maybe you shouldn't talk about running away, Kieran."

She wondered why she brought it up. She'd known at the time why he left her in Saskatchewan. It had made perfect sense then, and not one iota of difference now.

"I had to, Alexandra. I thought I could be a danger to you, after Lori was killed. I thought—"

"I know what you thought. You thought I wasn't strong enough to cope with what *you* thought you might be. My faith in you wasn't enough. And you didn't really need me anymore. Your instincts gave you an alternative, and you followed them. To this place." She heard the rising emotion in her own voice and caught her breath. "And I followed you, still believing you might—"

"Need you?" he finished softly.

She kept her words cool and level. "I only made things worse."

"No, Alexandra."

"There was a time when you needed me. But I can't do anything more for you now. Not when you have a place to belong, your own people to give you what you've been missing all your life."

"Such as love?"

She tensed her muscles so the shaking wouldn't show. "I believe you can have whatever you want, Kieran. You were always worthy of love."

His eyes gave her no quarter. "You're very sure of my future. What about the past? Our past?" He seemed to loom over her without moving at all. "Can you tell me the reason for everything that's happened? Why we were brought together so many years ago and found each other again?"

"I don't—"

"What about the night we made love?"

With that single sentence he made her remember and relive every moment she had been in his arms, every kiss and caress and murmured endearment. All the ache of wanting returned, undimmed by time or tragedy or the vast gulf she felt between them.

"We both wanted that, Kieran," she said hoarsely. "It was wonderful. It was . . . grabbing at life in the midst of so much uncertainty. It was a way to heal. A step in the journey we both were making."

"And you believe the journey is at an end."

She wanted to shake him. "Don't you see? You talk about purpose. Fate. You were brought *here* for a reason. I still remember what you said that night: 'I don't belong in the human world.' You have to have a chance to heal. This is that chance—to be what you are for once in your life without having to hide."

"I never had to hide from you, Alexandra."

His words were soft and utterly devastating. "It's not the same," she whispered. "I know how I would feel in your shoes. I'm selfish, Kieran. If I could have found a place where everyone accepted what I was, I would have given anything to go there."

Kieran closed his eyes. "It never occurred to you that it might be something other than this place I was looking for."

"You were looking for *yourself,* just as I was. But the call you felt didn't summon me here, Kieran—"

"Then what did?" He opened his eyes and focused on her with his predator's stare.

"I told you."

"What did it mean when you said you loved me?"

She closed her mouth, stunned into silence. He had heard her when she flung that desperate admission at him, and he had not forgotten.

"I . . . I knew I had to get through to you somehow, make you listen before you killed Arnoux."

"And you succeeded." He gazed up at the tops of the lodgepole pines that brushed the winter sky. "I did need you after all. You seem to know what I need better than I do myself." He smiled, a sad lifting of his mouth. "You'd sacrifice anything to give me what I need."

"Sacrifice? After all you've given me?" She flattened her hand across her mouth, as if that gesture alone could hold back the tears. "Once I wanted desperately to be a wolf. I thought they were better than people. I got my wish, in a way. I came closer than any human being could. I realized that miracles still exist, that I'm worth something after all. *You* gave me that, Kieran."

"Then there is nothing for you to give up when you leave, Alexandra?" he asked, searching her eyes. "Nothing to regret?" Before she could react he closed the space between them and took her in his arms. "Not even this?"

His mouth came down on hers. She tried to hold herself passive and still, but it was like trying to resist a force of nature. She welcomed his lips, his tongue, the strength of his body. She felt him claim her and nothing in her rational mind had the strength to fight back.

He could still make her want him so easily. His desire for her was unmistakably clear. But wanting wasn't enough.

She stiffened, but he didn't release her. He pressed his mouth to her neck just above the collar of her coat, biting with the gentlest of nips.

"You're my mate, Alexandra," he growled against her skin. "I won't let you go."

She turned her face from him and closed her eyes, unmoving. Gradually his caresses slowed and stopped. When she looked at him again his expression was grim and far from loverlike. He dropped his hands from her arms.

"I'm not a wolf, Kieran," she whispered. "I'm not a . . . *loup-garou*. I can't live like one."

He backed away as if she had struck him. "You're afraid, Alexandra," he said. "All the time I could have been a killer,. and you weren't afraid of me then. But now—"

"We're too different, Kieran."

"No."

"I can't be what you are!" she burst out. "I won't ever run with a pack or know what it's like to be a part of all this." She threw her arms wide to encompass the silent forest. "You *can*, Kieran. You were *meant* to."

Amber fire flickered in his eyes. "Arnoux thought he understood my true nature. Was he right?"

"You know he wasn't."

"But it isn't possible that you could be wrong as well."

She stared at him in shock. "You accept what you are. You must—"

"You would have me deny half my soul." He didn't move toward her again, didn't touch her, and yet he held her in an unbreakable grip. "I want the truth, Alexandra."

"What truth?" she whispered.

"Were you lying when you said you loved me?"

She couldn't answer. God help her, he must know she hadn't been. But he—*he* had never told her he loved her. Needed, yes. And wanted. As she needed and wanted him so desperately now.

His voice dropped very low. "If you want to leave because all this is too much to accept . . ."

Treacherous tears formed in her eyes. She stared past his shoulder, feeling him as she'd never felt him before— not with her body, but with her soul.

"A clean slate—is that what you want, Alexandra?" he asked. "To forget everything that's happened?"

The safety of her anger deserted her. "I'd think you'd want to forget," she whispered.

"No." He held his body very still. "Forgetting is like running. I won't run anymore. There's too much I want to remember."

His eyes told her what he remembered, wordlessly, in shattering detail. Alex felt herself beginning to come apart at the seams.

"What do you want of me?" she demanded.

"Only one thing, Alexandra. All I ask is that you deny it. Deny that you love me, and I'll let you go."

It should have been possible. She'd lied to herself plenty of times until Kieran had come into her life, and even afterward. *It's for his own good. I have to. . . .*

"I can't," she cried. "I can't."

He gave a great, gusting sigh and pulled her against him, pressing her face into the hollow of his shoulder. "That's why you'd leave me now, isn't it, Alexandra? Loving me, believing it's best for me that I stay with my people." He tangled his fingers in her hair and held on as if he thought she might escape again. "You'd take everything on yourself—look after Kevin's future, go back to Minnesota and face what we left behind there. Alone. For my sake."

She stiffened against him and he let her go just enough for her to look up into his eyes. "You can't go back," she said. "There's little they can really do to me. But you . . . you're still going to be a suspect in Peter's murder, Kieran. Maybe Lori's as well. They'll ask you questions, arrest you, put you behind bars. All the things we ran from in the first place. Until the truth comes out, there's no telling what will happen. I won't let you go through that."

He shook his head, but there was a gentleness in his eyes, a quiet strength that needed no posturing or raised voice to make itself felt. "No, Alexandra," he repeated. "The running is over. I know it must be faced, for both of us. But you're not doing it by yourself."

She balled her fists against his chest. "Damn it, Kieran, I don't want your sacrifice for my sake. *This* is what you've been searching for all your life. Your people, your own kind—"

"*You* are my kind, Alexandra."

"You won't have to wander ever again, looking for a place to belong. This is your home!"

He cupped her cheeks with his hands, catching an errant tear with his thumb. He stroked her skin, both scarred and smooth, his fingers forming a cage to hold her fast.

"You are my home," he said.

She felt the last shreds of her feeble resistance drift away like snowflakes in the wind.

"It doesn't matter what happens when we go back," he said, cradling the back of her head in his palm. "Wherever you go, I go. Nothing can change that." He brushed his jaw against her hair. "We're bound, Alexandra. No one can take anything from us ever again."

"But—"

"I love you, Alexandra."

Just as she began to shatter, as her knees began to give way and her bones dissolve, Kieran covered her mouth with his. He gave her his strength, his goodness, his acceptance in the kiss, gave her the love he had shown in a hundred ways. She buried her fingers in his hair and pulled him down fiercely, giving back in full measure.

And Alex knew that Kieran was right. It didn't matter that she was only human. She was his kind, as he was hers.

They were images in a mirror—not in form, but in spirit. When she looked within herself she could find no anger, no fear, no dark foreboding about the future that awaited them. Kieran was free of his past, as she was of hers. They were both through running.

She pulled back, coiling a lock of his hair around her finger. "I guess," she said wryly, "that you'd have followed even if I'd managed to get away."

He showed all his teeth. "Wolves are very good hunters."

"And I still think you'd make one hell of a wolf researcher. I even have a position in mind."

His eyes narrowed. "I also have a . . . position in mind."

She gave a little squeak of surprise as he swept her up in his arms. " 'Me Tarzan, you Jane,' " he quoted softly.

"You heard that!" she accused, remembering the day she'd discovered him naked in her bed.

He bent his head to hers. "Wolves also have very good hearing."

She returned his gentle kiss and touched his cheek. "You know it's not always going to be easy, Kieran."

He rubbed his jaw against the palm of her hand. "You and I wouldn't know what to do with ourselves if it were." Golden light sparked in his eyes. "But I think there'll be some compensation."

Epilogue

Alex sat on the porch and gazed down at the last blank page in her journal.

She hadn't touched it since the day after her first night with Kieran, when she finally dared to put her feelings into words. The feelings that Arnoux had tried to use against her, and failed.

Eight months ago, now. It seemed like forever. Alex rested her hands on the broad curve of her stomach and smiled. A very wonderful forever.

It was time to fill that final page.

She shifted the pen in her hand and began to write.

Dear Mother, I've come home at last. Truly home. Everything is more wonderful than I believed it could be. I spent so much of my life closing myself off behind bitterness, blaming myself and the world for things I couldn't control, instead of learning to change what I could.

I know now that you would never have blamed me for the accident, that you wanted me to live more than you loved your own life. I never needed your forgiveness at all; I needed to forgive myself.

I know now how lucky I was to have you, how much you gave me in the time we were together. You gave me the ability to dream. And you were right. You were always right, about believing.

Warmth and heat stole up on her from behind, strong arms caging her in a tender prison.

"Kieran." She sighed, leaning back. "Finished with your run?"

He rubbed his jaw against her cheek and nipped her ear. "I can never stay away from you long, Alexandra." He spread his fingers to encompass her belly, and the rhythm of his breathing became deep and slow.

"Trying to figure out if she'll be like her daddy?" Alexandra said lazily, rolling her head against his bare chest.

He kissed her temple. "Hoping she'll be like her mother. Beautiful."

Alexandra sat up, twisting awkwardly to face him. He could still take her breath away when she saw him as he was now, magnificently naked, gazing at her with pride and love.

"You know I want her to be like you," she protested.

He rocked back into a crouch, hands dangling between his knees. "Even if it makes her life harder?"

"It won't if we teach her right," she said seriously, frowning at him. "If we make safe places for wolves where she can be herself when she needs to be. Like you."

"She'll have a mother to teach her courage," Kieran murmured, taking her hands.

"And her father to teach her everything else she needs to know." She scooted closer to him on her knees. "She'll never feel like an outsider, Kieran."

"Not with all of Val Caché and Julie's family ready to stand as godparents." Kieran pulled her head against his shoulder and stroked her hair.

"If our daughter is like you, your people will have another reason to hope for the future," she said, nestling as close as she could in spite of her bulk. "There are still so few of you. If you and I can have a *loup-garou* child—"

"She'll be *our* kind, Alexandra—yours and mine— whatever she is. And she'll be loved."

"Yes." She looked up at him, at amber eyes so vivid with emotion that she could either kiss him or drown.

He responded with a soft growl, filling his hands with her heavy breasts. He began to massage them with utmost gentleness, stroking her nipples to delicate points.

"Kieran—"

He slipped his tongue between her lips. "Hmmm?"

She sucked on him lightly and then bit down just enough to get his attention.

"Kieran, there's a truck pulling into the driveway."

He started and let her go. Alex pushed herself to her feet, reached for his jeans draped over the porch chair, and tossed them to him.

"If you can manage to get them on," she said, glancing significantly at the base of his belly and blushing in spite of herself.

Kieran grinned and sniffed the air. "It's only Julie," he said.

"Still . . . " She brushed past him, trailing her fingers along his bare arm, and eased her way down from the porch. He tugged on his pants quickly and followed just as Julie got out of the truck.

"Julie!" Alex embraced her friend. "What brings you here?"

"Oh, just checking up on you guys." Julie's gaze settled on Kieran with teasing intensity. "Hope I wasn't interrupting."

"Not much to interrupt these days," Alex said, rolling her eyes.

That was not precisely true. Between the two of them, Alex and Kieran had discovered any number of ways to assuage their constant hunger for each other.

"Feeling all right?" Julie asked.

"Perfect." Alexandra leaned against Kieran as he curled his arm around her thick waist.

"Luke and his wife still coming down next month?"

"Yes. With their boys." Alex laughed. "They seem to think they should be here for the blessed event."

"I can understand that. Not that you won't have all the

help you need." Julie grinned. "My whole family feels pretty possessive of the kid already. . . ."

Alex listened to Julie chatter, letting her thoughts drift back to their return to Minnesota. It hadn't even been spring then; now the leaves were turning, another summer gone. In British Columbia Kieran had told her that the two of them could face whatever waited for them here, but even he hadn't counted on the help of his newfound people.

Luke had been the first to tell Alex and Kieran that he, his cousin Philippe, and two others of the *loup-garou* would accompany them home, to reinforce Alex's testimony of Arnoux's confession to the murders of Peter Schaeffer, Lori Carstens, and Julie's cousin. There was never any risk that the *loups-garous* would be exposed for what they were; they had learned long ago how to protect themselves, and Kieran could control his shifting now.

There'd been an investigation, of course. Police, and lawyers, and time spent in jail before the hearing. But Kieran hadn't been alone this time. He had faced his brief imprisonment with unshakable calm.

The facts of Lori's death had come out, including tissue samples taken from her fingernails that confirmed Arnoux as the murderer. A maid from the Merritt Motor Inn had come forward with a report of having heard Arnoux and Peter arguing in Peter's room only a day before his murder.

In the end Kieran had been cleared of all charges. But Arnoux had become the source of endless speculation.

Alex could still remember the restrained amazement on the judge's face when the witnesses related the bizarre story Arnoux had confessed before the villagers. That he'd believed he could change into a wolf, had gone mad and died of that madness.

Not of madness, but a massive heart attack, according to the coroner in British Columbia. His dying declaration had suggested a rare modern case of lycanthropy, the knowledgeable agreed. A man who'd believed he was a werewolf. Who'd killed the parents of a young boy and kidnapped him, murdered others, and tried to blame those murders on his former captive.

So the affair had ended. If the people of Merritt weren't entirely won over to Kieran and Alex, some were beginning to come around. Alexandra found more allies in her crusade for the wolves.

And there was Julie's family, who had at last been able to end a tragic chapter in their lives. Cheryl's murder had been solved. "The circle has closed," Julie had said. She explained how she'd sensed a connection between Alex, Kieran, and Cheryl's death almost from the very beginning but had been convinced of Kieran's innocence and the importance of his part in learning the truth.

She'd been right, as she was right about so many other things.

"All right, then," Julie said as Alex returned to the present. "I'll expect you two at Mom's house tomorrow night. Or should I say 'you three?' " She looked at Kieran with a mischievous gleam in her eyes. "The twins and Bobby can't wait to play horsey with you again."

Kieran glanced at Alex, who made a helpless gesture. "Don't look at me. I can still remember how fascinated I was with a certain wolf when I was a child."

They gazed at each other, sharing memories. Julie coughed.

"Uh . . . I think I'll be going now," she said, backing away. "See you tomorrow night!"

Alex made a vague wave in Julie's direction. She was distantly aware of receding noise and the dissipating smell of gasoline and hot metal. Then there was only Kieran. She stepped into his arms.

"How did the tracking go yesterday?" she asked, nuzzling his neck.

"Very well. The pack allowed me to approach closer than ever before." He drew back and brushed his knuckles along her jaw. "They're accepting me, Alexandra."

"I think I know why." She looped her arm around his waist, hooking her thumb in a beltloop, and pulled him back toward the cabin. "When the wolves tried to attack you before, it wasn't because you weren't either a man or a wolf. It wasn't because you didn't belong as a part of nature they could recognize." She leaned her head against his shoulder. "It was because you didn't accept yourself. They sensed that. And now—"

"Now they feel the difference in me," he finished.

"You still may never run with the pack," she said softly. "You're still not exactly what they are. Does that bother you?"

"How could it?" He swung her to a stop and kissed her brow. "I have my pack here. My home, and my world."

Her eyelids fluttered. "It's funny. Even the people of Merritt are starting to see us differently now that we've come to terms with ourselves. Maybe wolves and people aren't so different after all."

"They respect strength," he said.

"And love is the greatest strength there is."

He agreed with her fervently until she pulled away and got him moving toward the cabin again. "I still have a little unfinished business," she told him. "Wait for me inside?"

He kissed her in answer, making an erotic promise with his lips and tongue. "Don't be long, Alexandra."

When he had gone in, she sat back down on the porch and opened the journal again.

Julie was right, Mother. It's come full circle, just as it was meant to. Fairy tales are real. And so are miracles. She closed her eyes and smiled. *I know you'll always be with me. We both have our journeys to make.*

Good-bye, Mother. I love you.

She closed the journal, tucked it under her arm, and went to find her miracle on the other side of the door.

Afterword

I hope you've enjoyed *Prince of Shadows*. I have touched briefly on the issues of wolf recovery and reintroduction in such states as Montana and Idaho, and the current status of wolves in Minnesota, the only state other than Alaska which contains a sizeable and stable population of wolves. Any errors in depictions of wolves, wolf research and researchers are mine alone, and should not in any way reflect on the marvelous work being done by those who study these magnificent predators.

If you are interested in learning more about wolf study and reintroduction, and how you can help these very important programs, I suggest you write to the following organizations:

The Wolf Education and Research Center
P.O. Box 3832
Ketchum, Idaho 83340
(208) 726-2860
(Devoted to providing public education and scientific research concerning the gray wolf and its habitat in the Northern Rocky Mountains.)

Wolf Haven International
3111 Offut Lake Road
Tenino, WA 98589
1-800-448-9653
(Private, non-profit organization working around the world to develop a better understanding of the wolf. Provides sanctuary for wolves unable to survive in the wilds, and public relations with wolves on tour. Also associated with the Mexican Wolf Recovery Program.)

International Wolf Center
1396 Highway 169
Ely, MN 55731
(218) 365-4695
(Dedicated to educating public about the wolf through education center in Ely, Minnesota, and through college courses, exhibits, field trips, symposia and school programs. Produces a quarterly magazine, "International Wolf.")

Other organizations such as the Wolf Recovery Foundation in Boise, Idaho; Timberwolf Preservation Society in Greendale, WI; Timber Wolf Alliance in Ashland, WI; Preserve Arizona's Wolves in Phoenix, AZ; The Mexican Wolf Coalition in Albuquerque, NM; World Wildlife Fund, National Wildlife Federation and The Environmental Defense Fund also help support the wolf. There are also many wonderful books on these subjects available.

If you would like to contact me regarding this, please send a SASE to:
P.O. Box 272545
Concord, CA 94527

Or e-mail me at: S.Krinard@Genie.Com

Happy hunting!

Susan Krinard

About the Author

Susan Krinard graduated from the California College of Arts and Crafts with a BfA, and worked as an artist and freelance illustrator before turning to writing. An admirer of both Romance and Fantasy, Susan enjoys combining these elements in her books. She also loves to get out into nature as frequently as possible. A native Californian, Susan lives in the San Francisco Bay Area with her French-Canadian husband, Serge, a dog and a cat.

Susan loves to hear from her readers. She can be reached at:

P.O. Box 272545
Concord, CA 94527

A self-addressed stamped envelope is much appreciated. Susan's e-mail address is:

s.krinard1@genie.com

If you loved
Prince of Shadows,
*don't miss the new novel of
time travel, intrigue and romantic adventure
from the exceptionally talented*
Susan Krinard

coming from Bantam Books in Summer 1997

MacKenzie "Mac" Sinclair comes from a long line of adventurers, but caring for her beloved grandfather has always kept her close to home. Until he shows her a photograph of her world-travelling great-great-grandfather, Peregrine Sinclair, and his partner, Liam O'Shea. Mac is fascinated by their adventures, especially the handsome O'Shea's disappearance on a solo expedition to the Mayan jungles—so fascinated that she follows their story back to the same jungles . . . a century later. She takes the photograph with her, as well as a pendant handed down from Peregrine himself, as reminders of her connection to the past. But when a mysterious Indian guide leads her to an obscure temple, Mac is not so sure she's as adventurous as her forebears. And when she becomes disoriented inside the ruins and blunders into the arms of another explorer—a distractingly masculine one—Mac *knows* she has gotten more than she bargained for. Because she has in fact found Liam O'Shea . . . alive, well, and seductively real. In the year 1884.